REVENGE

THE NEW WORLD SERIES | BOOK TWO

Stephen Llewelyn

Published by Fossil Rock Publishing 2020

ISBNs:

978-1-8380235-2-2 paperback
978-1-8380235-3-9 ebook

For Sally

***Thank you for your unwavering
commitment to the cause.***

The author also wishes to acknowledge:

Mum and *Dad*, thanks for your continued encouragement.
Special thanks to the experts who took time out of their frantic schedules
to answer my emails and questions about our favourite subject. Cheers.
…And last but by no means least, to everyone who reads this book and
enjoyed the one before it, thank you.
The crew of the USS *New World* will return soon in

THE NEW WORLD SERIES | BOOK THREE | ALLEGIANCE.

No dinosaurs were harmed during the making of this book.

Prologue

"That's not possible!" exclaimed Kelly Marston, studying the object in her hands. "Professor? You gotta see this!"

Guy Schultz stooped under the low ceiling brace in the cave they were excavating and made his way on all fours to where Kelly was working. Schultz was the research professor supervising her doctoral thesis.

"What have you?" he asked, grunting slightly as he worked his way into a cross-legged sitting position. "And lose the 'Professor', will ya? It makes me feel old," he added.

Kelly and Guy formed part of a paleobotanical expedition in Patagonia digging for amber deposits. The sedimentary rock strata they currently worked had begun to form in the middle of the Cretaceous Period, roughly 100 million years ago, in a slim seam of relative stability between two layers of volcanic basalt. They believed the area to have once been a prehistoric forest, overtaken by a natural disaster of some sort. The forest had certainly been buried by a non-volcanic landslide, although they were yet to discern the exact cause.

"You're gonna freak!" said Kelly, placing a ragged piece of ancient resin into his palm. She shone a light through the find, to help him see.

Guy's research team were hunting for preserved seed deposits from ancient volcanic regions, their project design goal: To study the preserved genetics of ancient seeds and pollens, specifically those which exhibited some degree of tolerance to volcanic gas exposure.

The stratum they were excavating was ideal, because their finds showed not only the direct effects of volcanism, as exhibited by the stratum above, but also the long term effects on future generations of plant life. The hope of successfully engineering modern plants with more resilience to the pollution of the 22nd century was both key to their research and their funding. The summer of AD2102 was their final season in the field at this location, so the last thing they needed at this point was distraction.

Guy looked at the small, seemingly inoffensive item in his hands, straining his eyes in the low light. He rubbed soil from its surface, turning the sample over once, twice. Pouring a little water from his flask, he washed the find and rubbed it again. His frown of concentration suddenly cleared and he looked up, thunderstruck. "Oh my God," he said, "this came out of that seam?"

Kelly nodded, completely dumbfounded herself. Both professor and student immediately jumped forward to the ultimate conclusion of this find. No one had made a discovery like this before; it was world-changing.

"We need to say exactly *nothing* to anyone about this," said Guy.

Kelly looked incredulous. "Are you kidding?"

He shook his head. "This is dangerous, Kelly. This could well be something we were never meant to find – never meant to *know*, even." He pondered for a moment. "I need to get to the satellite phone and call the university. For your own sake, for all our sakes, don't say anything. Not yet, until we know what we have. There could be serious political fallout from this. Trust me – this is the kind of discovery that ends careers, maybe even lives. C'mon, let's get outta here."

Within two hours their camp and equipment had been abandoned, Professor Schultz separated from his students and the whole research team borne away in three black helicopters which appeared out of nowhere – their destination, unknown.

Chapter 1 | Declaration

Thick early-morning mist blanketed the plains and forest. The stillness was smothering, but did allow a single voice to carry on the breeze. Latin prayers drifted in and out eerily, haunting the fog.

The murk slowly thinned, gradually revealing huge walls from grey obscurity. Elements of a ditch and rampart crested by a wooden palisade became visible. Inside the ten-metre-tall enclosure, smoke augmented the murk as a large fire burned, fiercely engulfing four wrapped bodies. Within moments they were barely distinguishable from flame and fume.

This *dark ages* landscape became stranger still as the gargantuan, 550-metre-long hull of the NASA ship USS *New World* shimmered, mirage-like, into view. The gauzy gloom began to dissolve around her as the sun gained strength with each passing minute.

Georgio Baccini threw the wreath he had made from local brush flora into the conflagration. His twin, Mario, had been the first casualty on their extraordinary journey. The explosion which sent the *New World* back almost 100 million years to the Cretaceous Period, had been so destructive that there was no body for him to mourn.

"*Amo tuo fratello,*" he said quietly, retreating slightly from the intensity of the flames. The heat dried the tears on his face instantly.

1

Lieutenant Hiro Nassaki, chief engineer and closest companion to Georgio, gently guided him back to a safe distance and like a pagan ritual, heaven swallowed the smoke.

Hiro squeezed his friend's arm, smiling warmly but with great sadness.

Georgio tried to smile bravely in return but his face crumpled and he collapsed into Hiro's shoulder, sobbing. The chief engineer, so often at a loss with societal expectation, could only hold his friend, awkwardly. Not knowing what else to do, he simply stared balefully into the flames as a single tear ran down his own cheek. He was angry, he was afraid and he wished he could have his friend back. The sounds of Georgio's pain hurt terribly but also served to harden his resolve; someone had to pay for all this.

Patches of blue sky appeared as the fog continued to clear. The heavy hush abruptly shattered as the piercing scream of a giant flying reptile rent the air, high above. The Pterosaur surfed the early thermals as the climbing sun heated the new day.

Mother Sarah gazed at the soaring giant and took a moment to appreciate what she had and what she had been shown, despite the sadness in her heart.

Most of the people gathered were also looking up; some in awe, some in fear.

She watched the beautiful creature vanish from sight and smiled slightly at this congruity with her thoughts.

"I would just like to finish with a few words written by my uncle Joe, when I lost my father. They're not religious, but I found them healing. They helped me and I hope they will help us all to remember that no one is ever truly lost to us, maybe just out of sight." Her American accented English travelled more clearly now, the breeze no longer tearing her words away and as the morning mist began to lift, so did her mood.

Taking a deep breath, she spoke sonorously and by heart:

Hand on your shoulder, becalmed or by storm,
Shattered in past deeds, or futures forlorn,
Loneliness lies, by noon, night or dawn,
My hand on your shoulder, you need never call.

Untruths, black cares, heedlessly borne,
Hanged on quarters, this shame adorned,
Neither slighted in crisis, nor far away from home,
My hand on your shoulder, you are never alone.

Your heart made heavy, of world weighted stone,
Do you hear my voice, on the wind 'tis blown,
The pain I see is not yours to own,
My hand on your shoulder, you are never alone.

Sweet laughter's lament, shared between one,
You turn to tell, then remember I'm gone,
The eye may lie, yet the truth still be known,
My hand on your shoulder, you are never alone.
Look inside in the last light, on the last leg home,
This hand was ever on your shoulder, my darling, and you were
never alone.

Sarah struggled with the last couple of lines, her voice breaking slightly. A few tears carried some small measure of relief. Stillness followed, disturbed only by the crackling of burning timber, masking the sobs and occasional soft words from the congregation around the pyre.

Mother Sarah Fellows stepped down from the temporary podium erected for the funerals. She moved to stand next to Captain Jill Baines, but neither woman spoke for a time.

Eventually, Baines broke the silence. "That was beautiful, Sarah," she said in barely more than a whisper, eyes never leaving the flames.

Sarah looked at the woman next to her and without being asked, gave Baines a hug with a single squeeze before continuing her consolatory rounds.

Baines remained stationary, eyes locked on the hypnotic destruction burning up before her as she relived the last few weeks in her mind.

Captain Douglas had given himself into the clutches of the psychopathic Dr Schultz just two days previously and she had hardly spoken a word in that time. Meanwhile, the crew and passengers of the *New World* had started to give her a wide berth, waiting as it were, for the other shoe to drop.

After the initial sorrows of the funeral service, people began to talk and gather in small groups; there was even a little laughter here and there. Food, drink and the usual distractions were provided as people tried to look a bad day in the face and carry on.

An hour or so went by as people chatted and remembered. During that time Baines just stared into the all-reducing flames. People sensed her aura of 'leave me alone' and so they did. Eventually, she stepped up on to the platform from which Mother Sarah had given the service and looked out at the assembled people – now *her* people. She had never before addressed them as their captain. She cleared her throat a few times. After a couple of days of barely using her voice, she knew before she even opened her mouth that her first few words would likely be croaked.

The new society of the *New World* noticed Baines take the stand and began gathering once more, in expectation. Once everyone was assembled, she judged her moment and began to speak.

"Ladies and gentlemen," she cleared her throat one last time and then continued with more strength in her voice. "We've all lost so much over the last few weeks. Please remember that we are the innocents, we did nothing to deserve being thrown into this situation, this world. It was all done *to* us by evil people with twisted agendas. However, we may be innocents, but we are done with being victims!" She slammed her fist down on the podium as her anger, simmering for the last forty-eight hours, began to surface.

"We've said goodbye to some very brave, very special people today – people who gave their lives for us. Let us not forget that there was also someone else who sacrificed himself for us, so that we have a place to live, with heat, comfort, food and safety," she gestured toward the huge spaceship they now called home. "As you already know, Captain James Douglas gave himself as hostage to that mad bi— that *creature*, Schultz, along with our shuttle, to save us from losing our only refuge – indeed, everything we have. He saved my life too," she added a little more quietly, before firing up again. "He is still *alive* and he's out there. We've depended on him since this journey began and now *he* needs *us*, and I for one don't intend to let him down!"

Sounds of agreement and approval greeted her words, as the gathering looked from one to another with nods of determination.

"From now on," Baines continued, "we will build our defences whilst working on a plan to get the captain back. Every resource, every skill we have will be utilised to bring him *home*!"

Her words were sanctioned by a more vigorous cheer from the crowd and she let the noise abate naturally before continuing.

"We have four main tasks to fulfil," she counted off on her fingers. "One, we continue to build our defences – Captain Douglas' only wish was for all of you to be safe. Two, alongside that work, we devise a strategy to find the captain and bring him home. Three, we plan a larger compound and start planting the food we'll need. Four, and lastly, we continue to look for a way to travel home."

She brought both of her hands down and held onto the podium as she leaned forward animatedly. "We must remember that if these criminals have their way, most of the folks we care about back home will never even *exist*! So from here on in everything changes, from here on in we stop being on the back foot, we stop being led around by the nose by these insane terrorists who have tried to destroy us!"

Her eyes burned with emotion and she breathed heavily, her voice cracking slightly as she roared, "From here on in, people, WE ARE AT WAR!"

Later that day, in the early evening, Baines called a meeting of her senior staff. Present were Lieutenant Sandip Singh, the ship's Indian pilot and second officer; Lieutenant Hiro Nassaki, chief of engineering and Japanese national; Sergeant John Jackson, her English chief of security on the *New World*; Major Ford White, chief of Pod security, representing the United States' military; and finally, Captain Elvis Percival Gleeson, the Australian army demolitions expert of no fixed post at the moment.

Also present were Mother Sarah Fellows, the Catholic priest, also American and Dr Satnam Patel, one of India's leading minds in the field of astrophysics. These last two were not military, but were invited because they formed the remainder of what used to be a triumvirate government, along with Captain Douglas.

"Lady and gentlemen," Baines greeted them. She remained standing at the head of the table after the others had seated themselves. Full of nervous energy, there was no rest *in* her, only anger. Working hard to keep her emotions in check, she pressed on. "Thank you for coming. I know today was meant to be a rest and remembrance day but every second we waste or delay is another second that Captain Douglas is out there – as *her* prisoner."

"It's OK, Captain," replied Sarah, sympathetically. "The people need this time to grieve and lick their wounds but we here have to go on, for them and for James."

Baines nodded gratefully. "There are several things we need to discuss," she continued. "Firstly, our government, the triumvirate. Obviously, the captain was voted for by the people, and I still believe in the concept of three-way governance, so what do we do to replace him?" She held her finger up pointedly, "*Temporarily.*"

Patel spoke first. "James wanted you to take his place, Jill, and that's good enough for me – both as a governor and as leader of the military aboard this vessel." He smiled encouragingly at her. "I know what you're made of."

"Hear hear," added Sarah. "That has always been the form with democratic government anyway. The second in command takes charge if anything happens to the leader and stays in charge until a new election is due. I'm still hoping that Satnam, and that brilliant young Mr Baccini he's been working with, will find us a way home before we have to worry about *re*-elections."

"No pressure then?" asked Patel wryly.

Baines looked uncomfortable. "I'm not sure I can fill both roles the way James did. I'm just not sure I'm *good* enough."

"Well, you were the next most popular on the voting list anyway," Sarah noted, "before you stood down, that is. I wouldn't have been here at all otherwise. Thanks for that by the way!" she added with bright sarcasm, drawing tired smiles from the others present.

Baines nodded acknowledgement. "Sorry," she said.

"Never mind that," Sarah answered heartily. "We need you now, Jill. We need your strength, it was what James wanted, he said so more than once." She looked at Patel for support but he was already nodding his agreement.

Baines sighed heavily. She still could not bring herself to sit; she was too wired. "Alright," she agreed at last. "But I see this as a temporary shuffle until James is back and make no mistake, people – we are going to get him back!"

"We are," The Sarge vouched, speaking for the first time.

Baines nodded to them all and to herself. "Talking of shuffles, the last couple of days have been horrible for us all but I have had to consider, for the sake of the whole crew, who will be the new commander. Now, I see this as a temporary and largely ground-based position, although I do not mean this to be in any way demeaning to the officer chosen. It's just a matter of fact that when we bring James home, he's going to want his chair back, and I will be only too glad to return it to him! Then we can all go back to our day jobs."

"Who did you have in mind, Captain?" Patel asked courteously.

Baines nodded again thoughtfully, holding in her thoughts for one last moment. "The reason I've invited you all here is, excepting the non-military councillors, you are *all* on the list. I wanted Sarah and Satnam here so that the government knows what the military is up to. I think James would appreciate that."

The crew around the table looked from one to another uncomfortably – all hoping it was not going to be them.

Baines continued, "There are also a few changes, or amalgamations I should say, that I wish to propose. Firstly, let me say that I, *we*, so badly need you all where you are right now that I'm reticent to change anything. However, change has been thrust upon us, so here goes." She looked directly at Jackson and let go her first broadside. "Sarge, I considered making you up to Lieutenant."

The Sarge, who had just raised his coffee cup, slammed it back down unconsciously, as first shock and then horror registered on his face. "Me? An officer?" he muttered, stroking his sergeant's stripes like he was saying goodbye to a beloved pet. The other officers smirked as the hardest man on board wilted in the light of his own achievement.

"*But*," Baines pressed on, "I knew you would never forgive me for it. Besides, I wouldn't even know what to call you, if not *The Sarge*." This raised a few chuckles. "So my plan is to bring Pod and ship security under one banner with Major White in command," she looked at White, "and The Sarge as your second, Ford. You OK with that?"

Ford raised his eyebrows in surprise but nodded thoughtful agreement.

"Due to the new situation we find ourselves in, I intend to bring the whole security contingent under the direct control of the ship's captain." She held a hand up. "Now before you start worrying about this blatant grab for power, I fully expect that to be James Douglas in the not too distant future. Is everyone OK with this so far?"

"It's your ship, so it's your call, Captain," said Ford. "However, I'm fully behind the idea of bringing it all together. We need a clearer command structure if we're to take the battle to the enemy. I'm on board."

"Thanks, Ford." Baines gave him a small but appreciative smile. "Are you OK with this, Sarge?" she asked her *ex* chief of security. "I know this wasn't what you signed on for?"

The Sarge gave a rare chuckle, part relief, part humour. "I doubt you could find anyone who thought they were signing on for any of this, Captain. I agree with the major though, we need a clear chain of command. I'm a soldier so I'll obey your orders at the end of the day, but saying that, I'll be happy to serve under you, Major." He offered a small nod of respect, adding, "I do have a request that I hope you'll both consider, though?"

"Of course, Sarge, go on," Baines invited.

"I would like to recommend Jones for lance corporal, possibly even jump to full corporal," said Jackson. "With our new, extended security force, we'll need a few more experienced NCOs to keep it all working. Jones has really shown himself to be calm and capable in the last few weeks."

Baines looked to White. "What do you think, Ford?" she asked. "He'll certainly have no trouble calling for silence in the ranks – they'll be shaking in their boots."

Ford smiled, thinking of the house-sized Welshman. "I agree, and I think he'll do well. I remember when we were trying to restart the ship and we came upon two dead crew members. The situation was real bad, yet Jones was fully in control. He impressed me then, as he did when he stayed at the door controls when that forty-foot monster charged out of the Pod cargo bay into the outer airlock – right past him! That was ballsy. There are a couple of other men and women under my command, that I might also consider raising," he added.

"Good, that's settled then. Right, back to the appointment of the new commander. As I said earlier, we really need everyone where they are, doing what they're doing. But I want you to know that I would have been honoured to have *any* of you as my second in command." She looked specifically at Sandip and Hiro. "I hope you know that?"

They both nodded, grateful for the sentiment but more grateful still that it was looking less likely they would have to let the job they *had* signed on for, play second fiddle.

Gleeson was absentmindedly rubbing an abraded bruise on his forearm. This minor injury had been acquired recently, whilst running away from a terrifying Giganotosaurus. The crew of the shuttlecraft had hauled him and Major White up, pell-mell, out of the way of the T Rex sized killer just in the nick of time.

All eyes turned to the oblivious Australian army captain, until the silence in the room finally encroached upon his reverie. He looked up at his new audience, suddenly. "You've gotta be bladdy joking?"

The next day saw a new energy among the crew, with everyone determined to get to grips with their situation and put everything in place for when the inevitable confrontation came.

Chief engineer, Lieutenant Hiro Nassaki, was joined in the Pod manufacturing bay by Thomas Wood, the structural engineer; Jim Miller, the chemist and materials specialist; and Satnam Patel, councillor and physicist. They met to discuss the structural frameworks with which they hoped to support the *New World*.

A recent storm and flash flood had caused the enormous craft to list slightly to one side. The construction crew had dug several tons of soil away from the main cargo bay doors, allowing traffic once more. However, the engineers were concerned that, left unchecked, this sinking action might begin to cause serious stability or even structural problems for the ship.

The *New World* had support plates under her belly, close to each landing strut. They were designed for use when repairs to these landing struts became necessary. The engineers' strategy called for these to be used as jacking-up points. Once the earth around the landing struts had been excavated down to bedrock, they would manufacture a structure capable of supporting a quarter of the ship's mass alongside each strut, to carry and spread the load.

Normal procedure would see the Pod removed before an operation like this, to massively reduce weight, but their current situation made removal difficult and even dangerous – a last option in case of emergency.

With the ship's vast weight supported, the engineers planned to retract each landing strut, one at a time, filling the huge holes under each with a rubble-concrete pile. When fully cured, they would be left with a basic, four-point landing pad, allowing the ship to stand or even take off and land if necessary.

Their original plan was to construct a relatively lightweight unit, which might be moved from one jacking point to another, but this idea had been scrapped. Bearing in mind their limited resources, the mathematics had proved that anything strong enough, yet built from steel alone, would be too costly in material.

Subsequently, the engineers had decided on four squat, heavy duty steel lattice frames, formed in concentric box-like configurations. Once in place, they planned to shutter each, filling them with a strong concrete grout which could then be tamped and vibrated to remove any air pockets. Steelwork would be left jutting from the side facing each landing strut so that when the pile was poured, the whole construct would be bound together into one structure. When all of the concrete had suitably cured, the hydraulic rams which supported the ship on her landing skids could be lowered to carry her weight once more.

Scientists feed off ideas like hungry hippos and almost immediately a second plan began to germinate, where similar constructs might be used as support stanchions for a bridge across the river. This would allow ground vehicles much more freedom of movement across the plains.

However, at the moment these impressively strong monoliths were but scribbles on a light board, being animatedly augmented and rubbed out again by four bickering engineers.

Baines walked calmly onto *her* bridge. It would take a while to get used to that and she fervently hoped they would get Douglas back before she had to. She greeted Singh with a good morning, as she always did, and made herself a cup of coffee – as she always did. Singh liked to start his day with a cup of English breakfast tea. Noting the Lieutenant's favourite mug, the one emblazoned with the *Delhi Daredevils* cricket team, was not by his station, Baines poured him one.

Stepping out of the bridge's small galley with a steaming mug in each hand, she looked up to find Singh grinning from ear to ear.

"What?" she asked, quizzically.

He thanked her for the drink before spilling the beans. "As we have Cap— sorry, Commander Gleeson starting his intensive training on ship's systems here this morning, I thought it would be nice to make him feel at home. Especially as India, captained by myself of course," he made a slight bow, "absolutely *humiliated* Australia in the opening overs of the test match we started to play last night in my holo-room. So I made these, to make it up to him, so to speak."

He reached under his desk to pull out two pieces of apparel. Baines stared at these items of mischief for a stretched moment before her shoulders began to shake, followed by a shuddering laugh and even a few unbidden tears. Their deep medicinal laughter drove some of the darkness away. Eventually they regained control of themselves, wiping their eyes.

"Thank you, Sandy," said Baines, looking intently at the Lieutenant. "I needed that more than I knew."

"We both did, Captain." Singh bit his lip for a moment, adding earnestly, "We *will* get him back, you know. Captain Douglas is as tough, as the British say, as old boots."

Baines nodded and smiled at his kind attempt to keep her spirits up. "Yes, but until then I'm gonna keep his seat warm, his crew frosty and his whisky at room temperature," she said.

"He doesn't take ice?"

"Hates it. Says it ruins the scotch!"

The door chimed. Singh opened a window on his station's main screen to display the camera feed from outside the bridge. Baines had insisted security remain at the highest level, just in case the 'bad guys' had not completely left the ship. *Commander* Gleeson stood in the corridor, requesting permission to enter. Singh unlocked the door from his station.

"Morning, Commander," said Baines and Singh together as Gleeson strode in purposefully.

Gleeson nodded to them both in greeting. "That's gonna take a little getting used to," he said.

"Believe me, you're not the only one feeling it," replied Baines, "but you've proved your courage and leadership time and again already on this mission, and I know I'll be able to rely on you in this. Obviously, due to the circumstances we're under, yours will be a position of leadership and dare I say it, administration."

Gleeson's face soured at the last, and Baines smirked for the first time since… well, it had been a while.

"You're not going to be required or expected to fly the ship," she continued, "but I need you to know your way around. You'll have to understand ship's resources, capabilities, strengths and weaknesses, so you can make the calls when necessary. Make no mistake, *they* will be back and we *will* be attacked."

"You make it all sound so easy, Captain," replied Gleeson, sardonically.

Baines smiled. "You've got a week's grace to get up to speed and then I'm going to need you, Commander. I intend to begin sending out reconnaissance groups to find the location of our shuttle and most importantly, Captain Douglas."

"Sooner the better," said Gleeson. "So I can give you this job back."

"We're on the same page there, trust me," she replied. "Today, Sandy is going to help you learn your way around the bridge and also bring you up to speed on our plans to train up as many pilots as possible for the ten escape pods we have. I want you to learn to pilot them too. Have you ever flown?"

Gleeson pulled a face. "Only simulated. As you know, all military and construction staff on the mission had basic training for piloting the escape pods and the small shuttlecraft they use on Mars, which are similar." He shrugged. "But that's all I have, sorry."

"No need to apologise, Commander," said Baines. "You'll not find a better man to complete your training than Sandip. His piloting skills are second only to his fast bowl, I understand," she added, mischievously.

Gleeson nodded knowingly. "So that's my first lesson is it?" he asked.

Baines raised her eyebrows innocently.

"Get to work before *you two*, before you've had chance to gossip?" he declared, his tone rising at the end, making a question out of the statement.

Baines chuckled and patted him on the hand. "So glad you're a fast learner."

Gleeson sagged a little. "You know, you've had me lawyering, now I'm gonna be administering, when do I get to blow something up?" he asked, looking glum.

"Funny you should mention that," replied Baines. "Patel's team have begun work on some large-scale stunning weapons which can be ship-mounted, and I want you two," she included Lieutenant Singh in her gesture now, "to not only train pilots, but also to get the little ships kitted out with weapons."

Gleeson smiled for the first time, stating, "Now that I *can* do."

"Right," said Baines. "But before you start, Sandip has done his best to make the bridge feel a little more like home for you."

Gleeson glanced around; he had not noticed anything overly familiar. When he turned back to his fellow officers to ask what he must clearly be missing, he saw the hats. Both Baines and Singh wore broad-brimmed hats with numerous corks dangling from strings underneath.

"What d'ya think, sport?" asked Baines, smirking again.

Gleeson blew out his cheeks in a theatrical sigh. "I suppose a transfer's out of the question, Captain?" he asked.

"You may recall," answered Baines, "that there are only two ships in the whole world now and one of them is in the thrall of a despotic madwoman!"

"Right," said Gleeson. "And which one am *I* on again?"

At Hiro's request, Dr Portree had the construction crews out in their diggers and tippers, working the riverbed and near bank. The heavy machines dredged up bucket after bucket of sand and gravel to form the ballast component of the new concrete which would be mixed to support the ship. The Pod had been stocked with many tons of cement and structural steel for construction and mining purposes on Mars, so they would soon be able to begin. Eventually, they planned to send out survey teams in search of lime and gypsum deposits, but it was early days.

The ten-person security team, under the watchful eyes of the newly minted Corporals Dewi Jones and Jennifer O'Brien, closely monitored the situation.

O'Brien, already one of Major White's staff before the new shakeup, always presented a stern attitude towards discipline, danger and duty. During the last few weeks, this quality had earned her the clumsily ironic moniker of 'Iron Balls'. However, O'Brien notwithstanding, a relaxed routine began to settle over the rest of the work and security teams – much to her irritation.

As the machines moved to and fro, hauling many tons of ballast to their compound, the *texture* of the river seemed to change.

O'Brien noticed it first. Staring, it became clear she was seeing the bodies of dozens of fish sliding by just below the surface, and they were huge. Swimming upstream, almost salmon-like, they powerfully disregarded the adverse current. However, what made the event more noticeable from the shore was the scale of them; each fish was two or three metres long, maybe more. She wondered if these giants were also making their way back to the place of their birth to breed – perhaps to a pool or lake as yet unknown to the recently arrived humans – when as quickly as they arrived, they were suddenly gone.

Back on land, the large fires lit around the work site to discourage animals from coming too close, worked well for a while, but hunger is one of the most powerful forces in nature. Unsated, it can even attenuate fear. The controlled human operation exploded violently into turmoil as one of the excavators came under attack.

The comm on the Bridge binged. "Lieutenant Singh here – go ahead."

"Lieutenant, this is O'Brien. We have an animal incursion – some sort of giant crocodiles!" She was shouting over the comm to a background of hollering and screams.

Baines looked at Gleeson.

"I haven't even tried the chair out yet, skip!" he said, plaintively.

The giant yellow machine sat in the shallows, scooping great bucketfuls of gravel from the riverbed and depositing them on the back of a waiting lorry. The driver sang loudly and off key, as site workers have always done, when a set of two-metre-long jaws launched from beneath the river's surface, raising barely a ripple of warning. They struck his cab with stunning speed, crumpling its protective framework slightly. He screamed in shock and surprise as the side of his enclosure took the hit. Meanwhile, two more of the creatures snapped at the machine itself, injuring themselves but also causing damage to one of the tracks.

The operator panicked and tried to reverse, but the damage caused the tractor to turn right. He could spin around but was otherwise stuck in place. Finding himself even deeper in the water and effectively crippled, he attempted to steady his breathing and his nerves while he considered.

Quickly deciding on a course of action, he tried to pull himself ashore using the bucket arm and one working track, but the excavator began to twist and skip. His first attempt at movement had caused him to slip into the very hole he had been excavating under the water and his machine now listed. Dug in as he was, the danger of going over was simply too great so he gave up on the idea, trusting in the build quality of the machine while he waited for help.

The twelve-metre-long animals slunk back into the water, but sensing their quarry was in trouble, soon rallied for a second run. With huge jaws gaping to reveal a maw almost four metres high, they renewed their assault.

Although the lorry was no longer being loaded by the stricken machine, the driver was yet to notice. His attention focused on an e-zine article, while he listened to music through earphones. He jumped and nearly threw his expanded comm out of the window when Corporal Jones banged on his window bellowing, "WAKE UP *PEN COC*!"

Jones and two other security personnel, a man and a woman, climbed up into the back of the steel sided tipper, shouting for the driver to reverse into the shallows towards the stranded digger. "Don't fire at them in the water!" ordered Jones. "A high charge will fry the machines!"

Forty metres away Corporal O'Brien saw what Jones was doing and ordered the remaining six officers to jump up into the second lorry's load bed. Certain they were safe, she climbed up into the cab of the remaining thirty-ton earth-mover and squeezed in behind the driver.

This was a really workable defence platform against the low-slung crocodilians, but at that moment the whole nature of the attack changed.

Tim, Henry, Rose, Woodsey and Clarrie were encamped on top of the wooden palisade with a picnic. The teens peppered Tim with all sorts of questions about the creatures and plants they were seeing, while generally enjoying the lazy, warm spring day.

Woodsey took a swig of his drink. "Now this is how I like to watch work happen," he said, sighing contentedly as he observed the labour at the river's edge.

The entire mood of their situation went from paradise, to paradise lost, in an instant. The brutal animal attack which erupted before their eyes left the people out there – their people – suddenly fighting for their lives.

"*Sarcosuchus?*" Tim queried in disbelief, at once horrified and fascinated.

Almost immediately it became obvious that one of the excavators was in a lot of trouble, although the driver appeared to be safe for now at least. He was protected within the defensive structure Woodsey's father had designed to reinforce the cab. Another devastating crash rang across the plain as the largest crocodile hit the house of the digger again and still the structure kept the man inside alive.

"Damn it, Dad," Woodsey spoke in a reverential whisper. "You're *good*!"

They saw the soldiers scramble up into the back of the lorries to get away from their assailants. That was when the second attack came.

Gleeson ran down to the Pod's armoury to meet Major White and The Sarge, who were already gearing up to take a team outside.

"Congratulations on your promotion," said The Sarge, slapping a stun rifle into Gleeson's hands with an *almost* straight face.

The Australian's response was muffled as he donned his body armour.

Sergeant Jackson smiled. Gleeson was his kind of bloke.

"I wish we'd got the shuttle," said White.

"Tell me about it," Gleeson bit out as his head popped through the top of his vest. "We were just talking about bringing the escape pods into service not five minutes ago – and now this!" he gestured, generally outside.

"There's a personnel carrier in the compound, fully charged and ready to go," The Sarge announced. "I had it prepped in case we needed to sally out in a hurry."

"You must be bladdy psychic, mate," Gleeson commented, as he turned to leave.

"Not really, Commander," replied Jackson, as they ran together towards the main hangar. "In this place, all you need to do is plan for the very worst thing that could possibly happen ever. That's the number that comes up every time!"

Four more giant crocodiles swam towards the skirmish. Two of them crawled out of the water to snap at Jones and his companions as they stood in the tipper bed on the back of the lorry – a vantage point frustratingly close but just out of their reach. The remaining pair diverted back into the flow as the river began to boil.

This was not a function of temperature but an effect created by the monstrous shoal making its way upstream. If they were to join the small advance party, which swam by a few minutes earlier, this larger group would have to run the gauntlet. The bask of Sarcosuchi, mostly hunting the waters, were waiting for them. The riverbanks were also coming alive, as other interested parties began to appear from the forests and even the air.

A terrifying bellow rolled across the clearing behind O'Brien. She turned as best she could in the restricted space within the cab and gaped as yet more new players joined the game.

Clarrie screamed. All the teenagers froze, jaws dropping, as a nightmare unfolded before them – all except Rose.

"What can we do?" she cried, frantically.

Tim shook his head, unable to process, shocked by the ferocity of these living, breathing, fighting creatures. He was seeing them for the first time, undiluted by narrative, film or holograph. "Oh, crap," was all he could manage.

"Henry!" Rose grabbed her boyfriend and shook him. "There must be something we can do?" Henry hardly seemed to even notice this fierce treatment, so she looked around for inspiration and saw it. "Can you drive that truck?"

Down in the compound was a large four-wheel-drive people carrier. Rose turned Henry's head roughly and pointed at it. "Can you drive it?"

"Er… sure. What are you thinking?" he answered dumbly, barely able to tear his gaze from the mêlée.

"Those blokes and Sheilas in the tipper are gonna get it, mate," said Woodsey, finally adding his assessment as he pointed towards the latest intruders.

Henry turned back to see the new threat his friend was referring to. He scanned the riverbank and sure enough, there were the newcomers, swimming strongly to the shore. As they left the water, they did not crawl in a sprawling gait along the ground like Sarcosuchus, but used their powerful, upright hind legs to launch themselves the last couple of hundred metres overland, at a speed the crocodiles could never hope to match. They were certainly too fast for any human beings caught out in the open, but what made matters worse for the men and women crouching in the backs of the lorries, was that the heads of these latest arrivals were a good three or four metres above the ground.

"What the hell are *those*?!" shouted Henry, beginning to panic. "Two legged crocodiles?"

"Two legged, sprinting crocodiles, mate," added Woodsey, feeding on his friend's fear, "and I've seen 'em before in one of Tim's video nasties – they're Irritators, they are!"

Corporal O'Brien pointed at the new threat posed by the incoming Irritators and ordered the digger driver to intercept them.

He looked at her in disbelief. "This is a digger, Jen, not a jet fighter!"

"Get in front of that lorry!" she shouted. "Those guys are dead if we don't do somethin' right now!"

The operator relocated his thirty-ton earth-mover as ordered. It was painfully slow, but they only had to crawl ten metres, whereas the eight Irritators still had several times that far to run. He managed to plant the machine in front of the team exposed at bite-height, just as the hunting pack arrived.

The animals swerved and bobbed around them in frustration as he swung the bucket erratically – dangerously. They were quick for their size, so this motion failed to score any direct hits, either with the dipper or the bucket. However, the giant yellow-painted monster from another world did make them shy a little, and this provided an opportunity. The soldiers seized it and began firing their stun rifles, but with everything in motion it was difficult to get a clean shot, so their effectiveness was also limited.

This no-score-draw whipped up an agitated cacophony from the Irritators. Their anger was so thunderous that the terrified people in the back of the lorry had to release stock and trigger to cover their ears.

White, Gleeson, The Sarge and their team burst through the outer hatch of the personnel airlock and staggered, almost comically, to a halt.

"Where the hell is it!" bawled The Sarge, livid. "Someone's nicked the damned truck!"

Henry drove faster than he really felt he could towards the people being attacked by the dinosaurs.

"I hope you know what you're doing!" screamed Tim from one of the rear seats.

"*Hell*, no!" shouted Henry, as the ten-ton personnel carrier smashed through ferns, cycads and brush, tearing up the soil. The truck jumped and bounced alarmingly over the uneven ground.

"You're gonna turn us over, mate!" shouted Woodsey, terrified.

"I know what I'm doing!" Henry called back.

"You just said you didn't!"

"I *sort of* know what I'm doing, OK?!"

"Great, so we'll only be 'sort of' killed when you get it wrong then!"

"Will you just shut the f—"

"Watch out for that tree stump!" shouted Rose.

"—ront door, Woodsey! You're makin' me crash!"

"You're doing that all on your own, mate! Aaaargh!" The truck jumped again and Woodsey bounced, banging his head. "Where did you learn to drive? A pay-for-view simulator?!"

Henry slammed the brakes on in an attempt to regain control. The cabin was full of vibration and clatter, as the powerful anti-lock-brakes system worked hard, with all of the other clever onboard electronics, to compensate for the incompetent at the wheel and save everyone's lives. They pulled alongside the lorry with the six stranded soldiers on the back and opened a hatch in the roof.

The driver of the tipper lorry had stayed where he was because the only protection the six people behind him had from these, much taller, invaders was provided by the extraordinary skill of the digger driver in front of them.

The animals were furious but fixated, and as Henry drew up on the opposite side of the lorry they failed to notice them at first. The security team saw their chance immediately and jumped onto the roof and in through the open hatch.

Once inside the personnel carrier, Private Davies sat behind the designated driver, Henry Burnstein Jnr, as he turned the vehicle around.

"Go, go, GO!" he shouted. After a double-take, he added, "Didn't I arrest you last week?"

Henry booted the accelerator and the truck lurched forward as the drive-train and differential gearboxes tried to fulfil his desires and find some traction in the mud and vegetation. Without turning around, he said, "Is that you, Pete? Pete Davies? Didn't you hear? I beat that suspected terrorism rap and as this is only grand theft auto, can't you just give me a fine or somethin'?"

"Just watch the road!" shouted Tim.

"I wish there was one, dude!" retorted Henry.

The Irritators were much quicker off the mark than the personnel carrier. Encircling the tipper lorry, they ran straight into Henry's path. The animals may not have noticed the teenagers' arrival, but they certainly noticed their quarry disappearing into the belly of this new adversary.

Rose screamed as one of the creatures lashed out, snapping like a crocodile at the windscreen. Another animal jumped at the side of the truck and then another. Henry had to stop in order to prevent the personnel carrier from tipping over due to the huge forces created by these one-ton predators launching themselves at its sides.

Rose screamed again and then everybody screamed as the vehicle shook violently.

"If you wanna live to pay that fine, kid, GET US OUTTA HERE!" shouted Davies.

Henry gunned the powerful electric motor once more, knocking one of the dinosaurs aside in a desperate attempt to escape.

The driver of the recently vacated lorry also hit the accelerator, making his thirty-two-ton eight-wheeler shudder and jump into action. He aimed at one of the animals *buzzing* the rescue vehicle – a vehicle he had just realised was being driven by a kid – and knocked the hapless creature flat, crushing it mercilessly under his vehicle's colossal weight. Glancing in the rear view mirror, he saw dinosaurs, pterosaurs and archosaurs draw unto the feast en masse, wreaking havoc. The whole glade behind them rang with a bloodcurdling dissonance of calls, roars and screams.

O'Brien urged her kidnapped digger driver to approach Jones. For a moment, the whole fracas seemed to have moved away, leaving them within a little island of calm. In the sudden respite, the driver began to shake as shock replaced adrenaline. Nevertheless, he nodded and set his jaw, even as he set the machine crawling forward.

The personnel carrier appropriated by the teenagers drove side by side with the escaping lorry. They cut a swathe through the plant life with the enraged carnivores close behind, snapping at their rears.

Soldiers stood in the open gateway to the palisaded enclosure, watching them draw closer.

Hmm… lorries jumping and crashing through rough terrain, followed by furious dinosaurs, Gleeson thought. He looked from White to The

Sarge. "Does anyone else think we should start running?" he asked more calmly than he felt.

"That *would* seem appropriate, sir," replied The Sarge.

"Proportional response, I'd say," added White. "Give the order, Sergeant."

"LEGGIT!" bellowed The Sarge and the whole team ran like hell, heading for the ship at the speed of fright.

Nerve-jangling screeches came from the river, as giant pterosaurs wove and dove overhead, hunting the smaller of the piscine quarry. Some of them in turn fell victim to the waiting Sarcosuchi, as the crocodiles returned to the easier prey in the water. There were so many fish now that even a *do-you-think-he-saurus* would not have left empty-handed.

The Irritators also realised there were easier pickings to be had and peeled off, abandoning their pursuit to make their way back to the river.

"What *are* those things?" asked Davies.

"Irritator Challengeri," Tim supplied automatically. "A smaller cousin of Spinosaurus Aegyptiacus," he added for good measure. "We thought they favoured a fish diet. I suppose we can confirm that now, as they've gone back to the river. Looks like they're quite partial to other things as well though, doesn't it? Like us, for instance."

One of the soldiers in the back of the personnel carrier looked out of the rear windows and called up to the front, "Hey, they're heading back towards Jonesy! We need to turn around!"

Henry checked his mirrors. They were indeed heading towards the lorry where the Welshman made his stand, while attempting to help the stranded digger operator. "Hang on," he said, trying to keep his nerves as well as the vehicle under control. He spun the wheel, turning in the smallest arc he could achieve. Plant life and clumps of earth flew everywhere as the locked differentials kicked and fought against the tight turn. Gracelessly but doggedly, the truck completed its manoeuvre and accelerated back to the riverbank. At least the flattened ferns made the going easier to see, if no less lumpy to traverse.

The bigger lorry carried on through the open gates all the way to the, very closed, hangar bay doors.

Jones leaned over the rear of the tipper lorry's load bed, checking the ground and then the water behind them. Between them, the three soldiers began to relay information back to the driver as his rear-view cameras became submerged. As the huge machine backed into the shallows, Jones felt like he was locked in some bizarre, slow-motion dream. The clincher was the repetitive, *"Warning! This vehicle is reversing!"*

The Sarcosuchi did not appear overly concerned by the monstrous thing creeping towards them, issuing polite requests to make way. However, they did start to take an interest as the juicy titbits upon it, ever out of reach, began to get closer to the waterline.

The driver of the crippled excavator had tried to fend them off as much as possible but the angle of the machine had made any extreme manoeuvres perilous. If the bucket swung too far out and dug in, or even took on a ton of water at the wrong moment, it might have tipped the machine over completely. Then it would simply be a matter of being torn apart or drowning, depending on which way the digger ended up.

He brought the cab around so that his door faced the slowly approaching corporal.

A huge Sarcosuchus snapped at Jones, making him dive into the bed of the lorry for protection. They were now very much within the reach of these killers that even the dinosaurs feared.

The man in the digger almost collapsed with relief when Jones poked his head back up again. A deep, guttural grunting sounded from the water, as two smaller Sarcosuchi approached from the other side. They both opened their mouths ready to attack.

Faced by this terrifying group, this 'anger of Archosaurs', Jones could only wave the digger driver back into his safe shell, backing himself off, too.

Every time he approached, the crocodiles came on. It seemed that the majority of the huge shoal had now passed them by, despite heavy losses. Fortunately, this meant that there was a general quieting around them, as many of the predators began fading away to devour their kills in peace. *Unfortunately*, it meant Jones had the remaining Sarcosuchi's full attention.

"Lush!" the Welshman commented sarcastically. "Any ideas?" he asked the man and woman standing behind him.

As they pondered, the hatch on top of the lorry's cab opened, making the three turn around. The driver popped his head up. "What now, Corporal?" he asked.

The hugest of the three remaining Sarcosuchi chose that moment to attack. With a gargantuan effort, it jumped onto the back of the lorry, throwing all three people to the deck.

"GET US OUT OF HERE!" screamed Jones.

The driver dropped immediately but was unable to help them. The colossal weight suddenly landing on the back of the load area had caused the lorry to jump, cracking the man's head hard against the hatch. Luckily for him, he fell into the relative safety of the cab; unluckily for the others, they were now stranded and just a few feet away from the snapping maw of one of nature's most successful, time-proven predators.

When the personnel carrier drew alongside, completely unlooked for, Jones made a mental note to offer up a prayer of thanks at the earliest possible opportunity – but at that moment, he had to jump.

The roof hatch was opened again and helping hands dragged the three petrified souls inboard.

"What about the drivers?" someone asked.

The lorry next to them was bucking and swaying as the enormous beast on the back thrashed wildly to get either forward or off. It was beached.

Jones thought frantically and then an ear-splitting roar filled their entire world. The Sarcosuchus made an immense effort, using the power of panic to launch itself back into the water. It disappeared under the surface quickly and, with one furious thrash of its tail, was gone.

The passengers shouted, almost all at once, *"What the hell is that?!"* The rumble was shaking the whole vehicle and now so loud that no one could hear anyone else.

The first lorry to escape reached the ship, but instead of safety and relief, the driver found only Gleeson and The Sarge. Jumping up into the cab, they asked him the unthinkable. When he told them what he thought of their request, they *insisted.*

After a hasty three-point-turn, they drove back out of the compound, heading once more for the fiasco at the river's edge. As they approached, they saw a woman and two men – one of them the unmistakable bulk of Corporal Jones – leap across from one vehicle to the other. They had no chance to cheer this good fortune, because they were almost immediately overwhelmed by a ground-quaking roar.

Covering their ears and looking up to find its source, they saw something which rattled them far more than any terror of the ancient world.

Chapter 2 | I'm Captain Baines

Baines and Singh watched the debacle on the riverbank unfold via the *New World*'s security cameras. Without the shuttle, there was really nothing they *could* do but watch, and hope.

A sudden and deafening roar shattered that hope.

The noise, loud even through the bulkheads, was that of another giant vessel. It was not as huge as the *New World*, but it didn't need to be – this was a warship, black and more lethal than anything in this world.

Baines ran to one of the side windows on the bridge and her heart sank.

"What the hell is it?" Singh demanded, frantically. "I've got nothing on scanners, sensors, radar – nothing!" He ran over to join his captain, having to resort to simply looking. Part of him wished he had not.

A beeping started up behind them, from another console. Singh ran over to it and called up the information the computer was so desperate to impart.

"Oh no," he said quietly.

Baines turned slowly and walked back to him, her face ashen. "What is it?" she asked, unemotionally.

Sandip turned to her. "Another ship," then he requalified. "Not *that* one," he pointed back out of the window. "I mean *another*, 'nother ship."

Just a few minutes before these events, in the innocent past, it was quiet where Natalie stood in one of the subsidiary holds, deep within the Pod.

Dr Natalie Pearson, as the programme's zoologist, had originally signed up to consult. Her brief was wordily entitled: Consultation and supervision of the dietary requirements for the various animals allocated for introduction to the new environment on Mars. She was also to advise on any practical issues faced when creating suitable environments for these animals. Her experience in the field and in veterinary science had now been given a new direction, however.

A couple of days ago, she had quickly converted a largish container into a giant kennel of sorts for her patient. During her last trip outside with Captain Douglas, an animal had been injured saving the captain's life. Douglas had insisted the creature be brought back to the ship for treatment and it had automatically fallen to Natalie to look after it.

She smiled at her patient. The Mayor Dougli Salvator had been named partially by Captain Douglas himself. He had called him 'the mayor' because the little animal, alone, had welcomed the captain to prehistoric Earth – at least, if you considered being knocked to the ground and covered with saliva and urine a welcome. The rest of its name had been supplied separately by Natalie, and to Douglas' dismay, the name had stuck. Its name meant Mayor, Saviour of Douglas, in honour of the manner in which the little dinosaur had joined their crew.

By treating Mayor, for short, she was by her very actions studying him too. He had been seriously wounded by an adolescent Mapusaurus. The attacker had bitten a nasty chunk out of Mayor's side with its lethal, shark-like, serrated teeth.

"Up on your feet already?" she asked in pleasant surprise. Natalie shook her head in wonderment at the extraordinary toughness and resilience of animals, as she reached out and patted the creature's leathery skin. Already the Mayor had accepted her, realising she was the food provider.

Natalie had cropped a thick carpet of ferns from the new compound outside the ship and laid them on the floor of the container. They were for use as bedding, but also provided a modicum of comfort to the frightened animal in this stark, unnatural environment.

It turned out that the crop was also providing for a good deal of comfort *eating* too. She was sure there had been a lot more ferns and certainly a lot fewer pats in the container the night before.

Her smiled transformed into a grin. "I'm nursing a dinosaur. A dinosaur!" she repeated, unable to believe it.

Tim had not been able to identify Mayor's species exactly. The best description that they had for him was, 'like a Hypsilophodon', a small herbivore from the early Cretaceous Period. Mayor was around the same size, a little under two metres in length and around 700mm high, at the hip. He was an olive to green colour and usually walked about on all fours, but could run very quickly on his hind legs when necessary; quick enough even to outpace the deadly Mapusaurus, given a chance out in the open.

The description was pretty close but for two problems: firstly, Hypsilophodon lived around thirty million years before the crew of the *New World* had landed in Patagonia, and secondly, remains of that species had only been found in Britain and Western Europe.

Mayor limped around to face Natalie, expectantly. She reached down and picked up a large fern to feed him, whilst stroking his head dotingly.

She was not really sure if these ancient reptiles would respond to such tactile comforts, but it certainly helped her to connect with this miracle with which she had been entrusted. It did not matter a jot to Natalie which species he was, she adored him.

"Now we need to keep all of this pooh for your Auntie Patricia," Natalie spoke as if to a child. *Auntie Patricia* was actually Dr Patricia Norris, the microbiologist and Tim's mother. Patricia had requested that all of Mayor's dung be kept for the seed growing areas, set aside in the recently finished inner compound.

Natalie heard a noise from behind and turned. At first she thought she was hearing things, but lowering her gaze, she found the cause. Reiver sat in the open hatch of the container, polishing the floor with his tail.

"I thought I told you to stay in our quarters?" The question was rhetorical, of course. She knew the answer. The border collie did offer mitigation though; he yawned hugely and whined.

Natalie gave up, chuckling at her most loyal, if not always most obedient, companion. "Come in then, come and say hello – be gentle though."

Reiver entered the container slowly, perambulating erratically as he was driven on by his propeller at the rear.

As the two animals came nose to nose, Natalie could not help thinking she had stepped into one of those mushy movies, where the animal is the star. She petted them both and gave Reiver a kiss on his head. He grinned his border collie grin.

Introductions made, Reiver promptly raised his leg over Mayor's dinner.

"Reiver!" snapped Natalie.

"Ahem," someone said from the door.

Natalie looked up and saw Thomas Beckett, the once wealthy historian, standing in the entrance.

"Hi, Thomas," she greeted with a smile.

Against all odds, they had brushed aside the frosty beginnings of their relationship to become friends. A freak hurricane had almost killed them a few days ago, the terror of that shared adventure bridging any gap between them. Natalie had since begun to realise that, when returned to his comfort zone, Beckett was actually quite interesting. Moreover, he was wise and even witty when engaged. In fact, he reminded her a little of her father. He had never understood her need to go 'gallivanting off' all over the world after dangerous animals, either – but always loved hearing her stories about them, nevertheless.

"Come in," she invited.

Beckett looked a little unsure as he eyed the dinosaur and then the protective dog. "I've not had much experience with animals," he said.

"You'll be alright," Natalie encouraged. "Just come in slowly but confidently."

Reiver gave the historian the unbreakable stare; always the first warning. Natalie saw the signs and tried to break his line of sight, but it was like chewing gum to a shoe.

"This is just phase one, Thomas. He's not sure of you because you look tense," she said.

"Erm…" Beckett looked, if anything, tenser still. "Phase one?"

"Yes, phase two is the lip curl and show of teeth. I call it the Elvis," she chuckled. "Phase three is exhibited as aggressive growling and barking."

"What's phase four?" asked Beckett, tremulously.

"That's the point when, for centuries, postmen and women around the world have realised they've left it too late to jump the other side of the gate," she laughed, unconcerned. "Just walk in with confidence, ignoring the animals at first."

He tried to walk in like he belonged there but despite his best efforts at nonchalance this still led to phase two. "How long do I ignore him?" he asked nervously, trying not to glance downwards.

Natalie smiled. "Once *we've* spoken, you can greet Reiver. It's a pecking order thing. Speak lightly, in an animated, friendly way. They associate deep voices with aggression. Get this right and he will always think of you as a friend. Most importantly, *want* to make his acquaintance. If you don't, he'll smell it on you and won't trust you. We can often use our superior intelligence to influence dogs, even control them, but we can *never* hide our moods from them."

"Erm, right," Beckett said weakly. "And if I get this wrong?"

"Ah… well, yes, he'll remember that too, I'm afraid. It would be better if you got it right."

"Hello, boy," tried Beckett, kindly, doing his best. He let Reiver sniff his outstretched hand, keeping his fingers safely curled but not fist-like.

Along with his mistress's relaxed bearing, this was of course enough. The dog sensed the man's friendly, if clumsy, intent and displayed his understanding by giving Beckett's hand a lick. He wagged his tail and sat, panting slightly – Cretaceous Gondwana offered a rather warmer climate than the mountains of Northern England and Wales, for which he had been bred.

Beckett knelt to fuss Reiver's ears. "Good boy," he said, smiling now with relief. He was surprised how rewarding it felt, being accepted by this most vigilant of bodyguards.

Reiver *woofed*, startling the historian at first, but realising he was not actually about to be savaged, Beckett decided try his luck with the dinosaur. This was actually a lot easier. Thomas did not get the feeling he was on trial for his life with this one. Mayor was actually more interested in the fern Reiver had so recently *flavoured*.

"You did that well," Natalie congratulated warmly. "Just before you came, I introduced Reiver to Mayor and couldn't help marvelling at the way they just took it in their stride. 100 million years between them and many, many species, but no problems. We can't even get on with our own – and from our own time, no less!"

"Yes," Beckett nodded sagely. "As a historian, all I can say is, the more things change…"

As if on cue, a siren began to wail all over the ship.

"Oh, what now?" asked Natalie, exasperated. Her comm binged, as if in answer. She took it from her pocket. "Pearson," she answered.

"*Natalie,*" drawled an American voice through the small speaker. "*It's Doc Flannigan. Remember our little chat a few days ago, about joining my medical staff?*"

"Yes," Natalie stated cautiously.

"*Well, this might be the ideal time to earn your wings!*" he replied.

The main doors were already open when Baines arrived in the hangar. She watched impassively as most of the heavy plant made its way in, trailing mud everywhere. Everyone appeared subdued. The animal attack had been shocking, but the arrival of the warship dispelled any illusion of safety, even within their walls. Gleeson and The Sarge jumped down from a huge eight-wheel-drive behemoth and Baines approached them.

"Commander. Sarge. What's happening?" she asked, peremptorily.

Sergeant Jackson looked furious. "All hell broke loose out there, Captain, dinosaurs everywhere!" he said. "And those damned kids nicked the people carrier I had ready for just such an emergency!"

"What!?" asked Baines in disbelief.

"Never mind that," said Gleeson, looking waxen. "Did you see that bladdy great black warship?!"

Baines nodded. "We couldn't track it – stealth tech," she stated, disgustedly. "Sandip roughly worked out its trajectory and then he caught something else on the radar. We'll need to discuss that crisis as soon as we've dealt with this one. We've got a new reality here, and we need everyone to get busy. It seems that time's caught us up, gentlemen."

"Time – that's funny," said Gleeson, without any trace of humour.

The three looked around to find the personnel carrier already disgorging some very frightened looking people. After all the action and panic, shock was beginning to affect everyone involved.

Dr Dave Flannigan, Nurse Justin Smyth and the recently recruited Dr Natalie Pearson were taking people aside to sit them down and check them over.

This left only five very sheepish looking teenagers to jump down.

Jackson ran across the hangar towards them, bawling, "What the hell were you lot playing at?!"

When he reached them, Private Davies asked him for a quiet word before he tore them off a strip. As the soldiers huddled, Baines caught up with them. Corporal Jones intercepted Gleeson and took him to one side too.

"They shouldn't have boosted the truck, I know, Sarge," said Davies. "But they got to us just in time."

"We were on our way!" countered The Sarge, angrily. "At least we would have been if they hadn't nicked the personnel carrier to go joy riding!"

"I know, Sarge," Davies tried again, placatingly. "I know they did wrong, but what I'm saying is, we were absolutely down to the wire. If they hadn't got there at that exact moment, I think we'd have been lost – everyone outside the vehicles anyway. They were just ahead of you, Sarge. They acted. It was last second, Sarge. With all due respect, I think you would have been too late."

"We can't have people just taking vehicles, Private," Baines broke into their conversation, "however well intentioned."

"I understand, Captain," replied Davies. "It's difficult to condone, I know, but they were on point and they made the call. If they'd done as they should have, and got the hell outta there, back to the ship, I for one wouldn't be here to have this conversation, ma'am. That's all I'm saying."

Baines nodded and looked at the other officers.

"Davies has a point," Baines admitted, reluctantly.

"Captain?" asked The Sarge, looking scandalised.

"I know," said Baines, waving him down a little. "You're right in principle, Sarge, but maybe we need to adapt here. There's a good chance that if those little," she searched for the word, "*tearaways* hadn't lifted your ride, we'd be several people down right now." She sighed and thought for a moment. "Maybe what we need to do is accept that this is the end of the line for any mollycoddling, and start training *everyone* for situations like this?"

"So we *all* become the security force?" chipped in Gleeson, joining them.

"In a sense, yes," said Baines.

The Sarge frowned in thought. "There's merit in this, Captain," he said. "But don't forget, we've had years of training to help us make these sorts of decisions. I'm not sure about giving out the keys to the armoury and hoping for the best?"

Baines smiled at him, ever the security officer. "That's why we need you to keep 'em in line, Sarge," she stated.

Jackson gave her one of his sergeant-to-officer looks. This one, quite eloquently but with exquisite politeness, said, 'you're out of your damned mind!'

Baines approached the unruly teenagers with the three soldiers in tow.

"Anyone care to explain what you were doing out there?" she asked, menacingly.

"Er," said Henry. "Well…"

"We… erm," began Tim.

Rose glared at her friends with exasperation. "We were saving those people's lives!" she snapped at the captain. "What the hell did it look like?!"

Baines raised her eyebrows, the germ of a smile tugging at her lips. "Rose *Miller*, isn't it?" she asked.

The little group was suddenly broken up by a mob of panicked and irate parents, all seeming to arrive at once.

"We'll continue this conversation later," Baines said, squeezing out of the way of the flow.

Jim Miller pulled his daughter into his arms and held her close until she was fighting for breath.

Patricia Norris grabbed her son, alternating between holding him and straightening her arms to look up and threaten him.

Tom Wood wore a half smile as he looked Woodsey up and down. He shook his head before shaking the young man's hand. After a moment of manly respect, he pulled him into a bear hug, unashamedly shaming his teenaged son.

Mrs Chelsea Burnstein, already in tears, ran straight to Clarrie and Henry, also holding them tight. Mr Burnstein went straight for the captain, "What the hell are you guys playing at? Letting a bunch o' kids drive off monsters? That's your jobs, damnit! That's what you're all paid for!" he included the other officers now.

"About that," bridled Gleeson. "My last month's salary seems to have gotten lost in the mail – along with a hundred million years of back pay!"

Baines waved him down and spoke to the angry father of two. "Mr Burnstein, we are all upset that they took this into their own hands, but—"

"Upset?!" shouted Burnstein in disbelief.

"*But*," Baines continued, talking over him, "they acted quickly and they saved a lot of lives today. I don't want them to ever attempt anything like that again, but we should be proud of them."

"They all nearly got themselves killed!" Burnstein bellowed.

"And that is why," Baines was unfazed by the man's righteous anger, "we are going to begin training everyone, as best we can, in the sort of survival skills we'll *all* need from now on."

That brought silence down over the little congregation.

"We're also going to need pilots for the small fleet of shuttles we're converting from the *New World*'s escape pods."

A larger group was gathering now. It seemed that almost everyone had run down to see what was going on. *Right*, thought Baines, *this is as good a time as any*. She climbed up onto the back of one of the lorries, the better to see everyone and be seen.

She raised her hands for quiet. With the outer airlock now closed, it was almost absolute. "Everyone, we haven't much time, so I'll be brief," she began. "What happened outside was another animal attack, but as far as we know, everyone is OK – at least, for the moment."

As Baines gave the crowd some information to keep them satisfied, Gleeson caught The Sarge's eye, taking him aside. "I've just spoken to Jonesy. We've still got two blokes out there, Sarge," he spoke quietly. "The drivers of the digger and the lorry."

"I see," said Jackson. "Shall we get some privacy and see if we can radio them?"

They walked further into the hangar, picking up Corporal Jones on the way. Jumping up into one of the other trucks, Jackson fired up its radio.

"This is The Sarge to the stranded digger and lorry, come in."

White noise.

Sergeant Jackson looked bleakly at Gleeson when another Australian voice came back to him. *"Hey, Sarge, it's Bluey here. I'm in the digger."*

Jackson nodded, at once relieved and satisfied. He knew Bluey, he was solid and level-headed; he could work with him.

"Good to hear from you, Bluey. Sorry we had to scarper on you," The Sarge acknowledged. "Are you secure, for now?"

"I'm in the river surrounded by dinosaurs, mate."

Jackson winced. "Yeah, sorry me old mucker. Can you see the driver of the lorry? I understand he was knocked unconscious?"

"Not from here," the analogue rig crackled. *"But if he's outside, he's carked it."*

"No," said Jones, "I saw him fall back inside the cab."

The Sarge nodded with relief once more and reported this encouraging news back to the stranded digger operator.

"Well, he should be safe from the crocs up there, but those other baggers were a whole 'nother stretch o' road, mate," concluded Bluey.

"Any sign of them calming down?" asked Gleeson.

"The crocs have calmed down after the fish course," replied the Australian. *"They are sunning themselves on the banks now – three of 'em, I think. Those other ugly rooters went back to the forest carrying a load o' dead fish in their mouths after the shoal disappeared up stream. The flying critters have all but gone too. I think that might be down to the crocs hanging around though, 'cause there's still plenty of dead fish around."* White noise fizzed across the channel for a few moments before Bluey's voice returned, strong once more.

"I tell you what, cobber," he continued, *"if I ever get home to have a cold one with me mates, I'm gonna laugh their crocodile stories straight out o' the pub!"*

"We'll come and get you as soon as we can," replied The Sarge, grinning appreciatively at the man's courage. "Is there anything you need?"

"*Yeah,*" he replied. "*If this sort o' crap is gonna happen every time we go out in these things, you need to get one o' those engineers to build a dunny into 'em! It's bad enough bein' stuck out here like a galah, without having to cross m' legs as well. And no way I'm sticking me old fella outta the window, either, so get a wriggle on, mate!*"

Jackson chucked. "We'll be coming for you soon, bud. Hang on."

"*Fair dinkum, but, Sarge?*" asked Bluey, calling him back.

"Yes, son?"

"*That black ship...*"

"I know. Just hang on, we're coming for you, both of you, I promise. Sarge out."

He turned to Gleeson. "We need one of those escape pods now, Commander," he said. "We need to fly over those crocodiles and frighten 'em off. Then we can charge out with the personnel carrier and get our boys back."

Gleeson nodded and activated his comm. "This is Gleeson, calling Lieutenant Nassaki?" he said. "Nasso? Can you hear me?"

"*Hiro here, sir,*" the engineer's voice came back. "*How can I help?*"

"We need you to pop one of those lifeboats, now," said Gleeson. "Looks like we've got to rescue somebody."

A moment's silence. "*Is it urgent?*"

"Yeah, the clue was in the word 'rescue', mate."

"*Oh, but we haven't got a workaround for the explosive decoupler yet, Commander,*" said Hiro. "*If we do this, we may not be able to reengage the escape pod to its berth.*"

"We'll just have to park it in the Pod hangar, then," said Gleeson. "I need it now, Lieutenant."

"*Right,*" said Hiro. "*Meet me at escape pod five.*"

Gleeson looked momentarily unsure. Then his comm came back to life.

"*That's the escape pod bank at the rear of the ship, Commander,*" said Hiro.

Gleeson grinned. "Thanks Hiro, on my way."

He turned back to The Sarge and Jones. "Fancy a little drive out in the countryside, gents?"

The Sarge climbed back into the personnel carrier, while Captain Baines continued to speak in the background. Jones opened the inner hatch allowing Jackson to back the truck into the airlock. He began the closing cycle and walked around the vehicle to the outer hatch in anticipation.

Baines noted their movements, but did not break off her address. As yet unaware of the people left outside, she kept the crowd distracted, trusting The Sarge would have good reason for taking a vehicle out.

"…And whatever challenges we face," she intoned, slapping a fist into her palm, "we will meet them and beat them, together…"

After a few moments the giant steel doors boomed closed, cutting her off and Jones began opening the outer airlock. He jumped up into the cab as daylight streamed into the chamber. The Sarge reversed out and turned around, slowly letting the vehicle creep towards the gateway. The eight-metre-tall gates were now closed, securing the compound against attack. There was no hurry, he knew it would take a few minutes for Gleeson and Chief Nassaki to free the escape pod and fly over the river. This strategy had proved successful with the dinosaurs on previous occasions – he just hoped the noise of its engines would frighten these huge crocodiles away, too.

As the personnel carrier rolled up to the gates, The Sarge nodded up to the men who guarded them from the top of the walkway. One uniformed man, who turned out to be a woman, climbed down via a ladder to ask their intentions. Jackson ordered the gates opened so that they could sally out immediately as soon as the coast was clear. He also explained that, with any luck, they would be bringing the abandoned lorry back with them too. The stranded digger would have to wait for now.

The woman saluted and climbed into the ten-ton excavator parked at the entrance – her services training placing her at home at the controls of almost any type of vehicle. The machine was permanently posted by the gateway to remove and replace the pair of tree trunks being used as draw-bars, through the hoops on the back of the gates.

The system was simple and dirty, but it was strong and worked well enough for now.

"Kong at the gates," Jones muttered.

They waited.

Chief Nassaki and Commander Gleeson sat in *Lifeboat 5*'s pilot and co-pilot seats respectively. Hiro had already opened the external hatch, allowing them to see out of the front screen. He had chosen *Lifeboat 5* specifically, because its location on the hull faced the situation they were heading into. They could clearly see the stricken plant vehicles, temporarily abandoned in the shallows.

Gleeson sent a text message to the captain with a priority code, outlining their intentions and giving her the opportunity to warn the assembly that a bang and some structure-borne vibration through the ship might be likely.

"I hope she won't mind us destroying one of the escape pod bays," Hiro fretted.

"Don't worry, Nasso," drawled the Australian. "It's on me." He turned to the Japanese engineer and grinned. "Maybe she'll give me the sack and I can go back to blowing stuff up?"

"We *are* blowing stuff up, that's what's worrying me!" retorted the engineer. To further make his point, he hit the launch stud and the escape pod shot out with a boom, trailing pieces of scrap metal behind it from the linkages.

Gleeson knew, even the best laid plans can go awry, but the situation was desperate for the men out there, one of whom was not even conscious. Worse still, they had not really had time to *make* a proper plan. For now, he was working on the theory that half the time, half-baked knee-jerk reactions, come off. *Please let the glass be half-full today*, he prayed silently, as he commed Jackson and Jones.

"We're out – be real careful fellas, there's a lot of ways this can go cactus on us."

Sergeant Jackson and Corporal Jones waited just inside the gates. As soon as they heard the boom and the sound of the engines, the digger driver began removing the locking bars.

The comm crackled to life with Gleeson's warning. "Understood," replied Jackson. "We'll be on our way as soon as the gates are open."

"How do you want to play this, Sarge?" asked Jones. His voice was surprisingly high for such a huge man, his sing-song Welsh accent sounding at odds with the gravity of the situation they were about to plunge into.

"We park alongside," answered the no nonsense cockney sergeant. "Jump out of the top hatch onto the bed of that wagon, get our boy out of the digger and get him into the cab of the lorry. The driver of the lorry is probably still out, so I may need some help with him. Bluey's a handy sort of geezer, he can look after him while I drive. *You* climb back into *this* vehicle and we'll make our escape."

The Sarge glanced at Jones, to make sure his orders were understood.

Jones nodded, affirmative. "That's a nice, simple plan, Sarge," he said.

"Thanks," replied Jackson, quirking his lip slightly. "By the numbers – there should be no problems."

"Business as usual, isn'it."

"*Absolutely.*"

"What do you think will happen?"

"No idea."

Captain Baines had no idea what was going to happen next either. She broke off her address, dispersing the gathering in the hangar bay so that she could contact the bridge for an update. Lieutenant Singh was at his usual station at the helm and able to bring Baines up to speed with the rescue plan – such as it was. Hopefully, it would be little more than a mopping-up exercise, but either way, there was little she could do to help. Besides, Singh could certainly be trusted to organise any further support, should they call. So the captain decided to leave the boys to their rescue and recovery while she set about a mission of her own.

Their time alone had ended, it seemed, and she urgently needed answers.

Broadly speaking, her intention was to interrogate their prisoner. She should probably follow some kind of procedure – certainly that is what Douglas would have wanted. However, what little time they had left to them was just too precious to waste getting bogged down. Before she knew it, she was standing outside the brig. She hit the call button and waited for a response from the duty officer. As they were still on maximum security, the guard activated the view screen before opening the door. Corporal Thomas saw who it was and let her in.

"Thanks, Corp," said Baines, returning his salute casually and striding in more purposefully than she felt.

Her plan had been to hold an advisory meeting prior to this interrogation, but now this new enemy had arrived, and in force, there was no time. Although the commander of the warship had not made their intentions clear, Baines knew they must be the backup Schultz had threatened. After all, a rescue outfit would have landed, or at least introduced themselves. *No,* she thought, *that was a spectacle designed to frighten us, that's all. It damned well worked too!*

She stood in front of the prisoner. Her loathing of this man was surely even greater than it had been for Lloyd; at least as it stood before Lloyd had redeemed himself by saving Georgio Baccini, at the cost of his own life.

She could see no such path to redemption for this slimy creature. Her only solace came from the man's uncomfortable looking split lip and missing teeth, courtesy of James Douglas. She drew further pleasure from the bandages to both of his arms; traces of the fifty-seven stitches that had been required to remedy Reiver's handiwork, after the dog had taken him down as he tried to run away with the other terrorists.

"Well, well, well," she said at last, breaking the silence. "You look like you were talking when you should've been listening. Reiver's normally such a cuddly bear, and Captain Douglas… well, I suppose he's more complicated. You should choose your enemies with more care."

The man looked balefully at her, his previous, aristocratic *bonhomie* a distant memory.

She said nothing else for a long, long moment, letting the silence build. The fear in the man's body language grew, palpably. This wasn't a deliberate device, although it was nice to watch. The truth was, she simply did not know where to start.

Eventually, he cracked under her stare and blurted out, "OK, I'll tell you whatever you want – anything, everything! Just don't put me outside."

Baines continued to stare. Maybe no interrogation would be necessary after all. He seemed to be doing so well all on his own. She took a deep breath and let it out. Turning her back on the man, she walked a few short steps to the chair opposing the cell and sat down. Crossing her legs and making herself ostentatiously comfortable, she looked up and waited.

Del Bond whimpered, sinking to his knees. Holding onto the bars of his cell, he added, "I'm sorry." He sounded almost frantic.

Baines snorted at that, despite herself. "Tell me," she said, eventually, "who was in that ship which roared over a few minutes ago?"

"What ship?" he tried.

Baines sneered, uncrossed her legs and re-crossed them the other way, settling back into a comfy contempt.

"I mean," Bond sputtered, "I heard something, but…" He stopped talking, a shiftiness intruding on his look of fear. He was clearly working through what she had confirmed for him.

Baines uncrossed her legs a second time and leaned forward slightly. Quietly she asked, "Who?"

Hiro brought the little craft in low over the river and hit the landing rockets. He saw Bluey don his ear defenders to block out the noise. The Sarcosuchi had no such protection and after snapping impotently at the air, they slunk back under the water in a thrashing tantrum, rocking waves over the digger's cab. Bluey's view was temporarily obscured for a moment, until the front and side windscreen wipers self activated.

Another minute or so passed as the roar of the little ship's engines cleared the wildlife from the area. Hiro backed the escape pod off slowly. As far as he could tell, they had accomplished their mission.

Gleeson looked all around them and checked his instruments. "I think we've driven them away for now," he said, reaching a similar conclusion. Hiro turned back towards the *New World*, the swell of engine noise rolling across the plains, sending all sorts of creatures scuttling for cover.

Hiro radioed for one of the Pod hatches to be opened so that he might berth the little ship inside, for safety. The rescue attempt may then take place without blowing the ear drums of any people below. As they neared the ship, a man wearing ear defenders waved them in, using light batons.

Back at the river, the large, four-wheel-drive personnel carrier drew up alongside the tipper lorry. The Sarge backed into position, the rear wheels dipping into the shallows to draw level with the load bed of the much longer lorry. He wanted his vehicle facing their direction of flight when the time came, keeping the front wheels on dry land, just in case it sank in the mud.

Sergeant Jackson and Corporal Jones looked around, making a split-second threat assessment. Jones handed The Sarge a stun rifle – one of the Jerry-rigged devices the crew called Heath-riflesons after the Heath Robinson nature of their construction and appearance. Taking a second rifle himself, he looked to his superior.

"Ready?" The Sarge asked.

Jones nodded once. "Sarge," he replied, simply.

Jackson popped the top hatch and scrambled out onto the roof of the truck, making a full 360 degree check of his environment before calling Jones out after him. He offered a hand to his corporal and both men leapt from the roof of the vehicle into the tipper back of the waiting lorry. As they made their way towards the rear of the load bed, Bluey stood, taking off the ear defenders and dropping them onto his seat.

He tentatively opened his cab's door and waited, wisely checking for a crocodilian resurgence, before committing.

The Sarge nodded and both soldiers held their arms out, ready to catch the stranded construction worker. He leapt. The men caught Bluey and dragged him aboard just as a huge set of jaws launched from the water with an enamel-shattering *snap*!

Jones fairly launched Bluey out of the way as another wave of river water crashed into the back of the lorry soaking them all. Bluey flew and rolled to a halt halfway up the load bed. The Sarcosuchus slunk back under the murky surface, sending up a huge plume of air bubbles.

"The cheeky sod was waiting for us! Just under the water!" exclaimed The Sarge, incensed by the sneak attack.

Jones ventured a glance over the back of the truck. "Ha! *Twll dy din di, crocodeil gwirion!*" he snapped back. No one but Jones understood the remark but it caused a second Sarcosuchus to launch at him from the other side of the digger regardless, taking the corporal completely by surprise.

The Sarge's lightning reflexes saved him. He snatched the bigger man back out of the way and both went down, with Jones' significant bulk on top. The Sarge matched one ancient language with another, releasing a string of Anglo-Saxon invective.

"Sorry, Sarge," said Jones, jumping to his feet and unceremoniously grabbing the back of Jackson's combat jacket to drag his, slightly winded, superior to safety after him.

When The Sarge found his feet, and his breath, he ordered Jones back into the personnel carrier. "We can gloat later!" he admonished.

"Sorry, Sarge," Jones repeated. He leapt back to the other vehicle, disappearing down into its comparative protection.

The Sarge shook his head and pointed for Bluey to climb down through the top hatch of the lorry's cab. The Australian vanished down the hatch as ordered.

For a moment, The Sarge stood alone on the lorry bed and his senses suddenly heightened, making all the hairs on the back of his neck stand up as one. Someone or *something* was in his personal space – right in it. A heavy snort of hot, rancid breath on the back of his neck and the side of his face provided him with undeniable confirmation of this. Slowly, ever so slowly, he turned his head. His heart sank. "Oh, Turkish delight!" the Londoner muttered, under his breath.

"I can't tell you," said Bond.

Baines stood and approached the cell threateningly. "Come again?" she replied.

"They'll kill me."

"What happened to 'I'll tell you anything – everything!' Well, *Derek*?" snapped Baines, her anger rising.

He still twitched slightly at the use of his full name. "But if that ship is here now and I talk, I won't be safe, not even here!" he answered.

Baines frowned and squinted sidelong at Bond, pondering the words, 'not even here'. She filed it away, to come back to later.

"What makes you think you *are* safe here?" she asked with quiet menace, but also genuine intrigue.

"I've seen the way you do things," replied Bond, his confidence increasing a modicum. "I was at Lloyd's trial, remember? You're all still bound by the rules – a fair hearing, even for terrorists and all that *rubbish*. You won't kill me, even if I don't tell you about that ship."

Baines eyebrows shot up. "I won't?" she asked.

"You didn't kill Lloyd."

"He's not here, is he?" asked Baines, tauntingly.

A flicker of contempt crossed Bond's face. "He killed himself," he said. "Playing hero – like that would change anything with *you people*!"

"The way I heard it, he wasn't playing at anything. It was one of the few genuine acts he ever performed," retorted Baines, surprised that she was actually a little saddened by Lloyd's demise. She supposed it was more for the fact that he never had the chance to publicly reform and gain acknowledgement for his atonement.

Bond snorted with derision. "Lloyd was a weasel."

Baines barked a laugh of surprise. "And what the hell are *you*?!" she asked, incredulous.

"I'm a businessman."

"Well, let's do business then," she answered, calmly. "You tell me everything I want to know and in payment you will suffer less, how does that sound?"

"Or I could just wait to be rescued," said Bond, playing his last card.

"You won't be rescued," said Baines. It was simply a statement.

"You don't know what you're up against," he bit back. "I'm better off waiting for them to come for me – waiting with this crew, and its pitiful excuse for a government – than I am telling you about that ship."

Baines wore an expression of mock puzzlement. "But you were there, Derek. Hell, you caused it! So you must know better than that?" she asked, obliquely.

"I was there for what?" he enquired, his recently bolstered nerve unravelling slightly.

Baines summoned Corporal Thomas over to unlock the cell door.

"The regime change, of course," she said. "Captain Douglas is the very best of men, but you've driven him aside, haven't you?"

She stepped into the cell and Bond backed away, but not quickly enough. The woman's fist launched straight from the shoulder, Shotokan style, putting the man down and augmenting the mess his face was already in. Standing over him with a maniacal light in her eyes, she added, "Hi, I'm Captain *Baines*!"

The Sarge dove as the jaws snapped. There was no possibility of getting into the cab in time, so he simply threw himself over the opposite side of the lorry and prayed for a soft landing.

The mud *was* soft and, thanks to his training, he *did* manage to roll with it but he was badly winded and his shoulder hurt like hell.

Jones watched in horror through the windscreen of the personnel carrier as Jackson threw himself from the bed of the larger vehicle, landing right in front of him. He could see that The Sarge was hurt and more than a little dazed. As he opened the door to help, a monstrous head turned the corner of the lorry cab in front of him and *ROARED*! His eyes widened in disbelief and horror – he had no time.

The animal also appeared to size up the situation. With all the predacious senses of the hunter, it roared again as it surged forward.

Jackson came to, just in time to scream as the enormous jaws opened wide enough to swallow him whole. The stench was appalling but his attention really belonged to those huge, serrated teeth.

Baines left the brig and bumped into Mother Sarah.

"Sorry, Jill," said Sarah, distractedly. Then she noticed the overall appearance of the captain, the state of her hands and worse, the look in her eye. "What's happened? Are you OK?"

Baines took a breath, calming herself a little. Her rage felt like it was eating her alive.

"I'm fine," she said, stiffly. Then a question presented itself to her. "What are *you* doing here?"

"I came to try and talk some sense into that awful man," said Sarah. She raised her eyes to heaven, "Forgive me, Lord."

She looked back at Baines. "I thought that if I could get through to him then maybe he could... you know... help, with James."

"Don't worry, I just talked all of the sense out of him!" said Baines with more force than she intended.

Mother Sarah looked down at the captain's bloody hands again. "What happened?" she repeated, quietly.

"I told him he could talk to me or he could explain it all to the dog. He came round to my way of thinking in the end. I'll tell you what I learned in council. I need to get cleaned up. Can you pass the word, Sarah? I want all the heads and chiefs, usual round-up, meeting room off the bridge, one hour."

Sarah nodded. "Of course, Captain," she said.

As Baines started to walk, the priest gently took her arm to stop her. "I know it's been hard, Jill, and I know you've been angry." She looked away. "I don't normally force feed, as you know, but reading my Bible really helps me find comfort and peace when I'm angry or upset. Would you like to try it? There are some passages I could suggest which might really help."

She looked at the captain with so much love and concern that Baines bit back her initial irritation. Instead she sighed, saying, "I tried reading it once, Sarah, but I just couldn't get into it – *so* many adverts."

Sarah rolled her eyes and smiled ruefully. "I have a couple of older copies with me," she said, "printed before all that."

She looked around conspiratorially. "I had to stop using the Bible the diocese gave me, after I read out the first line of a double glazing ad, right in the middle of St Paul's Letter to the Corinthians during a wedding ceremony! They'd muddled all the lines up!" She intoned, "When I was a child, I spoke as a child, I understood new and used doors from just nine-nine-nine. When I became a man, I put away childish things down at Window Shack, for offers you can see through! – Yes, it was all rather embarrassing."

Baines snorted, laughing involuntarily and with her laughter came a few tears. She wiped them and nodded, smiling warmly at the priest with ever-growing respect. "Walk with me to sickbay, Sarah. Maybe I can get two salves for the price of one."

Sarah nodded and fell in alongside. "I'll message the others about the meeting as we walk," she said.

Jones blasted the powerful horn on the truck. The jaws of the Tyrannotitan[1] snapped shut like an enormous bear trap. The Sarge, though injured, nevertheless had time to throw himself back under the lorry he was so

---

[1]   When Tim eventually reviewed the attack from the camera mounted to the front of the personnel carrier, his identification of the animal forced him to update his informational database. He was pretty sure that the creature captured on memory stick, was thought to have either died out towards the end of the Aptian stage of the Cretaceous Period, or possibly have evolved into other strains of Carcharodontosaurs such as Mapusaurus or Giganotosaurus. Clearly this was not the case, because here it was, large as life, in the very late *Albian* Stage – a good 12 or 13 million years later. He put it down to the problems with radiocarbon dating, especially when fossils were preserved within sandstone and without benefit of two handy layers of volcanic rock to sandwich an accurate date for the scientist. This simple anomaly forced him to consider anew, just what else he might be wrong about in this time, too.

lately on *top* of – otherwise, he would have simply disappeared, forever. Jones' split-second distraction had saved him, but only for a moment.

The Sarge looked around. "Oh, Turkish Delight!" he said again, plaintively. The Tyrannotitan could not get to him, but from under the lorry he had spotted a sub-adult Sarcosuchus crawling with deadly purpose from the other side of the vehicle.

Jones' mind raced to find a way, any way to save his sergeant and comrade.

The dinosaur was getting frustrated and *very* angry. The truck's horn seemed to be exacerbating this, so Jones crept forward instead, hoping the slow and relentless threat of the large vehicle might scare the animal away.

The Tyrannosaurus Rex sized adversary clearly did not respond well to threats and reacted by attacking the windscreen with impressive force. The toughened, vacuum rated glass withstood the first blow but cracked at the second.

The multi-laminated material held its ground but Jones was in no mood to see what would happen next. He threw the truck into low-range, selected second gear and stepped on the accelerator. The wheels kicked, the tyres dug and ten tons of steel jumped forward into the very teeth of the furious carnivore.

Head down, muscles bulging, tendons straining to hold the vehicle in check, the creature slowly began to lose ground, its talons leaving great furrows in the soil as they too dug for purchase.

Even though the truck was gaining the upper hand, Jones was astounded by the awesome strength of the beast. However, this force of nature had not reached its maturity without knowing when to retreat and so, giving a final roar of defiance, it fled – there would be another time.

Sergeant Jackson rolled back out from under the lorry, crying out in agony as he went over on his injured shoulder again.

Jones' shoving match with the dinosaur had taken him past The Sarge, so he applied the parking brake and ran back through the vehicle to pop the rear hatch. After a quick check, he jumped down to help.

The adolescent Sarcosuchus, seeing first the angry Carcharodontosaurid, then his quarry about to flee, launched itself under the eight-wheeler, where The Sarge had been hiding just moments before.

It snapped at the men, catching the very back of the injured man's jacket. Jackson screamed again, this time not in pain but in full-blown terror.

Jones held on to him with all his prodigious strength, but even he looked pathetic in comparison with their adversary, half grown or no.

Bluey gaped from the side window of the lorry cab. The whole drama had passed in mere seconds but felt like an epic. Returning to his senses, he threw himself behind the controls and locked the central and all four of the axial differential gear boxes with a practised stroke of his hand – engaging full eight-wheel drive, he floored it.

A terrible noise filled the clearing; terrible and heart-rending. There was simply no stopping the machine as it climbed out of the river, throwing earth and muck everywhere.

The animal, still underneath, was crushed as the four rear wheels smashed its ribcage and spine. The sheer size and power of the animal meant it survived the blow initially, only to die horribly and agonisingly over many drawn out minutes as it slowly suffocated, paralysed and with punctured lungs.

The Sarge was not a cruel man where animals were concerned, but he spared not a second's thought for its suffering. He felt his jacket release from the creatures grasp and shouted a visceral, wordless cry for Jones to get him the hell out of there.

The corporal reacted instantaneously, virtually throwing his injured companion into the waiting truck. The Sarge screamed again but Jones had no time to worry about that now. He secured the rear hatch behind them and ran to the front of the vehicle, climbing into the driver's seat. Throwing the machine roughly into gear once more, he set off after the terrified Australian, who was already bucking and jumping a thirty-two ton lorry across the prairie at full tilt. Jones knew the only thing he could do for his injured friend now was take him back to the ship, where he could get the help he needed.

Bluey tried to wake his own companion, the lorry's original driver, who was alive but still unconscious. As the lorry bounded across the rough terrain, the man slipped from his awkward sprawl across the passenger seats onto the floor of the cab, leaving a smear of blood from a nasty head wound. "Sorry, mate," said Bluey, without slowing.

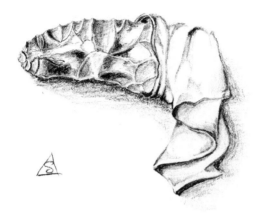

Chapter 3 | Three Sides to Every Story

The click-clack of one stone being bashed against another rang across the small clearing. A rustle in the undergrowth spat out a broken flint – followed by a strong oath.

The man had awoken cold and was trying to bring his fire back to life. He had fallen asleep again in his small cave. He kept doing that, day or night. Drowsiness overwhelmed him constantly, since the accident, and he was always cold. He knew, intellectually, that the weather was temperate, even warm and so put it down to his weakened state.

It must be two, no, three days since I was left alone, he mused. Temporarily giving up on fire, he mussed his hair and rubbed sleep out of his eyes before reaching for the meal he had been unable to finish that morning.

Three days earlier
He had no choice but to leap. The cliff face was almost sheer but tree studded. He crashed straight through the smaller branches near the top, barely slowed, but with every metre he fell the branches became more robust. This robustness quickly translated into pain for the falling man, but it did slow his descent. By the time he came to a stop he found himself

wedged, not high in the branches, but just high enough. This piece of luck, although costly, saved his life. Had he made it all the way to the ground, he would surely have been preyed upon by who knew what before the end of the day.

Pain tore through him. A small branch had gouged a deep gash up his side during the fall, causing much blood loss. Fortunately, the injury did not appear to have pierced any organs, his agony testimony that everything was still working. However, this was where any glimmer of good fortune deserted him and sure enough – lost alone in the Cretaceous Period, trapped up a tree in excruciating pain, unable to move and bleeding copiously without so much as a sandwich to sustain him – he was finding it hard to count his blessings.

He applied as much pressure as he could bear on his wound and waited, hoping for rescue.

Many hours passed. No rescue came. He swore at the unfairness of his situation. At least his wound had coagulated enough to allow him some, very careful, movement. All he could do was try to find a position where the pain was dulled enough to allow him to sleep. He dozed fitfully.

He awoke to his second day alone. Confused by his surroundings, he unthinkingly attempted to stretch some of the unbearable stiffness from his joints. The sudden agony flashed so quickly through his nervous system that it switched off his consciousness like a light bulb.

By the time he came round, half the day had gone. A little more cogent this time, he moved sparingly. After several minutes testing his limits, he spent the next hour trying to leave his tree. Very gingerly, he lowered himself, praying his wounds would not tear open again.

The red sandstone of the cliff changed to limestone at the bottom. He made a cursory search of his immediate area and spotted several pieces of flint lying around on the forest floor. Despite having no idea how to knap it correctly, several attempts, and a few random blows, eventually provided an edge. The man tied his handkerchief around the stone where the bulb of percussion created a natural handle for an improvised knife.

"Great, so now I'm in the stone age," he acknowledged, sourly. After a sigh, he added, "Well, I suppose I'm heading the right way in time, even with this Palaeolithic effort!"

Pocketing some other pieces in his jacket, for use as fire lighters, he moved out.

By late afternoon, thirst and hunger warred with fear and pain to set him about finding sustenance and a better hideout. After a broader investigation of the vicinity, he found what would have been a fairly easy route to scramble back up, had it not been for his condition. The climb up to the shelf from where he had tumbled, the evening before, was torture. He rested for several minutes at the top to catch his breath, knowing he was not safe, but unable to do anything about it.

When the fatigue faded a little, he began scouring the plateau for anything he could use. He was back where the crew, *his* crew he supposed, had made the remarkable discovery of two, twenty million year old, human graves.

A deep depression threatened to take him over as he stood looking into the still open graves, when he spotted two items which allowed him to go on.

The first was a battered lunch box with 'Thomas Beckett' handwritten upon a purpose-made nameplate set into the lid. Inside, there were some sandwiches and snacks which were still edible. More importantly, it also contained a flask of tea. Considering the hurricane and the beating the box seemed to have taken, this was nothing short of miraculous. He turned this tiny piece of civilisation over in his hands, marvelling. "If I ever get home, I need to buy one of *these*."

The tea was cold, but it tasted like the elixir of life to the battered, resourceless outcast.

The second item looked a little more difficult to attain. It was a stun rifle – juiced-up to unleash a massive electrical shock, it was capable of making even an enormous dinosaur think twice.

From his elevated position, the weary, wounded man spied the weapon hanging from a tree at the bottom of the near sheer incline – very close to the place where he had first awoken.

He let go another very long and very heartfelt string of expletives at the injustice of this. Eventually, he realised there was nothing for it and, bracing himself against the pain, he struggled back down to reach this unexpected, but oh so typically difficult to obtain gift.

Once the effects of the effort expended and the pain endured ebbed a little, he was forced to accept that this was actually an immensely fortunate find. Whoever had lost it in the recent storm had even been kind enough to tape a couple of spare power cells to the stock for him. He certainly would never have had the strength to hunt without it.

Darkness began to fall. He had so far been incredibly lucky not to cross paths with any predators big enough to threaten him, but the idea of being out in the forest at night was terrifying. Climbing another tree in his condition was out of the question. If he tore his wound again and lost more blood it might be the end of him. So, moving as quickly as possible, he restarted his search for a bolthole. Life had provided little that he wanted lately, but he seemed to have just a little credit left with regards to what he needed, and his continued reconnaissance of the area soon turned up a small cleft in the wooded, rocky outcrop. Following it cautiously, a tiny, but most importantly empty cave revealed itself.

The space inside was just about big enough for one to sit or lie comfortably, while still leaving room for a small fire at its mouth. He quickly gathered some firewood in what remained of the daylight. Laying some dried brush among the sticks, he took a couple of pieces of flint from his pocket and chipped away until he managed to spark a small fire to life. Bending to blow essential oxygen into the tiny conflagration almost made him pass out. Luckily the fire caught, because it was a while before he could tell whether the sparks before his eyes were real or the flashes of a fading consciousness.

Now

"This healing is hungry work," he muttered to himself. Although still in bad shape, for the first time, he was beginning to feel a little more like himself. He took a bite of the drumstick in his hand. "Hmph, it seems that chicken is the universal default, whichever era you're in."

He had eaten his earlier meal too exhausted to even notice the taste; his body had simply required fuel. The man chewed whilst he stewed, on his situation. He was still feeling the cold. Three days after the fall, his cave was still providing much needed shelter for rest and recuperation; a secure foxhole which even afforded a moderate vantage point. He had managed to pot-shot a couple of small dinosaurs that morning, only leaving his sanctuary to collect his prizes. The first was about the size of a pigeon, the other slightly larger. With some effort, he had plucked and cooked them, devouring the smaller creature entirely. Despite the dubious benefits of Beckett's sandwiches, he had been unusually famished.

Now he was thinking more clearly, he understood the need to 'eat for heat' and decided to tuck into the second... *bird*? It was close enough and certainly tasted similar. Moreover, he did not want to think too hard about what it actually was. After eating it, he almost immediately fell asleep again.

He awoke to a low rumbling noise which was growing gradually louder. His first impulse was to curse his stupidity for falling asleep without a fire, but eventually, the noise became so loud that he had to cover his ears. He limped to the mouth of his small refuge to look out, fearful of what he might find. His jaw dropped.

A huge black warship roared overhead, shaking the very rocks he stood upon. Small animals skittered in all directions across the little clearing before him, all desperate for the cover of the forest.

As the ship passed him, it appeared to slow. For a moment he wondered whether he had been spotted but quickly pushed *that* thought aside. Even if they had seen him, he could not imagine them making any detours on his behalf.

It occurred to him that the ship would probably be headed for the clearer landscape on the other side of the mountains. He knew something of the lie of the land, as seen from the windows of the shuttle a few days ago. He did not know who was in the ship, but he was pretty sure he knew what they were about.

As the swell of the engines' roar gradually died away, he fancied he could hear another set of engines on the wind. These were smaller and higher pitched and he thought he recognised them as those belonging to the *New World*'s shuttle. "A rescue party?" he wondered aloud.

Turning around, tilting his head, he attempted to get a bearing on the sound. "If that's the shuttle, it's coming from the opposite direction from the *New World*. They must be meeting up with that battleship. There's more going on here than I know," he said and the thought filled him with trepidation, as did the realisation that he seemed to be spending a lot of time discussing things with himself. He put his hands together in front of his face, prayer-like, and sighed heavily. He simply did not know what to do. He checked his weak ankle, another souvenir of his fall, to see how well it would support him.

"Hmm," he grumbled to himself. He shook his head in frustration and pulled a face, while reaching for the crude crutch he had manufactured from a long stick with a handy 'Y' shaped top. It was not too uncomfortable to the underarm – he begrudgingly had to thank his flint knife for that small comfort.

"So, what to do?" Once more aware that he was talking to himself, he asked the trees and stones for their opinions. "Step forward or backward? Known or unknown?"

Mulling over the pros and the cons for a while, he calculated allegiances, risks, pitfalls – possible outcomes.

Eventually he began packing up his little camp. He would have preferred to wait, at least until his ankle had healed, but clearly things were in motion and it was time to move on. He roughly fashioned a strap from a slender vine, which he placed through the handle of Beckett's lunchbox. With it thrown over one shoulder and the rifle over the other, his arms were free to use the crutch and generally keep his balance. He looked out over the forest towards the plain where the *New World* lay, many miles hence and well out of sight.

After another moment's pondering he turned to look in the direction the black ship had taken. It had definitely slowed. If the people aboard decided to land at the first available plain or plateau on the other side of the mountains, they could be as close as fifteen or twenty kilometres away. The *New World* was surely closer to thirty, in the opposite direction.

He tried putting weight on his ankle and grimaced again.

"Damn," he said, leaning on the crutch once more. "OK, this way then." Limping towards a most uncertain future, he kept his eyes open for any other signs of man – or for any signs of anything which might wish to eat man.

Baines sat alone, awaiting the arrival of her senior staff. There was real fear on board ship now and it was far more tangible than at any previous time. This was no natural disaster they could get through by 'sticking together' and 'mucking in'. The people on that warship would almost certainly be trying to kill them soon – or render them homeless, which amounted to the same thing.

Baines felt the fear too, relying on anger to keep her afloat. She reminded herself that, firstly, she had some extraordinarily capable people behind her and should take heart from this; and secondly, she must listen carefully to their views and not let anger push her into making mistakes.

This cogent logic helped her feel that she was still, at least nominally, in control. However, despite the enormous worries crowding in on them, she was also prey to smaller niggling doubts. It was impossible not to wonder whether the fear would have been as great had Douglas still led them.

Not for the first time over the last few days, he took over her thoughts completely.

James...

She sighed deeply. Although confident she had the crew's respect, this did not necessarily mean they trusted her the way they had trusted him – did she, for that matter? For the first time, it really struck home, just how much she relied on Douglas' presence. Simply knowing there was always someone to whom she could go when the chips were down made all the difference.

They had all been walking a tightrope since the explosion which destroyed the wormhole drive, but now she had lost her private safety net too. Now she was the leader and it scared her. She briefly wondered if Douglas had been afraid too, when he was 'the man'. It was hard to imagine him feeling like she did inside, right now, but maybe he did. Maybe he always had, but was more skilled at hiding it. *Perhaps! Maybe!* Her thoughts raged. *All I know for sure is that I miss him* so *much!*

Douglas himself had made her captain – to her mind, out of direst necessity – but she knew he would not have felt that way, and his confidence in her was like a knife in her heart. She would rather die than fail his trust and it made her feel ever more the understudy. She was capable of putting on a show or two, of course, to get them out of trouble, but what about the long haul? If she fluffed her lines on this stage, people might die, and it would be her fault. She did her best to shrug that thought aside before it paralysed her; besides, it was time to break a leg.

Captain Baines greeted everyone as they arrived. All the usual faces, but she had also included Tim Norris. The decision was not made lightly. Some of the topics for discussion would be gritty. In the end, she had opted to listen to her own, earlier advice – all mollycoddling is *over*, we need his input, end of.

"Thanks for coming at short notice," she began. "We've got a lot to go through and little time. There's no perfuming this turd. This is probably the worst crisis we've faced yet."

The assembled military and experts looked from one to another with concern.

"As you will have noticed, we have a new face here. I don't know if you're all familiar with Corporal Dewi Jones?" she gestured at the giant Welshman. "He was in the thick of it all out there, earlier today, as he so often is, and was in no small way responsible for getting everyone back alive – even The Sarge, for whom he is sitting in."

She paused to let everyone absorb this information. Gradually, people around the table began congratulating Jones for his courage.

Unused to this sort of praise, he felt awkward, but accepted their goodwill quietly. Normally speaking, if The Sarge gave him a nod of approval, he knew he had done well. "The Sarge saved my life, not thirty seconds before he was injured," he ventured softly. "Getting him home seemed like the right thing to do."

This drew appreciative smiles from the people gathered. Major White gave Jones a comradely pat on the shoulder and a nod of respect from one soldier to another.

Baines spoke again. "Unfortunately, as Corporal Jones said, The Sarge was injured in the rescue attempt and is undergoing surgery on his shoulder as we speak. Thanks to Dewi's quick actions, he was not hurt too seriously. As he obviously can't be here, The Sarge himself asked Dewi to stand in for him, as Major White's second."

She looked at Jones directly. "With what we have planned next, I'm sure you'll earn that seat." She smiled at him with reassuring pride.

Jones smiled back weakly – his face was not really designed for it. "I would just like to say, Captain," he said, "that if Tim and his mates hadn't come back for us, I doubt I'd be sitting here now, isn'it." The Welshman nodded to the lad, who went tomato red.

"Quite right," said Baines. "It was an astonishingly brave thing to do."

"It was all Rose's idea really and, well, Henry drove..." Tim spoke quietly, fading away as he caught his mother's look of consternation.

Jim Miller visibly inflated with pride at the mention of his daughter's clear-headed courage, even though it had shocked him at the time.

"Yes, I'll be keen to keep an eye on Rose's progress," Baines smiled archly at Miller. "It seems she's full of surprises. She certainly appears to have Burnstein-the-younger well trained."

The adults chuckled at that, doubtless remembering their own teen years.

She looked back at Tim. "We don't have time to thank you and your friends properly for your courage and quick thinking. All I can say is thank you, from all of us." She leaned forward on the desk towards Tim. "And don't do anything like that again," she said with a combination of pride and menace. "Please pass *both* of those messages along."

She smiled at the sixteen year old to ease his discomfort before straightening up. "Right," she checked her notes. "First up, I've spoken with Del Bond."

"Wow," Sam Burton commented. "With everything, I'd forgotten about that dag!"

"Yes, I must confess, I couldn't face him right away," Baines admitted. A shadow of sorrow crossed her face for an instant but she drove it away. "You'll be gratified to hear that he needed fifty-seven stitches after Reiver dragged him back into the fold. Apparently, Dave Flannigan had nearly finished sewing him back together before he realised that, with everything, he'd forgotten to anaesthetise him first. Hey ho."

White leaned back in his seat, relaxing with his hands behind his head. "Hey, accidents happen. I'd like to hear more of that story when we have time."

"Anyway," continued Baines. "It was my intention to hold a meeting to decide how to treat with him and what to ask, but when that ship roared overhead it pushed our schedule forward. I got him to talk, eventually."

"Yep, that's the word around the ship," interjected White.

"What *word*?" asked Baines, frowning. "This was barely an hour ago!"

White grinned again. "Which is ten times longer than the story needed to get around – you know *that*, Captain. 'Bad-ass Baines', they're calling you."

"My team couldn't talk about anything else, when I left," said Patel, subduing a smirk. "Something about a new style of leadership, was it?"

Baines drummed her fingers. "Look, we're getting off topic," she said, finalising the point. "He said that he wasn't safe from them, not even here. Now, I wasn't sure what he meant by that. At first, I naturally thought he was saying that they would attack and we would be virtually defenceless – but I couldn't shake the feeling that there had been a double-meaning, so I had to get to the bottom of it."

"You thought there may be other insurgents still aboard? Who could reach him?" asked Jones, tentatively.

Baines raised an eyebrow. "You don't say much but when you do…" she nodded appreciatively. "That's *exactly* what I thought, next. Eventually I got it out of him. He told me there is another agent on board that not even the other terrorists know about – saving Bond, and Schultz presumably."

Mother Sarah visibly sagged. "And we still have to hold some kind of funeral for Dr Hussain," she said quietly.

Hussain, a chemist working for Jim Miller, had turned out to be one of Dr Schultz's henchmen and a hidden terrorist aboard ship. Schultz murdered him in cold blood to make a twisted statement to the crew, just moments before she took Captain Douglas hostage, along with the *New World*'s shuttle.

Baines' expression hardened. "I know I've complicated things for you, but there was no way he was going to be part of the service we held for those brave men and woman yesterday, Sarah."

Memories of kidnapping and containment flashed through her mind – all to lure Captain Douglas into Schultz's grasp. Her anger simmered as she relived the raw shame of that debacle.

Mother Sarah broke into her thoughts, "We have several people of the same faith as Dr Hussain. I asked them all if they would help me to give him an appropriate funeral. He was another human soul after all, just like the rest of us."

Major White frowned, his normally genial face setting hard. "What did they say?" he asked, in a taut voice.

Sarah looked down the table towards him. "Some said they wanted nothing to do with him, dead or alive, after what he'd done. Honestly, I don't think they appreciated my request for help. Probably concerned about association, I expect. It's understandable. One lady told me to throw him in a ditch and another gentleman told me that in order to give him an 'appropriate' end, I should feed him to the dinosaurs and set fire to the dung."

A bark of laughter escaped Gleeson, but noticing Sarah's misery, he turned it into a coughing fit with quite uncharacteristic tact.

Still standing at the end of the table, Baines reached out to put a hand on Sarah's shoulder, giving it a gentle squeeze.

The priest looked up at her. "Is there no end to all this treachery, Jill?" she asked bleakly.

"I know you'll do the right thing, Sarah. You always do." She smiled encouragingly. "Let's not lose heart. We're still here and we still have each other. We'll get through it."

Singh spoke deeply, using his empty glass to distort his voice, "I find your lack of faith disturbing."

Sam Burton burst out laughing. Baines tried not to. Tim hid a snigger behind his hand, shoulders rocking.

"Am I missing something?" asked Patel.

"It's a rather old joke but think I can elucidate," replied Baines. "Sandip lent me some of his classic literature – actual, honest-to-goodness books – for the journey. Remember? When we were on our way to Mars and everyone was bored?"

"Ooh, lovely," said Sarah, brightening. "What were they? Wuthering Heights? Jane Eyre?"

"Actually, I'm still on The Empire Strikes Back at the moment."

"Oh," Sarah acknowledged, lifelessly.

"Hey! Don't dis the holy trinity!" Singh exclaimed, speaking ahead of his thoughts, as ever.

"I would *never*!" replied Mother Sarah, scandalised.

Baines cleared her throat. "We may be speaking the same language, but there are two very different conversations going on here. Could I bring everyone back, please?" They were all nervous and it was distracting them.

Trust Sandip to say something inappropriate, but she was pleased to note that their spirits had not been completely crushed by events.

"Right, back to Del Bond," Baines continued. "He told me we have another undercover lunatic at large." She let that sobering thought rest for a moment. "As always, the problem is we don't know who he, or she, is."

"I thought you said Bond and Schultz knew about this person?" asked White.

"Bond knew *about* them, but not their identity. It seems that some of *Grandaddy's* secrets are known only to Schultz herself. Apparently, this person has even been genetically altered to become, for all intents and purposes, someone else. New fingerprints, eye colour, face, the lot – Heidi's perfect little ace in the hole!"

"Er... Grandaddy?" asked Patricia Norris.

Baines looked at her, gesturing expansively to take in their situation. "Yes, apparently we have him to thank for all of this, Heinrich Schultz, our illustrious doctor's grandfather.

"Look, long-story-short, Schultz told us, and Bond reinforced this, that she comes from a long line of Nazi sympathisers. Based in South America, they have been growing more powerful with each passing decade.

"At this stage, I should mention that regardless of Schultz's family and any hangers-on, the German people are an essential partner in the Mars programme and have nothing to do with this madness, as a nation.

"Schultz said that many of the world's terror organisations are funded and directed by this hidden group, mostly without ever suspecting the truth of where the cash comes from. Of course, they probably don't look *too* hard."

"You're telling me that half of the religious terrorists in the Middle East are funded by the Nazi Party?" asked White, incredulous. "What the hell?!"

"Oh, it doesn't stop there," continued Baines. "They've got fingers in every pie! Government, defence, virtually every corporation and conglomerate you can think of, and they're global."

"Don't tell me they own Four-X?" asked Gleeson, looking traumatised.

"Doubt it," muttered Singh. "Tiger's the drink for men, after all."

"So why's there a picture of a big pussy on the front then?"

"Gentlemen, *please*," said Baines. "Captain Douglas told me an interesting little story just after we landed – a story about time travel.

"Apparently, some students digging more or less exactly here, about ten years ago – our time – found an amber deposit with a ring-pull from a beer can inside it."

Everyone looked blank.

"It turned out to be quite old but the amber had preserved it perfectly. Would anyone like to take a guess at its age?" she asked.

Tim put his hand up. "99.2 million years, Miss?" he speculated and then reddened – old habits die hard.

"Give the lad a gold star!" said Baines, nodding that he was correct. "Circa 100 million years was the verdict. Now let's not get bogged down, at this point, with how it got into the sap. The chances seem good that we are responsible for the deposit and subsequently for the very idea of time-travel being fully realised and then hijacked by these insane criminals."

Gleeson looked shifty. "Was it from a Four-X can... *Miss*?" he asked, quietly.

Baines gave him a look.

"I mean, I may have had a little tinny or two, you know, outside, at the funeral and er..."

Baines continued to glare at him, realising for the first time that if she was the new Douglas, then Gleeson must surely be the new *her*. Eventually she said, "I don't think that really matters at the moment, Commander. What does matter is this – after realising that time travel was possible, these cracker-boxes set about making it happen. The quickest, dirtiest way of getting this ship back in time was with a bomb in the wormhole drive. Enter Lieutenant Lloyd!"

"Did Lloyd know all this?" asked Jim Miller, shocked.

"I don't think so," replied Baines. "They gave him only what he needed. Apparently, he was supposed to place a very small and very meticulously calculated amount of explosive at the event horizon of the wormhole when it opened. He bottled it and shoved a whole pack of plastic from one of the lifeboat release systems in and, as you know, the rest is history. Or prehistory as it turned out.

"The idiot was only meant to send us back 100,000 years but that's what happens when you don't tell people the whole plan and they improvise, thinking it won't matter!"

Her audience was overwhelmed by this, to many at least, new information.

Baines gave them a moment only to process. "Sorry people, we need to press on. Now we have one piece of good news. According to Bond, the bad guys *need* this ship."

White sat back, relieved.

"You've seen it?" Baines asked him.

He nodded. "They're not gonna risk destroying the *New World*," he stated.

"Exactly so, and that's our power," Baines affirmed. "Of course, that won't stop them kicking in the front door, so we need to be ready. Which brings me onto the bad news – we have an enemy loose on this ship and if we don't catch him or her, they may not even *need* to kick the door down!"

"Aahh!" shouted Hiro, jumping to his feet.

Baines looked taken aback. "Hiro? Are you OK?"

The engineer remained standing but his eyes and mind were clearly far, far away.

"Hiro?" Baines jogged him again.

"Captain, I need to see photos of the whole crew roster," he said. "Right now!"

She nodded to Singh, who touched a flat button in the tabletop. A section of the surface slid back allowing a transparent monitor to pop up. After a few seconds of manic skittering across the accompanying flush-mounted keyboard, he networked it to a large screen behind him in the wall. The opaque glass wall took on the appearance of liquid, as it too transformed into a large monitor.

As crew photographs scrolled, it turned out to be number fifty-seven that made Hiro knock his chair over in an attempt to get to the screen to stop them.

He looked at the man for a long moment. Eventually, he turned back to the room and simply said, "*Him.*"

Corporal Jennifer 'Iron Balls' O'Brien marched down the corridor with purpose, six fully trained soldiers at her back. Each was armed with a Heath-Rifleson, a stun pistol, a commando knife and a tazer. Their boots rang down the passageways with menace as they headed towards Dr Patel's workshop and offices within the Pod.

O'Brien's orders were to arrest Julian Bradford and take him to the brig, where he was to be kept under heavy guard at all times. Major White had made it quite clear that Bradford had no legitimate reason not to come quietly, but if he did not, she was to take his *body* straight to Dr Flannigan's morgue.

The orders were pretty unequivocal and, after everything they had been through, O'Brien intended to carry them out without question.

"What tipped you off to, to, Julian *Bradford* was it?" Singh asked.

"Never heard of the man," replied Hiro, honestly.

"Why are we sending in the heavies, then?" asked Gleeson.

Hiro thought about it for a moment. "About a week or so ago," he began, "I was taking my lunch in the Mud Hole. I sometimes go there between shifts when I need to think, away from engineering."

"To think or to drink?" Gleeson quipped.

"I was on *duty*," replied Hiro, genuinely shocked by the very idea.

Baines grinned. "Go on, Hiro."

"Well, this guy walked past my table and said hello. He used my name. I nodded acknowledgement but I hadn't a clue who he was. That's not unusual for me, I'm not brilliant with faces – people all tend to look a bit alike to me. Now if you give me a motherboard and ask me to identify the manufacturer or reel off the serial number then that would be a different matter." He frowned as a thought struck him. "You know, I was in one of the stock rooms on deck nine yesterday and I found one of the old P35S boards. Do you remember those, Sandy? The ones we used for—"

"What made you suspicious?" Baines interrupted, reining him back in.

He looked at her and blinked before continuing, "Oh. Well, obviously, as a senior officer, I wasn't overly surprised that he knew me but there was something about him… just something that I almost recognised, but couldn't quite place. Because I'm pretty hopeless with faces, I put it down to that, but it wasn't really the way the man looked. It wasn't even the way he spoke, he sounded similar to The Sarge, so I guessed he was from the same part of the world, but I'm not brilliant with accents either."

"So what *did* you recognise?" asked Singh, beginning to worry they had just taken a lottery, and Bradford had lost. "I hope you picked the right photo, Hiro, or our Julian's about to have a really bad day!"

"Yes, I'm sure. Well, I think I'm sure."

"Hmm." Singh was unconvinced, knowing Hiro as he did.

"It was a, what's the word, the way he was," the engineer continued.

"A mannerism?" Jim Miller chipped in helpfully.

"Yes, that was it," agreed Hiro. "Thank you. Something about the way he moved. I had completely forgotten about the incident until the captain said that we had someone on board hidden in plain sight – possibly even from their own people. Then I realised that the person I had seen may not have been the person I had *seen*, if you follow me? Their mannerisms may have been all that remained of their true identity."

He looked at the captain. "After you told us that this person had been genetically altered, it all popped into my mind in a flash and I realised that the accent could have been affected too. It all came together and I got another picture of him in my mind with a different face and a different voice but the same *way* about him. Finally, his real name popped into my head!" He ran out of words, dumb-struck.

Everyone waited.

"Hiro, you haven't told us the name yet," Baines nudged him gently.

Hiro looked up in surprise and then dropped his bomb-shell, "Sargo Lemelisk."

Bradford heard the unmistakable noise of approaching soldiers. Looking up from his work station, he saw them enter. The leader, a female NCO, went straight to the duty supervisor and began questioning him.

"I think I'll take a little break," Bradford said to the woman at the next desk. He made his way around the lab as nonchalantly as possible, using the large fixtures as cover. At the earliest opportunity, he slipped out of another door.

O'Brien followed the supervisor over to Bradford's station only to find him gone.

"Well, that explains a *lot*," said Patel.

"What's that, Satnam?" asked Baines.

"Why his work is so poor."

"Really?" asked Gleeson. "That must make him stand out like a turd on a fairy cake around here?"

"Erm, quite," agreed Patel, weakly. "I always wondered how he *had* got here – on this mission, I mean. His qualifications are very impressive, as you would expect, but the substance just isn't there."

"So is there *anything* about this guy that isn't fake?" asked Baines, rhetorically.

"As far as I know," continued Patel, "he's from London and one of my environmental engineers. If we had reached Mars, I would have had to let him go. Obviously, with everything that's happened since, it just didn't seem important anymore and it's not like I could send him home."

"Once Ford's people have caught this guy, what then?" Burton asked the captain.

"We put him away somewhere very safe for now and hope he's our guy. Either way we should know in a min—"

White's comm binged, interrupting her. "White, go ahead."

"Sir, it's O'Brien. He's given us the slip."

White sat back, rolling his eyes to the heavens.

O'Brien continued, *"I've called all the NCOs, except Sarge Jackson and Corporal Jones. We've got everyone back on duty searching the ship."*

"OK, Jen. Post guards at engineering, both on the ship and the Pod and make sure you get people to the lifeboats and vehicle pool, too. If he's looking for a way out, they'll be on his list."

"Don't forget the lifeboat we parked in the main hangar, after we scared the crocs off," reminded Gleeson.

White nodded. "Did you hear the commander, Jen?"

"Actually, that lifeboat isn't there anymore," Baines interrupted. She shared a secret look with Sam Burton.

White relayed the message, "Scratch the lifeboat in the hangar bay, Corporal. Apparently, the captain has it stashed elsewhere."

"Yes, sir. Could the captain make an announcement, please, sir? Anyone in their own quarters should lock themselves in – all workers should remain in groups and stay put at their stations."

Baines nodded.

"You got it. Keep me appraised, Corp. White out."

The captain made the announcement. "Well, that's tipped our hand, rather," she said afterward.

"But it's all we need to know," said Gleeson.

"What do you mean, Commander?" asked Sarah.

"He did a runner, didn't he? Sounds like Hiro's right on the money. Just one question though, who the hell is Sargo Lemelisk?"

Dr Patel's team were progressing well with their current project, despite the potentially worst efforts of Dr Bradford. The small escape pods, about to be pressed into service as mini-shuttles, were naturally without weapons of any kind and this presented a problem in such a dangerous environment.

However, Patel's engineers had now fitted one of the little ships with the first prototype of a large-scale stunning weapon.

It was based on the rifle technology already in use and, when fired in the laboratory, had produced tremendous results. These tests used the Pod's main power plant to create the charge. They were yet to charge it from the small, onboard reactors, which provided much of the lifeboats' power requirements. However, calculations suggested that the weapon would deliver a similar punch, but due to power limitations, would only be able to cycle every fifteen seconds. Rapid fire would not be possible – at least, not yet. Some questions remained about the effectiveness of the concussion mountings, but as the whole project had been thrown together so quickly, the risk of teething problems was inevitably high.

Regardless, one man was perfectly willing to give it a go. All he had to do was steal the little ship and then he would be only too happy to try the weapon out on anyone who followed him.

He expected the rear lifeboat stations to be fairly quiet at the moment, the majority of the action currently taking place in the lab and manufacturing bay.

Bradford turned the corner carefully. Good, no one there.

He made his way to *Lifeboat 7* and was just about to open the hatch when a shout commanded him to halt. He did not think, he merely acted – the small throwing knife he had pocketed left his hand quicker than sight, taking the man in the neck. The stricken guard gurgled and went down. Bradford followed him almost immediately, when O'Brien shot him in the back from the other end of the corridor.

She ran to her fallen comrade, calling into her comm for Dr Flannigan to get to them on the double. She ordered the other two guards in the area, a man and a woman, to take Bradford to the brig and lock him up.

"Is Donavon gonna be OK?" the man asked, deeply concerned.

O'Brien looked meaningfully at him. "I'll stay with him," she said.

The other gestured to the downed Bradford with her rifle. "Should this one go to sickbay first, Corp?" she asked.

"The brig," she said with finality. "Then we'll decide whether it's worth the Doc's time to check on him later. Take him away."

With one last look of disgust at the unconscious prisoner, they roughly dragged him away by his heels.

The injured man was coughing. "Jen," he croaked, plaintively.

"Sssh," O'Brien said, trying to comfort him. "It's gonna be OK." She placed her hand over his throat wound, applying pressure around the blade to help staunch the bleeding. She did her best not to restrict his breathing, while they waited for help. "Doc Flannigan will be here any second."

Sure enough, Flannigan, Nurse Smyth and another guard turned the corner on the run, carrying a stretcher with them.

Flannigan got straight to work, wrapping a bandage compress around the wound. The injured man finally blacked out. "I dare not remove the knife here. We'll need him in sickbay, stat," he said, standing. "Get him on the stretcher, Corporal, you're with me. Everyone grab a corner, put your backs into it!"

They lifted the man and ran back to sickbay as fast as they could with such delicate cargo.

The guards who dragged Bradford away reported back to O'Brien within minutes, stating that he was secured in a cell, but out like a light. Although, they had to confess that he may have bumped his head a few times on his way there. Mindful of the major's warning, she ordered an extra pair of guards posted to the brig before reporting the incident to White.

"Good work, Jen," said White. "Keep him on ice until we need him. Who was hurt, Donavon? Is he gonna be OK?"

"Don't know, sir. Sonofabitch got him in the neck with a blade. I've sent someone to bring Donavon's wife to sickbay – just in case."

White winced. "Right, keep me posted. If he needs anything, he's got it, OK?"

"Yes, sir. O'Brien out."

The major looked ashen after receiving the report, deeply concerned about the injured man under his command. He had lost so many in such a short time. Before he could dwell on this fact, a welcome surprise brought him back to the moment.

"What have I missed now?!" asked a familiar voice from behind him.

White jumped out of his chair and grabbed the man's free hand. "Sarge! I didn't hear you come in, how the hell are you doin'?"

Jones was about to give up his seat but White dragged one over specifically for The Sarge, who had an arm in a sling but otherwise looked well enough.

Baines smiled too. "You OK, Sarge? You gave us quite a scare."

"You should have seen the scare *I* had today," Jackson replied with grin. "I won't sleep tonight!"

"We heard," said Baines. "Glad you're still with us."

The Sarge waved away their concerns. "Thank you, Captain, but I'm fine. Fit as a butcher's dog!"

Baines' expression was secretive. "Well, you're just in time to hear the plan," she said.

"What plan's that, Captain?"

"I'm just about to tell you all how I plan to get Captain Douglas back and destroy the warship that's casting a shadow over my, usually so sunny, disposition."

There was a general, sharp intake of breath.

"When did you come up with this?" asked Sarah, rallying first.

"Whilst I was *interviewing* Del Bond."

"We don't have any weapons that can take that ship on, Captain," Ford White noted with concern.

Still standing, Baines leaned forward, placing her hands on the table. "I beg to differ, Major. We have everything we need. Firstly, two of Dr Burton's people have taken the lifeboat we had in the hangar and loaded our, now fully complete, spy satellite into it. They set off, flying at low level across the ocean, to the northeast. Once far enough around the planet to avoid detection from that warship, they have orders to shoot up into orbit. With any luck, they'll have released it already, by now."

"Won't the enemy find the thing, I mean, with their scanners, or whatever?" asked Sarah.

"It's a possibility but, firstly, I doubt they know we have it, and secondly, we've taken steps to make it hard to find. Obviously, we don't have the sort of stealth tech their ship is made from, but our satellite has a few advantages – basic, but no less valid for that. Over to you, Sam."

Burton cleared his throat. "As some of you will already be aware, we've been working on this since we first had the idea, so we've been able to pack it with a few extra goodies.

"As well as the communications equipment and basic manoeuvring systems it came with, it now has cameras that can see in the visible and infrared spectrums. We've also added a full spectroscopic suite – so that we can see what our world is made of and find the best mining sites. Last, but not least, we've given it a self-destruct mechanism, so we can deny it to the enemy if necessary.

"Our plan is to launch it into a retrograde orbit. When added to the natural rotational speed or the 'prograde motion' of the Earth, this will give it the appearance of travelling at a colossal speed from the perspective of anyone down on the planet."

Baines nodded her approval, as did some of the other people around the table.

"But what I'm really happy with is the paint job!" the New Zealander stated proudly.

"Eh?" Gleeson asked.

"Yeah," said Burton, clearly chuffed with himself. "I found some matt black paint in one of the vehicle containers. It may not be stealth tech, but finding it'll be like bobbing for an apple in Lake Taupo!"

"OK," said White. "That all sounds great, but how can it help us destroy that ship? You didn't think to pack it with awesome death-lasers, did you?"

Burton slumped, theatrically. "You know, I checked but we were clean out."

"All we need are its eyes," Baines assured them, with a disconcertingly manic twinkle in her own. "It will find us the cover we need for our diversionary operation. That's why Tim's here with us today, to help us choose our cover wisely, and that's how the satellite's going to bring us our victory!"

White threw his hands up. "OK, I give up! Lay it on me."

Baines treated him to her trademark grin, which both exasperated and ingratiated.

"Right, here goes," she said. "When we have a feed from the satellite, we will scan the area around that ship, naturally. Now, we don't know exactly where it is but Sandip was able to plot its last known trajectory by eye and using landmarks – hopefully we'll be within a few degrees of true. What we know for sure, is that our shuttle is just the other side of the mountain range to the west. It's probably no more than fifty kilometres from here. When that monster flew over us, we may not have been able to track *it* with the sensors we have, but our own shuttle showed up like a flashing beacon on our instruments. I think it would be a fair guess that their ship rendezvoused with our shuttle on the other side of the mountains.

"Of course, when the ships descended behind the mountains we lost them from our terrestrial scanners on the ground here. However, just before this meeting began," she added excitedly, "we got the best news we've had in days. When Schultz took the shuttle, she switched off the homing beacon that allows us to track it from the *New World*. A little over an hour ago, it was reactivated!"

"The captain!" said Hiro.

Baines nodded, swallowing back her emotions.

"What if it's a ruse?" The Sarge remarked darkly, back on form.

"You mean they're trying to lure us?" asked Baines.

Jackson nodded sombrely.

"It's definitely a possibility, I'll grant you, but either way it tells us where they are. They've no fear of us, you see? That flyover was gratuitous posturing in the extreme. It served no purpose but to make us wet ourselves!" she finished angrily, slamming her fist down on the table.

"I'd like to see them try and put me in a nappy, isn'it," rumbled Jones, pokerfaced.

The Sarge gave a rare bark of laughter.

"A nappy?" asked White.

"A diaper," explained Mother Sarah. Smiling at the enormous Welshman, she added, "I think you'd look sweet, Corporal."

White chuckled. "OK, we've dried ourselves and treated any rash, now what do we do?"

"Commander Gleeson is going to blow that ship up for us!" stated Baines with relish.

Gleeson stared at her like she had sprouted another head. "He's gonna *what*?!"

"Play to your strengths, Commander."

"Not like the cricket, then," Singh interjected, quietly.

Gleeson glowered at him. "You got lucky last night, bucko! There's a lot of overs left in that game."

"But not tomorrow night, chaps," Baines cut them off. "Because tomorrow night you'll be leading a team of six skilled combatants on Hiro's electric dirt bikes, which will be finished by then, and you're gonna blow the engines on that ship!"

"Tidy!" said Jones, rubbing his hands together.

Gleeson looked like he was lost in a bad dream.

The Sarge sighed, looking down at his damaged arm and shoulder. "Looks like I'm sitting this one out," he said disappointedly.

White gave him an understanding look. "I doubt this will be the last battle before we're out of this mess, Sarge," he offered.

"I'm recommending Jones to take your place, Sarge," said Baines.

Jones just nodded stoically. "I would suggest that we also take Iron— O'Brien, Captain," he said, remembering himself at the last moment.

"Agreed," said White. "I'll come too."

"Actually Ford, I'm going to need you here," said Baines.

White looked surprised. "You think there will be trouble here, while all *that*'s going on over there?"

"I'm not sure, but these people are going to need protection and the Pod will have to be defended, just in case."

He looked at her sidelong. "So where will you be, Captain?" he asked quizzically.

"I'll be over there," said Baines, pointing to the west.

"Now hang on a minute," said Gleeson. "If I'm the first officer, you should be here, surely?"

Mother Sarah coughed politely. "I think Commander Gleeson has a point, Captain. Maybe you should stay with the ship."

Baines smiled at them both. "I *will* be with the ship – I'm taking the *New World* with me."

"Sekai!" shouted Hiro, standing up in alarm, "Doesn't have any weapons... Captain," he added slowly, sitting back down.

"I know that, Hiro. All I need is her power and I need all of it, so we're leaving the Pod here."

Now *everyone* stared at her like she had sprouted a *third* head.

Gleeson spoke first. "Please tell me there's more to this plan, because at the moment it's looking we've got less chance than the Poms at The Ashes."

The man stepped out of the woods onto a large plain. It was probably two or three kilometres to the opposite tree-line. He was still in the mountains, but the gaps between them were becoming larger.

The foliage to his left creaked and shook, like it was being ravaged by high winds. Peering cautiously around a colossal redwood, he saw a herd of equally huge dinosaurs. Massive necks arched and long, muscular tails swished. They were no more than a few hundred metres away. He tried to remember what they were called from when he was a child, *sauropods?* Whatever they were called, they were doing what they did best it seemed – eating, clearing, clearing and eating.

They rumbled and flicked their tails, in constant communication with one another; the smaller members of the herd, particularly, always keeping a watchful eye out for killers on the prowl.

He took in the otherworldly scene and despite his predicament found just a moment's peace and wonder. He calculated that crossing the plain would save him a good hour, perhaps more, but there was no cover. It would be an all or nothing gamble if he took it and although he was armed, he did not fancy his chances. The skies were fairly clear at present and these relatively peaceful giants were the only animals he could see, but he had been here long enough now to know that big game brought big predators.

He sighed once more in frustration. His ankle was killing him, his side ached like hell and he was starving. Checking his side, he was dismayed to find that his wound was bleeding again and to make matters worse the sun would be setting in a couple of hours too.

Before darkness fell completely, he needed to find a tree which would be climbable in his state, but inaccessible to any potential man-eaters.

"So, find a hotel, catch some dinner. How hard can it be?" he said to himself, trying desperately to keep his spirits up. "Unfortunately, I really will have to *catch* some dinner!"

At least he had found a fresh stream earlier, enabling him to refill his flask, but all he really wanted was to find a place to curl up and give up. A simple call of nature, some fifty metres back in the woods, had provided significant challenge to a man with a deep gash down his side, one good ankle and the rather pressing need to keep a rifle in his hands. Thankfully, very large leaves had been plentiful.

He remembered reading somewhere that, before they became extinct at the end of the 21st century, polar bears liked to sneak up on people as they crouched, so to speak. What he would not have given for a mere bear in his situation.

The trees were a nightmare too. Full of aggressive little bird-like creatures, to his untrained eye. He was not sure if they were dinosaurs, but they were not fun to be around, he *was* sure of that – especially high off the ground, and even more especially, in the dark. Then there were the scorpions, millipedes and who knew what else.

The stinking *concrete* jungle of his memory, full of murderers, muggers, scammers, pushers and every flavour of criminal, not to mention suicide bombers, all seemed so gentle and safe to him now. So much so, that remembering it all left him bereft.

After a few minutes searching he found a likely tree, and was about to attempt it, when a small red-feathered creature shot out of a hole in the trunk, all teeth and claws aiming straight for his face. By a stroke of utter good fortune, he caught it in his fist while it was just inches away from his eye. The animal screamed bloody gore at him, jaws wide, needle teeth savage. It was clearly livid, struggling insanely to break free of his grasp. He looked at it in wide-eyed shock at first, then his stare turned into a glare as the violent little critter became both the vent for all his anger – and supper. He *squeezed*.

After a few moments of applying deadly pressure, he faltered and almost let the suddenly pathetic little thing go – but he knew he had no choice. He had to eat or he would not be strong enough to make it to his journey's end. He did not want to lose an eye, either.

Distracted by the dilemma, he was blind and deaf to the crack of timber behind him in the forest. Nor did he hear the sniff, sniff of blood, and other bodily material, scented.

Trapped in his moment of agony, he keenly felt the reality of taking a life, *any* life. This was no flick of a switch, nor pull of a trigger with the protection of a thousand yard stare. The little animal fought with all its being, for every precious second of the meagre time allotted to it in this world, but in the end, all it could do was submit to the great cycle. Even bare-handed, the man felt like the bringer of death, watching the light of life leave as eyes so bright with spirit became dead things.

He wept – and the tears came hard. He cried for what he had done, for *all* that he had done and for everything that had been done to him. Never a believer, the idea of God, 100 million years before Christianity, was little more than a ridiculous abstraction to him. However, despite all the logic, the derision and disdain, he prayed. Leaning against the tree, he prayed. As his legs began to collapse, he prayed, for he truly had nothing else, nothing at all.

Whether Nature is God or God is in Nature, the answer he needed came to him just in time. Less than a second passed into history before raw instinct awoke, hardwired and much faster than the speed of thought, it shoved all mind aside… Something was behind him – something big.

The man stuffed the tiny, limp body into his jacket, dropped his crutch, freed the rifle from around his shoulders in one fluid movement and, his own life roaring in his ears, turned to face the cycle.

Thousands of miles above a primitive blue green planet, a small piece of technology fired its tiny rocket thrusters to adjust position as it settled into a retrograde orbit. The diminutive satellite photographed the little ship as it dove back towards the exosphere, rapidly leaving it behind. This *parting shot* was transmitted down to the world below, specifically to the *New World* below.

For several minutes, Lieutenant Singh had kept an expectant eye on the screen set into the table in front of him, waiting for the image feed.

Baines noticed his attention divert to the monitor. "Do we have a signal, Sandy?"

In answer to her question, Singh passed the image to the wall monitor triumphantly, for all to see.

A crisp image of an escape pod diving down towards Earth could be clearly seen. "Our eyes in the skies are online—s," he finished smugly.

"Needs work," said Baines, rolling her eyes with a smile. "How long before we get a feed on our target?"

"Several hours, Captain," replied Singh. "They will have launched the satellite into orbit a little over 22,000 miles above our heads." He looked up whilst performing a rough mental calculation. "One orbit for our camera should be about 170,000 miles – in round figures. As Dr Burton's guys will have launched it on the other side of the planet, to hide from the black ship, it will need to traverse somewhere in the region of about 80-90,000 miles before it's over us."

"How fast will it be travelling?" asked Mother Sarah.

"Roughly 17,000 miles per hour," replied Burton, jumping in, "but the retrograde orbit will increase its speed tremendously from our perspective down here." He swapped his attention to Baines. "A full orbit should take a little under six and a half hours – so working on that, maybe three or three and a half hours to reach target, Captain."

"By target," interrupted Major White, "do I assume you mean the bad guys' ship?"

Baines nodded. "The satellite will scan the whole planet to give us our first picture of home. Upon reaching the zone above the enemy, and us, it will start collecting more detailed information. We need to know as much as possible about the region we're in. Of course, our immediate objective is to locate the enemy ship, our shuttle and any animal movements in that area."

Still standing at the head of the table, Baines leaned forward onto her knuckles and gave them a predatory smile. "Our enemies will be confident in their fortress – cocky even. I very much doubt the thought that *we* might contemplate 'bringing it' to *them* will cross their minds. We're going to give them a surprise they will never forget. They sowed the wind, and now they are going to reap the whirlwind!" A nasty little chuckle accompanied her words.

White raised an eyebrow. "Air Marshall 'Bomber' Harris?" he asked, referring to her quotation.

"It seemed appropriate," she agreed. "We didn't start this and if we can successfully execute my plan, the effects will be shocking. However, there will be two main differences. Firstly, Harris' campaign, although terrible and damaging, did not destroy Hitler's ability to make war – if it works, ours will. And secondly, there are no innocents to get caught up in the destruction here. If our shuttle is indeed under the protection of that battleship, our enemies will be in plain sight."

White nodded, his interest piqued, but before he could ask further questions his comm binged. Excusing himself, he turned away from the table to hold a hushed conversation. When he turned back to the group, he was beaming.

"Good news, Ford?" asked Baines.

"Indeed. That was Doc Flannigan. He managed to stop Donavon from bleeding out and somehow fixed the artery. He's gonna be OK – won't be saying much for a week or two, but he's gonna be OK. His wife's with him. In other news: Bradford is still unconscious."

With such a scarcity of good news lately, Donavon's survival and expected recovery was well received.

"OK," said Baines. "On that positive note, I think we should call a halt to this meeting now and try and get some rest. If sleep eludes you, think on how we can cut Captain Douglas out of that horrible black trashcan once we've disabled her. Unfortunately, I'm going to need you all back here in four hours time. We'll have sorted the information we want from the satellite by then." She looked down at their youngest member. "I'll need you here too, Tim."

Tim nodded and rose with the rest of them as they filed out. It was getting late in the evening and in all likelihood the next few hours would be all the rest they would get this night. It had been a hell of a day but tomorrow looked as though it might be even more dangerous.

It looked like a crocodile. The man fired and screamed, but the stun bolts bounced off the creature's thick hide, only making it angrier. Although the predator was certainly crocodile-*like*, it had much longer, more upright legs. This gave it the appearance of a fast, ambush predator; it certainly had the appearance of ferocity.

The stun rifle was dialled down to hunt a small animal for supper, without frying the meat to destruction. Unfortunately, events had overtaken the lost human before he realised his mistake.

The beast snapped for him. Somehow, he managed to fall to the side, keeping the giant redwood he had so recently been peering around between them. He scrambled to his feet, almost passing out from the pain in his side. His only hope of eluding this vicious crocodile-line archosaur was to hop further around the trunk, favouring his weak ankle.

At the periphery of his senses, and outside his immediate crisis, he registered another loud roaring sound coming from somewhere further off. Three flashes of realisation struck him in rapid succession as he twisted around the tree in a bizarre one-legged dance. The first was that he had no right being alive at that point. The second was that his aggressor was *truly* stupid, luckily for him. Lastly, the roar was growing louder and sounded like the combined snarl of several high-powered diesel engines.

Barely daring to glance away from the creature, he caught the approach of three armoured vehicles as they crossed the plain out of the rapidly westering sun. Their tracks churned up muck and undergrowth as they came on at speed. The large machine guns mounted atop the leading vehicle opened up, firing just above the man's head and to his considerable consternation. Brush, timber and bark flew everywhere as the fifty-calibre rounds struck the foliage, shredding the smaller trees and flora all around him.

The large carnivore ran for the cover of the forest, disappearing as quickly as it had attacked.

Covering his head against the fallout from above, the man's ears rang from the assault which was quickly replaced by the bass bellowing of the giant sauropods. The herd had been startled at first, by the scent of a predator, but had since had the time to work up into a frenzy as three fast moving, completely alien devices carved up the plain towards them.

The gun-fire tipped them completely over the edge, causing the enormous animals to stamp in circles, knocking over trees and shattering them to matchwood in their rage. Smaller members of the herd suffered full-blown panic, fleeing death under the smashing anger of their larger relatives to crash through the forest. As the path began to widen, others followed, cutting a swathe to another plain.

The three vehicles came to a stop at the edge of the trees, cutting their engines one at a time. The immediate area fell eerily silent. Crying out in pain, the man picked himself up from where he had eventually fallen and cast about to find his crutch. Upon locating it, he simply hobbled out of the tree line to face whatever was to come – his destiny no longer in his hands.

A hatch in the top of the foremost vehicle popped open. The man watched, incredulous, as a beautiful young blonde woman, wearing military style fatigues, climbed out of the belly of the vehicle to sit atop it with her arms crossed.

She smiled indolently before speaking in German accented English. "Hello again. Small world."

"H-Heidi?!" sputtered the man in disbelief. A wave of exhaustion overcame him and he leaned heavily on his makeshift support.

She smiled coldly. "Guess who's winning?"

He closed his eyes and bowed his head. "Oh, Christ…" said Geoff Lloyd.

Tim and Patricia returned to their quarters. Tim was bursting with information overload and so raced into his room to comm Woodsey.

He was rewarded with a drowsy sounding, *"Wha?"*

"Hey," said Tim excitedly. "The Captain has thanked us for our bravery. Of course, she then followed it up straight away by telling us never to do anything like that again, like old people always do!"

"*Do what again?*" A loud yawn. "*What are you talking about, dude? I was just falling asleep.*"

"The rescue, you know? You *were* there weren't you?"

"*I'm going back to sleep, mate.*"

"Aren't you interested?! The captain herself said—"

"*I'm the hypnagogic king, why should I care what mere captains say...*"

"Hypna-what?"

A groan and a sniff. "*Eh? Don't tell me I actually know a word that you don't? It was almost, but not quite, worth being woken up to find that out. If it helps, think of it as 'word for the day', mate, and look it up.*" He yawned loudly. "*I'm going back to sleep, I'll see you tomorrow.*"

"Woodsey, you really are a pillock sometimes, d'you know that?!"

"*Yeah, yeah.*"

"But we're about to go to war!" snarled Tim, but the only response was a gentle snore. Exasperated he added, "Well at least close the damned channel!"

Tim had left his door open, so Patricia walked in. "Who are you shouting at?" she asked in surprise.

Tim looked nonplussed. "Woodsey. I was telling him about what the captain said, and that we are about to go to war but he fell asleep!" He knitted his eyebrows. "By the way, what is a hypnagorra... hypna... oh, never mind!"

Patricia's lips twitched with amusement. She sat down on the bed next to her son, rearranging his fringe. It took about an eighth of a second for Tim to put it back over his face again. "I'm so proud of you, son."

Tim rolled his eyes, "Muuum."

She laughed lightly. "Get some sleep, darling. We've got to be back with the captain in a little under four hours. I've asked the computer to wake us." She stood and kissed him on the head.

"Muuum," he repeated, irritably.

She smiled and did it again. "Get some sleep. Goodnight."

"'Night," Tim responded half-heartedly.

He lay down and pondered. Eventually, he decided to get undressed and under the covers, but sleep was beyond his reach. His thoughts turned to Captain Douglas in that terrible place. He had believed in Tim, given him a chance to be more than just a kid; had given up everything, in fact, possibly even his life to save them all.

After an hour of staring at the opposite wall, Tim finally fell into a fitful doze, but his mind continued to work.

Bright light shone through heavy lids. Lloyd could not open his eyes, though he tried. Vaguely conscious of people around him, his mind felt heavy, like his awareness was wrapped in cotton wool.

The last thing he remembered, at least with any clarity, was a lightning pain as he was moved into one of the armoured vehicles; pain, then safety of sorts leading to relief, juxtaposed with the clear and present danger of his rescuers, and then finally, blackness.

He vaguely understood that he was troubled, but somehow only in a peripheral way. *Is this safety?* he thought, wearily.

"Damn…" he mumbled, the blackness coming to his rescue once more.

Jim Miller arrived back at his quarters to find his wife, Lara, watching recorded footage from a reality show, set inside someone else's house, entitled, 'What Are *You* Looking At?'

"Hi, sweetheart," he said. "I don't want to interrupt the plot for you, but have you seen our daughter? I want to tell her something."

"There isn't a plot, it's just someone else's house," replied Lara.

A question crossed Jim's mind but he internalised it, pushing it down. "And Rose?" he asked delicately.

"She's gone to the Mud Hole with that American boy. That's what she told me anyway, who knows where they really are or what they're really up to."

Woodsey christened the pub and restaurant aboard the Life Pod 'The Mud Hole' during a general meeting held just after the *New World* landed on ancient Earth. The name was in honour of the 'squelchy' nature of that landing, and as the name suggested, it had stuck.

"Don't you like Henry? He seems a nice lad to m—" Jim gritted his teeth. He just may have said too much.

The holo in which Lara was engrossed showed someone asleep. She turned towards him. "He's too old for her. Lads of that age are only interested in one thing!"

Jim seemed to remember that most girls of that age were similarly interested but he absolutely did *not* let that comment out. He decided on a slightly safer tack.

"Too old, darling? About 18 months between them, isn't there?"

"Exactly."

He was pushing his luck here, but his logical mind was screaming to be let off the leash. "But I'm *three years* older than you, my love."

As soon as the words left his mouth he regretted them; he almost ducked away from the coming storm but the response was surprisingly mild. It must have been a really good episode of 'What Are *You* Looking At?'

"That's different," replied Lara, distractedly. "A man should be older, it's only natural."

Jim's face twitched, contorted and twitched again as he struggled in silent agony to unpick this spiral rationale. In the end he retreated completely, simply saying, "I'll see if I can find them."

As he left his quarters he blew out his cheeks heavily, part relief due to narrowly avoiding an argument by the skin of his teeth and equal part utter bafflement and exasperation.

Jim entered the Mud Hole and looked around. He quickly spotted Rose and Henry. They were holding hands and chatting quietly in a completely innocent way. Jim could not help being relieved by this, even though he knew, like all fathers everywhere, that he was burying his head in the sand.

"Hi, guys," he greeted cheerfully.

Henry released Rose's hand like he had received an electric shock. He stood up and said, a little too quickly, "Hello, sir. We were just having a drink."

Jim smiled warmly. *Did he just call me 'sir'?* he thought. *Bless.*

"It's OK, Henry. I don't want to keep you long. Thank you for the courtesy but please, Jim will do. Looking at you guys makes me feel old enough as it is, without being *sirred*!"

Rose laughed and grabbed Jim's hand on the tabletop, as he sat next to her.

"Could I get you a drink, si—Jim?" asked Henry, nervously.

"That's kind, yes please. I'll have whatever you guys are drinking. Thank you."

Henry was trying to surreptitiously place his half empty beer bottle on the floor as he ventured, "Ah gee, a tonic water with lime then?"

Jim laughed out loud with genuine delight and so did Rose. He knew well enough what teenagers were about, his memory was not that far gone, but the fact that this young man took the trouble to hide it from his girlfriend's father spoke to his sense of decency. It fooled no one but it was the thought that counted. Jim let him off the hook with a wink. "I'd rather have another one of those beers you're hiding under the table."

Henry flushed red to the roots and made his way to the bar mumbling, "Yes, sir."

Rose gave her father a playful slap on his arm and told him how horrible he was, as they laughed together at Henry's expense.

Presently Henry returned with three beers and a sheepish grin.

"Cheers," said Jim, nodding his thanks. "I just wanted to tell you that Captain Baines mentioned you both, and your friends, in the meeting earlier. She said that you were extraordinarily brave in saving those men and women's lives earlier. She also said, *please don't do it again!*" he added, good-naturedly.

Rose and Henry grinned at one another.

Jim studied the teenagers for a moment. "I'm immensely proud of you – both of you," he added and squeezed the younger man's arm across the table before lowering his voice. "Tomorrow the *New World* is going on a mission and the Pod will be staying here. We will have a hell of a lot of work to do down in the manufacturing bays but if you want to be with me, Rose, and you Henry, you are welcome."

His expression darkened slightly. "We're going into great danger tomorrow, some of us more than others. I know you're not children and

I'm not going to insult you, which is why I'm telling you that I don't know how this will all pan out."

The three sat in solemn silence for several heartbeats.

Henry reached across the table and took Rose's hand again before looking at her father. "I understand, Jim. I swear I will take care of Rose, whatever happens."

Jim smiled at them both but with a hint of sadness this time. "I'm not going to tell you what to do, but I will say again, if you want to be with me tomorrow, you will *both* be most welcome."

He let that idea settle for a moment, taking a couple of good pulls from his beer. "I've got an important meeting in a few hours, so I need some shut-eye. Try not to be too late, darling," he said, kissing his daughter's head as he stood. He nodded to Henry and walked away.

As he reached the door to the bar, he turned to look at his baby once more, disguised in the body of a beautiful young woman. He also looked at the very decent young man she had chosen.

"They deserve better than this," he said quietly to himself. His eyes moistened as a wave of tiredness and emotion washed over him. Almost immediately it was replaced by a surge of anger; uncharacteristic for him. He drank in their image one last time before striding away with determination in his heart.

0300 hours

Baines waited for the shuffling and scraping of seats to abate. "Thank you, everyone, I know you've not had much sleep. We should receive full satellite telemetry in the next few minutes. Then we can look over the sections we're especially interested in to put the finishing touches to our plan."

She was pleased to see everyone looking bright and more confident than they had earlier. It may have been merely the medicinal power of a little sleep but she suspected that it was more than that. They now had a goal, and come what may, they were going for it, today. Only one face looked less than gruntled.

Gleeson put his hand up, as if in school. "I move to call it a *desired outcome* – I've yet to see a *plan*."

"Commander, you've been asking me when you can 'blow stuff up' ever since I promoted you. Aren't you the least bit excited by this proposition?" replied Baines.

Gleeson's response was deafening, although he neglected to say anything.

Baines smirked. "Right, Sandy, how's it going with that satellite?"

Singh grinned. "The Death Star is moving into position and the rebel base will be within firing range in seven minutes!"

Baines grinned back broadly, that instant making a conscious decision to use her fear to fuel excitement. "He means that we are almost there," she translated for the majority of the others present.

"Whilst we are waiting for the intel to download, I wish to outline our objectives as I see them." She counted off on her fingers. "First and foremost, we cripple or destroy that ship, *nothing* supersedes this – all our lives depend upon it. That thing is the biggest threat on this entire planet. Second, we get Captain Douglas back. Third, we take back our shuttle if possible. However, this last item is very much on the wish list, truth to tell."

Patel put his hand up to interject.

"Satnam?" Baines encouraged.

"Sorry, Captain, but I see another objective which must be at least as important as the first two."

"Please go on."

"Thank you. The way I see it, that warship contains the knowledge we need to get home and stop all this madness at its source. They clearly had the technology to find us and get here. Now, I know it's dangerous to assume, but we have to work under the hypothesis that they have a way back, surely?" Patel threw the last word out as a question to them all. Some nodded, others merely looked thoughtful.

Baines' expression darkened as she lapsed into thought for a moment. "Ford," she said at last, looking up at Major White. "What sort of complement would a warship that size typically carry? Fifty crew?"

"Typically, but she could carry far more than that on manoeuvres. There could be three times that many, along with general equipment for a unit in the field, armoured vehicles, weapons..." He tailed off, shaking his head, his concern obvious and understandable.

Baines nodded thoughtfully once more. "I'm not sure how possible it will be to get aboard and find the information we need, Satnam. It's going to take an extraordinary effort just to find James. I take it you don't believe we can discover a way home on our own?"

"I don't know for sure, but certainly not quickly, Captain. That ship represents our best, and certainly most expedient, opportunity."

"But don't we have all the time in the world?" Mother Sarah chipped in. "Almost 100 million years, I believe?"

Baines shrugged at the simple truth of that statement. "As long as we stop the enemy within our lifetimes, and without too much damage, there should still be hope for the future," she said at last.

"No," said Patel simply. "They might do any number of things to disrupt the timeline, Captain. Any small event could cause vast and unknowable changes down the line – imagine the old ripples on a pond analogy. We need to act quickly and leave this time as soon as we possibly can. It's our only hope of leaving the future intact."

Murmurings of concern followed Patel's summation and Baines began to worry that this curve-ball might seriously disrupt their meeting and the disclosure she had planned.

"OK," she said loudly. "We'll consider that later. It's a very important and valid point but it will have to come in *behind* our primary objective, sorry Satnam."

Patel nodded, also noting that his observations were having a deleterious effect on their focus. He decided to let the matter drop for now.

"We have telemetry," Singh reported, for once with perfect timing. He fired up the big screen to display the satellite's information, instantly grabbing everyone's attention. The feed came in real-time, barring a few seconds delay due to distance. A vast amount of information was transmitted to the *New World*, in very fast, very short bursts. There was a danger that the transmission might be detected by the battleship's scans, but they had only one chance to collate this intelligence and if that meant spending the resource, then they really had no choice.

"Phase one of my plan," Baines began, as the information continued to scroll in, "requires a team of six highly trained soldiers on dirt bikes to make their way to the enemy ship, carrying explosives in their backpacks. The team will be led by Commander Gleeson with support from Corporals Jones and O'Brien. I'll let the commander choose the rest of his team later this morning."

She strode around to the monitor, which now showed the newcomers' landing site. Fortunately, due to favourable atmospherics, the picture was surprisingly detailed and clear, despite the ghostly, grey glow inherent to infrared footage.

"Once here," she pointed to the black ship, now in plan view as the satellite saw it, "we will set our explosives in the main rocket nacelles at the rear."

The new arrivals had clearly been busy. Already a floodlit compound had been set up around their ship. They were still on the dark side of the planet but this illumination allowed quality images to be taken, even by the daylight cameras on board the satellite.

Baines shook her head. "They have no fear of us at all."

Nestled in next to the warship it was possible to make out the *New World*'s shuttle, glowing white in the floodlights, and tiny next to its giant neighbour. "Anyone care to tell me what this might be?" she asked wryly as she pointed it out.

"Well, that confirms it," said Gleeson with a nod. "No doubt they're the enemy now. Just one question, how exactly are we to sneak up and blow their ship from around them? They'll know we're coming as soon as we enter the valley. If not before," he added tersely.

Baines studied the people around the table. They all appeared concerned. "That's why Tim is here," she said simply.

Eveyone turned to Tim Norris like *he* was the one with the answers they all craved. He was dark-eyed, clearly had not slept well and now looked uncomfortable, too.

Baines continued, "He's going to choose a herd of animals that will mask our presence and get us to within striking distance as safely as possible. We will drive them, spook them if necessary, in the direction we need them to go. Then we pounce. No one will see us coming or hear our electric bikes in the middle of a stampede."

Gleeson wore a look of horror, clearly wishing he had stayed in bed.

Tim absorbed the captain's words in silence for a few moments, before he spoke. "I might have another idea which could help us," he offered, at last.

His words came quickly at first, almost like he was blurting out his thoughts, but despite this shaky start, his voice gained strength as his audience warmed to his idea. He shed the effects of a broken sleep before their very eyes, becoming more animated with every point that he made. After rolling out his plan, he chose an appropriate herd for them, within moments of studying the satellite feed.

The adults were agog, marvelling at him.

0800 hours

Baines glared at Julian Bradford, also known as Sargo Lemelisk, attempted murderer and perhaps even the man responsible for the death of Aito Nassaki, Hiro's brother, three years previously. She had broken up the earlier meeting at 0500 hours, ordering everyone to get another couple of hours rest. They would never need to be sharper than on this day, but for the moment, Baines was unsure what to think. Alongside her in the brig were Commander Elvis Percival Gleeson, Lieutenant Hiro Nassaki and Sergeant John Jackson, his arm still in a sling.

No one had yet spoken. Del Bond sat in the opposite cell, trying to make himself small, but straining his ears to catch every syllable.

"Sargo Lemelisk," stated Baines at last. It was by no means a question.

Bradford did not even flinch. "Is that supposed to mean something to me?" he asked at last.

Hiro stepped forward and quietly spoke through the bars. "What actually happened to Aito? Did you kill him?"

Aito had died mysteriously about three years ago – AD2109 in the crew's timeline.

"I don't know anyone called Aito and I don't know you."

"You knew my name when you greeted me in the Mud Hole a week or so ago."

"Everyone knows *who* you *are*," the prisoner answered with a disdainful shrug. "You're Hiro, the chief engineer."

"So you're not Sargo Lemelisk then?"

"Never heard of the man," he stated, witheringly.

The Sarge looked at him sidelong. "Where are you from?" he asked, forestalling the chief's next question.

"London."

"Where?"

"Elephant and Castle, why?"

The Sarge did not answer but continued to stare intently at the prisoner.

"OK Sargo, forgive me, *Julian*," continued Hiro with just a hint of sarcasm.

Baines was surprised. Hiro was blunt but never deliberately so; a wide-eyed idealist and rarely given to scorn or derision. Irony was a foreign country he had *never* been able to find his way around. She was also surprised he had taken the lead in this interrogation, especially unasked. Clearly there were powerful forces at work here. She glanced at the chief wondering what else he might do this morning, but allowed him to continue uninterrupted.

"Why don't you tell us why you were trying to steal one of our lifeboats and why you tried to kill Pt Donavon?"

"I wasn't trying to steal anything. They attacked me."

Hiro nodded, as if to himself and then tried again. "That's the wrong answer, *Sargo*. Why don't you try telling us the truth? It will be better for you in the long run."

The prisoner curled his lip at that. "I don't know what the hell you're talking about!"

Hiro tutted and nodded once more. "That's two wrong answers, Sargo. You're not doing very well, are you?"

"Go and shove your head down the Kermit!"

"Down the what?" asked Hiro, genuinely mystified.

"Kermit the frog – bog. It's rhyming slang, you wouldn't understand."

"No it ain't," interrupted The Sarge. "Kermit means road. Kermit the Frog, frog and toad – road; and you ain't from Elephant and Castle, not whilst I've still got a hole up my ar—"

"Oh dear," interrupted Hiro. "That's three wrong answers in a row, Sargo."

The prisoner leapt at the bars reaching for the engineer. Baines cried out a warning but her shout was partially strangled by a third surprise. Before the man could reach Hiro, he was thrown back across his cell only to land on the floor twitching. The cables from a device which appeared, almost magically, in the chief's hands, had clearly delivered a very high voltage charge into the man's body, completely disabling him.

Hiro switched off the power. The others watched in horrified fascination as their, usually so awkward but well meaning, engineer knelt down level with the prisoner. "Let's start again, shall we?" he said.

Bradford or Lemelisk was shivering and coughing now.

"Oh," Hiro added quietly, as if to remind himself, "and just so that we understand one another." A second high voltage jolt surged through the prone man, making him scream and then gibber as the power stopped. "Now tell me what happened to my brother!"

1100 hours

Gleeson was in his happy place – he was building bombs. He failed to notice the presence behind him until he reached around for a tool from his box and looked up in surprise.

"Hey Cap, didn't see you there."

"I could see you were busy. What shape are we in?"

Gleeson scratched his cheek as he reached across his workbench for one of the completed devices. "Top banana! I've built enough of these weekend spoilers to ruin someone's whole year!" He grinned proudly, tossing it to Baines. "Nice, eh?"

Baines held it like she had been forced to hold a baby who had laid an egg. "Is it safe?" she asked cautiously.

"Bladdy hope not, mate. It's a bomb."

She looked up sharply, concerned, only to see Gleeson laughing silently at her. She put it down on the bench and gave him a playful slap on the arm. "Alright – one-all, soldier!"

They both chuckled.

"What did you think of Tim's plan?" she asked him.

"I think it's insane," he answered frankly. "But what isn't, these days? It's no crazier than anything else we've done since we landed in the zoo from hell."

"Using a herd of several thousand small dinosaurs – named by Captain Douglas, after one of them knocked him down to lick his face – as a cover for our charge, does sound a little unusual now you come to mention it," she grinned.

"Yeah," agreed Gleeson, deadpan. "Gets a bit surreal after that, though."

Lieutenant Nassaki was also in his happy place – engineering. He and Georgio Baccini had really been in the zone over the last couple of hours since the chief returned from the brig. The *New World*, or *Sekai*, as Hiro referred to her, was about to undertake manoeuvres for which she was certainly never designed.

Impossible engineering problems, ludicrous deadlines – the engineers were in paradise. It was several seconds before they realised their work was being observed by the captain.

"Captain?" asked Hiro, eventually. "I didn't notice you there."

"I could see you were bus—"

"Captain?"

"Never mind – déjà vu. How are the preparations coming?"

"Good, si—ma— …er, Captain." He saluted to cover his confusion.

Baines smiled as he tripped over his words. Hiro was a good man but not good with people – although, he hid a remarkable talent for getting information out of them, it seemed. She was still rather shocked about the interrogation, but covered her discomfort by putting an arm around her chief engineer and leading him over to a couple of seats. It *was* good to see him back to his dear, socially inept self.

"She will be ready for tonight as promised," continued the engineer. "I wish we'd had the time to build the concrete piles under her, though. For takeoff, I mean. Still, without the Pod dragging us down we should be able to lift off. When we get back, I suggest we hover to lift the Pod into place. It will use a lot more fuel but will be far safer than trying to put down with any precision in the muddy, collapsed field we are in. Especially with the Pod capsized as it is."

"That's great, good work. Now, how are *you*, Hiro?"

"Erm, fine...?" he asked, a little confused.

"That must have been hard this morning."

"No."

Baines raised her eyebrows. "No?"

"Sargo Lemelisk was involved in the death of my brother, he was involved in the death of Georgio's brother and he was involved in getting Sekai lost in the Cretaceous."

She waited for more but clearly the engineer thought he had covered all the bases there. Perhaps he had. Shrugging, she rose from her seat and said, "I can't argue with that, Hiro, but of all the people on this ship, I never expected..." she let the sentence hang. What *had* she expected?

He helped her out. "They don't see us as people, Captain. Just tools to be used. So I saw him as a tool which wasn't functioning correctly, I simply applied more power until it did. I think it worked?" His eyes sought vindication or at least some consolation.

Baines nodded.

"We found out where to look for the wormhole drive and where the brig is on that ship, didn't we?" he asked.

"Yes, we did," Baines admitted.

Always such an innocent soul, she could not help wondering if something had broken within the chief. *What are these creatures doing to my poor, poor crew? They don't deserve this and I have to stop it, even if it destroys me, I have to,* she railed within.

Keeping that thought to herself, she asked, "But do you think we can trust the information?"

"Yes."

Baines raised her eyebrows questioningly.

The chief looked blank.

"Can you elucidate?" she asked, remembering who she was talking with. "*How* can we be sure?"

"*I* rigged up the device. It was cannibalised from one of the security tasers Major White's team use. It's quite difficult to describe how it delivers the pain…" his brows knitted in thought for a moment before his expression cleared. "I could draw you a graph?" he offered, earnestly.

She threw her head back and laughed before leaning forward to pull the chief into a brief hug. "Bless you, Hiro. I'll see you later to discuss the final arrangements." She walked away leaving Hiro looking bewildered.

He shook it off quickly and got back to work. At least he only had to ready over half a kilometre of spaceship for a daring attack she was never built for – people were just too complicated.

Major White was *not* in his happy place. He was about to be left behind for the most important mission they could ever hope to undertake in the circumstances, and it was eating him alive.

He just could not settle down to anything and someone was *shuffling*. More than that, they were re-filing and clearing things away, across his entire office. Although he had requested this, today he would have preferred the mess. For some reason, these simple acts seemed to be taking over his entire focus. The little noises, randomly timed, without any sense of rhythm or obvious purpose were destroying his concentration and gnawing at his nerves. After reading the first line of a speech he was working on, at least five times in the last minute, he wondered how much more he could stand.

A door slammed, a drawer slid open partway and then the rest of the way, as the person considered what they were looking for. They closed the drawer, but not fully and then opened it again, before finally *slamming* it shut. Another drawer was opened and the process repeated. Datasheets were moved, shuffled and sorted through so that, almost before he knew it, the drawer operation could begin all over again. The banging of the filing cabinet drawer, on the third attempt after removing a protruding file, was a nice touch. Once successful, another cupboard was opened immediately, causing something which rattled to fall out and clatter across the floor. Apparently, it had been in the wrong place and needed to be placed in yet another drawer, no, not that one it seemed. Slide, *slam* – nor that one. Slide again and a rattle as the item was forced into position – bang. The drawer would not close and needed to be emptied and tidied to make room for the item which had been placed in the wrong place and now could not be *re*placed. All the while the office chair they leaned on creaked with every movement. The chair now appeared to be in the way of another drawer opening – slam. It needed to be moved – slam. Apparently, it would not fit between the desk and the cabinet – *slam...*

White, usually so affable, was developing a twitch. Without realising it, he crushed his coffee cup, spilling the hot beverage onto his hand. He jumped, pouring it all over his desk and, joy of joys, into his crotch too.

He leapt out of his chair, which shot back to bang loudly into another cabinet, dislodging a stack of data sheets from the top. The autumnal grace with which they cascaded all over the floor was completely lost on the major, distracted as he was by the piping hot coffee which had just penetrated his trousers all the way to his groin.

Bending down to urgently adjust his dress, he forgot that he was still holding the cup and the remainder of the coffee liberally spattered these fallen data sheets. Perhaps unsurprisingly, the sheet on top just happened to be his first ever report, as head of ship's security, to his new captain – at least, it used to be. Naturally, his speech had been the first casualty in the coffee cascade.

He let out a roar like an enraged bull, straightened and drew back his arm to throw the offending cup all the way across his office, knocking his white board clean off the wall, when—

"Is this a bad time for you, Ford?" asked Captain Baines, innocently.

White seethed like the death of a pressure vessel. Returning to himself, he snorted and both officers laughed as Baines bent to help him tidy up the mess he had made.

"Was this report for me?" she asked, unhelpfully.

The person tidying the office made a strategic withdrawal in the background.

White grinned lopsidedly. "Yeah, it's the new coffee-mat format – latest thing before we left." He gestured toward the mess on his desk. "As you can see, I'm completely prepared for my address to the Pod crew and residents this afternoon, otherwise."

"Just keep it light, you can fill in the details when we get back," she suggested calmly, straightening up to give him a direct look. "It's OK, you know. We'll be back before you know it. We'll be barely more than fifty klicks away."

White sighed, attempting to re-sort the fallen datasheets into order. "It's not the distance, Jill," he said, simply.

"I know," she acknowledged.

"I'm still not sure I should give this address. It tips our hand and might even start a panic."

"If this were a purely military unit, I would agree with you. Trouble is, we have families to protect and if the *New World*, their only way out of here, were to suddenly lift off without them there would be a stampede, never mind a panic."

"I guess, but the saying 'everything we have in one basket' springs to mind. Not to mention I want you guys and all these people to be safe. I can't help feeling useless, staying here with what you're going into."

"If we fail, you'll be the only hope for these people, Ford. I *need* you here. Lead them well."

"If you fail, I can't see how we can..." he left the thought unfinished. "Just come back in one piece – all of you!"

She smiled kindly at him. "Just remember, the enemy won't risk destroying this Pod. They will do anything to avoid even damaging it and that's your strength."

"And they'll pay a high price for it, if anything happens to you, that I swear. We have two working stun cannons now, a hold full of explosives and a real bad attitude!"

She put a hand gently to his cheek. "Good luck, Ford."

"Good luck, Captain."

She turned and strode away. As he watched her go, he pondered their last words, hoping 'good luck' did not mean 'goodbye'. He shook the thought aside brusquely, returned to his desk and sat with a heavy sigh, glaring at his ruined speech.

"Hi, Jim," greeted Baines as she walked into the Pod's manufacturing bay.

Dr Jim Miller looked round and waved as he saw the captain approach. His daughter, Rose, was with him, along with Henry Burnstein Jr.

Rose Miller was a stunning beauty and always immaculately dressed in the latest feminine fashions, so Baines was rather surprised to see her wearing military style fatigues and hiking boots. She still looked fantastic, Baines thought enviously, trying to remember what it was like to be sixteen. She nodded to the teenagers. "Helping out the old man, Rose?"

The young girl smiled in welcome. "Just making sure he's safe."

"And trying to learn as much as we can," added Henry.

"I haven't had a chance to thank you for saving those people yesterday," said Baines. "It was very courageous."

"It was Rose's idea really," said Henry. "I was too shocked to think straight but she was amazing, came up with a plan straight away."

"So I was told. When the *New World* takes off later, Major White will be in charge and he will need all the help he can get. I don't want you to put yourselves into any unnecessary danger, but if you get another brilliant idea," she looked at them both intently, "don't keep it to yourselves." She smiled at them and gave Henry an encouraging squeeze on the arm before turning back to Jim.

"The cradle is nearly finished, Captain," he said.

A cradle was being fabricated to carry one of the personnel carriers under the *New World*. There would be no time to stop and set down when they arrived at their destination. Ergo, the truck would need to be dropped off quickly if it was to provide support for the people on the ground - that and a way back home when the *New World* left the theatre of operations. It had to be carried, there being no way a ten-ton truck could hope to keep up with Gleeson's dirt bikes over such rough terrain; it would also blow their cover. However, once the operation was complete, the insurgency team would need its protection, from wildlife at the very least.

The truck would also provide means of evacuation for any casualties. No one had actually said it, but they had no idea what state Captain Douglas might be in when or if they got to him.

Captain Tobias Meritus sat on the bridge of the *Last Word*, watching the armoured patrol drive towards his ship on a heads-up combat display. They were returning from a twenty-four hour reconnaissance mission. Meritus had insisted they test the entire area strategically, looking for any weakness in their location. Routes which might be used by the people aboard the *New World* to launch a ground assault on their position, however unlikely. He knew they had no aircraft capable of threatening him.

Schultz had vouched safe that the crew of the *New World* had no means of mounting an attack of *any* kind. Furthermore, without Captain Douglas, they would lack the backbone to try.

Meritus was less sure. Schultz's confidence was absolute but he saw only hubris, so he kept the *Last Word* on high tactical alert. It was his call. He knew they appeared to be holding all the cards, but there was something about Douglas' reputation that rankled. Enemy or no, the man was worthy of admiration. He would be unable to help his old crewmates directly, Meritus had seen to that, but he *was* the sort of leader who inspired people. They might just come after him yet, regardless of the danger.

Despite the awesome size of the *New World*, his battleship had the power to destroy it in the blink of an eye. At 150 metres long, the *Last Word* was a vast flying tank, stacked to the roof with the technology of war and stealth. Unfortunately, they needed the *New World* intact, which complicated things, but it was a hurdle Meritus knew he could overcome. His only real concern in this venture was the attitude of Dr Heidi Schultz and the unswerving belief she held in her grandfather's omniscience.

Her family were funding the whole operation and if he intended to prosper, or indeed live, in the new society they were to forge, he had to toe the line. He agreed with the principles which drove their mission, he believed that the human race had gone terribly awry and needed to be fixed. If this meant throwing the reset switch and starting again then so be it, although he did not necessarily believe that their new world should be seeded only from the Schultzes' preferred stock. Meritus saw this as a limited vision, but there was more to it than that, something about Schultz herself. He found it unpalatable. Her grandfather was worse, much worse. Even Meritus could see that Heinrich Schultz was pure evil and *he* worked for the man. However, as a soldier, he realised that sometimes great wrongs are necessary to do a great right, and so long as the technology worked as advertised, so would their plan.

At the moment Meritus, as captain of the *Last Word*, was the mission's second in command, but he knew that would change when the others, including old man Schultz himself, joined them.

Meritus may be first amongst the captains. After all, his was the flagship and the mission to take the *New World* from the enemy, paving the way for *Operation Dawn*. However, when the *Sabre*, the *Heydrich* and Schultz's personal yacht, the *Eisernes Kreuz* arrived, he would suddenly find himself little more than just another flunky – unable to reap the rewards of *his* actions.

The construction of the *Last Word* had stretched even the Schultz family assets to breaking point. The three ships to follow were mere forty metre long attack ships, no more than a tenth of the mass of the *Last Word* and nowhere near as deadly. He, Meritus, had the power, and they expected him to just give it up to an old man, his psychopathic granddaughter and their menagerie of sycophants.

The rest of the 'Dawn' fleet were waiting for his signal, along with exact space-time coordinates, before jumping through to take his command away from him – once the bloody business of soldiery had been done, of course. He could stop that from ever happening if he arranged for the favoured granddaughter to have a little accident. The Cretaceous was a phenomenally dangerous time, after all.

It was not like he needed the fleet, he already had everything he required and with the *New World* he would be unstoppable – he could cripple the timeline so that there *was* no one to come after him, he had good breeding stock aboard the *Last Word* and, after he had sifted the wheat from the chaff, the *New World* would probably yield yet more.

His musings were interrupted by a comm call from one of the patrol vehicles. Meritus nodded for one of his bridge officers to patch it through to him.

"This is Meritus, go ahead."

"Captain, I need medics and a stretcher sent to the cargo bay immediately."

"Very well, Dr Schultz. Have some of your group been injured?"

"No. We found someone from the New World. *Just do it!"*

A muscle twitched in Meritus' jaw. "Very well," he said simply, keeping all emotion out of his voice. "They are on their way – out."

He nodded to the same officer again to carry out the order. *Yes,* he mused, *the Cretaceous was a very dangerous time to live. Anything might happen.*

1630 hours

The triumvirate sat around the table in the meeting room off the *New World*'s bridge. It was a while before anyone spoke. Anxiety thickened the air as the time drew near for the first team to leave.

Baines opened her mouth to speak when Lieutenant Singh entered from the bridge, in a heightened state.

"Captain," he blurted, "I've just downloaded the latest telemetry from the satellite. This is the third pass and I think it will be the last!"

Concern crossed the faces of the council.

"What's happened to it?" asked Patel, peremptorily.

Singh sat down and called up a monitor from the table, networking it to the large screen in the wall. The video footage they were shown needed no explanation.

The satellite was filming a very dangerous looking, two-man, orbital attack vessel which had manoeuvred into its path and was about to swallow it. As the rear hatch opened they saw a small cargo hold. Once inside, the hatch presumably closed behind the satellite, sealing it in. Lights came on with the gravity and the satellite dropped suddenly hitting the deck hard.

The picture was now canted over to one side as they watched a uniformed man enter, grinning at this little piece of technology which had dropped in from the void.

"We can't let them have that asset," said Baines, her voice raised. She looked at Singh, her mouth set. "Detonate it!"

Singh's eyes widened. "It's *inside* their ship."

"I can see that – *do it!*"

The young man on the screen knelt down to look more closely at the satellite. He still appeared to be grinning but the sudden exposure to atmosphere had caused ice to flash-form over the satellite's frigid carapace, obscuring the lens.

"Jill!" Mother Sarah called out, jumping to her feet in horror. Satnam said nothing, simply remaining seated.

"Not another word!" snapped Baines, raising her index finger. She turned back to Singh. "*Damnit*, Sandy! Do it now!"

Singh had prepped the self destruct but was now just staring at the monitor as if in a dream. Baines leaned over and hit return on the keypad. The satellite feed snapped to white noise for a second before the screen, sensing the loss of signal, went to standby.

Silence…

"Geoff?"

Lloyd stirred but just barely. He was not quite sure if he had heard—

"Geoff?"

Ah, he *had* heard. He must be awake – ouch. Yes, he was awake. The pain he felt was unequivocal.

"Geoff? It's… are ye… be OK… hear me? It's me… *Geoff?*"

It was like listening to an analogue radio which was not tuned correctly. The voice phased in and out and he only caught snippets of it.

He tried opening his eyes – ouch, that was a mistake. His injured side felt like his insides might become outsides any minute. He steeled himself...

"Wha?" he tried.

"Geoff, it's me."

It was a man, he could tell that at least. He was very briefly glad that it was not Heidi Schultz – maybe that had just been a bad dream? He had spent days on his own, almost going out of his mind with fear, loneliness and pain. Despite this, there were very definitely two people whom he never wished to see again and Schultz was certainly one of them. The other was—

"It's me. James, James Douglas."

"Oh, Christ..." said Lloyd, again. He hated his life.

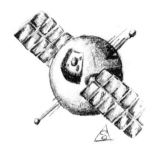

Chapter 4 | The First Stroke of War

"You killed that man!" Sarah was shaking in shock.

Baines turned on her, angry. "I was saving *our* people! What do you think is going on here, Sarah?"

"But…" The priest was still standing, unable to move or function after what she had just witnessed. Patel stood slowly and walked around behind her, gently helping her back into her seat.

"I had no choice!" shouted Baines, a tear brimming in her eye.

Patel raised his hands placatingly. "We know, Jill. We know." He moved around the table to help Baines into her seat too.

Singh was still staring at the monitor. Other than swallowing, he had not moved a muscle.

Patel returned to his seat at the head of the table between the two women and took a hand from each in his own. He spoke softly. "If they had been allowed to keep that satellite, they *would* have used it against us, maybe even found a way to break into our comms from there and caused all manner of damage. It had to be destro—"

"But that young m-man," stuttered Sarah, her lip trembling.

"Was a man who happily signed up to kill us, Sarah – and not only us. If they get their way they will wipe out the entire human race and start again with their own 'version' of humanity." A little emotion crept into his voice at this last. "Everyone we knew, everyone who was or ever *will be* born, throughout the entire history of man, gone. Can you imagine that? Jill had no choice, Sarah, and now we must help her."

Baines' face crumpled and she pulled back her hand to wipe a tear from the corner of her eye.

Singh took a deep breath and came back to himself. He stood and stepped closer to his captain. She jumped as he put a gentle arm around her shoulder. Kneeling next to her chair, he pulled her into a friend's embrace. "I'm sorry," he said, quietly. "I should have done that, I froze…" he tailed off.

Baines leaned back, giving him a direct look. "No, Sandy. I wouldn't want you to have this. It was bad enough seeing Hiro electrocute that man this morning. I want to save you all from this, so you can be the people you have always been. Whatever the cost, I will protect you – I swear it." She choked and was unable to say any more.

Mother Sarah stepped around quickly to hold her, too. "I'm sorry, Jill," she said in a shaky voice. "You're not alone. This is on all of us."

"No!" stated Satnam, irrefutably. "This is on the people who perpetrated this chain of atrocities. The men on that ship were killers, or soon would have been. They had to be stopped and the enemy had to be deprived of both our satellite and that attack craft. Now, be steady, people. This is just the first stroke of war."

Chapter 5 | Battleship

Captain Baines sat alone. The rest of the crew were all working at breakneck speed to bring the ship to a state of readiness for liftoff. Equally busy were the crew and residents aboard the Pod, many of them buzzing about the *New World* providing support to her depleted engineering team. In a little island of calm, Baines needed some time alone to prepare her mind and spirit for what was to come.

Her head was full of the last few hours, a confusion of conversations held, images beheld and feelings buried – with limited success. She attempted to work through it all in this precious moment of peace.

Major White's address had received a mixed response, apparently. She had deliberately stayed out of that, feeling that it was vital for the people aboard the Pod to see Major Ford White as their leader, should anything go wrong with the mission – and *so* much could go wrong with this mission.

However, she *had* been present when Commander Gleeson's away team met with Tim Norris.

Fortunately, one of the first tasks the crew carried out, before venturing far from the ship, was to calculate magnetic north. Extrapolating the bearing allowed them to continue using standard compasses.

Baines reflected on their final briefing…

Tim had clearly worked hard to correlate the data gathered during the satellite fly-overs. His information identified the creatures shown by the satellite, alongside others which the insurgency squad might reasonably expect to encounter. A simple talk, with associated imagery, condensed the animals' expected behavioural patterns and dispersals, along with some of their more obvious physical characteristics, into something the soldiers could memorise easily. This 'general expectations' approach to the fauna by basic type, along with a brief look at the landscape, accompanied by a satellite map of the region, were the only guides available to them.

A herd of animals grazing not too far away from the enemy position were selected to provide cover for their operation. Tim based his decision on three factors, the first being their location, which was pretty good for the team's purposes. A little rounding up and a few prods in the right direction should enable the men and women, mounted on electric dirt bikes, to start a stampede towards the enemy – *hopefully*.

The young naturalist voiced some scruple about this, however. He was passionately against any of the animals being harmed in any way.

Gleeson's response was rather more pragmatic. "Look, Tim, we won't do anything to deliberately hurt these guys, but a stampede is a dangerous place to be. Once everything kicks off, my first concern will be for the mission and my people out there in the thick of it. The lives of everyone aboard this ship depend upon our success."

Tim pushed for more assurance but it was not forthcoming.

The second point guiding the young man's choice balanced the size of the individuals within the herd against their effectiveness as a diversion. The chances of surviving a stampede would reduce as the bulk of the creatures increased. These animals were fairly small – the very largest of them no more than three metres long, and almost half of that was tail.

"The animals I've chosen will hopefully prove fast enough to keep up with your bikes over the challenging terrain," he explained. "Their small size should make them easier to intimidate and direct, too – so you can herd them. Mayor is fairly skittish and we have no reason to believe that his brethren will behave differently. Although that in no way means that they'll be safe to be around. Fear can be *devastating* in animals."

"Thanks for the vivid image," Gleeson commented. "I'll have to remember that one, 'devastating' – surely a word that's worth a thousand pictures."

Baines smiled slightly at Tim's discomfort, trapped in front of a roomful of hardened soldiers glancing uneasily at one another, and staring balefully at *him*. "Quite right, Tim," she spoke up. "We don't want anyone to think they can get comfortable out there. They'll need to keep their guard up at all times."

Tim had nodded his gratitude before continuing. "Thirdly, putting aside that the Mayors are a newly discovered species for a moment, we've acquired more knowledge about them than any palaeontologist before us – or after, depending on how you view our situation – could ever rival. We're living with one! More than that, Dr Natalie Pearson has taken several scans of the animal's physiology while treating him for his wounds."

He referenced the many hours spent with the zoologist, studying and interacting with Mayor over recent days. Although, it transpired that their observations of his temperament were of the most import, as far as the mission was concerned.

"I know," Tim continued, "that one individual can hardly be said to be an exhaustive study, but it's all we've got. Anyway, as I said, there's no suggestion that Mayor isn't typical for his species and thankfully he's fairly placid, if inquisitive. He shows many of the characteristics sought in domesticated animals. Of course, a herd thousands strong will likely be more of a handful, especially when spooked."

Gleeson's frown returned. "He may be calm on his own, son, but it's springtime out there. Back home we called that 'the rutting season'. I hope I don't have to draw you a diagram?"

Tim nodded his understanding and agreement. "But if you want to start a stampede, then the more edgy they are the *better*?" he winced again, apologetically under Gleeson's stare. He raised his hands placatingly. "I'm sorry, but look, I fully acknowledge that you'll be putting yourselves very much in harm's way, well before you even sight the enemy."

He paused to smile awkwardly, looking very young once more. "You're all *so* brave and we're all *so* grateful for what you're about to do. All I can tell you is, I think this gives our plan the greatest chance of working.

The large herd of Mayor Dougli Salvator are our best option for providing cover. There are no palatable options, just worse ones, I'm afraid."

Brightening slightly, he added, "At least we can say that the species was named after, and partially by, Captain Douglas himself. That does lend a certain circularity to our choice, doesn't it? One of these creatures saved his life once already. Hopefully this will prove a good omen for all of us, but most importantly, they're by far the safest bet from what's out there in the area we're looking at. Of that, I'm absolutely confident.

"I don't know if this will give you a little more assurance but, well, when we think large reptiles, we tend to think crocodile. Mayor's behaviour appears to be nothing like that. Nor does he seem particularly birdlike, either. Aside from occasional spats of petulance, if you remove the fern he's eating, he shows none of the violent aggression we often see in birds. Many of us love to hear birdsong, but what we think of as 'song' is more usually a frank invitation to 'get the hell off my branch or I'll peck your eyes out!'.

"It's impossible to directly compare Mayor's behaviour with the mammalian herd animals we're familiar with, but I have to say he does seem to behave more like a sheep than a crocodile or a bird. I think that's encouraging. I hope that this gives you... hope," he concluded weakly.

The commander's team left soon after, quietly, despite all the hopes travelling with them. "Your courage is a light in the darkness for us all," Mother Sarah said, seeing them off with a prayer and a hug. There were no atheists in a foxhole.

Baines tried not to dwell, turning her mind back to Tim. She was always impressed by the young man's informational talks. His enthusiasm tended to push back his obvious nervousness, even when facing some fairly imposing adults. It never took long for him to envelop them with his knowledge and love of the subject. Even so, she had been gobsmacked when the teenager rolled out his audacious plan to reduce the enemy threat, earlier, in the small hours of the morning. His augmentations to the plan she herself had tabled were radical, perhaps even unasked for, but just possibly doable.

Her initial idea was simple: Carry one of their personnel vehicles, with a complement of six troops, under the belly of the *New World* within a purpose made cradle. Upon reaching the enemy, deploy it in the field right next to the warship. They hoped to be upon them before the enemy could react, especially in the aftermath of the planned explosions Gleeson's team were about to rig.

Baines then planned to release the cradle and hopefully damage one or more of the opposing force's ancillary craft. The personnel carrier would be left behind to provide the teams with protection. Terrified animals would doubtless be running all over the site by that point.

With the enemy battleship hopefully disabled, their troops could look for a way inside, if possible. This final element seemed like wishful thinking, to say the least. They had no clear way of retrieving Captain Douglas, but it was all they had. Maybe, if their diversion was successful, it could even provide an opportunity for the captain to make a break. It was pretty thin, she knew, but doing nothing would *guarantee* their demise. Most importantly, they had to move quickly.

It was all about diversion on top of diversion, whilst relying on the assumption that Nazi arrogance would likely write off the *New World*'s crew as incapable of defending themselves, let alone launching any kind of meaningful attack.

She sighed, wearily. *If these events stack up, and with a little luck, maybe we'll catch the enemy with their trousers down for just long enough to... what? Pull a rabbit out of the hat in the ensuing chaos?*

She massaged her temples. So many unknowns, and retrieving Douglas from inside the enemy vessel, for they were bound to have him in their most secure facility, presented a problem with no obvious solution. Even for the elastic imagination of their teenaged genius. Baines' hope that structural damage to the ship from the planned explosions might offer them a way in was just that, a hope. Crippling the battleship had to be their number one priority. It was the single greatest threat on this Earth.

At least, after Hiro's interrogation of Sargo Lemelisk, they had some idea of the internal layout of the vessel – shocking though it had been to witness. Eventually, Lemelisk had fallen unconscious before Hiro managed to find out the facts about his brother's death. Aito's fate would have to wait. Other events were more immediately pressing. At least until this desperate assault was concluded, for better or worse.

On the ground, the warship was like a fortress, prickling with the deadliest weaponry mankind could produce. If the enemy were allowed even a moment to gather their wits about them, the *New World* would be blown to pieces.

In the part of her mind where she segregated her misgivings from her will, Baines accepted that hers was not a great plan but it did have two points in favour. Firstly, the enemy would be unlikely to suspect such a bold move and secondly, it could be executed quickly and with minimal preparation, hopefully before the new arrivals could put their own strategies into effect. She could not shake the feeling that moving quickly was more important than anything else. Once Schultz's people got their act together they would be unstoppable – especially as the crew of the *New World* had virtually nothing with which *to* stop them.

Baines rubbed her eyes. She felt a little disjointed, knowing her thoughts lacked order. She prayed the explosives would be enough to disable the enemy vessel and the officers on the ground would be able to take advantage of the general confusion to create, or steal, an opportunity to save Douglas.

James...

A small tear escaped and she wiped her cheek gently, studying the moisture on her finger. They would soon be *so* close to him. There had to be a way to bring him home, there simply had to be.

She took solace in the fact that Gleeson would be on point. If anyone would have the quick thinking nerve, nay the damned cheek, to pull this off, it was surely the Australian. She smiled through her sadness, remembering his reaction when she had promoted him. Gleeson was one in a million, there was no doubt, but so was young Mr Norris.

Her mind drifted back to Tim's plan, for surely it was his. Wild, gung ho, it might even be called a little crazy perhaps, but if successful, it could well redress the balance in one fell swoop.

The teenager had eventually confessed that, unable to sleep properly, he had spent most of the ordered rest period tossing and turning, as he worried about the warship and poor Captain Douglas trapped within it. The topographical surveys, provided by their short-lived satellite, provided a sharp focus for his nebulous ideas. After that, it all came together.

The images showed the enemy ship on a steep sided plateau at the end of a heavily wooded valley. The position was naturally defensible; a steep bank in front and to the side of them, a thick forest to the rear. The distance between the opposing forces would take a couple of days to traverse on foot and vehicular access would be extremely difficult. Schultz knew they had cycles but would not be expecting fast moving, powered transport, capable of making such a difficult journey, to be available to them.

Without the satellite, the *New World*'s crew would have had virtually no chance of finding them on the ground. It seemed plausible that the enemy had also factored for this, clearly thinking their position so strong that they may well have switched on the shuttle's homing beacon as a lure.

Tim had reasoned that the enemy leadership would feel secure from any kind of ground attack within the timeframe they needed. As far as *they* knew, the *New World* had no weapons or fighter craft, either, so they owned the skies, too. There were, of course, some *very* large 'birds and wildlife' but none of the animals could threaten the heavily armoured battleship directly.

Of course, thought Baines, *they may think they have us exactly where they want us – and maybe they have – but they haven't factored for Tim's plan to use the topography they've chosen for its very defensibility, against them.*

Baines shook her head ruefully as she pondered the details. It was an *insane* idea. "I don't think they'll see *this* coming," she muttered softly to the empty meeting room. She desperately wished to contact Gleeson for a situation report, but the enemy would certainly pick up any long range comm traffic. It could blow their whole mission. So she stewed and hoped, her mind whirling in binary orbit with her stomach.

Sighing once more, she consciously blew out her anxiety, grateful for the little solitude she had been granted. Her mind freewheeled, her thoughts wandered. She found an odd contentment in this moment, could feel herself sinking into it, with the temptation to just let go and never move again.

Mother Sarah's words in this very room just a few days ago intruded on her reverie, echoing, as if still in the air, "*We need you now, Jill. We need your strength. It was what James wanted, he said so more than once.*"

No, Baines could never truly let go. The pressure of providing hope for their people weighed on her, but that tether was also a lifeline, pushing back at despair. She had left standing orders to the crew. She would make herself available to any who needed to see their captain. It was her promise, and as that thought surfaced, so the door chimed. Baines put her head in her hands, taking a deep breath, "Come."

Entering on a bow wave of aroma, Lieutenant Singh bore a coffee mug and just possibly the most wonderful thing Baines had ever smelt.

"Wow!" she exclaimed, the threat of caffeine snapping her back from the funk she had been slipping towards. "I knew you could do it really! All that slop you've supplied us with over the years, just so that we never asked you to get a brew on!"

Singh beamed. "Ah well, this is a special occasion, after all. *So* special, in fact," he looked a little sheepish now, "that I ordered Mary to make it for me."

Crewman Mary Hutchins, the *New World*'s cook, cleaner and dogsbody, beloved of all, was well known for her skill and ingenuity with both chocolate and beverage.

"I knew that if I gave you my usual sludge," he continued, "you'd just be forced to smile politely and then tip it into the nearest plant pot."

"We don't have any plant pots up here."

"You see the problem."

Baines snorted. "No bickies?" she asked hopefully.

Singh looked stricken. "Oh, sorry, Captain. I knew there was something else."

"Never mind," said Baines. "Thanks anyway, it was a lovely surprise – just what I needed. Please pass on my regards to Mar—" Before she could finish, Singh whipped out a packet of double chocolate cookies.

"*Sandy!*" she laughed. "You know there is probably a regulation somewhere which says that lying to a superior officer can land you on washing up duty for a month!"

"Ah, but there's also the counter regulation which says that you can get away with almost anything if you bribe said officer with chocolate," he replied, grinning his brilliant smile.

"Damn! I need to read that book again – my staff are running rings around me!"

Singh sobered slightly. "I've a visitor who's requested to see you. I told her that you were preparing for what's ahead and she insisted that she's here *because* of what's ahead."

"Who is it?"

"Rebecca Mawar. You know, the spiritualist?"

Baines frowned. "Did she give any detail?"

"Not to me. I can ask her to call back at a more suitable ti—"

"No," Baines cut him off, putting her hands up. "I promised I would let people see me if they needed to. Where is she?"

"Waiting – I left her in the corridor outside. I know it's rude but as we're short staffed, I didn't want anyone left alone on the bridge right now."

"Or ever, it seems," agreed Baines, sardonically. "Alright, I'll see her. At least I've got coffee!"

Singh gave her a comradely pat on the arm and left to show their guest in.

The medium entered the meeting room cautiously, looking around and seeming to commit every detail of this 'inner sanctum' to memory. She stopped in front of the flush-mounted keyboard set into the tabletop. It was not active, but her hand hovered over the keys as if sensing something or feeling for a heat signature.

Baines studied her for a moment before inviting Mawar to take a seat, doing her best to seem positive and welcoming despite how she was feeling inside. "Beck, isn't it?"

The woman nodded. "Yes, Captain. Thank you for seeing me. I know you're busy, so I'll get right to it. Firstly, Captain Douglas is alive."

Baines felt a thrill of panic at the sound of James' name being spoken by this woman, famous as she was for communing with the dead. Finally, the entire sentence registered and she sighed with relief, surprised at herself, as she had no *be*lief whatsoever in Mawar's talents.

"I'm very glad to hear it," she replied, weakly.

Beck smiled at that. She was used to polite scepticism – often without the polite. "The second thing I came to tell you is not so positive, I'm afraid."

Baines leaned forward, piqued, despite herself. "Go on, Beck."

"Earlier today, I felt an energy – a negative force. It appeared to start far away but then seemed to take hold around this part of the ship. It's here now, although it is not as strong at the moment."

The captain's eyebrows rose and she stared at the other woman for a long moment. "I'm afraid I don't understand."

Beck nodded. "I'll try to explain. I know that there is a lot going on at the moment and naturally, not all of it's for discussion in the public forum, but I felt something bad happen here today and its effects are still in this room." She took a sharp intake of breath as a look of fear darted across her face.

"Beck?"

"Sorry, Captain, but as we're talking about it, it's growing stronger again. I can only describe it as a *malevolence*. I can't associate whatever it is with a person yet. It can take time for them to learn how to communicate fully, from the astral plane. Did someone die here today?"

The directness of the question caught Baines completely by surprise.

"There was an *incident*," she replied, before she could think better of it and then hastened to add, "but not in this room."

Beck nodded as if to herself. "Sometimes when a dark soul passes over, it gains power. Through history we have known such spirits. Even Christianity has a name for them. You might have heard them referred to as demons." She reached across the table and took Baines' hand in her own before she could pull away. "Captain, be careful. There's something going on here, and you are at the centre of it."

"You don't say," said Baines, drily.

Beck shook her head, looking serious.

"I mean something *more* is going on," she added. "Look, since we came here there has been very little spiritual activity. There's a lot of *energy*, vast amounts, but all natural from the life surrounding us.

"Please believe me when I tell you, this was big news for me, when we arrived.

"Apparently the human soul, without its host, is only capable of travelling forward through the continuum. For the first time in my life I've been more alone than you could know. If it hadn't been for Mario, I think I would have gone mad."

Baines raised her eyebrows slightly but said nothing impolitic about Georgio Baccini's deceased twin, or his alleged link with the psychic.

"Mario was lucky," she continued.

"Lucky?!" Baines could not help interjecting.

Beck nodded. "More than you know, Captain. The wormhole had activated for a split second before the explosion, so poor Mario actually died in the Cretaceous era or period or whatever the correct term is. Otherwise, his soul could have been trapped at any point over a hundred million years, completely alone, forever. He would be on a separate timeline, with no way of ever meeting up with his people before his energy became so thinly spread throughout the universe that he would truly cease to be."

This sent a chill down Baines' spine. She was happy to risk her *life* for her people but suddenly this did indeed seem bigger…

Her training and position reasserted itself once more and she shrugged it aside as fantasy. She decided to bring the interview to an end when the medium spoke again.

"I was alone until he found me," Beck continued with an almost wistful look. "However, as several of our number have sadly fallen, they too have started coming to me. I've even seen Dr Hussain, although he likes to hide and I haven't tried to speak with him.

"But this here, this remnant of what happened today, feels very different. For a soul who has only just passed, they must be incredibly strong to gather such energy to themselves so quickly.

"Strong and evil."

Baines sighed. *I really needed this at the moment*, she thought privately. *I'm already in a monster movie, now I get a horror flick too! I couldn't have landed in the middle of a nice steamy romance, oh no, not me. Even a soppy one would have been acceptable when compared with all this!*

Once again, her thoughts and her words danced a different jig. "Look, Beck, I appreciate you coming to see me, but I really don't have much time just now."

Beck held her hands up to forestall the captain's next words, which were bound to be to ask her to leave. "Please, Captain, I don't expect you to be able to sense any of this, but I need you to know that there are two wars going on here. I will do all I can to offer you protection. I can also tell you that our crew mates, who crossed recently, are right behind you. They're working hard to further prop up your defences, especially as your own guides have been left behind in the future."

Baines looked blank, utterly baffled now.

Beck smiled at her confusion. "Yes, they can do that. All I ask is that you wear this stone." She proffered a small pendant hung from a necklace of natural leather.

Baines took it cautiously.

"It will enhance your aura and help our spirit friends to find you. Just think of it as a lucky charm if nothing else," Beck added with a wan smile.

"Thank you."

"It will cost you nothing to wear it, Captain. Please?"

Baines put the necklace over her head and studied it. The pendant was a type of soft grey stone with sigils carved into the face. "Thank you," she repeated, a little more warmly. "I will wear it today, I promise." *Why not,* she thought, *where would be the harm and if it gives even one of our people a little peace of mind then it's the least I can do.*

She stood to see Beck out.

Just before she left, the medium turned back, looking around the room one last time. "Thank you for seeing me, Captain, and by the way, Mario says that you should look out for someone you *don't* expect to meet. I'm not sure who he means, maybe you know?" Beck surprised Baines further by giving her a brief hug. "Good luck, and thank you for doing everything possible to protect us."

"Thank you and good luck to you too, and all of us."

Just as she left, Singh came back with another visitor, two in fact. These were not people who required an appointment, however. Baines was happy to welcome Tim and Patricia Norris into her meeting room. At least, she was at first.

"Hey, guys," she greeted, directing them to seats. "What can I do for you?"

Tim spoke first. "I should come with you."

She stared at him in disbelief and looked to Patricia for support. Tim's adoptive mother already appeared uncomfortable, even angry, but said nothing.

"I'm always glad to have you with us, Tim," Baines began, delicately, "but I don't think it would be safe for you to join us this time out."

"I know that," said Tim, flatly. "But what if the *plan* doesn't work as... as *planned*," he finished lamely.

Baines smiled. "Tim, we have some very experienced officers on the ground – people who are used to making these kinds of urgent decisions. They'll make the right calls, whatever happens," she finished with a lot more confidence than she actually felt. "You should be here with Major White and your mum, they'll need you."

"But what if *you* need me, Captain? Let's face it, if this fails will it really matter where I am or where my end comes?"

"Tim!" Patricia snapped.

"It's OK," Baines placated.

"It's not OK, Captain," said Tim. "And I'm sorry, Mum, but what I said is true!" He looked back to Baines. "What if I could make a difference but I wasn't there? I could only give those brave soldiers a few minutes instruction about the animals which appear to be in the area, but what if there are others? Or perhaps some other situation presents itself which I may just know something about?"

Baines smiled kindly at the teenager. "You're very brave, Tim, and very clever but I don't want to take you into this."

"You want to protect me – I get it," he said irritably, as an afterthought adding, "and I'm grateful. But please, Captain, we only have one chance and every asset we have should be at hand just in case. I may *not* be able to add anything and I know just how brave and how good our people are, but what if you did need me? And I was just hiding here, waiting for the end – with my *mum*?" His voice rose slightly with the passion of his argument but Baines was not offended.

"And what do you say, Patricia?" she asked Tim's mother.

Patricia rubbed her brow with a shaking hand. "I hate this idea, but... I don't know, Jill. What if Tim's right?" she asked eventually.

Baines sat in silence for a moment, thinking. "Look," she said at last. "We are about to take this ship into an extremely dangerous situation and no one really knows how it's going to go down. If our timing is off, or any of a dozen things go wrong, they might easily blow us out of the sky!

What I'm saying is, we'll have our hands more than full without worrying about civilia—"

"Then don't," Tim interrupted. "I will be there as a resource should you need me, nothing more. I'm not going to be screaming or running around in your way, Captain."

"We!" interjected Patricia. "If the captain allows you to go, it will *only* be under the proviso that *I* go along with you."

Baines sat back, her brows furrowed in deep study. Eventually, she looked at Dr Patricia Norris once more, who gave an agitated shrug of tacit approval. "Alright," she acceded, "but there will be ground rules."

Gleeson's small squad was making good time. The six hastily rigged dirt bikes, re-engineered by Lieutenant Nassaki from the heavy-duty cycles originally designed for use in the mines on Mars, had carried them faithfully so far. Hiro's addition of a powerful electric motor, upgraded brakes and a headlamp made the formidable little vehicles ideal transport for the rough brush, plain and rocks of the Cretaceous.

The soldiers managed to pick a trail towards their destination without too much difficulty, only occasionally having to dismount and carry the bikes over their shoulders. This was tiring, burdened as they were with heavily laden backpacks, but fortunately, the vast majority of the kilometres went by under power.

The westering sun lowered in the sky and the beautiful spring colours took on an added glow as the ultraviolet increased with the dying of the light. This strange anomaly on the universal spectroscope had occurred every day since the very first atmosphere clung to our world, and would happen every day thereafter, for so long as it endured.

The soldiers were not immune to the beauty of light and nature, but this day, they simply could not spare the time it undoubtedly deserved. Their stomachs lurched in and out of rhythm with the lurching and bouncing of the bikes. Destiny was drawing them in as they skipped, slithered and jumped across the landscape. The 'home-made motocross' may even have been fun under better circumstances. However, their thoughts, as much as their attention could be diverted away from simply hanging on, were focused on what awaited them at journey's end.

They burst from a tree line onto another plain which extended a good way down its valley. Well into the mountains now, they spotted their quarry at last. This was their first connection.

The herd of small green dinosaurs named Mayor Dougli Salvator called and grazed across the valley peacefully – and there were *thousands* of them.

Gleeson raised an arm for the other riders to draw up next to him.

O'Brien whistled. "That's a lotta steaks," she said.

"I think you mean chicken drummers, isn'it," provided Jones.

"So what now?" asked O'Brien.

"Back home, I used to spend my summers out in the bush riding the huge sheep farms in Victoria," Gleeson answered, wolfishly. "This'll be just like that."

"I know things are different in Australia, Commander," said Jones, looking more than a little concerned, "but where I'm from, sheep don't look like that."

"Did they wear pretty dresses?" asked Davies with a grin.

Jones turned on his bike and gave the man a stare.

Davies looked down. "Sorry, Corp."

Gleeson barked a laugh. "Don't worry Jonesy, just follow my lead. Listen, this is what we're gonna do."

Geoff Lloyd woke again. If anything, he actually felt a little worse than before. *What a crappy dream that was*, he thought, his enemies all back within his orbit. He was quite relieved to wake, despite his renewed pain and discomfort.

A voice cut through his reverie. "Geoff? Are ye awake?" it said, with an unmistakably Scottish cadence.

"Oh, *Christ*!" said Lloyd, yet again.

"Ah'm sorry Ah cannae do more for ye," said Douglas with concern.

"You've done enough already," said Lloyd, witheringly.

Douglas' mouth twitched with a smile. "Ah see you've still got your sunny sense of humour."

"I can't believe that with everything I've been through, I'm now stuck, in what is essentially a jail cell, with the man who put me here."

"Actually, Geoff, if you spin that back a little further, Ah think you'll find that it was actually you who put me here to put you here. Or have you forgotten the little field trip you orchestrated when ye blew up ma ship?!"

"Alright, alright, we can argue about who's to blame later."

"Ah wasnae arguing – it's you!"

Lloyd sighed deeply. "OK, alright, enough please. I'm in enough pain as it is without you giving my backside a headache!"

Douglas laughed at that.

"I don't suppose you've managed to come up with an escape plan during your days of R and R?"

Douglas laughed at that too, but with less enthusiasm. "They bring food, they take away the empties – repeat. Ah've only been out of this cell once, when Ah was allowed to shower and my clothes were laundered. They've been remarkably genteel about the whole thing. They've even brought me material to read. Ah've been told to exercise once a day, too. Ah cannae help feeling like a prize turkey in December."

"I dare say they want to keep you in good shape, mind and body. Until they've no further use for you, of course. You wouldn't be much good to them if you forgot all your security access codes because your mind was addled, would you?"

Douglas grunted tacit agreement. He had been reasoning along similar lines. "So how come they threw you in here with me?" he asked eventually. "Ah thought you were meant to be on *their* side?"

"Is that what you really think?" asked Lloyd. Douglas could not tell if the pain in Lloyd's voice was emotional or physical.

"Why don't *you* tell *me*?"

Lloyd sighed. "I know what I did was wrong, James, but I had no idea where it was going to lead. All I saw was a dead-end career that was going nowhere on board a ship where everyone loathed the very sight of me. Then I was offered a shed load of money to do something *very* naughty. Did I know that it might get people killed? I'm not sure, maybe I did deep down, but I hated my life so much that I just didn't listen to that voice.

"Before you say anything, I know how despicable that makes me sound, OK? I've already said I'm sorry and I meant it, there just isn't a damned thing I can do about it – ouch!" He tensed and clenched his teeth, his eyes shut tight against the pain. After a moment he added, "But just so we're clear, I still don't like any of you!"

Douglas snorted at that. "Well, Ah'm sure that many of the people back aboard ma ship would pay good money to see you in this much pain."

"Thanks."

"But Ah'm not one of them, Geoff. If you felt so low that your only recourse was to do something as bad as this, then Ah'm at least half to blame."

Lloyd looked at Douglas like there was a bad smell under his nose. "How d'you figure that out?" he asked.

"Ah'm your captain, or Ah was. Who knows what Ah am now," offered Douglas, thoughtfully. "Ah should have tried to help you, or at least given you the chance to transfer."

"I thought that was Nassaki's job?"

"Come on, Geoff. You know how it works. Ah was captain, not Hiro. The buck stops here."

"So you're willing to take responsibility for what I did because you were the captain?"

"That's what 'captain' means. It's also how any decent person would feel. Why are you looking at me like that?"

"Like what?" Lloyd snapped crossly.

"Like someone swapped your hotdog for a dog log?!"

"Maybe you just make me sick!"

Both men sighed, uncomfortably together but magnetically opposed.

"You really are a dickhead, Lloyd!"

"Good, finally something we can agree on! Now can we move on?"

Douglas did not answer, so Lloyd asked another question. "By the way, what happened after I was stranded in the jungle with only the most dangerous predators in history for company? And why didn't you look for me?" he pressed accusingly.

The anger in Douglas' face faded and was replaced with sadness, maybe even a little shame. "We had no idea that you'd survived, Geoff, we—"

"No, you didn't bloody well look either did you?!"

Douglas sighed. "Ah'm sorry," he said. "You probably won't believe me, but when you went over the cliff with that dinosaur, well, it looked like chips for ye. Ah would never have left you behind if Ah'd thought there was the slightest chance…" he tailed off under Lloyd's glare.

"You know what, Douglas, I actually believe you. You are that *wet*!"

Douglas bridled again. "Moral fortitude really doesnae factor highly on your list of priorities, does it?" he hissed, waspishly.

"Just tell me what happened next, damnit! I might not live long enough to hear the rest of the story at this rate. I hope you didn't leave that *luney* in charge?"[2]

"Ah left *Captain Baines* in charge," Douglas rejoindered, pointedly. "Ah promoted her myself."

"While you were still there? Ha! That was stupid. Perhaps it explains how you came to be sharing the Presley suite here with me though, eh? Eh?" Lloyd indicated their very utilitarian surroundings ironically.

Douglas clenched his fist and blew out an exasperated breath, trying with all his might not to explode.

Tim and Clarissa stood to the side of the open hangar bay doors, watching the bronze light settle over the compound. Activity buzzed all around them.

Knowing he had to leave, Tim first called on his friend. He would have hated going without seeing her and explaining a little of what was to come, just in case things did indeed go badly for them.

As his short explanation came to a close, the young girl looked up at him searchingly, glancing from one eye to the other. He had no gauge, of course, but instinct told him that this was no ordinary look.

---

[2]   Luney or *loony*: A slang term coined in the late 21st century to describe people who lived on the lunar sphere – Jill Baines was listed as the first human being ever to be born on the moon, making her the first 'luney'. This would normally be something to be very proud of, but words can be so cruel.

"You're so smart, Timmy," she said at last, with feeling.

"And you're so beautiful, Clarrie." Tim had no idea that he was about to say that, the words just *fell* out.

A moment happened. Tim's heart banged as his stomach crested and troughed in sinusoidal panic. Without warning she threw her arms around his neck and kissed him, hard.

He had not had much of a childhood, but neither was he yet truly a man. He wavered one last moment in the waiting room to the adult world, as her kiss threw open the doors in a rush. Forces beyond his control shoved him through, stumbling, on legs trembling and new.

Another moment passed before she pulled away slightly, as shocked as he. Tim drew her back into his arms and hearing that door slam firmly shut behind him, returned her kiss.

Everyone around them vanished as the world collapsed to the size of two teens...

An indeterminate time later, a deep bellow rang off the metal surfaces in the hangar bay. Tim thought that it might be the sound of his inner mojo, off the leash and on an endorphin crazed, chest beating rampage, but a subsequent roar brought him to his senses.

He looked out into the compound and saw a giant head peeking over the huge eight-metre-tall gates.

Clarrie looked dazed and confused, eyes still closed.

Laughing, Tim grabbed her hand and ran out of the bay doors up to the rampart walk.

The teenagers arrived breathless. A couple of armed guards were already up there but recognising Tim, let them through.

Cautiously approaching the massive wooden gates which bisected the palisade, they crept to within arms' length to avoid startling their visitor. Tim realised belatedly that he had dragged Clarrie the last few metres and turned to check on her.

Clarrie looked at the giant with a fear that was natural, but also with a wonder she could not hide. "Is it safe?" she asked.

"Of course," said Tim. "We need to be careful though," he added, unhelpfully.

He reached out and gently stroked the animal's snout as one would a giant horse. The creature must have been fifteen metres long at least, maybe slightly more. A good deal smaller than the Argentinosaurus they encountered upon arriving in Cretaceous Patagonia, but still a huge beast. It was perhaps just a little longer than the terrifying Mapusaurus but much more massive.

This particular 'nosy neighbour' was certainly no predator though. The long neck and tail marked it clearly as a sauropod dinosaur. It leaned against the ominously creaking gates to get a view into the compound.

Tim laughed for the pure joy of this incredible moment. Not able to believe what he was doing or the events of the last few minutes, he was lost in a madness he prayed would never end. As he turned back to Clarrie, tears welled in the corners of his eyes, but although his beatific smile was certainly more than skin deep, his inner analyst never slept.

"I think he might be Agustinia," he said, almost choked, before the power of intrigue restored him. "That's the name of his species *and* family. Originally named Augustia, but unfortunately that rather 'august' designation had already been given to a beetle, apparently!"

He was grinning now. "When initially classified, it was unclear which branch of the sauropod family the remains belonged to, as they showed both characteristics of Titanosaur, like the mighty Argentinosaurus, and Diplodocid, like the famous Diplodocus." He turned away, irresistibly drawn back to his new, giant friend.

Clarrie was left shaking her head slightly and smiling dotingly on them both.

"*Remains...*" he repeated dreamily, marvelling at the beautiful creature before him, so full of life and power. He touched his brow to its skin lovingly, still stroking the animal's face. "Where's your herd, fella? You lost, eh?"

As if on cue the Agustinia called out again. Tim stepped back quickly, covering his ears but laughing like a lottery winner. An answering call came from the distance, out of sight for the people on the palisade walk. Tim's eyes drank deeply of the miracle before him. He just could not stop laughing, though his ears were now ringing.

Eventually, he pulled himself together, wiping his eyes with a little embarrassment as a thought struck him. "Oh," he said. Pulling a nutribar out of his pocket and peeling back the packaging, he offered it for the animal to sniff.

The huge mouth opened to receive this strangest of bounties and the bar vanished.

"Oh," Tim repeated himself, turning to Clarrie. "He ate the wrapper!"

Clarrie laughed and, deciding that she too was now 'in it to win it', leaned forward to stroke the creature's face. It blinked innocently at her, giving her hand a hopeful sniff.

The guards behind them grinned, themselves caught up in wonder and disbelief.

"You don't wanna hang around here, big guy," Clarrie spoke kindly to their huge visitor. "There's gonna be a whole bunch o' noise soon, when the ship lifts off."

After petting the dinosaur, she sniffed her hand and pulled a face.

Tim failed to notice, his eyes sparkling with barely checked tears. "You know, we may be in an awful mess but I would not change a thing. Not a single thing!"

"Me either," she agreed.

He kissed her again.

"Oh!" he repeated for a third time, pulling away.

"What is it, Timmy?" she asked, suddenly concerned.

Tim stared, looking stricken. The huge head merely waited with bovine patience for another morsel.

"*Timmy?*" Clarrie asked more urgently.

Remembering she was still there, Tim gave her the hunted look of a naughty schoolboy as he whispered intently, "I hope he doesn't have a nut allergy!"

1845 hours. Major White entered the brig of the *New World* trailed by a four-strong security detail. Corporal Thomas saluted as the officer entered. White returned the salute casually, fixing Bond and Lemelisk with a stare.

Bond looked nervous and backed further into his cell. Lemelisk was inscrutable.

"You two are going on a little holiday."

Bond looked very concerned now. "We haven't done anything wrong, Major," he ventured.

White chuckled softly. "It's just adorable, the way you say that with a straight face." He looked at Thomas. "Corporal," he said, nodding towards the cell doors.

"Yes, sir."

Thomas unlocked Bond's cell and, after a brief pause as they waited in vain for him to move, two of White's men went in to retrieve and cuff him.

Lemelisk turned, also waiting to be cuffed. Clearly this was not a new drill for him.

As the guard grabbed one of his wrists, he spun quickly and in one movement locked the *officer's* wrist, whilst delivering a reverse-round-house kick to the side of his head. There was not room for a full-force swing but the man still fell sideways, stunned.

The other guard reached for his taser but Lemelisk was quicker. He released his first assailant, allowing him to fall, whilst back-fisting the second to the temple left-handed and kicking at the man's shin simultaneously with the blade edge of his foot, just below the kneecap.

Stepping over the prone men, he regained his posture ready to bolt.

He bolted straight into White's waiting fist.

Ford wasn't a huge man like Jones, but he was strong, fit and well trained. Lemelisk's arrested 'runner' doubled the force of the impact and he went out like a birthday candle, leaving the major sucking his knuckles and swearing like a *sergeant* major.

Bond's guards threw him roughly back into the cell and locked the door again, readying themselves to help secure the situation.

White was already helping the closest downed man up. As he rose, he tried to rub his head and shin at the same time, making him hop around in circles.

"You OK?" asked White.

"Sir! Yes, sir!"

Once the guard had regained his composure, he used his boot to give the unconscious Lemelisk some bruised ribs to commemorate his moment of freedom.

The other guard also righted himself and began dragging Lemelisk up whilst standing on one of the prisoner's hands. "Oops," he commented half-heartedly.

After securing Lemelisk, White ordered them to carry the prisoner to the holding cell down on the Pod, as a reward for losing control of the situation.

He nodded once more to Thomas. "You may as well come back with us, Corporal. Nothin' more for you to do here and this crazy mission is expected to kick off any time now."

"Sir," Thomas replied and fell in behind them, locking down the brig on his way out.

Both prisoners were soon locked away safely inside one of the two holding cells within the Pod's security station. Bond seemed very unhappy with his new situation and kept staring at his cell mate like he had been banged up with a snake.

White smirked. "I thought you were all buddies?"

"I'm 'planning and policy', I don't deal with the likes of *that*," sniffed Bond, waving away his co-prisoner, foppishly.

The major snorted and turned away as the Pod's New Zealand born chief of operations, Dr Sam Burton approached.

"Hey, Sam. How are we doing?"

"Ready for separation, Ford. The final adjustments have been made to the ramparts too, so that we will still be secure when the *New World* leaves."

"*New World* leaves?" asked Bond, dialling his panic up another notch as he ran over to the bars.

White was looking at Burton, but nodded sideways towards Bond as he said, "*Her* Majesty here, was just telling me that she didn't appreciate being locked up with the help."

"Poor sod," said Burton, without feeling.

"Actually, I do have royal blood in my veins, if you must know," Bond retorted, pulling himself up to his full aristocratic height. "My grandfather was the illegitimate son of a British royal duke."

"You don't say," answered Burton.

Bond nodded regally. "I would have been in line to the throne had my grandfather not been a bastard."

"Well baggar me, if his grandson wasn't born one too!"

White guffawed, doubling up.

Burton joined in, laughing at his own joke.

"What precisely do you mean, the *New World* is leaving?" Bond tried again indignantly, speaking over the laughter.

White put an arm to Burton's back and guided him out towards the door. "Better show me where we're at," he said.

"Major," Bond called after them. "Major! I demand to know what is happening."

"*Absolutely*, Your Grace," White shot back, still chuckling.

"Yeah, he's a real darling," added Burton as the two men left Bond remonstrating to the air.

"YEEEAAAHHH!" Gleeson screamed, revelling in the chase. "Round the side! Jonesy left, O'Brien swing right… swing *RIGHT*!"

The roaring and bellowing of the powerful little herbivores was deafening. They could really move, and the dust they threw up into the air made it hard for the squad to see where they were going. The six bikers shouted instruction and encouragement to one another, jumping and criss-crossing over the land, trying to work together as best they could. For most of them this was more than a little outside their area of expertise.

One man, however, could not have been happier. "Woo-hoo!" the commander hooted as he popped a wheelie to bring one of the Mayors back to the herd.

Meeting up in the thick of it, Jones and O'Brien exchanged a meaningful look, the look meaning, 'who *is* this guy?!'

"I grew up with kids like that," said Jones, shaking his head as they parted again.

After several minutes of trial *bike* and error, the *team* finally began to behave like one, getting their eye in and their act together. As the herd slowly turned in their desired direction, they began moving towards the enemy at last.

Inevitability hung in the air... A long snout sniffed the same air.

Lower down the valley, a river shallowed, widening as it turned east. The assault team drove the herd downhill towards this point where possible, although some animals baulked, causing commotion at the shoreline.

Confusion turned to bedlam as the one thing they hoped not to see, from the satellite images, turned out to be two things.

"Whooaaa!" screamed Gleeson, using their short range comms now.

"*What was that?*" someone asked on the air.

"*Dunno,*" someone else replied. "*Sounded a bit like Elvis.*"

"Hilarious!" snapped Gleeson. "Regroup, regroup!"

He hated his forenames – Elvis Percival – they were just one more thing for which he had to thank his estranged family. It was perhaps not surprising that this caused much merriment amongst the rest of the crew.

They gathered around their leader. "For your information, my name is sir or commander. Anyone who doesn't want to be left standing outside with the dinosaurs when we get back should try and remember it!"

"Yes, sir," his team answered dutifully, trying not to smirk.

"Will you look at that," said Gleeson, distracted again by the vista before him. His eye followed movement to the right of their chosen fording point. Too late, he noticed a similar movement on the left as well. A convergence was in process. "What the..."

The herd crossed. They bucked, they brayed, they sank, they swam.

Morale in Gleeson's ranks merely sank.

"Well, gentlemen, how was the reunion?" The beautiful blonde woman crossed her arms, smiling unpleasantly.

"What do *you* want, Schultz?" Douglas replied, roughly.

"I want the *New World*, this has not changed." Heidi Schultz spoke with a strong Bavarian accent but the coldness was all her own. "You will now give me your access codes as we are going to take it away from your mongrel band this very night."

"Ye might no' find it so easy." Douglas taunted with a bravado he hardly felt.

Schultz grinned. "They will be completely incapable of mounting any kind of defence against this ship. And after the recent flyover, I doubt they will even try. I'm sure they shiver in terror as we speak, waiting for us to break down the door."

"You might be surprised," snarled Douglas. "Ye'll no' take ma ship that easily."

"*Your* ship?"

The inflection in her voice made her meaning clear. The muscles in Douglas' jaw bunched.

"Why am *I* in here, Heidi?" asked Lloyd petulantly, raising his head slightly from his bunk. "You wouldn't have gotten any of this off the ground without me. Why am I imprisoned with... with *him*?"

Loathing and betrayal crossed Douglas' face as he glared down at Lloyd.

Schultz caught the look and grinned broadly. "So that is how your reunion went, yes?"

Douglas rounded on her. "Ah'll no' tell you anything, ya psychotic harpy!"

Heidi laughed, a tinkling little laugh. "I hoped you would take that line, *Kapitän*. I have things to prepare, I will return within the hour with one or two toys specifically designed for extracting the truth. As for you, Geoffrey, you were paid to do a job and you messed it up!"

"Messed it up?! How? We're here, aren't we? The *New World* and its resources *are* at your mercy, aren't they?"

"Yes, we are here, you stupid little man, but *here* is not where we wished to be, is it? You were meant to follow your instructions to the letter, so that we were transported 100,000 years into Earth's past. You brought us almost 100 *million* years into the past. Trusting I have the mathematics correct, this is as close to 100 million years out as to make no difference!"

"*Yeah*? Well, I haven't got my money either, have I?" sniped Lloyd.

"Problems in paradise?" Douglas sneered at them. "You two may have stitched me up from the shadows, but Jill knows you're coming now. You may just live to regret making your 'big statement'."

"Big statement?" asked Lloyd.

Douglas looked down at where he lay. "She made them fly this giant bedpan over ma ship, just with the intention of scaring everybody." He turned back to Schultz. "If Ah know my first officer, no, if Ah know *Captain* Baines, all *ye* will have done is made her angry!"

"Am I supposed to be afraid, Captain?"

"Ye havenae the imagination."

Captain Baines was indeed angry. Very angry.

At the metaphorical eleventh hour, she had received a message from Major White calling her to the embarkation area of the Pod to calm a potentially explosive situation. She was being summoned to answer to *the people*.

The time of the *New World*'s departure drew near. Indeed, so near that Sergeant Jackson sat by an open high-level hatch, pointing a pair of electrobinoculars and a laser microphone in the direction of their stolen shuttle's homing beacon.

A quick search of the area through the powerful binoculars revealed a cliff face, well over half way towards the enemy encampment. It was close to the horizon, even from his elevated position and subsequently, on the limits of his line-of-sight equipment. He trained the laser mike on a flat section within the vertical face, hoping the colossal sound waves from Gleeson's planned explosion would slam into the rock, causing it to vibrate. When they came, these tiny, almost imperceptible vibrations in the rockface would create minute variations in the time the light took to travel back to his equipment. The electronics would then convert those variations in light back into audio and, via the miracle of technology, he should hear the bang even before the speed of sound carried it to him.

He fully expected to see the impending firework show in the night sky and possibly even hear it with the naked ear, but this was no time for taking chances, so he had broken out the hardware. All set up, he waited in silence…

Captain Baines strode into embarkation. A large gathering already waited expectantly, while still more people milled to find seats. A woman seemed to have the crowd's attention from the stage area at the front of the arena. Baines was normally very good with names but this one escaped her for the moment. She stepped up alongside the podium where the woman had activated the built in microphone.

"What's this about?" Baines asked, angrily. "We're about to leave on the most critical mission we've undertaken since arriving here and we're on the clock!"

"That's why you were summoned here, Captain," replied the woman in a very friendly, passive-aggressive manner. Her accent was fairly neutral, but certainly British.

Baines bridled at the word 'summoned', taking an instant dislike to the woman *and* her manner. *What the hell is her name?* she thought.

"I am Ms Alison Cocksedge, Captain. As I'm sure you already knew."

Baines raised an eyebrow slightly. "Of course," she acknowledged simply.

"Captain, it's about this mission that we wish to question you."

"*Question* me?"

"Yes," continued Cocksedge, unabashed. "Quite a number of us believe that we should not be taking military action against the new vessel without provocation. It is our—"

"Without provocation…?" Baines repeated.

"—belief that we should make no aggressive move without meeting with these people first and seeing exactly what it is that they want."

"Did you miss the bit about the terrorist bomb which blew us 100 million years into the past?" asked Baines in disbelief.

"The actual facts of that situation have still not been fully explored, Captain."

"Our people have been murdered, one in that very explosion, our captain has been taken hostage and has undergone God knows what sort of treatment—" Baines was working up to a full-blown explosive event. She could feel the edges of her vision blacking as rage tore through her soul. Cocksedge chose that moment to interrupt again.

"But they may have had very real concerns, reasons for believing that that sort of atrocity was perhaps their only recourse. We may simply have left them no choice. We need to at least listen to them, in order to understand the motivation for their actions."

Baines was finding it hard to concentrate further on Ms Cocksedge's words. Her body felt like an earthing rod for her fury, the deck plates just weren't soaking it up, any minute now the meltdown would come. A memory of the young, recently deceased Mario Baccini smiling and sharing a joke with his equally charming brother, Georgio, flashed through her mind providing the final ignition.

She opened her mouth at flashpoint but before the actual eruption occurred, a surprise defused the situation. To Baines' mind, it was a big one too.

Hank Burnstein Snr spoke out. This was not the surprise, he often did this, the surprise was that Baines completely endorsed his well considered interruption, as he stood and bellowed across the large auditorium.

"That's just a bunch o' horseshi—"

"So, despite everything, you're still the enemy?" asked Douglas.

"Let me ask *you* something, Captain. Do you intend to try and get out of here if you get the opportunity?" asked Lloyd.

"Of course."

"Well I can't, can I? Look at me."

Douglas had to acknowledge that Lloyd was in a bad way.

"So that's your excuse for betrayal?"

Lloyd sighed. "If you were in my position, what would you do?"

"Ah would stay true to my people and the ideals Ah believe in."

Lloyd sighed again. "OK. What would you do if you weren't a selfless martyr and had more than haggis for brains?"

Douglas considered, ignoring the feeble insult. "So you're playing both ends against the middle." It was not a question.

"No!" said Lloyd with unexpected force which made him wince. It took him a moment before he could continue. "There is nothing I can do at the moment, so I am trying to survive until I am in a position where I can."

"Do something to help yeself, you mean?"

Lloyd merely glared at Douglas, noncommittally. Eventually he simply looked left and right exaggeratedly to make a silent point.

Because Douglas had been kept alone since offering himself hostage, there had been no reason to be concerned about being monitored. Lloyd's point found its mark and he nodded very slightly.

Seeing Douglas had caught his drift, Lloyd continued. "All I would have to look forward to if I came back with you, Captain, is incarceration. That's in the unlikely event that we even survive the coming encounter with this far superior force. I picked my side a long time ago. There's nothing in it for *me* to change now. Schultz is annoyed with me at the moment, but it'll pass. She knows that I know more about the *New World* than anyone else, or she wouldn't have patched me up. Anyone barring Nassaki that is, but he won't last long when she gets her hands on him, that I *can* tell you!"

"Shut up," said Douglas simply, turning away. "Just shut up."

"Oh, that's just champion!" snapped Corporal Jones.

As the soldiers stared down the valley towards the river crossing, it was obvious that the waters were much deeper to either side of the wide, stony shallows.

The inspiration for Jones' comment came from the sails. There were two of them, both red, one moving in from each direction. They came on with purpose, as the panicked herd attempted to ford. The smaller approached from the left, the larger, more brilliantly coloured, from the right.

As the river shallowed, two magnificent creatures stepped out. Water sheeted off huge, steaming flanks, their hides all the furies of scarlet and flame in their reigning glory. They *ROARED*, almost in unison. Their primal cry was nerve shredding and with it came chaos.

Screams of terror echoed all around the valley as the river crossing turned to boiling insanity. Life clung and scrambled in the dying light, to the soundtrack of the hunt, and against this thunderous music of the universe, one human voice rang out clearly…

"Are they those bladdy wossnames Tim warned us about? Oxyacetylenes or some bladdy thing or other?"

"Oxalaia, Commander," O'Brien chipped in helpfully. "The kid thought that, as it's spring time, if we saw two together they might be a mating couple. Apparently they're related to the Spinosaurus he showed us the picture of."

The watching humans could clearly see the massive spiny sail on each animal's back which gave the family their name and which made them appear even huger. The larger of the pair, with the more brilliant sail, could have easily weighed in at seven or eight tons. They guessed it to be the male. With a head almost a metre and a half in length, jaws fully loaded with crocodilian teeth and powerfully clawed hands, Gleeson thought it wise to take a moment to consider before moving on.[3]

"Great," he said. "So, not only have we stumbled across two enormous carnivorous dinosaurs, we've also broken up their little tête-à-tête? I'm

---

[3]   Tim had explained to the assault team that Oxalaia Quilombensis were very large dinosaurs of the Spinosaurus family. Although not as huge as the North African Spinosaurus Aegyptiacus itself, at up to fourteen metres long, they may possibly have been the largest carnivorous dinosaur to have lived in South America during the middle Cretaceous. Gleeson felt obliged to categorise them as 'bladdy ugly rooters'.

trying to blank this vision from my mind already, but have we possibly interrupted a little *moment* here?"

O'Brien looked horrified.

"If he's looking to buy her dinner, better hope it's not us," Davies commented.

"No worries, mate," said Gleeson. "I'm way too delicate for her palate."

"So what do you want to do, Commander?" asked Jones.

Gleeson grinned. "Follow me, fellas," and he set off without another word.

"Fellas?" asked O'Brien, nonplussed.

Davies twisted a half smile at her. "After you, Corp."

They set off after the Australian, who appeared to be heading straight for the centre of the herd, which now skittered, slipped and leapt across the whole fording area. The thousands strong Mayor Dougli Salvator brayed in fear, anger and pain as they trampled one another.

All the while the two giants closed steadily. With such an abundance of prey, they had no need to rush. Simply standing amongst the herd made catching dinner about as difficult as reaching for water in the middle of a river. No ambush was necessary.

The satellite had spotted a single Oxalaia earlier, but that was much further upstream. Of course, that was several hours ago. On the face of it, this was terribly bad luck but the commander was still determined to turn it to his advantage.

He picked a line and went for it, slipping between the terrified herbivores as they scattered in all directions, their only bearing *away*. Many hundreds had crossed the river already. Gleeson was hoping to catch up with them to continue his run on the battleship, when his short range comm crackled in his ear.

"This was your whole plan? *Charge*?!" asked an irate female voice with an American accent.

"Don't worry, O'Brien, just keep moving – all of you *keep moving*! And watch out for the stones in the river, they're a nightmare!"

"The stones?" asked O'Brien, in disbelief as dinosaurs filled her entire world. "Yeah, we'd better watch out for those!"

Gleeson laughed. He felt more alive than at any time since boarding the *New World* at Canaveral, weeks ago. "Just another croc in the bush, mate. Don't let 'em get you down. Keep chasing the roos – they're running all over the bladdy place!"

Captain Meritus posted a perimeter guard around the small, ring fenced compound. Within it nestled his complement of four tracked and armoured vehicles, two remaining orbital attack ships and of course, the shuttle taken from the *New World* by Dr Schultz.

The *Last Word* carried three small fighting ships, but having lost contact with the third almost three hours ago, Meritus grew more concerned with each passing minute. Schultz had acerbically told him to stop worrying 'like a little school boy', suggesting they were simply searching for the tiny satellite on the opposite side of the planet. She may have been right, but he could not shake the feeling that something was wrong. As a military man, he knew better than to simply ignore these instincts.

As the satellite was no longer transmitting, it would be the very devil to find, this much was true. With no orbital communications system in place yet, there simply was no way of finding out for sure. Even so, he mused.

To hell with Schultz! he thought. Making up his mind at last, he opened a comm channel to one of his pilots. Within a few short minutes, a second attack craft was scrambled and away into the rapidly deepening twilight, the first stars already twinkling in the evening sky.

Meritus watched moodily, as the little vessel fired its afterburners to gain altitude, rapidly leaving them behind. Before it had even left his sight, Schultz appeared next to him.

"Why have we launched another ship?" she demanded.

"To find the lost one – we've been scanning for two hours now. No sign."

"I want those ships back right away!" spat Schultz, peremptorily.

"So do I, that's why I sent it," answered Meritus, coldly.

Schultz turned to face him directly. "I need those ships this evening for our attack on the *New World*, *Kapitän*. We need to show them what they face if we are to get them to surrender without a struggle. I don't want my prize damaged in a fire fight. Do you understand?"

"I *do* understand your plan, Doctor – believe it or not. But one of my ships is lost out there and I want to know what has happened to it before committing to anything else."

Schultz eyed him coldly. "The *first* ship will still be hunting for the satellite, *Kapitän*. We know it stopped transmitting very suddenly and will subsequently take time to find. I put it to you, that the two men on that first ship understand the importance of finding it, and in *not* disappointing *me*."

They glared at one another in a charged silence.

"One hour, *Kapitän*. If they have not made contact in that time, recall the second vessel. We embark at 2100 hours as planned."

It pained him to do so but Meritus clicked his heels and nodded in acquiescent salute.

The small fighting ship powered steeply towards space, leaving a swell of engine noise rolling and rebounding across the valley. The noise ripped the ancient night, gradually fading to leave something else in its wake.

The guards on the ground outside the battleship began to *perceive*, rather than hear, a rumble from the surrounding forest. As the rumbling became louder, it was augmented by other sounds. At first it was unclear what these ancillary noises might be, but as they drew closer individual cries and squeals could be heard.

The patrols, almost subconsciously, began to bunch together. It quickly became apparent that what they were hearing, far from being the ordinary sounds of the night, was actually the clamour of mass panic – on the move.

In the faded dusk, a slow-motion hellscape unfolded before their eyes for just an instant. Shock seemed to freeze time for many of the Nazi troopers and before they could gather their wits, they were steamrollered by a wave of life at the visceral edge of screaming terror. The few survivors from this onslaught were in the uniquely unenviable position of being able to see what followed.

The scale of what was clearly a stampede continued to escalate through the valley, then the pair of giant Oxalaia smashed their way into the clearing, roaring slaughter. The few petrified sentries who remained were surrounded by the angry bellows of all manner of creatures. So varied in volume and pitch was the cacophony which commanded the night, that it became indiscernible white noise.

The huge male Oxalaia stepped off a low bank right onto the wing of the remaining attack craft. In order to provide the strength and rigidity required for any sort of aerobatics, the structure within the wing was a triumph of engineering. Subsequently, it resisted the creature's colossal weight steadfastly, until the landing gear gave way, slamming it into the ground.

The adrenaline crazed animal roared in fury, tearing at the little ship's flanks in an attempt to keep his balance. This capsizing motion, the shifting of weight and the point-load impacts as the creature unleashed its anger upon the machine, finally proved too much. One of the wings failed fatally, damaging the fuselage and leaving the whole vehicle just so many billions of dollars of scrap.

Anarchy... and in the middle of it all the *New World*'s tiny squad, providing token direction. Gleeson's team continued navigating groups of stragglers towards the enemy compound for maximum disruption. Staying well clear of the giant carnivores, they tracked and jumped among the host towards their goal, muffled and all but invisible amidst the confusion they had wrought.

Commander Gleeson felt halfway between a hell's angel and a hell*hound* as he rounded up his abyssal herd. With no plan to close the gate at trial's end, all he could do was *ride* – straight for their prearranged meeting point at the rear of the ship, under the main engine nacelles – trusting his people to do likewise.

Aboard the *Last Word*, the distraction began as a tremor through her deck plates. Meritus and Schultz stared at one another for one more second, confusion replacing anger on both faces. The rumbling became audible as they quickly moved to a console where an officer was already scanning their surroundings.

"You reacted very quickly, Lieutenant Hemmings," Schultz remarked, unusually impressed.

"I've been scanning all afternoon, ma'am," she replied.

Schultz raised an eyebrow to Meritus.

"I don't share your confidence in our safety here, Doctor," he stated, adding with just a hint of temerity, "Looks like I was right."

The screen before them was populated with hundreds, possibly even thousands of life forms smashing their way out of the forest in a torrent – and some of them were giants.

Jones found the commander first. Together, they hid under the massive warship, trying to stay behind one of the enormous landing struts which supported her. It was the only cover available from the flow of terrified creatures all around.

Gleeson saw the first problem with their hastily laid plan, almost immediately. There was no way on Earth they would be able to extend the lightweight, telescopic ladders, strapped to Jones' back, inside the maelstrom flowing under and around the ship. They would be swept away in seconds.

As the animals streaked past the men's tenuous shelter with alarming ferocity, they streamed straight over the edge of the promontory on which the *Last Word* sat. The bank was not sheer but it was steep. The noise grew more intense as the stampede slipped and rolled downhill in total disarray.

Elements of the terrified menagerie attempted to pull up at the edge, compounding the general pandemonium further.

Davies and one other, Fredrickson, managed to pick a way through to their comrades by the skin of their teeth. Fredrickson had to leap at them, as the back wheel of his bike was caught by a flailing tail and torn away in the rush, eventually disappearing over the edge. Jones caught the grateful man, steadying him.

"Where's O'Brien and Ross?" asked Gleeson, looking around the gathered men in growing alarm. "Anybody?"

Another loud roar sounded nearby, making them all jump. At first, they were unsure what it was as something loomed even blacker in the darkness between the stampeding animals. The sound was that of a diesel engine, a weirdly human sound in the midst of nature's cacophony.

This small comfort was shattered immediately as an armoured personnel carrier pulled up in front of them. It rocked slightly on its tracks, sporting a very serious looking brace of 50-cals. The guns were mounted to a small turret atop and to the front of the vehicle.

A hatch below the barrels flew open and the head of Corporal Jennifer O'Brien popped up. "Need a ride, boys?"

Gleeson nearly collapsed in relief. Quickly pulling himself together, he barked the order, "Open the rear hatch."

"Hang on," shouted O'Brien, disappearing below once more. She turned the vehicle 180 degrees on its axis and threw open the rear doors for her compatriots. Looking into the roomy interior, Gleeson tossed his bike inside and jumped in after it. The rest of his team, who still had a bike, followed his lead.

"Good work, Corp. Get us under those engin— what the—"

"Something wrong, Commander?" asked O'Brien.

Gleeson recovered his composure. "Who's laughing boy?"

He referred to the Nazi trooper, who was zip tied with a large red welt spreading across his forehead.

"I *know*," said O'Brien. "Can you believe they left the keys in this thing?"

Gleeson understood what she actually meant was, she needed the officer's retinal scan to start the vehicle. He surmised that the rather nasty contusion on the man's brow stemmed from a collision with the dashboard. "Couldn't you just take an eyeball?" he asked. "Did you have to bring the whole Nazi?"

"Think of the mess that would have made of my new wheels," she rejoindered. "I hope you boys wiped your boots on entering! Besides, he was already in here. I spotted him just as he cut and ran out on his buddies, leaving them outside to die whilst he climbed in here on his own – I followed him, gave him that facial decoration you saw and zipped him up!"

"Good work. Alright, before I have another heart attack, get us under those engines, Corp."

The tracked vehicle moved slowly through the panicked animals, which were thinning now, but still coming from the forest behind. The buffeting inside a vehicle weighing well over twenty tons was alarming. They really would not have stood a chance outside on a ladder.

Gleeson felt a boulder in his gut. "Has anyone seen Jane Ross?" he asked.

The silence spoke volumes. He lowered his head for a moment, took a breath and prepared himself for the next task.

"I don't have time for this charade, Miss Cockshed!" shouted Baines. "However—"

"Ms," interrupted the woman, raising her voice and index finger in the manner of a school mistress.

"Fine! *Ms* Cockshed—"

"Cocksedge."

"*However,*" Baines spat, glaring at her antagonist, "*Miss* Cocksedge, I really must thank you for introducing me to a genuinely new, and not *altogether* unpleasant experience – that of agreeing with every word Mr Burnstein just said! We have a lot of work to do and anyone here who doesn't, should stay the hell out of the way of anyone who does! *Good evening!*"

"Captain, we're not finished—"

"I disagree," answered Baines, rounding on Cocksedge once more. "The last 'someone' who tried to sow sedition like this was Del Bond. Are you another of his little buddies, still among us, Cocksedge? Huh? Or do you think this little scene will somehow build you a profile, maybe garner you a little power?"

A passive-aggressive specialist, Cocksedge raised her hands in a placating manner with obvious but carefully deniable condescension, as she interjected, "I see that you are under a great deal of pressure, Captain. This paranoia is perhaps just a sign that the strain of command is too great. No one would think any less of you were you to take the decision to step down."

Baines let that one go. "*Yeees*, I remember you now. I also remember your face when you weren't selected for the triumvirate, weeks ago. The reason why you'd slipped my mind was because, as an unremarkable career politician, you've absolutely none of the skills we need to get things done. Yet we still feed you, protect you and provide a safe place for you to live. Perhaps you should be grateful for that and take your damned agitation some place else! Or do I need to have you put somewhere secure until this is all over?"

"*Captain!*" Ms Cocksedge exclaimed, conjuring up just the right amount of outrage to appear genuine, despite getting exactly the opening she had been hoping for. "Are you suggesting that we are all under martial law? Are our voices not to be heard in this new military autocracy of yours, for fear of being banged up? Is this what the people wanted when they *voted* for you?" She ceased her righteous attack suddenly and smiled an understanding little smile. "Oh, but they didn't vote for *you*, did they?"

Baines suddenly saw where this was going and sure enough Cocksedge's next words immediately confirmed her suspicions.

"Maybe we should consider a revote," the politician continued, reasonably. "And, as Captain Douglas isn't coming bac—"

Baines gritted her teeth, spitting her reply like nails. "In answer to your *first* question, I am not *suggesting* anything! Every man, woman and child on this ship could find themselves outside with the dinosaurs, if we don't destroy the enemy's ability to make war on us.

"You're British for God's sake! Your ancestors were the people who gave everything and endured, alone at one point, to bring the Nazis down when the whole of Europe was aflame. People were being killed just because of their race – a regime Schultz has already proven she would be only to happy to reinstate! Now you think we should just roll over and take whatever the bully wants to give us? Perhaps this time it'll be different, huh? Or perhaps you think we should just stand up and be counted with *their* new world order, even though they've declared war against humanity itself and used terrorism and tyranny to bring us to this point? And—"

"War?" interrupted Ms Cocksedge. "Who says we *are* at war? Only *you*, it seems, and *your* military."

"I'm not finished!" Baines bellowed. "*And* furthermore, if I hear you spreading word that Captain Douglas won't be coming back, just to further your own ends," she lowered her voice dangerously, "your Westminster holiday will come to a swift and very unspectacular end – please trust me on that."

"Are you threatening me, Captain?" asked Cocksedge, appearing shocked.

"Oh, spare me the command performance. This ship could always use another restroom cleaner and it might just be you! What *exactly* are you trying to achieve here, *Miss* Cocksedge?" Baines glared at her before turning to assess the main group, many of whom looked outraged, many more simply afraid.

Cocksedge was silent for a moment, calculating. "If there *is* war," she tried again, still with a calmness perfectly engineered to conflagrate, "it's a war which you started, Captain."

"*What*?!" asked Baines, shaken, after a moment adding, "Does anybody else believe that?"

The crowd were mostly silent, either baffled or scared by these proceedings. However, Baines did hear some voices ring with a clear and emphatic "*no*". Once again Mr Burnstein came through for her.

Mother Sarah and Satnam Patel entered embarkation at that moment, answering Major White's call. Cocksedge smiled very slightly at this fortuitous timing.

"So you *deny* carrying out the cold blooded murder of that poor young man on the ship in orbit, Captain?" Her projected righteous indignation, with the side order of shared humanity, would have been a triumph on any other stage.

A protracted "*Oooh!*" blew through the crowd following her accusation. Baines was breathless.

Major White stepped up to the podium. "That 'poor young man' as you described him, was a Nazi stooge and if he'd got in here, it would be to do murder!"

"So *you* say, *Major*. Another military opinion," she added, turning once more to her audience.

White ignored her and looked around the multinational, multiracial group in front of him. "We know, *out of their own mouths*, that these people are here to reboot the human race from their own stock. Anyone they don't feel lives up to their ideals will be executed. All the folks we left back home won't even get the chance to *exist!*" He shook his head sadly, taking a deep breath. "There's a lot of good people in here that I don't wanna see come to harm. Even if it costs my life to defend you, I will."

Several people applauded this, standing and nodding demonstratively.

Mother Sarah spoke up loudly so that all could hear. "Captain Baines and the brave men and women under her command are all that stands between us and a *great* evil – potentially the end of the human race as we know it, not to mention the end of most, perhaps all of *our* lives."

"Yes, but we only have *your* word that this danger is real or indeed that any of this has been said by the other people," Cocksedge pressed on. "They could be here to rescue us for all we know. *We* didn't see how poor Dr Hussain died, for instance. Perhaps you'd like to tell us about your involvement in that fiasco, Captain?"

The other people, Baines thought, suddenly distanced from her surroundings. *Is that what they're calling them?* She could feel shock and outrage beginning to woolly her thinking.

"That is not so," shouted out a voice from the crowd. Dr Klaus Fischer stood to address the people around him. "I saw Schultz kill that man, *her own* man, in cold blood, with my own eyes! We can expect nothing but slavery or death at the hands of these animals!"

A whoop of approval followed Dr Fischer's rejoinder which allowed a little hope to enter Baines' battered and bruised heart.

"Hear, hear," shouted Burnstein above the din. "Captain, go get those Nazi sons of bitches!"

Baines felt yet another strange emotion towards Burnstein; this one bordered on gratitude.

"There's no more time," said Major Ford White through the PA with finality. "Go save us, Captain, and God speed."

Clapping began, here and there, followed by cheers as others joined in. Eventually most of the people in embarkation were on their feet roaring their approval, but not all.

Baines gave White a quick hug. "Thank you, Ford," she said quietly. "Take care of them all – well, most of them at least. You can strap *her* to the outside of the gates to frighten the monsters away!"

White gave her his lopsided grin. "I'll deal with this, Jill. Don't pay it any mind at all. Good luck and thank you – for everything," he said seriously, squeezing her hand gently in a double grip.

As she left, Baines heard Cocksedge speak again. "Perhaps this is not the right moment, but I must speak out. I believe in the peace process, and tolerance, most of all. I'm sure I am not alone in being *deeply* concerned about the path our leaders seem to be taking us down. I suggest that we should consider a re-election as soon as possible and furthermore—"

The door closed, cutting her off.

Baines left it all behind, wandering as if in a dream. At the time she most needed to hone her determination to a lethal edge, she felt shattered and heartsick; her soul in darkness. Inner thoughts running scared, she searched desperately for a reason why anyone would want to crush the spirits of those about to do battle for everyone's lives – indeed for *everything*. What could they hope to gain if all was destroyed? Could *anyone* be that short-sighted? It must be deliberate, or maybe they just don't care which side wins as long as they float to the top in the aftermath.

She muttered to herself. "Our plumbing must be really broken if we can't flush a turd like Cocksedge. That must mean that I'm failing... *me*. Some of the people in there believed her, or might by the time she's done confusing them."

Baines had thought herself at her lowest ebb when they lost James Douglas; could she be sinking even lower?

The ship-wide alarm sounded, making her jump in shock. She fell against the bulkhead panting like a trapped hart, desperately trying to gather herself. This was *it*.

Chapter 6 | Resolute

Jones stood atop the tracked personnel carrier steadying the ladder. The stampede which had been flowing around them seemed to have stalled. He looked down from his island amid the sea of life below, in horror. The animals milled about them, confused and afraid. He knew that any spark could ignite the chaos all over again. The armoured vehicle suddenly felt very small and not nearly so safe.

He called up to Gleeson and Davies. "Hurry up! They'll have us all down the valley, they will!"

Jones was not easily perturbed but this was hardly lambing in Llanberis, after all, and he became more edgy with each passing second. Some of the smaller animals were now jumping onto the vehicle to avoid the crush, well within his personal space.

Gleeson continued with the cool bearing of a career explosives man. Davies on the other hand kept looking around nervously. "Hurry up, sir. *Jonesy*'s gonna explode if we don't get outta here soon."

"Patience, mate, you don't want me to rush these babies."

They were deep inside one of the rocket nacelles at the rear of the enemy battleship, setting a large bundle of high explosives. Gleeson was just syncing their charges and detonators, so that they could all be set off as one.

Their outrageous scheme of starting a dinosaur stampede appeared to have worked so far, as a cover. A little luck had come their way, too. The armoured vehicle had been a nice, unexpected bonus. Also, had it not been for the mating pair of Oxalaia, gingering up the chaos outside, the stampede would probably have abated long since, maybe not even getting as far as the enemy.

However, Jones, who *was* outside, struggled to see it that way. Indeed, the movement of something huge, out in the darkness, made him feel more and more that *his* luck was actually up a well known creek. Out in the noise and the murk, the 'something' was nevertheless clearly headed his way. All the floodlights set up by the invading force to light their compound had been torn away by the stampede and it was almost completely dark now. He squinted at it, trying to discern its form.

The beasts all around him were less confused by the darkness, their other senses telling them, unequivocally, to run.

In the dim light, the herd's sudden jerk to movement, for the Welshman, was like standing in the middle of a flock of birds as they change direction. Why this happens is often incomprehensible to humans. Jones, on the other hand, was only too aware of why this startled reaction occurred, while fervently wishing not to know.

A shape coalesced from the darkness. It seemed the proverbial creek had not merely swallowed his paddle, but also his life jacket, homing beacon, radio, map, compass and emergency rations – along with any chance at all of survival.

It was terrifyingly close now, and even more terrifyingly large, making noises that were neither friendly nor welcome.

Well, damn me, thought Jones. *No paddle and now there's a hole in my boat as well, isn'it!* "Commander!" he screamed, his voice trembling. "We're seconds from death! *Seconds*!"

Jones was as brave as a lion but he really had no alternative but to abandon the ladder and drop into the vehicle below. The jaws snapped shut, exactly where he had been balancing on the bottom rung a mere second ago. The ladder simply disappeared. They never even heard its lightweight alloy remains strike the outer hull of the vehicle, deafened as they were by the colossal roar of the beast right overhead.

Its snout followed Jones down his rabbit hole and jammed, inches away from the Welshman's chest.

"Aaargh!" he screamed

"Close the hatch," shouted O'Brien, angrily.

"Wha'?!" cried Jones, terrified almost beyond speech.

O'Brien ducked into the back of the vehicle wearing a furious expression which instantly turned to wide-eyed amazement as she saw what was happening.

The Oxalaia pulled its snout back a little and roared again in frustration before lunging once more, only to be stopped for a second time by the armoured hoop of the hatch. The three soldiers covered their ears as the animal bellowed. Inside the steel-sided vehicle, the thunderous roar echoed with a hard ring that momentarily stunned them.

The creature retreated once more, readying for a third try. Jones shook his head before seizing the opportunity to fling himself further back into the load area.

Above it all, standing at the edge of the rocket nacelle, Davies shouted, "It's too late, sir!"

Gleeson walked to the edge and looked over. "Where's me bladdy ladder?!"

"Gone, sir!"

The commander looked down at the Spinosaurid trying to break into his newly acquired hardware like a tin of tuna and grimaced. "No you don't, matey," he said, tearing open a Velcro pocket in his jacket and pulling out two cigar-shaped cylinders, each around fifteen centimetres in length.

He turned to Davies and grinned. "Dingo wingers," he said, as if this explained everything. "Cover your ears."

Flicking a small switch on each device he dropped them both onto the animal's head and turned away covering his own ears.

The flash bang was *loud.*

Vocalising something between a continuous roar of indignation and a whimper of fear, the huge male Oxalaia turned and fled, head down, back into the forest like a spaniel from a bee.

Gleeson watched him go with a half grin. "Now, I don't pretend to be Dr Doolittle, but I swear I understood every word of that."

It was almost dark but from their vantage point up in the rocket exhaust of the enemy ship, the two men could just about make out the other, slightly smaller, female Oxalaia in the middle distance glutting blood, bone, flesh and bowel from a downed Mayor.

"He's split and left her behind," Davies commented.

Gleeson turned to him once more. "Maybe they weren't that serious?"

The voice boomed out of the Tannoy. "*Attention all crew and passengers: This is Lieutenant Singh. The* New World *will be separating from the Life Pod in 'T' minus five minutes. All personnel should make their way to their stations immediately before the hatches are locked down. Captain Baines to the bridge, repeat, Captain Baines to the bridge – Singh out.*"

It had not been possible to set a time for Gleeson's attack due to so many mission variables. They aimed to hit the enemy ship as darkness fell or as soon as possible afterward. All the crew of the *New World* could do was 'be ready'. Singh had sounded the separation warning just as the last light of day faded to dusk. The Sarge still watched and waited from his eyrie near the top of the ship. The engineering staff still ran their final checks prior to launch. Only the captain was not where she should be.

She decided to put that right and set off at a jog through the empty corridors of her ship. With every step her heart beat a little harder, forcing blood, oxygen and adrenalin around her system and with it returned the confidence and vigour born of movement. The further she ran, the better she felt. "When in doubt," she panted, "doing anything feels a lot better than doing nothing. Hang on, James, we're coming!"

The atmosphere was highly charged when Baines re-entered the bridge to take her seat. Singh was at the helm, with Tim and Patricia Norris taking seats at a couple of the science stations. Catching a few calming breaths, Baines' hand hovered over the controls for the public address system.

As Singh turned and nodded, she opened a ship-wide channel once more. "This is Captain Baines," she said, forcing calm into her voice. "The *New World* is about to separate from the Pod. All hatches will be sealed in sixty seconds. This is your last chance to reach your stations."

Pausing to allow any stragglers to understand the message and act upon it, she pondered what to say next. She needed to give them hope, but her recent experience had left her feeling fractured. Taking another deep breath, she continued.

"We will do everything possible to prevent the enemy from bringing their weapons to bear on our position here. This is a military situation and I expect you all to follow any order from Major Ford White as if it were my own."

The calmness she was able to affect replenished her strength, the one feeding on the other in a sort of internal loop as she took one last moment to steady herself.

"To all our people, it has been my honour to know you and to serve you. Stay united and stay strong. We will be launching shortly and fully expect to return to you shortly after that. Should we..." she paused. "Should we be delayed, I wish Major White to take my place on the triumvirate with Mother Sarah and Dr Patel until I or Captain Douglas return. Good luck everyone, and take care of one another – Baines out."

She closed the channel and watched the remaining seconds drain away before ordering Singh to lock down all the hatches and release the docking clamps which tied the *New World* to the Pod.

Hydraulics hissed and whished along the top, front and rear of the Pod as the mechanisms disengaged. There was no discernible movement, with both Pod and ship settled into the soil as they were.

"This is Baines to The Sarge, anything to report?"

Sergeant Jackson's voice came back strongly through the internal comm. "Nothing yet, Captain. Rest assured, when it kicks off you'll be the first person I call."

Baines smiled. They would soon be going hunting.

There was a loud bang on the top of the armoured vehicle which made the three soldiers inside jump, in spite of themselves.

"Ow! That was further than it looked. Davies, be careful, try and roll with it. Ow, baggar! Are you three on a coffee break in there?! Where's the bladdy hatch, I can't see a damned thing!"

O'Brien climbed up to help Gleeson find his way down into the hatch as another bang followed by a string of expletives hit the roof of the vehicle. Passing the commander down, O'Brien went back to help Davies, who was whimpering bravely.

"I think I've broken something, Corp. I landed on… on a… I don't know what, sticking up from the top of the tank, I can't see. Aargh, *hell*!"

With everyone inside, she battened down the hatch.

Gleeson helped Davies to a seat and felt his ankle through his boot, reaching for some painkillers from his jacket. "Leave the boot on and keep it tight, but you already know that, right?" he said, calmly. Over his shoulder he called, "O'Brien, get us around to our shuttle on the other side of the compound, towards the front of the ship. And don't try and leave the area 'cause they're bound to shoot at us! Drive steady, like we belong her—"

Before Gleeson could finish his sentence, the vehicle's comm crackled to life.

Schultz looked out of one of the portholes at the side of the bridge. It was almost dark, the stampede now diminished to a few stragglers, when movement caught her eye; something large.

"*Kapitän*, one of our personnel carriers is moving out there."

Meritus looked surprised. His previous calls had gone unanswered and he feared the worst. "We have survivors? This is great," he said, activating the comm.

"This is Meritus to the driver of the personnel carrier. We're glad you made it. Do you have any other survivors with you?"

No response.

Gleeson joined O'Brien in the cab of the armoured vehicle and stared at the comm – which flashed at them accusingly.

"What do we do, Commander?"

"Drive. *Slowly.*"

O'Brien continued away from the rear of the ship cautiously, making her way around to the far end of the compound as instructed.

The comm crackled again. *"This is Captain Meritus to the driver of the personnel carrier. Please respond. Meritus to any sentries, please respond."*

On the *Last Word*'s bridge, Meritus frowned. He was about to activate the comm again when Schultz snapped at him. "You're wasting your time, fire on that vehicle!"

"What?!"

She rounded on him now. "Clearly, this stampede was the first phase of an attack."

"Attack? By whom? You assured us the *New World*'s crew were a broken and beaten people, left without a credible leader," replied Meritus, with just a hint of irony in his voice. "Besides, that vehicle has borne the brunt of a massive stampede by hundreds of *dinosaurs*! It's quite likely damaged. It's not much of a stretch to believe that the driver might not be receiving us, or perhaps he or she is, but can't answer."

"Do it!"

"By a miracle they survive that cataclysm out there and you want to blow them up?"

"That's a direct order, *Kapitän.*"

Meritus' response was lost in the explosion.

"Captain, this is your call!"

"Thanks, Sarge, seal your hatch and get yourself to the bridge. We're going for a ride!" replied Baines. "Sandy?"

Singh nodded and turned to his controls. "Hang on, everyone. We are still partially capsized, so this is likely to be a bumpy take off!" He opened a channel to engineering. "Hiro, are you ready down there? We've got the green light."

The answering voice was that of Georgio Baccini. "*Hiro is just finishing something off, Lieutenant, but he's giving the thumbs up so please proceed with your engines' pre-start.*"

"Thanks, Georgie."

Within a minute The Sarge entered the bridge, taking a seat at the scanning station. "I carried all that fancy gear up there for nothing," he said.

"Quite a show, was it?" asked Baines.

"*Oh* yes. The flash lit the sky. I hope Commander Gleeson hasn't overcooked the pudding!"

"He's knows his trade, Sarge," replied Baines, quietly. "Is everyone strapped in?"

"*We're ready, Captain.*"

Singh turned one last time to Baines. "And so is the *New World.*"

"Do it," she said simply.

The thrusters fired and the ship began to vibrate. A small lateral movement made everyone grab the arms of their seats.

Outside, the clinging mud resisted, refusing to let go of her landing struts. A monstrous *sucking* noise came from the earth around the struts as the ground trembled and liquefied. The friction caused the *New World* to jolt against the hull of the Pod, causing a deafening clang which rang out across the plain.

In the circle of green around the ship, the local birdlife, thinking themselves settled for the night, erupted from the treetops in flocking havoc, a thousand strong. Dormant for the last few weeks, the behemoth was breaking free of the Earth once more.

With a juddering, jerking motion, the *New World* rose, retracting her landing gear as she climbed. Huge clods of soil and muck, accompanied by hundreds of gallons of water, sheeted away as she ascended like a pale goddess of fire, dwarfing even the gargantuan creatures under her gaze. The rocket thrusters reached a pitch that would have blown the ear drums of any creature unprotected beneath her, had they not already vacated the area at the first signs of her wrath.

The team assembled in the four-wheel-drive personnel carrier out in the compound had been ready for this, for over an hour. Even protected by the vehicle's bulkheads, they had to cover their ears.

Hiro was at the grappling controls in engineering. He lowered one of the hooks on immense cables and snagged the top of the carry-cradle in which the lorry stood. With ridiculous ease, twelve tons of lorry and cradle were plucked from the earth like an empty milk carton and drawn up into the huge space normally reserved for the Pod. The *New World* turned on her axis towards the west and set off in the direction of the enemy. Once clear of the Pod and environs, the main engines fired and she was gone.

The sirens and klaxons were muffled, as were the screams and the shouting. Secondary explosions tore through the *Last Word*. Within a split second, safety protocols took control, closing valves, gates and bulkheads all over the ship. But a split second was all it took for fire to find a way through the fuel system to devastating effect.

Meritus picked himself up and screamed for an immediate damage report. Even his own voice seemed far off to his ringing ears.

"An explosion in one of the main engines, sir," shouted one of the bridge officers. "That's all we have at the moment."

Lieutenant Hemmings stood from her console controlling the ship's sensing equipment and approached Meritus with a quick salute. "Captain, the internal sensors have been damaged – I should get to engineering to find out what's happened and see if I can help."

Meritus nodded. "Yes, go. Report back, *asap!*"

She saluted again. "Yes, sir." Turning away from the captain, she stopped once more at her station to remove a small memory card from the console. Quickening her step, she left the bridge heading down into the bowels of the ship.

Meritus glared down at Schultz, who was stirring sluggishly. She had a head wound which was bleeding profusely, doubtless caused by slamming into a hard surface on her way down. He approached her with a snarl and lifted her by an arm. "A broken and beaten people, eh?"

She gazed at him, not seeming to understand. Disgusted, he let her drop, and turned around to bark orders at his security team.

Douglas regained consciousness. "What the..." he breathed, blearily, feeling blood on his face from a cut above his eye.

Sirens were going off everywhere.

Throwing a piece of decking plate over, he stood shakily, looking around. Gradually he realised that a miracle had just occurred; perhaps more than one. Whilst taking his daily exercise, he had been jumping on the spot, bringing his knees up to his chest. On his last jump, the floor seemed to have followed him. A mere nanosecond after pushing off, the deck had buckled under some extreme force, launching him through the air towards Lloyd's bunk. From the feel of his head, they had connected, but his timing had indeed been miraculous. Had he been on the way down from his jump, the force would have shattered his legs.

Turning, he observed his second miracle. The deck had distorted so badly that the bars to his cell were bent out of shape, breaking the door completely away from its runners.

Hoping for a hat trick, he stumbled over to Lloyd and removed a few pieces of debris from the prone man. It seemed his third miracle was lost; Lloyd had a pulse but he was a mess.

"Geoff?" Douglas tried. "*Geoff*, can you hear me?"

Lloyd moaned and his eyes fluttered open. "Wha' happened?" He groaned more than spoke.

"Ah don't know. But there's been a fairly catastrophic explosion by the looks."

"A rescue?"

Douglas shook his head. "Ah cannae tell. Come on, whatever's happening we've got our opportunity to make a run for it."

Lloyd coughed and cried out in pain. His side was haemorrhaging, the sheets of his bunk already soaked in blood. "I can't."

"Ah willnae leave ye!"

"Wrap me up quickly, so I don't bleed out and go. Please!"

Douglas wrapped Lloyd's abdominal area as best as he could with a sheet. "Come on, Geoff, will ye no' at least try? We'll no' get another chance like this."

"Douglas, leave me. I can't move – *look* at me!"

Douglas stared, stricken with indecision. "Lieutenant, we just got you back from the dead—"

"I'm not an officer under your command," snapped Lloyd, interrupting him. "Or any kind of officer at all, come to that!" Pain and exasperation made him crotchety once more. "Court-martialled, remember?"

Blowing out a huge sigh, he calmed slightly and continued more gently. "James, you must go. Be the hero, save our people. That was always more in your line than mine, anyway," he smiled sadly.

Douglas wavered still.

"*Go*, you damned fool!" shouted Lloyd with one last tongue of his old fire.

"Ah'm sorry, Geoff."

"We're *all* sorry! Now get the *hell* out of here while you still can!"

"*Whoa*! That was a *big* one!" shouted Gleeson, grinning at his handiwork. He turned to the others, most of whom were trying to crane into the cab.

"What's that?" asked Jones, rubbing his ears.

"I said, that wa— ah, never mind." He leaned forward towards the small windscreen. "How much damage have we done?" he asked O'Brien.

159

"What?" she asked in return.

Gleeson shook his head in irritation and pushed his face close to the screen. There was light now, mostly firelight, but it lit the compound nevertheless. Flames belched from several cracks in the ship's superstructure around the engines, but a few were further forward.

"The fuel system must have carried the destruction throughout the ship," said the commander. He was still grinning, but catching Jones' expression he stopped. "What is it, Corporal?"

"I was just wondering where Captain Douglas was inside that thing, when we blew it up."

Gleeson swallowed and looked back to the ship. Slowly he nodded his understanding, but there was nothing he could do about it right now.

"OK," he replied instead. "We're gonna have company any minute, so we need to look for a way to board that ship and keep it in our back pocket until the cavalry arrives. There are fractures all over it. There must be a way in."

Douglas left his cell with a final backward glance at the man he had to leave behind. He cursed, hating it, but Lloyd would die if he moved him, so he had to remain where he still had a chance, even if that meant leaving him with the enemy.

Making his way cautiously to the end of the short corridor, he glanced around the corner for the briefest second. There was another short corridor leading away. It was empty. Continuing to the next corner he walked straight into one of the *Last Word*'s officers – who happened to be armed.

"Sixty seconds out, Captain," stated Lieutenant Singh.

Baines opened a channel to engineering. "Hiro, this is Baines. We'll be on top of them in less than a minute, are you ready down there?"

"Yes, Captain. Bring us in nice and low so that we can release the truck before moving on to our final operation."

"Will do – bridge out."

"Coming down the valley just above the canopy, Captain," said Singh, "just as the chief ordered."

"Let's not be too literal, Sandy. I don't want this to *actually* be our final operation!" replied Baines, opening a ship wide channel. "Strap in everybody, we're going in!"

A continuous rumbling began to vibrate the *Last Word*, growing louder. Many of the screens were out of commission, most of the others showing only frantic warnings and diagnostics.

"What *now*?" Meritus muttered angrily to himself. "That had better not be more damned animals!"

Giving up on the technology, he looked out of a window into the darkness. He looked out and then he looked up, his eyes widening in disbelief. "What the hell is going on out there?!" he shouted at the top of his lungs.

"Captain," reported one of the few remaining bridge crew still at their station, "the scanners are damaged but it appears we have incoming."

"I can see that! It looks like *everybody*!" Meritus dove to the officer's station. "Show me!"

"It's something big, sir."

"What, like a dinosaur?" someone called out.

"No. Like the *New World*!" shouted the scanner operator, beginning to panic.

"What the hell are they doing?" Meritus spun round and snapped his fingers at another officer across the bridge. "I want weapons, *now*, Lieutenant!"

"Most of our weapons are unresponsive, sir. There is so much damage to all the circuitry throughout the ship that trying to re-route it will be... no, wait. Stand by... got it! I've got one of the top cannons to answer, sir!"

"Good work. Now, I wonder if you would be kind enough to blow that giant flying trashcan out of the sky, *please!*"

"Yessir!"

The gunner activated the single working top cannon and began turning it around to face the incoming ship.

The *New World* roared down the valley through the darkness, clipping tree tops and generating tremendous sucking winds in her wake. The few animals remaining in the area after the stampede and the subsequent explosion finally gave up and fled for their lives.

"We've got their ship on the scanners, Captain," said The Sarge from his station. "Calling up night vision."

The heads-up display showed a scene of utter devastation.

"Set down the truck and our troops, Hiro," Baines commanded.

"Already underway, Captain," replied the engineer, lowering the cradle and its payload.

"It looks like a *stampede* has been through the place," noted Singh.

"A rather redundant simile, Lieutenant. Although in all honesty, I don't think I could've put it better myself," admitted Baines. "You were right, Tim."

"Captain?"

"When you said that fear in animals can be devastating. God help anyone who was on the ground down there a few minutes ago," she finished quietly.

The *New World* hovered like the angel of death, lording the darkness over fire and destruction. The bridge crew's reverie was broken by a crackling from the comm. "It's a secure channel, Captain," reported The Sarge. Baines nodded for him to acknowledge it.

"*Where've you guys been? The barbie's nearly gone out!*"

Baines' face lit up. "Commander! Are you all safely out of the way?"

"Yes, ma'am, we left the heavy lifting for you guys." Gleeson saw no reason to report his 'missing in action' just yet. There was nothing Baines could do for Ross and now was not the time for sorrows.

"We're on our way – Baines out."

Lieutenant Singh waited for their people on the ground to drive to a safe distance before inching the *New World* forward for the final stage of the mission.

"Get in there," ordered Douglas' captor, pointing with her automatic pistol to a room off the main corridor. Having little choice, he obeyed.

The room was small with banks of equipment along one side. Once in, he spun round to face her, hoping for an opportunity to turn the situation around. This was unnecessary, however, as his third miracle had clearly been biding its time until just this moment.

The *Last Word*'s officer clicked her gun's safety on and handed it towards him, grip first. It took Douglas a moment to work out what was happening.

"I'm Lieutenant Elizabeth Hemmings," she announced, pushing the weapon into his unresisting hand. "Captain, we have seconds only. There are no security cams in here, we're fortunate. Take these three extra clips for the gun, here is a comm unit and most importantly you need to take this." She handed Douglas a small data card.

Douglas' mind finally caught up. "What is it?" he asked, glancing at the card before pocketing it.

"It's important. You need to get that to your scientists on the *New World* – they'll know what to do with it. Everything depends on this, Captain. *Everything!*"

"Who are ye?"

"I told you, I'm Lieut—"

"No, Ah mean *who* are ye?"

"Hiro, we're in position," shouted Singh into the comm. "Are you ready?"

"Just a second, I need to get at least four grapnels in place for this to work."

"For the love of God, Hiro, there's a cannon turning towards us! Can't we just go with three?!"

"It won't work – we will only damage the mechanisms," replied the engineer, crossly. *"You saw the calculations, in order to get enough lift we need to—"*

"HIRO!" bawled Baines and Singh together.

"Alright! Alright! I'm almost there!"

"Long story short, Captain," said Hemmings. "They have their spies, we have ours." A look of anger crossed her face. "I was contacted by the US government after *Grandpa* Schultz had my fiancé murdered."

Douglas winced slightly. "Murdered?"

She swallowed her emotion. "I am related to the Schultz family. I was pulled into their world and was told that as long as I did as I was told, Stuart would be safe."

"Your fiancé?"

She nodded affirmation. "He was not, shall we say, of approved stock. Heinrich Schultz could never allow anyone of his bloodline to 'intermarry' so he broke his word and murdered the kindest and best man I have ever known."

"Ah'm sorry."

She accepted his commiseration with a nod. "Naturally, when Homeland Security contacted me, I was in the mood to talk. Most of my family are gone now – all the ones I cared about anyway. I learned not to have friends. They die. At least if *you* can stop this madness, my family, and

Stuart, will still get their chance to exist in the future… perhaps things will even turn out differently, huh?"

The gunner's voice wavered. "Captain Meritus," he said. "I've turned the cannon but don't have full control. It won't elevate enough to hit the target, sir."

"Are you kidding? That thing is over half a kilometre long!"

"I know, sir, but she's also several hundred metres in the air and I can't get any of the missile launchers to respond. The controls are mostly dead, sir. We might be able to fire a missile manually from the launchers," he spun his seat to face Meritus, "but there's nothing we can do from here, Captain."

"Come *with* me, Lieutenant," Douglas urged. "Together we can—"

"No," she shook her head fiercely, cutting him off. "I have to remain undercover here, Captain, because if you fail, *I* will have to stop them."

"But even if you succeed, that's a one-way trip."

"I know, but they've already taken everything I cared about away from me. The least I can do is return the favour." She gave him a brittle smile. "In order to continue with my cover, I'll need you to knock me out."

Douglas admired her courage, but before taking drastic action had to first try further persuasion. He opened his mouth to speak when the whole world turned upside down.

"Get someone down there, immediately!" Meritus ordered the gunner before turning back to the officer at the scanners. "What are they trying to do to us?"

Before his subordinate could answer, the ship lurched.

"Oh no," said Meritus, quietly.

Another grinding pitch, this one considerably more severe, threw most of the crew to the deck as the *Last Word* began to yaw. Worse still, they were being dragged towards the steep embankment which, until so lately, had been their defence.

The forces in play between the giant vessels made even the territorial battles of the mighty Carcharodontosaurs seem like mere pygmy skirmishes. Slowly, very slowly the *Last Word* capsized to the point where she crashed onto her side, smashing her starboard wing in the process, as the awesome power of the *New World* dragged her relentlessly towards the edge.

"Pour it on, Sandy," shouted Baines. "Don't spare the horses!"

Lieutenant Hemmings and Captain Douglas crashed hard against the bulkhead. They were both completely out of control as the ship continued to turn over. Douglas landed on the woman, increasing the force of the blow dramatically.

He coughed, struggling for the breath to ask if she was hurt, when the ship tipped one final time and they were smashed again, now into the opposite wall. The rolling motion was shocking and destructive, but there was another feeling of movement which was even more frightening. Douglas felt as though the whole ship was being dragged by giant hands. Then came the falling…

Meritus was thrown across his bridge to land on Schultz, who was still conscious but had done little more than moan since her first collision with a bulkhead. The *Last Word* was upside down. All of his crew had been thrown out of their seats, some were calling out or screaming. Others were dead or dying.

He tried to regain his feet but the whole ship lurched again as she was dragged over the edge. With one last effort, he gave all he had to throw himself at the vacated gunner's station, just managing to hit the firing stud before his ship groaned and began sliding into the ravine below.

"We're nearly there!" shouted Singh, excitedly. He turned to Baines. "Captain, it's going to work! It's going to *work*!"

Baines was suddenly breathless as the enemy vessel began her descent. They had done it, they had the result they so desperately needed – but at what cost? Resolute, she looked on, unable to do anything more, unable to speak even, as Singh began to manoeuvre the *New World* away. A single thought burned through her mind like a raw nerve – *James*!

As the last deep blues blacked away to full darkness in the valley, the nose of the ruined ship dipped and dug in, ploughing a huge trough down the embankment. The *Last Word* began to turn, plunging ever downward until she struck a rocky outcrop. Her bow slowed, but the majority of her vast bulk continued to push from behind, breaking her back. A vast debris cloud plumed high, hiding her from sight as she ground to a final halt. The dust glowed luminous under ancient starlight, but quickly began to fall, covering her rest with a wraithlike glimmer and from within that cloud, a violent flash overwhelmed all night vision. The accompanying boom thundered across the landscape as a single cannon spoke, delivering the dying battleship's last word.

The sudden fire in the sky lit the entire valley as an explosion tore through the USS *New World.*

Chapter 7 | Broken

"Major, that woman is threatening what small measure of stability we have left," said Dr Satnam Patel. They were seated in the privacy of Major White's security office, just minutes after breaking up the gathering in embarkation.

White kneaded his brow in silent frustration. After a few moments' introspection, he turned to the other member of the triumvirate government present. "What do you think, Mother Sarah?"

"Satnam's right," she answered immediately. "Cocksedge is dangerous. She just wants to use this crisis for her own ends, so that she can soak up the limelight and elbow her way into authority. We've seen enough politicians like her over the years. Far be it from me to take against another human soul, especially as we have so few right now, but she could bring us to ruin. We cannot afford the damage she could do to our authority right now."

She looked a little apologetic, but pressed on. "I know how bad that sounds, but I've come to trust the senior staff on this mission. Trust them with my life and the lives of my fellow survivors. Being shipwrecked in the past is terrifying beyond anything I could have hitherto imagined, but they've helped me believe that, just maybe, we can find a way to survive the tragedy that's been unloaded on us.

"Weak leadership now, along with who knows what kind of crazy deals she might want to make with the Nazis, would almost certainly see the end of most, if not all of us."

She looked pointedly at Satnam, taking his hand in hers. "I am a woman of peace, true peace, without political agenda. But that said – I will stand with my friends, against all who would wish them harm, simply because of their birthright or race."

Patel smiled and squeezed her hand in return. "Thank you, Sarah," he said and then turned back to White. "It's not just me or the other races aboard this ship who we must think about though, Major. If they destroy the timeline, they will wipe out the majority of their own people too, the good and the bad, along with almost everyone else.

"These people, our people – the human race to follow – even the vastly powerful, such as the Caesars and the Napoleons of our history, are like babes in our arms at this point – completely unable to defend themselves from oblivion, if we give up our foothold in this time.

"There can be no deals with the Nazis and any weakness on our part will assuredly mean the end of everything and everyone we have ever known. I get the feeling that Ms Cocksedge cares nothing for this, her only agenda to come out on top. She clearly thinks that she is clever and subtle. I'm sure she believes she can bring the hound to heel. However, sticking with the same metaphor, this cannot be done when the dog is mad."

White blew out his cheeks with a deep sigh. "My every instinct is to simply take her away and lock her up in a dark hole somewhere until this is all over – maybe not let her out even then!" He rubbed his eyes again, clearly exhausted. "If we do that, we play right into her hands though, don't we? We exhibit exactly the kind of behaviour she's accusing us of and she knows it. So what *do* we do?"

"If she wishes to talk with the enemy, maybe we should let her?" said Patel.

Sarah and White stared at him in surprise.

"Well," he continued, "she knows very little strategic information about this Pod or the *New World*. We could send her out to meet with them and leave her there, perhaps? Is there any doubt that we would be safer if she wasn't here among us?"

Sarah and White looked at one another.

"That does make sense," said Sarah slowly, working through the idea. "What about her followers? Some of the folks in embarkation were actually buying her rhetoric."

"You do realise that we are discussing the removal of a political rival here," White could not help stating. "That's about as unconstitutional as it gets!"

"True," said Patel, simply. "But back in our own time there are billions of people crowding the world. Here, our survival hangs by a thread, and it would take but one fool to cut it. Besides, if she wants to talk to them, let her talk to them. She wants to find out what they want, let them show her. I doubt we'll see her again."

White nodded, viewing his fellow councillors with a new respect. He knew it was wrong to presume, but he had expected more dithering and handwringing from a scientist and a priest. He could hardly call them ruthless, but they were certainly serious about the survival of the group, which sounded like the full band to his ears. "Alright," he said. "I can't argue with your logic, but first things first, we need to wait until we hear from Captain Baines. We can't do anything until then." He looked to Sarah. "Other than pray," he added genuinely.

Gleeson watched the strike, unconsciously covering his mouth in disbelief. The grappling cables had released the enemy warship, retracting as planned, when their cheers were suddenly strangled.

The explosion erupted from underneath the *New World*, near her bow and to the port side. One of the huge heat-resistant plates, which covered her landing gear whilst retracted inboard, had been completely blown away, partially vaporised. The huge hydraulic strut housed there showed damage clear even from the ground, although from that distance it was impossible to discern the extent.

This alone would have been problem enough, for the ship could not put down without all four of her stout landing struts, but Gleeson's gut really clenched as he saw the destruction continue aft. The shell fired from the *Last Word*, as she turned that final time, had struck the hovering *New World* obliquely, damaging not only the landing gear but also skipping into one of the rocket thrusters which held the ship suspended above her victim.

The crew on the ground could only watch in horror as this twisted déjà vu unfolded before their eyes. For the second time in just minutes, they saw secondary explosions carry through the hypergolic fuel system of a giant ship, crippling her.

The system was less critical than the main engines he had destroyed upon the *Last Word*, but the *Last Word* had been on the ground in a completely powered-down, passive state. Although the explosion which struck the *New World* was a full order of magnitude less powerful, she was little more than a cargo ship, despite her vastness; merely a lorry to the *Last Word*'s battle tank and in no way designed to repel cannon fire.

Her safety systems came to life almost immediately, cutting fuel supplies and sealing off damaged areas, but the laws of physics would not be so easily assuaged and the huge vessel began to drift forward, listing down and to port.

The bridge rocked with a deafening explosion. Through buzzing ears the crew were assaulted by myriad alarm calls from the systems all around them. The ship rocked again as secondary explosions tore through her belly. It took but a fraction of a second for the *New World* to suffer extensive damage, as did all their hopes along with her.

Captain Baines got to her feet and almost fell again as she tried to regain her seat. She had cracked her head on the deck and could feel her left eye starting to close. Gritting her teeth against the pain, she shouted above the clamour of alarms, demanding a report.

Lieutenant Singh, Sergeant Jackson, Tim and his mother Patricia Norris also picked themselves up. Thankfully no one appeared to be seriously hurt, yet.

Singh called up a damage report list while The Sarge used his good arm to quiet the sirens and klaxons going off everywhere.

"An explosion in one of the bow thrusters, Captain," Singh yelled above the whistling in his ears and the din all around him. "Automatic fire suppression and emergency protocols have been activated."

He took the helm once more and began to arrest the wayward movement of the *New World* as she tipped slowly into gravity's irresistible embrace.

It took a moment for Baines to realise that the comm was also shouting for attention.

"Bridge here, this is Baines."

"Captain, we've been hit by a shell from the enemy vessel," babbled the frantic, disembodied voice of her chief engineer.

"We know. We thought we had a kill, but it seems she had one last trick up her sleeve," Baines answered. "Are you all OK down there?"

"It'll be us who are killed if we don't land!" shouted Nassaki, direct as ever.

"He's right, Captain," added Singh. "We're barely in control of her. Also—" Lieutenants Singh and Nassaki spoke in perfect tandem, *"the landing gear's been damaged."*

"And by land," Hiro elucidated further, *"I mean crash – as gently as possible!"*

"Can we effect repairs to the landing gear whilst we're still in the air?" asked Baines.

"Captain," answered the chief, *"we can crash-land the ship in a controlled manner immediately or allow her to crash all on her own when she fails to respond to the helm altogether – either way we are going down!"*

"Sandy?" Baines looked to the pilot for any shred of hope.

"I can give you a minute, maybe two," replied the pilot on open channel with an edge of despair in his voice. "Choose a landing site right now!"

"What if we put down over water?" asked Tim, intruding into the panicked exchange.

"We won't make it to the sea," replied Singh, head bowed over the controls.

"No," said Tim, rushing over to the scanning suite where The Sarge was seated. The grizzled veteran gave up his chair so the young man could pull up the maps they had put together for the region. "When we went out recently, to undertake the first survey of the area with Captain Douglas, we found a wide valley clearing with a large body of fresh water. Do you remember, Lieutenant?"

"Er... vaguely," commented Singh, splitting his attention from the uncooperative helm.

"If we hit water at the wrong angle it will be like hitting concrete," Hiro warned, through the comm.

"I know," said Tim, "but Sandip won't allow that to happen, will you?"

Lieutenant Singh rolled his eyes. "Give me a direction, *now!*"

Tim fed him the coordinates, allowing the pilot to begin his work. He turned to Baines. "Captain, the lake is only a few degrees off course from our way back to the Pod. We should be able to put down no more than five or six miles away from them. Close enough for them to help us, yeah?"

The young man was shaking involuntarily with fear and shock, but still looked determined. She needed to provide him with hope, true or false; she owed him that – owed all of them. She smiled at Tim specifically, despite the pain in her head. "That's right, Tim. Well done, that'll give us a good chance of landing safely and fixing any damage."

Singh turned and raised an eyebrow. She caught his gaze and shook her head almost imperceptibly.

Patricia Norris waited painfully for Tim to finish his task before checking him over.

"I'm OK, Mum." He resisted his mother's interference tetchily.

Satisfied that this was indeed the case, she moved on to Baines. "Captain, you've really caught yourself a good one," she said, referring to Baines' florid black eye and the blood running from a cut on her brow. "Let me see. Hmmm, you'll need a few stitches when we get back. I think you've a small concussion too."

"Not much we can do about it at the moment," replied Baines, grimacing as the pain stabbed at her again. "You, Tim, everybody – strap yourselves in. That goes for everyone down in engineering too, Hiro. This could be a very, very bumpy ride! Sandy, you're getting really good at crashing this ship – please ensure that this one is another triumph!"

Douglas opened his eyes and wondered if he had. It was pitch black in the little room where he had been temporarily holed up with Hemmings.

"Lieutenant Hemmings?" he called out. "Ah cannae see you. Elizabeth?"

Crawling in the direction he believed the door to be, he felt his way around in the dark. By feel, he came across the controls but they were dead. He gripped the edges of the door and pushed, sliding the panel sideways. This afforded him a little illumination from the emergency lights in the hallway. Turning back into the room, he resumed his search for Hemmings.

He found her slumped and unmoving in a corner and knelt to check her vitals. When the ship had turned the first time, the force with which he struck the wall had knocked him sick. However, Lieutenant Hemmings had spared Douglas the worst of the blow, by granting him a semi-soft landing. He saw now, in that awful light, that his luck had come at a cost; the very highest.

"No," he said softly, sitting back and closing his eyes against tears. Taking a steadying breath, he leaned forward once more. The brave young woman lay lifeless before him. Her neck, at a sickening angle, was clearly broken.

Putting his head in his hands he sobbed silently as desperation clawed at him, dragging him towards darkness. He knew his ballistic weight had killed her, had felt the crunch at the time, without realising the full consequences. Leaning forward one last time, he closed her eyes gently.

"Ah'm sorry, Elizabeth. Ah'm so sorry. God bless."

Wiping his eyes, he got to his feet and took another deep breath, standing to attention. He saluted his fallen comrade. "Lieutenant Elizabeth Hemmings, it was my honour to know you, even for such a short time. Ah swear, Ah'll never give up until Schultz has been stopped and as long as Ah live, you'll be remembered."

He brought his hand down smartly, turned on his heel and strode out of the room – his mind ablaze with thoughts of revenge.

Sargo Lemelisk eyed Del Bond with disdain. Bond looked away, unwilling to meet his glare. Their guard had left them for a little while. It was not as if there was anything they could do from a locked cell. Bond, on the other hand, realised that *he* was feeling rather exposed without the protection of their captors.

"You coward!" Lemelisk spat. "If you'd helped me we could've made a break for it. Clearly there's some sort of crisis going on. That was our chance."

"I'm not a field operative," Bond replied huffily.

Lemelisk literally spat this time, following it up with, "You're a nothing, *Derek*!"

Bond flinched at the hated use of his Christian name. "I fail to see how I could have helped you anyway, we were outnumbered and overmatched—"

"You failed alright! What good is a pen pushing politician like you on a mission like this?"

"You may eat those words yet!"

Lemelisk jumped to his feet and strode across the cell towards his co-prisoner, making him raise his hands over his head protectively, as he slid into a corner.

"You're pathetic," he snarled. "Not even worth the effort to put you out of your misery."

"I tell you, you're wrong," said Bond, continuing to cower in the corner. "I heard the guards talking before you came round. Apparently, the illustrious crew of do-gooders aboard this Pod are having some political problems of their own just now. There's talk of a new piece on the game board. Another politician apparently – I'm sure you'd hate her."

Lemelisk looked down at Bond quizzically. "One of ours?"

"I'm not sure. You know how Old Man Schultz and his mad granddaughter like their little secrets. All I know is, this new player is getting everyone all worked up and building factions amongst our captors. This can only be good for us. You may mock me for being weak, Lemelisk, and I'm sure you are a master of your trade or you wouldn't have been hired. But you need to realise that revolutions don't happen without politicians, no matter how much you revolutionaries pretend to the contrary. Politics is everything and I too am a master."

"Ha!" mocked Lemelisk. "I could kill you with hardly an effort."

"I don't doubt it," rejoindered Bond, "but people from my profession can kill a world with a word. You won't believe what I'll accomplish when I get out of here."

Joining the corridor again, Douglas felt doubly grateful to Hemmings. Not only had she saved him from being smashed into the bulkhead – tragically, at the cost of her own life – but had she not forced him into that small room, he would probably have fallen to his death as the ship tipped over the edge of the escarpment.

The corridor was about fifteen metres or so in length, but due to its current orientation, that fifteen metres was now almost straight down.

Douglas looked across the corridor to another open doorway opposite. The distance to the other room may only have been a couple of metres, but the drop yawning below him was like stepping across a lift shaft, without the elevator.

Clearly his options were limited, so he backed up ready to take the jump.

One, two, three steps and *leap…*

Landing awkwardly in the threshold he grappled for dear life to find a handhold. Not wishing to enter the room without knowing its size, Douglas had jumped cautiously. If the room was large, he might face a drop similar to the one offered by the capsized corridor.

It was difficult to make out the room's limits, full as it was with thick, swirling dust. He coughed, pulling his shirt up over his mouth and nose. Gradually the billowing murk cleared a little. Straining his eyes, Douglas began to discern the dimensions of the space before him.

As the weak light from the corridor's emergency lighting permeated further, Douglas became dimly aware of the opposite wall. The reason there was so much dust in this area was due to the gaping crack in the hull of the ship. Carefully lowering himself down to his floor, which was actually a wall, he made his way to the outer hull.

Climbing up the other side, he looked out into the night; nothing but more dust and debris. He sighed, which started him coughing again. Stepping through a hole in the hull with no idea of where he was in relation to the ground, sounded extremely dangerous, but then the shouting and movement from the bottom of the corridor behind him did too.

Gleeson opened a comm channel as the *New World* began lurching to one side. "This is Gleeson to Baines, come in. Captain?" he waited without response. "*New World*, come *in!*"

The seconds passed like hours for the small team in the armoured personnel carrier, when the comm crackled to life.

"*Commander, this is Baines. We need to put down immediately. Team up with Corporal Thomas' squad and get to a safe distance.*"

"But Captain, what about Captain Douglas?" Gleeson asked.

Baines clenched her teeth and swallowed before answering. "*I'm not giving up on him, but they may have other attack ships still out there on patrol. If they have, it would be better if you're all somewhere else. We can reassess when we know more.*"

"Understood," replied Gleeson. "And you're right – we heard a ship lift off immediately before we hit their camp. As the shuttle's still here, there must be another ship. The fact that we heard it take off through the canopy, and in the middle of a stampede, suggests that it's a powerful ship. Are you in good enough shape to land, Captain?"

He could almost hear Baines' grimace.

"We'll keep you appraised, Commander," she replied. *"We're heading back towards the Pod but we'll have to put down before we reach it. I'm sending you the coordinates of our planned landing area. If you cannot help James, then head for us. It's possible we may need you, and Commander, thank you all for your courage and exemplary work. Well done and good luck – Baines out."*

"Good luck, Captain," said Gleeson, uncharacteristically subdued.

No one spoke as they watched the *New World* limp away. Once she was out of sight, Gleeson nodded to O'Brien. "Open a short range comm channel to Thomas."

"Whoaaa!" Douglas could not help crying out as he slid down the outer hull. Falling into a black abyss, with no points of reference but the sheer wall he was sliding down, was terrifying. Desperately, he clawed at the side of the ship to slow his descent.

He only fell about five metres, his outstretched reach from the crack in the hull bringing the distance down to less than three, but it felt a lot further to a man falling blind. He used whatever wits he had left to keep his legs bent and braced for landing.

His leap of faith was crazy, he knew it, but his only other choice was recapture. In the light of what, he had to assume, had been unleashed upon his captors by his crew, not to mention his subsequent escape, he was *very* unsure of his welcome. However, fortune can favour the bold, as the saying goes, and his daring was rewarded by a relatively soft landing. The warship's slide down the hill had churned and turned the earth over providing a spongy, uncompacted loam to break his fall.

Winded but in one piece, Douglas knew he had to move fast. Clearly there were survivors inside the ship and he had no wish to run into them. The dust was still thick in the air and it was hard to breathe but at least direction was not a problem. He just had to climb.

After scrambling his way up to the crest of the promontory, he came across many corpses of animals, mostly Mayors. He recognised them even in the starlight and this saddened him. Yet more lives destroyed because of these people's actions.

In the distance he could hear the moan of what sounded like a powerful diesel engine. The *New World* had no diesel plant; they would have been useless in the thin Martian atmosphere. He could only suspect the return of an enemy scout party.

Thinking quickly, he looked around for inspiration. He needed to get out of there, certainly, but which way to go? Looking across the remnants of the Nazi enclosure, he saw one small piece of serenity amidst a scene of devastation. Nestled in the far corner, glowing dimly under the starlight, was his shuttle.

Douglas looked up at the stars and offered a silent thank you. The little ship had been far enough from whatever had happened to survive in one piece. Scanning the plateau, he marvelled at the destruction his people had wrought. It looked like the aftermath of a major stampede. *What the hell have they done?!* he wondered.

Making his way across the compound he heard a deep growl which turned into a guttural roar. Behind him, something huge out in the darkness had his scent. The hair rose on the back of his neck and he bolted forward. The frenetic energy of fear gave him wings and he cleared the distance at a sprint. Collapsing against the shuttle's hatch with his chest heaving, but with no time to recover, he worked quickly, keying his pass code.

Nothing…

He tried once more… nothing again.

"Damn her!" he swore vehemently. Schultz must have taken the computer's systems apart over the many days of his imprisonment, locking him out. He had provided the access codes for them to fly the shuttle as part of the deal to save Baines' life and now all he could do was curse in vain.

Douglas threw himself under the shuttle. The animal stalking him closed on his position. It was too dark to see clearly but whatever the creature was, it was truly massive and it stank of death and rotting flesh.

Sliding further under the shuttle as silently as he could, Douglas tried not to gag. He could hear two things. The closest and more urgent was the snuffling of the animal tracking around the shuttle. Clearly, the beast sensed that he was still close. The second sound his mind picked out of the night was the diesel engine again, but as the creature drew closer, the machine seemed to draw away.

Douglas closed his eyes, silently raging against his situation.

They snapped open again as a thought struck him. Riffling through his jacket pockets he drew out the comm Hemmings had given him. Further searching revealed the data clip. He had no idea what was on it but with the enemy battleship down and Hemmings dead, he reasoned that getting the information to the *New World* was more important than risking being caught. He decided to send the information on a maximum strength, coded frequency to increase the likelihood of the information arriving intact. More importantly, he decided to send it now, before the information died with him in the belly of a giant carnivorous dinosaur.

"This is it, Captain. We're going in... *again*," shouted Lieutenant Singh. "Hang on!"

The *New World* tore across the dimly lit plain. The fauna ran for their lives in all directions as the anchored flora bent double in obeisance to the sudden wind. In a dizzying rush, the ground gave way to water as the ship pitched downwards to zero metres. Huge waves rose into the vacuum left in her wake, even before the landing gear touched the surface, creating blinding spray and white noise. The drag twisted the ship off course as only three of her four supports could extend. She would have spun straight into the lake had not the pilot been working with the remaining systems to reduce her speed and bring her back to course.

The velocity required to bring the *New World* to their chosen 'soft landing' site, before she fell out of the sky, was working against them now. Singh fought with the controls to bring her down on an almost flat trajectory whilst shedding speed where possible. He was striving for a balance which he knew was unobtainable. All he could do was minimise – minimise speed, minimise spin, minimise damage.

The 550 metre long NASA ship USS *New World* hit the surface in a mostly controlled belly flop, creating a bow wave almost 100 metres high.

However, the water had played its part, slowly soaking up most of her forward energy as she dug deeper into the lake. Unfortunately, the huge ship soon ran out of lake and leaving the water once more, carved a deep valley into the opposite shore.

The ship's speed gradually approached the pilot's best case scenario – a leisurely twenty metres per second – but the momentum created by tens of thousands of tons of spaceship still brought the approaching tree line to them with alarming suddenness. Singh had been unable to fire the forward facing thrusters as the *New World* descended. He had barely been in control of the spin as it was, but now they were on the ground he powered them to maximum to arrest their forward movement.

With a colossal grinding, rending sound the *New World* hit the forest before coming to a full stop. Her bow cut a swathe into the trees a hundred metres long, smashing giant redwoods to kindling and cutting deep into the earth. Without the Pod, the ship's back arched over several hundred metres of plain all the way to the edge of the lake, where her rear landing gear and engines sat in a riptide as the waters crashed back to their natural low point. The huge cutting left by the bow of the ship also filled up like a canal beneath the *New World*'s belly.

Cutting power to the engines, Singh silenced all the screaming alarms. Only then did he release the breath he had not even known he was holding.

"I think I may have set the forest alight with the forward thrusters," he said into the silence. "Whilst possibly flooding the rest of the valley," he added.

The silence continued...

He turned in his seat. "We seem to have dug deep into the earth as well."

Baines removed her harness and walked towards him. "Water, earth *and* fire," she said, squeezing his shoulder companionably.

Singh acknowledged with a stiff nod, his nerves still knotted. "I don't think I damaged the air. Unless you count the oxygen burned when I set the trees alight," he added sheepishly.

"Well done, Sandy. It could have been worse – so much worse. Is everyone OK?" she asked.

Affirmation came from all quarters as everyone breathed a collective sigh of relief, all except Singh.

"Are you OK, Sandy?" asked Baines with concern.

He nodded dumbly. "I think the ship's in a bad way, Captain. Hiro's going to—"

The comm binged, interrupting him. The captain leaned across him to acknowledge it. "Baines," she answered.

"It's bad, Captain," said a distraught male voice with an Italian accent.

"Georgio?"

"Yes, Captain."

"Are you OK down there?"

"Mostly."

"And Hiro?"

"Hmm. Physically," he lowered his voice. *"Emotionally, I'm not sure he will ever be the same again. He keeps repeating, Sekai, over and over again. The ship is very damaged, Captain."*

"Are we talking 'hundreds of man hours and gritty determination', or are we talking 'never fly again', damaged?"

"This is preliminary and wildly speculative, but I reckon we've a month's work before we can even limp back to the Pod – and that's with their help. On the up-side, I don't think she's dead, Captain. I'll know more when the chief, erm... returns."

"Returns?"

"Yes, Captain. Hiro's not in his happy place at the moment. I'll try and find out more for you but it will be much easier to run a full ship-wide diagnostic with Hiro's help. I think he's in genuine shock. It was a good call to get almost everyone off the ship. Some areas got very badly bent from the crash, not to mention the shell which hit us. Of course the downside is – we got everyone off the ship! There's no one but us and your bridge team to inspect all the damage."

"Understood, Georgio. I'm glad you're both OK, that's the most important thing to me."

"Yes, Captain, likewise. Hiro on the other hand... well, I think he's going to need a friend. If you could start a damage assessment at your end, it would be a great help."

"Of course. We'll compare notes soon but the first thing I would like to you to do is check hull integrity. The last thing we need right now is an invasion of wildlife. Please keep us appraised – Baines out."

The Sarge unfastened his safety harness and was about to stand when he noticed an incoming comm channel.

"Captain, we've got a message. Incoming."

"Acknowledge it, Sarge. Who is it?"

Jackson spun in his seat, shock clearly registering on his face. "It's a data burst, Captain," he said.

Baines could clearly see that something had rattled her almost un-rattle-able security sergeant. "What else?" she asked darkly.

The Sarge grinned. "It's signed, James Douglas!"

"This is Major White speaking." One of his security staff had forwarded a hail believed to be from the *New World* to his comm.

"*Major, this is Lieutenant Singh,*" a voice responded through the tiny speaker. "*We took damage during the attack and have crash-landed about five miles west-north-west of you. I'm sending you the coordinates now, sir.*"

"Sandy, it's great to hear your voice! Are you all OK?"

"*Pretty much, sir,*" replied Singh. "*The* New World *is in a bad way though.*"

"Well, thank God you're all alive," replied White. "Was the battleship destroyed?"

"*As far as we can tell, the rest of the mission was more successful than we could have hoped, sir.*"

White sighed with relief. "That's fantastic news. Now, how can we help?"

"*We're going to need a large engineering team, sir. Captain Baines suggests waiting 'til daylight. She thought the bulldozer might be pressed into service, if the adaptations to the cab are complete?*"

"We'll make sure they are tonight. What's her plan?"

"*Send the people and material we need in trucks, following the dozer to clear a path. We will need to create a roadway from us to you. If we can patch the ship up, it'll take a while, sir, and we'll need a decent supply run. You should be able to carry smaller items with the escape pods but we will*" almost certainly need to manufacture much of what we need, and it will be heavy equipment. We'll have to move it by truck."

"Any news from the ground crews, Lieutenant?" asked White. "Obviously, Commander Gleeson's team got the job done, but are they on their way back?"

"They were safe and well when we left the theatre, Major. The captain ordered them, and the second team we deployed, to join up and make their way to our position here."

"Thank God," said White again. "Sandy, is there any news about Captain Douglas?"

Singh surprised White by laughing. *"Yes, sir! We received a coded transmission from him just minutes ago. He's alive and has somehow managed to get himself out of there!"*

"YES!" White shouted, punching the air and startling everyone around him. "That's the best news I've had since we landed here."

"But that's not all of it," continued Singh, his grin travelling through the comm channel without need of video. *"Don't ask me how the hell he got it, but he's transmitted us a full set of schematics for the wormhole drive they had aboard that ship – the one that allowed it to travel through time!"*

White was struck dumb for a moment. "Say again," was all he could manage.

"That's right, sir. I don't know how long it will take for the boffins you have back there to build it, but we're going home!"

White collapsed into his seat, not daring to believe this change in their fortunes.

"It's not all chocolates and flowers though, Major."

White's spirit wilted just slightly as he replied, "What is it, Lieutenant?"

"Obviously, Captain Douglas is out there alone, on the ground, sir. It's hard to imagine being in more danger and so..." he paused.

"Go on," prompted White.

"Captain Baines has taken one of the lifeboats and gone after him, sir."

"Oh," said White. He had been expecting worse. "Isn't that good news?"

"I'm not sure about that, sir."

"How so?"

"There's still the matter of the small attack vessel the enemy has in their possession, sir. One we destroyed in orbit, another seems to have

been severely damaged during Commander Gleeson's stampede, but we suspect a third was missing when we attacked."

"How do we know that?"

"Commander Gleeson confirmed that, sir. He said the engines were extremely loud, so the chances are it's another orbital attack vessel. Its pilot will soon notice that he or she is unable to get a signal from the battleship or the battleship may even have managed to get off a distress call. Either way, they will almost certainly be on their way back and the captain is completely unarmed and overmatched. She may as well have gone to war in a golf cart, sir."

"I assume you brought this to her attention?"

"Certainly did."

"And?"

"Made no damned difference at all, sir."

"Didn't you *try* and stop her?"

"Major, when Captain Baines wants something to happen, she gets 'that look' and it's best to just stand back, as our enemy have just found out. Who'd have thought it possible to destroy one of the most deadly warships ever built with a few pygmy dinosaurs, some cables and a flying van, sir!"

White rubbed his hands down his face in exasperation. "Understood," he acknowledged with a resigned sigh. "If you still have sensors, keep a bead on her. We're all getting very split up and that makes me nervous in this crazy world full of enemies and monsters."

"Agreed, Major," replied Singh reasonably. *"But with respect, Captain Douglas is out there alone in that crazy world now and somehow he's still managed to hand us a way home."*

"You're right, of course. I just hope she's OK. I hope they're both OK. We'll get everything ready over here and come get you at sunup. It must have been a hell of a night. Well done, Sandy. Well done to all of you – White out."

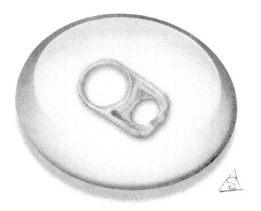

Chapter 8 | Copse & Robbers

Baines felt slightly faint. Less than half an hour since the *New World* had been hit by enemy fire and her injured head hurt like hell. The recent concussion she sustained was affecting her vision too.

After little more than a minute, she was over the enemy camp once more, throttling right back to circle the site. All her instruments were set to infrared and the area was awash with heat signatures. At a glance it was difficult to sift between animals, people and destroyed machinery. Several fires still burned, further diffusing her readings. She asked the computer to search for the specific heat signature given off by human beings. Most of the dinosaurs they encountered had body temperatures in the region of three to four degrees warmer than people, so the equipment easily sorted by type. There were a few on the escarpment where the warship had sat, just a quarter of an hour ago. Many were beginning to cool, which confused the results further. She assumed those were either incapacitated personnel, going into shock, or dead bodies.

Baines sighed at the waste as she noted a few people climbing over the edge of the embankment. She also noted their sporadic small arms fire as it began to ping off her hull.

James couldn't possibly be down there with them, she thought irritably. Widening her search to take the lifeboat out of range, she scanned a larger area. The computer beeped and her screen zoomed in on a figure moving through the forest towards the hills to the north. The trees obscured the shape of the body. "37.2 degrees – that sounds about right for a man running up a hill," she spoke to herself, more to buoy her spirit than anything else. "Now, if I was lost and alone here, that's where I'd go, to get a view of my surroundings as soon as the sun came up."

A proximity alarm screamed at the exact instant that tracer rounds ripped through the night past her port side, tearing up the terrain below. Instinct made her bank right before she even understood what was happening. The escape pod she had pressed into service as a rescue vehicle rocked like a boat at sea in the wash from the orbital attack craft which shot past her.

"Oh, *crap!*" she cursed. Banking further north, she throttled the little engines to full and shot off at a respectable lick. It took several seconds for the fighter to turn and sit back on her tail. Baines jinked and juked as wildly as she dared, her head spinning in sympathy with the craft. She had trained in fighter planes and was a fair pilot, although her combat experience was limited and several years ago. Nevertheless, her tactics bought several seconds before the explosion took the rear of her little ship and the engines died.

Her choices were limited. Escape pods did not come with escape pods, after all, but by their very nature they were incredibly tough. She still had a little aerodynamic control and made the most of it. Tightening her crash webbing, she just about cleared the second mountain ridge north of the enemy camp, before her ballistic trajectory began to flatten and eventually fall. Cresting a smaller, more rounded mountain top, she pushed the control yoke forward and skipped down its northern side. The steep, forty degree incline did little damage but little to reduce her speed, either.

Fortunately, the enemy pilot figured he had done enough and honourably discontinued his pursuit.

This left Baines alone, attempting to coax the forces of physics to favour her. The mountain must have been about 2000 metres in height, so she had a few precious seconds before she reached the bottom. Her shuddering, bone shattering descent began to slow, as crack after deafening crack veered the little ship to the left. Baines knew that if she rolled, she had had it. The cracking and crashing was the sound of snapping tree trunks and it grew with every passing second – she was hitting the tree line. As long as the trees were not too big, this action should arrest her speed, making it possible for the ship to come to rest, hopefully in one piece. For one moment, she began to hope. "Come on, come *on* – slow down, please, come o—"

Nothingness…

Douglas saw the fire-fight overhead and scrambled up a rocky bluff to get a better view. In the light of the tracer bullets, he could make out one of his own lifeboats from the *New World*. The pilot was putting on a hell of a show, but ultimately was impossibly overmatched.

"Jill?" he guessed. The sudden explosion vibrated through the stone on which he stood. "Oh, God, no!"

Powerless, he watched the escape pod's engines flower red, losing all propulsion along with chunks of superstructure. The hit was not devastating, but without engines, it may as well have been. The little craft began its descent between two peaks.

Having done its worst, the fighter circled back toward the ruin of the enemy's encampment.

Douglas followed it with his glare, clenching his teeth in anger, but at least he had a heading to follow and no time to lose. With the stars and a new moon to light his way he climbed toward the gap in the mountains. The show in the night sky would probably cow the wildlife for a while and he had to make the most of that time.

Major White made his way towards manufacturing to meet with Jim Miller and his technicians. There would be no rest on the Pod this night. His mind was far away, full of concerns for his friends. In a distracted state, he turned a corner and walked straight into Ms Cocksedge, knocking her sprawling in his haste.

"Oh wow, I'm real sorry, ma'am," he said, instinctively bending to help her up. "My bad. I was totally in a world of my own." He could hear other footsteps approaching from further up the corridor. Cocksedge heard them too. Now on her knees, she gave White a spiteful smile and palmed herself hard in the nose. Blood spurted all over her face and blouse as she threw herself to the deck.

"What's going on here?" shouted a booming male voice.

White turned to see Burnstein Snr, his wife and another couple from the so-called 'paid seats' round the corner.

"We collided..." White spoke, not quite sure what *was* happening.

"He punched me to the ground!" shouted Cocksedge, eyeing him triumphantly before bursting into tears.

Chelsea Burnstein ran to help the poor victim. Hank Burnstein looked at White with surprise but not anger. The other couple helped Cocksedge to her feet, fawning over the injured party.

White finally found his voice. "That's a complete lie!" he shouted, utterly outraged.

"You're supposed to protect us!" Chelsea rounded on him. "You men are all the same! Always using your power to bully everyone – especially women. You should be ashamed!"

"Wha—?" asked White, unable to fully grasp what was happening. He looked to her husband. "You can't believe this, Hank?"

Burnstein evaluated White for a moment. "So what do *you* say happened, Major?" he asked finally, in thoughtful tones.

White sputtered. "We... we just collided. I mean, I was walking quickly and she was coming from the other direction around the corner and we bumped into one another. I apologised, naturally shocked that I'd accidentally knocked her down, and I bent to help. Just as I was reaching down, she hit herself in the face and threw herself to the floor. Then you were all here and—"

"Liar!" spat Cocksedge. She turned to face the other women. "He punched me to the ground – obviously he didn't like what I was saying earlier this evening, about the military taking us down a road to ruin and trampling all over our rights. Looks like I must have hit pretty close to the mark, wouldn't you say?" She held a handkerchief to her bloody nose and glared at the major.

White searched his pockets and found his comm. "White to Doc Flannigan."

"Flannigan here. Go ahead, Major."

"Dave, can you treat Ms Cocksedge for a minor injury, please? She'll be in her quarters directly. She has punched herself in the face and I'm not entirely sure she's in her right mind."

"How dare you! You're not going to cover this up, Major White. I'm going to make sure everybody knows what you've done here," Cocksedge seethed.

"I'm sure you will," White replied coldly. "Please be sure to let me know which of them believe you. Now if you'll excuse me, we have lives to save."

"Would these be more lives you and your violent ways have put in harm's way?" Mrs Burnstein asked accusingly.

"Chelsea!" Burnstein warned.

"Oh that's right, we'd better all do as we're told, hadn't we? Or we'll get another beating," she rounded on her husband. "Now everyone has to live under the threat of violence, huh? Forever? Nothing changes!"

Cocksedge's eyes glittered from behind her handkerchief. She could not believe how well this was going. The other woman seemed less convinced. Major White had always been popular, so this was to be expected. She would invite both ladies back to her apartment and work on them and they would in turn work on their men and before they knew it, they would all be voting again – for her.

Jim Miller checked the ship's chrono. "OK folks, Ford must have been held up. We'll just have to proceed and he can catch up. We've got a provisional list of equipment here which will need to be loaded onto lorries, ready for transport to the *New World*'s crash site."

This statement caused a big stir.

Miller blinked. "Haven't you been told?"

Clearly the news had not reached everyone yet. Jim quickly told them the little he knew before assigning work. "The most important task, at the moment, is getting the bulldozer's cab secured. We are going to have to shove our way through who knows what to reach them – especially after the recent hurricane. The tracks between the forests are going to be littered with debris."

Jim spotted his daughter with her boyfriend, Henry – Burnstein's lad. She was trying to attract his attention. He frowned. "Right, everyone. Are there any questions? OK, we'd better crack on then. This is going to be a busy night."

The group broke up and were quickly about their assignments.

Miller beckoned Rose to him. "What is it, sweetheart? I'm a bit busy at the mo—"

"Dad, it's Major White!"

"Ford? What's happened?"

"He beat up Ms Cocksedge," supplied Henry.

"*What*?!"

The young man nodded seriously.

"That's only what that woman said," Rose objected. "She's obviously lying."

"My mother saw it happen," Henry argued, not willing to be swayed.

"Ford beat up a *woman*?" asked Jim, astonished.

"*Allegedly*," Rose stated scornfully.

"Rubbish!" said Jim.

"No, sir," Henry confirmed. "Ma saw it happen."

"I'm sorry, Henry," said Jim, "but there must be something else going on here. I cannot imagine Major White ever—" His comm beeped, interrupting him. He held up his hand to forestall the teenagers' comments. "Miller."

"*Jim, it's Sarah. We've got a situation here. Can you make your way to embarkation please? It's real important.*"

"Give me a few minutes, Sarah. I need to make sure the work is going as planned – we don't have long before we have to go out to rescue the *New World.*"

"I know, Jim. I'm sorry but come as soon as you can. Ford is in trouble, people are calling for his arrest. This is bad, and guess who's at the bottom of it?"

Jim whished. "I can guess. Be with you ASAP – out."

Henry looked satisfied. Rose looked furious.

The tracked and armoured personnel carrier smashed its way through the brush and detritus left by the stampede. O'Brien drove what she seemed to regard as her 'new wheels', using infrared cameras to find her way. The four-wheel-drive truck, dropped from the *New World* for Thomas' team, lumbered and crashed after them. The two disparate vehicles were joined push-me-pull-you style, by a five metre, telescopic tow-pole. So far they had used this technique to great effect, keeping momentum even through the boggiest of forest bed.

After about a mile they slowed. Ahead were the heat signatures of several bodies, slowly cooling. O'Brien gave Thomas a click through the comm, warning him she intended to stop. Upon receiving his answering click, she pulled up, staring solemnly at her screen.

"Commander," she said quietly, summoning Gleeson to the cab.

"What is it?" he asked, equally quietly.

"Human. Cooling. I think it's…" she left the sentence hanging.

"Jane Ross," he completed, in little more than a murmur. Taking a deep breath, he said, "Wait here, Corporal. I'll take Jones and have a look."

As Gleeson and Jones stepped out of the rear hatch of the tracked vehicle, Thomas jumped down from the passenger's door of the truck behind. "Trouble?" he asked.

"We lost Ross on our approach to the enemy camp. We may have just found her," Gleeson answered, nodding for Thomas to follow them.

They walked ahead of the vehicles. Using night vision goggles, they made their way carefully along the thoroughfare created by the stampede, little more than an hour ago. There were numerous boulders across the route at this point and several bodies lay scattered across the new game trail they had created. Clearly many creatures had come to grief upon these unexpected obstacles during their twilight charge.

"Commander," called Jones. He had found the remains of one of their homemade tracker bikes, the front wheel and forks completely mangled in a pothole between two large stones.

"OK," said Gleeson. "She can't be far."

"Sir," Thomas beckoned.

Gleeson and Jones jogged the seven or eight metres between them to see what he had found.

"Oh no," said Jones.

Gleeson merely put his head in his hands, exhaling loudly.

"I take it this is Ross, sir?" asked Thomas, unable to recognise the remains. Although certainly human and partially clothed, their identity was unclear.

"She's wearing our fatigues and Jones just found what was left of her bike over there," he pointed vaguely behind him. "We must assume so. We can't leave her here like this."

The body had already been partially pulled apart by scavengers. It was impossible to recognise the young woman's face. Thomas nodded and strode back to his vehicle, returning a few moments later with a body bag and some extra help. "We came prepared," he said simply. He placed a comradely hand on Gleeson's shoulder. "Why don't you leave this to us, sir? She'll be treated gently and with respect. Maybe you and Jones could salvage the bike, perhaps?" he added kindly.

Gleeson nodded dumbly and walked away towards the wreck. Jones lingered a moment longer and saluted the body before following him.

Two minutes later they were back inside the armoured people carrier. Their hostage had awoken while they were outside. He was still tied at the hands and under the watchful eye of Davies, who had his damaged ankle raised and a stun pistol aimed at the enemy soldier.

"What's your name?" Gleeson asked, bitterly.

The man stared angrily back at him. "Let me go, you scum!"

Gleeson bent slightly to roundhouse punch the man in the face, smacking his head against the bulkhead and rendering him unconscious once more. "Hang it all! That conversation can wait 'til I'm in a better mood," he said, stepping past the slumped form on his way back to the cab.

The vehicles continued back along the trail, heading for the river ford. No banter or cheer remained for their hard-won success and only the mournful dirge of the diesel engine broke the peace.

"Listen, I'm going to have to take the other lifeboat and find her," said Singh. He had been pacing the bridge for about half an hour, completely unable to get down to any of the vital work which was required of him.

Patricia placed a comforting hand on his arm. "Sandip, she ordered you to begin checking the ship over," she reminded him.

"She's gone down, I just know it! I can't just leave her out there! I have to go. This is just a ship, just a *thing* – we need Captain Baines—"

"*You can't leave the ship,*" Hiro retorted via the ship-wide, open comm channel. "*Not at a time like this! Wherever the Captain is, she needs us to fix Sekai—*"

"Damn you and your bloody Sekai!" snapped Singh, lashing out in his frustration. "She's more important than getting this broken down heap running! Besides, all the repairs will still be here to do tomorrow, Jill might not be!"

"Captain!" Tim shouted across the bridge, storming towards Singh. The Indian Lieutenant looked at him askance. "That's right, Captain!" Tim repeated.

Patricia gave her son a look of puzzlement. "We're talking about the capt—" she began.

"You *are* the captain," the teenager cut across her harshly, prodding Singh in the chest. "If we're to live, we all need the *New World* and we need you, *here*, now more than ever, *Captain.*"

"*The boy's right, Sandy,*" said Hiro. "*You can't leave the ship like this, Captain Singh. Now, what are your orders, sir?*"

Singh knew he had been trapped, expertly. What made it worse was that the trap had been set by a kid barely out of school. He gave Tim an exasperated shake of the head but nevertheless patted his arm in a comradely fashion. "OK. We continue with the full damage report. Once we're sure that the hull has not been breached, and we're safe from the wildlife, we begin an intensive inspection of the section where the shell struck us. If we're quick, we may be able to add a few extra items to the delivery list before the Pod crew set off on their first run over here at dawn.

"It's going to take them a long while to reach us the first time, as they're going to have to create a new roadway. Anything we can add to this first drop will speed our progress dramatically – so let's all get to it, people," he said, his confidence growing as he gave them direction. "I'll solicit advice from Major White about Captain Baines – maybe he'll have the manpower to send out a search party."

"Are you all outta your Goddamned minds?!" bellowed Burnstein. "We're in the middle of a war here! We don't know what the hell is going on out there and you wanna arrest the only senior soldier we've got left to protect us, because some chick says he beat on her? Can't this wait?!"

"Mr Burnstein is right... *sort of,*" agreed Mother Sarah. "I can't believe there is one word of truth in this allegation, but even if there were, this most assuredly is not the time."

"Absolutely right," added Patel. "We are all in terrible danger. The enemy could still strike at us any minute. Major White is our only hope and I, for one, trust him implicitly!"

White, in as much as it was possible for a senior military man, slouched. He felt like the adolescent Mapusaurus that invaded the Pod a week ago, completely at a loss to understand or defend himself from these pygmy aggressors. Sarah watched him with growing concern and was about to speak again when Cocksedge stepped forward.

"People of the *New World*," she addressed them, grandly. "The way I see it, we have to down arms, not *escalate* this struggle. We have been told there is an enemy – how do we know they are our enemy? All I see is a world full of monsters. Surely, the few humans on this planet should not be fighting one another."

"They're animals, not monsters, you stupid cow!" Natalie Pearson was on her feet, red in the face, quite uncharacteristically enraged. "The only monster in here is the one trying to turn us all against one another, and this man, Major Ford White, has never done anything but risk his life to help us, over and over again!"

"*If* I could finish," said Cocksedge, speaking over the zoologist's outburst. "The military," she glared pointedly at Patel and Sarah, "and their sycophants, have made a shocking mess of this whole situation from the very beginning. It was people like them who caused the attack in the first place, in all likelihood, by not allowing these people a voice. Is it any wonder the disenfranchised turned to such extreme measures to make their point when the system always ignores them so freely?"

The councillors heard a depressing number of 'hear hears' from the crowd.

Burnstein was aghast. "What the *f*—"

"Funnily enough," Sarah shouted above the growing din, "Captain Douglas was dead set against the military being in control of this mission from the start. Hardly the actions of a power-crazy despot! We – all of us – *forced* him to be part of the leading council. Why? Because we needed his knowledge, strength and experience if we were to stand even a cat in hell's chance of surviving our predicament, that's why. We all voted for him—"

"Not all..." interjected Cocksedge.

Sarah raised her eyebrows. *So she was the one who didn't vote for James*, she thought. *I always assumed it was Burnstein – just shows how wrong you can be.* "An overwhelming, democratic majority voted for him and he never let us down – never once! He sacrificed himself for us – does anyone doubt this? And *he* was a military man!"

"He certainly was a military man," Cocksedge rejoindered. "He practically started a war to save the life of one of his own, the then *Commander* Baines. He never stopped to consider the ramifications for the civilian populace—"

Burnstein rose to his feet again. "What the *f*—"

"Furthermore," continued Mother Sarah, unperturbed by either outburst, "these people you are suggesting we lay down our arms before, these 'disenfranchised' as you call them, are a bunch of super-wealthy

Nazis bent on erasing the human race from time, so they can set up a new civilisation for their buddies!"

"You are confusing two issues there," Cocksedge bit back. "The first is that we only 'know' this," she emphasised the word using good old inverted comma bunnies, "because the military told us it was so. The second is that, if the other people are indeed militaristic, and we have no hard proof of that yet—"

"They sent a *warship*!" someone roared.

"This is a dangerous place," she deflected. "They have a right to protect themselves. But if they are militaristic, then surely setting one military against another can only ever result in a single outcome. It's peace we need, not another war!"

Sarah was flabbergasted. "You're suggesting that fighting back against an unprovoked attack is somehow wrong?! We should just let them kill us? Or at least all the folks here who aren't on their 'friends' list?"

"I'm *suggesting* that soldiers only know how to hurt people. Major White proved that earlier by attacking me, simply because he had not the wit to counter my arguments in a civilised manner." A low, disgruntled murmur rolled through the crowd. "Maybe we *should* 'turn the other cheek', *Mother* Sarah – at least until we know their intentions. Isn't that what the Bible teaches us?"

"God teaches us to forgive those who trespass against us, he does not advocate standing idly by while innocents are put to the slaughter! Evil must be faced and stopped!"

Cocksedge raised her voice once more to cut through the hubbub. "I'm simply saying that we haven't explored *any* peaceful options with the strangers yet," she stated, reasonably. "The strangers whom *we* attacked!"

"What the *f*—"

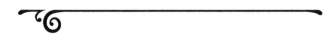

First light. Schultz sat atop the bank throwing stones at the wreckage in the valley below. Her hatred was such that she could barely rein it in. Her every nerve ending wished to dole out summary executions to the incompetent fools around her. She breathed deeply, twisting the ring-pull on a can of German beer, salvaged from the ruined ship.

Ring-pull design had evolved specifically to eradicate the need to separate them from the can. She twisted it further, until metal fatigue caused it to snap, then flung it down the embankment into a tree, against all the odds, still standing after last night's disaster. The tiny piece of machined metal fell through the canopy, sticking fast in a flow of resin seeping from one the larger branches...

...I will kill them all for this outrage, she thought, vengefully.

Meritus kept his distance. It was all he could do not to execute her on the spot for incompetence. Were it not for the chance that the other ships in the Dawn Fleet might still pick up their beacon and find them, he would have.

Incensed, he raged in the privacy of his own mind. *A spineless people, she said. Leaderless without Douglas, she said – Pah! And where is Douglas? Gone! Our key into the* New World, *and more importantly, its Pod, has escaped. We still have Lloyd, of course – the man seems indestructible – but he's a minor player. I need Douglas.*

However, at that moment, he knew that what they really needed was to gather themselves and count their losses. The *Last Word*'s complement stood at 156 men and women before the catastrophe. Schultz had brought another eight with her, including herself and excluding Douglas. Sixty-one of them had been killed last night, plus another twenty-seven seriously injured, either in the ship's destruction or during the stampede prior to it.

Their ability to make war had been seriously curtailed. They retained three of four tracked personnel carriers, of which only one was armed; one only, of their three orbital attack ships survived; they still had the shuttle captured from the *New World* and whatever hand weapons the survivors carried with them.

He still had teams exploring the dangerous wreck below, in the hope of ascertaining what else, if anything, could be salvaged.

Meritus stared east, wondering what fate had befallen the *New World*. He was pretty certain the shell he fired had found its mark; it would have been virtually impossible to miss from that range and with the angle he had when the ship turned over. Had he destroyed her? He hoped not – but what else could he have done under the circumstances? It looked like the end of the mission and very probably the end of them. He had to lash out. Now, things were changed. Salvaging her would be his only chance to get free of the Schultzes' insanity and begin again – his way.

He glared at Heidi's back, as she sat throwing stones down upon the wreck of his ship – *his* ship! Meritus took his sidearm from its holster and checked the clip. With an almost superhuman effort he returned it to its holster once more. He watched her for a few extra silent moments, his loathing concentrated to a single point, like magnified sunlight on a leaf. *Your days are numbered, my girl*, he thought.

Douglas awoke. Having walked through much of the night, he eventually succumbed to fatigue just before the dawn. Looking at the sun, he guessed he had slept two, maybe three hours? Four metres above the ground and in the arms of his conveniently shaped cradle, half way up a tree, he stretched awkwardly. How he had slept in that position he would never know, he thought, as he rubbed his neck – absolute exhaustion and depression he supposed. Still, no time for that now, whoever had crashed that ship needed him. He was probably the only human soul who saw where it went down.

Shaking himself out of this torpor was easier than expected. It is remarkable how quickly the effects of sleep evaporate when one awakens covered in scorpions the size of chihuahuas. He stood, shaking and batting himself mercilessly, before half scrambling, half jumping from his tree.

"Get with the programme, Douglas, you're no' camped out in the borders now, laddie!" he chuntered to himself.

Making his way to the top of the ridge where he had spent the night, he stood, he surveyed... he needed the loo. Stranded in a jungle full of dinosaurs, he knew he would never take the simple lavatory/cubicle ensemble for granted again.

From his vantage point, he could see the twin peaks the escape pod had passed the previous evening and after a brief *discomfort* break, he set off towards the gap between them.

It was a hard march, especially in the rising heat of the day. He came across a stream of crystal clear water en route and was able to, very basically, wash himself and drink his fill. Unfortunately, he had no means of carrying water with him, so he would become thirsty again fairly quickly.

The peaks were mostly bare rock. There were clearly seams of rusty iron running through them and just a few tenacious bushes and plants which clung to life within the crevasses, breaking up the largely grey with green. The shoulder between the two peaks was fairly peaty and covered in low-growing scrub and ferns. He smashed his way through, finally cresting the top.

The valley below was forested, rising again to the north. The mountain before him topped out below his current vantage point, its summit more rounded than the one on which he stood. It was the largest of a rolling set of hills which appeared to fill the heart of a huge circle of rocky pinnacles, like dragon's teeth.

Or killer dinosaur teeth, thought Douglas, darkly. *The crash site must be hidden the other side of that mountain.*

He had carefully observed the angle taken by the little craft, after it navigated between the peaks. The course must have either crashed it *into* the mountain opposite, or allowed it to slide down the other side. There was no sign of a crash site that he could see, so he hoped for the latter. If the other side had a good long slope, the pilot may have survived, assuming they gauged their descent correctly. All ifs and maybes, he knew, but judging by the dogfight he had witnessed, whoever it was knew how to fly.

Douglas shook his head. He was not sure how, but he knew it was Jill Baines. Who else would have tried something that crazy, obviously looking for him? Who else would have attacked the *Last Word* at all? He scratched his stubble. "Ah hope she's alright," he said, setting off down into the valley.

Light…? Or perhaps it would be more accurate to say, less dark.

Movement...? Maybe. Baines could not open her eyes. Everything hurt. A weight pressed down on her chest and she groaned as the darkness swallowed her once more.

Light. Black graded to red. She was now looking; this was an improvement, even if her view was merely the back of her eyelids. Awareness returned. The weight on her chest was gone. She was not fully cognisant of where she was. Vaguely, she checked for her side arm – it seemed a sensible place to start. It was gone.

Heaving herself into a more upright sitting position, the room, if indeed it was a room, spun madly, causing her to once again collapse into unconsciousness.

Light. This time she was sure, it was definitely sunlight. A rustling...? Yes, definitely. Someone was checking her pockets. "Hey!" she cried out.

"Hush now, remain calm," someone said, and that *someone* sounded male and pretty old.

"The hell I will. Who *are* you? What happened? You're robbing me?!"

"Questions, questions," said an irritatingly calm voice. "I'm trying to help you. Please keep still a moment longer."

"Where's my gun?"

"We have it—"

"*We?*"

"Please calm yourself, Jill," this second voice was certainly female and also sounded elderly.

"You know me?"

"Oh yes," said the man. "We remember you. Well, I do. Now, we're going to try and move you onto this stretcher. Bear with us, we're a bit creaky these days," he chuckled.

With a little help from Baines, the old man and woman managed to slide her onto the stretcher. With great effort, they lifted and stepped out of the wrecked lifeboat.

Once outside, Baines could see the trench her craft had carved down the hillside, before finally crashing into a small copse. The main tree line began lower down the slope. She had been lucky. Those trees were much larger – had she hit those first, her vessel would have been smashed to pieces and her with it.

Lowering Baines to the ground, the man threw a rucksack around his shoulders. Lifting her once more, they set off, slowly and carefully down the slope towards what appeared to be a long, low hill, covered with dense foliage. Baines felt guilty, being carried by a couple of pensioners, even if they had stolen her treat bars from the lifeboat's emergency rations. However, flitting as she was between consciousness and oblivion, she remembered little else of the journey.

When she awoke again, it was to a shock – she was alone and lying in a comfortable bed within the *New World*'s infirmary. "What the hell?" was all she could manage. Then she began to note little differences, small things at first; the position of a console on the wall, the orientation of the scanner bed. Flannigan never moved his sickbay around, always extolling the virtues of being able to put his hands on things, even in the pitch black. He had been tested and proven correct on several occasions recently, but Baines was perplexed – how could this be?

The hatch leading from the corridor hissed gently open, admitting the old man into sickbay. Seeing that she was awake, he approached with his hand out. "Hello again, Jill," he offered warmly. "It's been a long time, a very long time."

"Why, how long have I been out?"

The man chuckled lightly. She recognised that laugh and for the first time studied him closely. "Commander Morecombe *Hetfield*?" she asked incredulously.

He smiled, with just a hint of sadness. "Don't mind if I park my old bones, do you?" he asked, sitting on the side of her bed. "I'm seventy-eight, you know!"

"Mor? Is it really you? How is this possible? How come you weren't with the *Newfoundland*?"

He appeared a little uncertain about what to say. "But I was – am," he added, frowning. "You're aboard the *Newfoundland*, Jill."

"Ooooh," moaned Baines as the room began to spin again.

Douglas was moaning too. "A hundred million years ago, on the other side of the world, and Ah'm still taking the damned high road!" he grumbled and stumbled up the other side of the forested valley. "Damn but it's hot!"

He stopped to catch a breath and once still, he noticed the skittering sounds all around; just little cracking and rustling noises, as though several small creatures were running through the brush to encircle him. "Oh, *no!*" he whispered. Gently, very gently, he slid Lieutenant Hemmings' sidearm from his belt and removed the safety.

A small dinosaur, about the size of a spaniel, hopped from between the ferns and chirruped. Douglas slumped. Sighing with relief, he replaced the pistol's safety.

The little creature bobbed and swayed slightly, sniffing the air between them. It was clearly unsure what to make of him. Like a bald eagle, its head was scaly skin but, beginning from a brightly coloured ruff at its neck, the rest of the little body was covered in a fluffy plumage. Sticking out straight at the rear, the creature's stiff tail ran to scales again. In a bizarre way it put Douglas in mind of a double ended chicken drumstick. The feathers were a mixture of blues and aquamarines from the neck down to the rump, but the skin at the top of its neck was purple grading up into the reds and oranges which coloured its head. The tail was also russet with three distinct red circles near the tip. "Ah hope that doesnae make ye a third dan," said Douglas, smirking. He was about to replace his gun but the sound of his voice seemed to unnerve the little creature.

"Hey there," said Douglas, kindly. "Ah didnae mean to startle ye."

At about one and a half metres in length and maybe forty centimetres in height, it was certainly a striking, arguably even beautiful, little animal. Douglas approached very slowly, not wishing to frighten the dinosaur away. He need not have bothered. As he stepped closer, he noticed the impressive sickle-claw on the second toe of each foot. The animal tapped them on the earth, as if in agitation. Douglas tried desperately to recall Tim's dinosaur class. Frowning, he said, "Buitreraptor?"

Yes, he had it now. The young man had said that although small, these creatures were extremely... Before he finished the thought, the animal opened its jaws threateningly, suddenly revealing jagged rows of teeth – its reptilian eyes widening with a sudden look of murderous insanity. "Dangerous," he finished flatly, with the supplementary, "Oh, crap!"

"Woah!" he cried out involuntarily, stepping back. Worse still, he suddenly remembered the other part to Tim's warning, as this shocking change in behaviour heralded the arrival of six of the creature's mates – its pack.

Douglas, horrified by his abrupt change in circumstances, spun to take them all in as they encircled him. His mind wished he had Tim with him, to tell him what to do; his conscience glad the boy was safe elsewhere.

He expected an attack from all directions and was surprised when the dinosaurs suddenly regrouped further up the hill, in front of him. Then they were gone. A frantic rustle through the bushes and he was alone again.

"That was weird," he said, letting go a deep sigh of relief. Their rationale soon became clear when he heard the sliding, scraping sound, very definitely from behind him.

"Oh, crap!" his curse was but a whisper this time. He stood completely still, took a deep breath, let it out and dove. Basic training took over and, with the pistol still in his right hand he reached forward, rolling up his arm and across his shoulders to leap back to his feet facing back the way he had come. Bringing both arms up for a double-handed pistol grip, he fired.

When Baines came round again, Hetfield had been joined by the elderly woman who had helped carry her from the wreck.

"Take it easy, Jill," said Hetfield, helping her into a sitting position, while the woman buffed up her pillows. "You had a good beating in that crash. Aside from a nasty concussion, you've fractured your left tibia."

"My what?" Baines asked, groggily.

"Your left shin bone. Kelly set it for you."

"Kelly?"

"Forgive me, you haven't been introduced. Commander Jill Baines, please meet Dr Kelly Marston – palaeobotanist and the woman who actually found proof of time travel. Few people knew about the ring-pull—"

Baines shook the older woman's hand. "Actually, Mor, it's Captain Baines now and I do know about the beer can thing – James told me when we landed here," she said.

He brightened. "Congratulations!" he said, but as soon as he did, his smile faded. "When you left Canaveral, you were a commander. Does this field commission mean that Captain Douglas..." he did not finish the thought.

"He's alive," Baines placated him. "At least, he was last night."

Hetfield looked relieved. "I think you might benefit from some back story," he said.

"Er, *yeah*!" she answered sardonically.

The snake was vast. Partially coiled around the branch above, it could easily have been eight or even ten metres in length and thirty centimetres in girth. The head appeared less advanced than any snake Douglas had ever seen, its jaw line more basic. This interesting footnote was largely lost on the captain, however, diving as he was, for his life.

Not for the first time, Douglas screamed, completely unmanned by these often incredible, and even more often terrible, creatures. He rolled again and fired a second time. The snake lowered to the ground before rearing and opening its jaws wide in threat. The jaws did not hinge fully open, to swallow a Douglas sized creature, but this offered little comfort and he had little doubt that the bite would be devastating. Having no intention of being eaten, whole *or* in pieces, he fired again. The snake was clearly in pain, and very angry. It struck for him once more, but although Douglas was able to evade the lunge, the creature seemed to be all around him now and there was absolutely no doubt that it was an enormous constrictor. He knew he had to deal with this fast, so he fired for the head but between his diving and the snake's lunging, a killing shot eluded him.

Douglas stole a quick glance around, searching for an escape route. The moment's loss of concentration proved costly and the snake's tail slapped him to the ground from behind. Winded, Douglas rolled onto his back to stare up into the salivating maw of a giant reptilian head. As the jaws parted once more he fired six rounds into the creature's skull in rapid succession. He expected death throes, like something from a badly choreographed movie. What he got, was a hundred kilo dead-weight drop on him like a stone.

Douglas braced with his arms, to prevent his ribs from being crushed, but the blow knocked the breath from his body and pinned him to the ground.

For a moment he could not move.

Fighting for breath, eyes bulging, he managed to twist from under the huge bulk of this once magnificent creature to crawl away. The combination of being crushed coupled with extreme stress made him vomit. Coughing and retching, he scrabbled around for his gun. Unable to find it, he crawled back to the snake. Just peeking out from under the body was a pistol grip. He knelt against the side of the dead animal and heaved with all his might. The entire body must have weighed the better part of a ton. The gun was pinned.

He was about to try again when the snake's head turned and snapped at him, biting deep into his left arm. Douglas yelled out in agony and shock. Grabbing the firearm from the floor, he emptied the clip's remaining six rounds into the creature's face. This time it went down for good, but not before causing him serious injury.

His arm was bleeding copiously. He tore off his sleeve with his good arm and, using one hand and his teeth, managed to wrap a tourniquet around the damaged bicep.

Closing his eyes against the pain, he forced himself to his feet. Opening them again, he turned back to the slope he still had to face. The vicious little dinosaurs which ran from the snake had returned. "Och, not ye again!" He took two threatening steps towards them, shouting, "Awa' n' bile yer heed, damn ye!"

They ran.

Right, thought Douglas, *that worked* once – *time to obey my own orders and run for it.* "Eat that damned big ugly snake and stay the hell away from me ye little swines! Ye ken?"

With that, he resumed his climb.

Noon came and went as Jim Miller rode the first lorry behind the bulldozer. His driver was the Australian construction operative known as Bluey. Rose also travelled with him. He had wrestled with the decision to bring her along. He had no idea how much danger they were heading into. Unfortunately, he *did* know that the enemy survivors would be coming for the Pod and they would not be happy. Trapped between these unpalatable choices, he opted to have her with him – for better or worse they would be together. At least they had temporarily calmed down the preposterous situation with Major White and were able to leave him in charge, with the support of Mother Sarah, Dr Patel and the remaining military staff.

He suspected that Rose wanted a little break from Henry too. She had certainly been shocked by his attitude towards the major. Jim, reading between the lines, could understand how living under Burnstein Snr had affected him and why the lad had staunchly believed his mother. He was sure Mrs Burnstein would not lie about such a thing, especially after what she had no doubt been through, but people often saw what they wanted to see. Rose had pointed this out and Jim was proud of her perceptiveness in this regard, but it had not gone over well with Henry. *Ah well*, he thought. *What will be, will be.*

Since the disaster which led them all to this point, Jim had begun to notice a distance growing between his wife and himself, too. Although, maybe that was not strictly true, perhaps he was keeping *her* at arm's length. It saddened him. Their relationship had always been a one-way street, this was undeniable, but he could not help his feelings for her. He also feared her. She had the power to take his daughter away from him – at least, she used to have. That would no longer be possible in their new, necessarily streamlined society. As he pondered these mixed emotions, Rose grabbed his arm.

"Dad, look!"

He glanced down at the screen she was holding and shook his head ruefully. He was staring at a king's ransom.

The small, flat monitor on Rose's lap was connected wirelessly to scanning equipment situated on the cab's roof, just above their heads. The apparatus searched their surroundings, compiling a detailed record of the geology and flora through which they travelled. It was a similar, if simplified, version of the suite aboard the *New World*'s shuttle. Jim had reasoned that, if they had to make the trip, they may as well squeeze every piece of knowledge they could from it. Rose's screen showed a formation of quartz to their left. The strata reached from the surface down, many metres, and crushed in amongst the seams was gold – lots of it.

"Wow!" Jim exclaimed. "We're rich!"

"You're already rich, Dad."

"Ha – not any more. Maybe we could dig this little lot out and rebuild the Miller Empire, eh? What do you think, Bluey? Fancy jumping on the digger for a piece of the action?"

"How much gold is there?" asked the Australian.

"Ooh, about eight tons," replied Jim, casually.

Bluey shrugged. "Nah, I wouldn't get outta bed for that," he said, winking at Rose.

Rose laughed. "Will you come back for it though, Dad? When things get back to normal, I mean."

Both men laughed at that.

"*Normal?*" asked Bluey.

"I know," agreed Jim. "That's just what I was thinking!"

A colossal bang rocked the lorry, cracking the side window next to Jim's head. "What the— Aargh!" he suddenly screamed as the immense Tyrannotitan lunged again, its roar deafening at such close quarters, even within the cab. "Get us out of here!"

"How can I?" Bluey shouted back in terror. "We're jammed in, in front and behind – there's nowhere to go, mate! That's the same mongrel that tried to eat me last time, when The Sarge and Jonesy saved me down by the river. I recognise the scar on the ugly rooter's face!"

The titanic tyrant shoved the lorry again, attempting to turn them over to see if the underbelly was any softer. The vehicle was too heavy, even for this giant, but the people inside were shaken about like dice in a cup.

"*Dad!*" screamed Rose. "Do something!"

Miller gave his daughter a look of utter disbelief, but before he could begin to formulate an answer, a huge push from the bulldozer at the front of their train cleared the way for all four vehicles. They burst through the tree line onto the shores of a large lake. Bluey saw his opportunity and gunned the powerful motor to shoot around the side of the giant earthmover, leaving the Tyrannotitan to turn on the next vehicle in line. The lorry behind, and the personnel carrier behind that, also charged around the dozer in an attempt to flee the enraged carnivore.

The dinosaur gave chase to the last vehicle for about a hundred metres before eventually giving up. She slowed and roared across the water in frustration, having lost a couple of teeth in the encounter, but they would grow back. This watering hole was her territory and she could afford to wait for one of these new arrivals to make a mistake.

A mile further along the shore, half in and half out of the lake, was the vast bulk of the *New World*, scraped and battered but still shining mostly white in the sunlight.

"OK," said Hetfield. "After the *New World* disappeared, a reconnaissance mission was sent to her last known coordinates, as you'd expect. It found no sign of her – at first. After spending a few days sweeping the area they found some evidence that a wormhole *had* been created, along with a cloud of debris, so thinly spread that it was almost undetectable. The remains had been atomised.

"The samples they brought back were analysed thoroughly. As the evidence now suggested that the *New World* may have jumped elsewhere, Captain Bessel naturally started kicking up a fuss to go rescue her! You know how close he was with James Douglas."

"They were childhood friends," agreed Baines.

"Well, upon examination of the fragments, the egg-heads thought there was proof that the ship – your ship – had jumped through time, rather than space. Something to do with the fragments being smashed by extreme gravity or some such – it was all well above my pay grade. Anyhow, Bessel really got the bit between his teeth and kept pestering the chief of staff until he eventually got his way.

"Roughly six months after you vanished, a mission was drawn up to hunt you down. That's when things began to go wrong – for some of us, very wrong. It turned out the terrorists had influence over government and not just in the US, but globally. All sorts of public and private sector organisations seemed to have been infiltrated, at every level.

"The crew of the *Newfoundland* began to receive *visits*. Basically, it all came down to this – the *Newfoundland* was to find the *New World* and secure the factory Pod she carried. The team of marines who were to travel with us would undertake this task and *we* were to do anything and everything to assist – or there would be *consequences*."

Baines frowned. "What sort of consequences?"

"I was just twenty-eight back then, and unmarried. The youngest commander in the fleet," he added proudly, remembering. "Kelly here was thirty-four – she's my *older woman*."

He winked disgracefully and Baines laughed with the couple.

"Now, where was I?"

"You were unmarried," prompted Baines.

"Oh, yes. Right, so they began showing me holos of my parents and my brother's kids going about their daily routines – these were followed by threats against their lives. If I spoke out or failed to do as I was told, they would be murdered. The only crew member who didn't get a visit was Lieutenant Jansen – Audrey. She had no living family, you see. They held Bessel to ransom too, with his family, but you remember Arnold. He decided to fight back. He reasoned that after we'd left, they wouldn't know what the hell we were up to, so he'd try and stop 'em!

"He chafed for months leading up to the mission. We all tried to calm him down, afraid for our families, but he was a force to be reckoned with." The old man smiled with pride at the memory.

"So Captain Bessel was no traitor then," stated Baines, thoughtfully. "James was right – he said it could never be."

"What's this tale?" asked Hetfield, perplexed.

"Don't worry, Mor, I've got a quite a story for *you* too. But please continue."

The old man frowned. "OK," he said, slowly. "When we arrived in the past we calculated the leanest burn for a landing and figured you or your pilot would have worked along the same principles. What was your pilot's name again?"

"Lieutenant Singh. Sandip Singh."

"Yeah, forgive me – it was all such a long time ago."

"Not for me," said Baines, flatly.

"Of course," he agreed, kindly. "Right, so we landed and it was clear that you guys weren't here. We sent out messages all over the planet. It seemed pretty obvious that, if you *were* lost here, you would have been only too keen to respond, so the decision was made to move forward in time. That was when the trouble really started."

"What happened?"

"Bessel refused. He asked for the crew to support him but…" he tailed off, looking ashamed.

"You didn't?" Baines asked, guessing the answer.

"No," he admitted sadly.

"We were all too afraid for our families," said Kelly. "The soldiers they sent with us were brutal, too. We couldn't understand how they even came to be selected for a rescue mission at first. Of course, it all came out later. You see, they were all trusted and highly decorated men and women. We believed, and still believe, that something happened to them in the Middle East."

"What were they doing *there*?" asked Baines.

"Looking for the base that launched the black warship," replied Marston, staring down her personal past. She shook her head, also reliving the memories. "That was a worrying time. An extremely advanced battleship took off from the Middle East – no one knew who owned it or who was on it, or what their intentions were."

Baines dragged her hands slowly down her face, releasing a deep breath. "Oh my God. And this was fifty years ago, give or take?" she asked, feeling like the universe was unravelling.

Hetfield nodded. "What's wrong?" he asked.

"Nothing, I'll tell you in a minute. Please continue, Kelly. These marines, you say?"

"Yes," continued Marston, "we thought they must have been altered somehow – psychotropic drugs or some kind of deep hypnosis, perhaps. We never did find out for sure. Anyhow, they were pretty terrifying to live with."

"Yeah, but the captain wasn't afraid," said Hetfield, taking up the story once more. "Arnold decided he was going no further and he wouldn't allow them to get back to tell any tales, either. It was a hard decision for him. You see, to save his and all of our families, he had to maroon *us – his crew* – here."

"What did he do?" asked Baines.

"We didn't know at first. He took Audrey Jansen with him and left the ship in a small four by four. The bad guys chased them down, I guess, but we never found out what happened to them," he admitted, sadly.

"Actually, I can help you there," said Baines. "We found a fossilised tyre track, not far from here. It had been left twenty million years ago and under it, in the rock, were Bessel and Jansen. Their fossilised remains, anyway." Seeing the sadness in their faces, she added, "I'm sorry. They had been buried there all those ages already, by the time we arrived. It was quite a puzzle I can tell you – especially as *we* left home *first*."

Hetfield and Marston looked at one another with great weariness. Such a vibrant couple, for the first time they seemed their age. "So they killed them then," said Hetfield, at last. "We feared that was the case."

"Possibly, we were unable to ascertain an exact cause of death from the fossils," explained Baines.

The old man let out a great sigh and then cheered slightly. "And now you've been picked up by a couple o' living fossils, huh?"

"You speak for yourself, Mor," Marston corrected him.

"Hey, I'm younger than you, my girl," he teased.

Baines smiled at them again. "Did any of you have children?" she asked.

"No," said Marston. "Everyone who undertook the mission was surgically sterilised – no exceptions." She saw Baines' look of surprise and added, "Not permanently, but the procedure could only have been reversed once we returned to our own time. We had neither the knowledge, nor the equipment to undo it here. This was deliberate of course, the mission planners were protecting the timeline as much as possible – they couldn't have us churning out even more people, millions of years too early, after all! We all agreed. We believed in the rescue mission, despite the threats we were working under."

Baines was puzzled. "But that was twenty million years ago. How did the *Newfoundland* arrive here and *now*?" she asked.

"When the search parties came back without the captain or Lieutenant Jansen, we assumed the worst. One of their men was a pilot, so we left and hopped forward in search of the *New World*. That's when we found out what Arnold and Audrey had done. They had sabotaged the ship."

"That's right," said Hetfield, taking up the baton once more. "After the ship jumped and arrived here, almost fifty years ago, the wormhole drive exploded and so did her main drives. Arnold had left us control of the thrusters, so we were able to land safely, but she would never fly again. Not far anyway. We carried a search and rescue Pod with us, which we still have, under all the jungle which has grown over us. As you know, they were much smaller than the Mars Pod you carried. We had none of the manufacturing capability or knowhow that was aboard the *New World*. We were stuck – forever."

"So what happened to the marines?" Baines asked, feeling a little nervous for the first time.

"Oh, they died," said Marston. "Most of them a long time ago, now. We buried the last one two years ago." A small tear ran down her cheek and she wiped it away.

"You stayed with them all those years?" asked Baines.

"Where else was there to go?" replied Hetfield. "Besides, after a few months they began to change. Like we said, they had been altered somehow and whatever was done to them began to undo itself. There were thirty three of us back then, all stuck here, together. Sadly, eighteen of us died in a single incident. We took an expedition up on top of the mountains encircling us here, to take a look at our world. When we descended to the plains in the south, we were attacked. A single animal – God knows what it was, one of the big ones that look like T Rex. It killed them all. They shot at it, of course – would have been the height of rudeness not to! But they couldn't stop it before it got them. I was the only survivor, and I was in a hell of a state by the time I found my way back here, I can tell you."

He squeezed Marston's hand. "Kelly nursed me and saved me – brought me back. That was when she fell madly in love with me."

Marston slapped his shoulder, scandalised, and Hetfield winked again, as only a cheeky old man can.

"So what did the sixteen of you do?"

"We buried the hatchet, of course. This place is deadly enough. We certainly couldn't afford squabbles – righteous or otherwise. No, these were the lives we were given and the cards we were dealt and all we could do after that was survive."

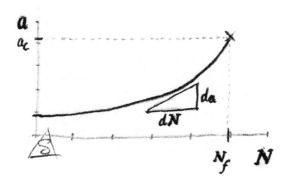

Chapter 9 | Splinter

"Your face still looks bruised, Ms Cocksedge." Chelsea Burnstein appeared full of concern as she leaned forward to help herself to another biscuit from the coffee table.

"Call me Alison, please, Mrs Burnstein," Cocksedge oozed.

"And you must call me Chelsea. In fact I insist – I wish I'd never heard that name."

"But you have two lovely children from your marriage, Chelsea."

"Yes, I've done everything I can to protect Henry and Clarrie, but they are getting to the age where they won't need me much longer. Especially now we're here. I guess it took me this long to recognise that *his* hold over us is finally broken."

"What made you realise?" asked Cocksedge, eagerly.

"You did," replied Chelsea Burnstein, frankly. "The way you stood up to that man and all the military – stood up for our rights. It was just great. I realised right then that I should follow you and hang the consequences. Hank can't hurt the kids here – he has no real power over them. You see, back home, he was one of the richest men in the world and no one, not even the president wanted to get on his bad side. Here, he's nothing. We're free of him and there are people willing to protect us from his kind."

Dangerous territory, thought Cocksedge. *I don't want her to realise that the people I'm up against are actually the ones she's relying on for protection. Better not let her think too deeply on the details. I'll just pour more fuel on the fire – she clearly has years of anger to burn.* "I'm very grateful for your support, Chelsea," she said instead. "I swear that I will stand up for all of our rights and not let these *men* of violence control our destinies. I believe we can make peace with the other people, if we're just willing to listen to their concerns and work with them to create a fairer, more equal society for all of us here."

"The attack ship has reported back from orbit, sir," said a young officer at the science station on the shuttle's bridge.

Meritus had made the stolen shuttle his temporary headquarters since the battle. He nodded to the lieutenant. "Go ahead."

"We have telemetry for the *New World*, sir, but what's most interesting is that she's separated from the Manufacturing Pod – seems to have crashed in a lake some six miles away from it." He turned to Meritus. "Details are still coming in but we have photographs of an expeditionary force leaving the Pod, presumably to assist the ship, sir."

Now, that is *interesting*, thought Meritus.

"Sir," the lieutenant spoke again. "Are we going to make them pay for what they've done to us and our mission, sir?"

Meritus placed a hand on the young man's shoulder. "*We* are going to take that Pod and anyone who stands in our way will be destroyed. We still have more than enough firepower to bring them to their knees and that's what we're going to do."

"And the civilians, sir?"

"Our original mission parameters still stand, Lieutenant. We save only the people we need or fit our profile. As for the others…"

The young lieutenant smiled nastily. "Yes, sir. Thank you, sir."

"Hey! Son of Captain America!" Woodsey shouted across embarkation.

Henry turned away from the porthole to which he appeared to have glued himself, to see his friend trot across the large space between them. "I thought you were helping your old man?" he asked.

"Nah, mate. I think I was doin' his head in," Woodsey laughed. "What are you doing in here? Mooning after Rose? She'll be back in a few days, mate."

"Yeah," replied Henry, moodily.

"Wassup? She chucked you already?"

Henry frowned. "No! At least, I don't think so. I mean, she hasn't said... Do *you* think she's broken up with me? She's broken up with me, hasn't she?! Would you believe it! Like it was my fault my mother saw that major beat on the British woman!"

"Eh?" asked Woodsey, for once at a loss.

Henry pulled out his comm.

"What are you doing?" he asked.

"I'm ditching her before she can ditch me!" snapped Henry.

"I thought you said she'd already given you the sack?"

"Well, I'm not sure, am I? They don't tell you things like that, you know."

Woodsey's head spun. "Woah! Slow down there, cowboy! You don't know if she's chucked you, so you're dumping her just in case? You know that's crazy, right? What actually happened and what did she say?"

"Not much, you know women."

Woodsey's brow furrowed. "Yeah, er... do I? Look, dude, I'm not really sure what you're talking about, but Rose and Tim are out there at the moment. It could be really bad and if something did happen, you'd never forgive yourself, mate. We're all split up enough as it is and no one seems to know what's going to happen."

Henry paused, message unsent. "Clarrie *has* been hard to handle since Tim went off in the *New World*. I doubt she'd ever get over it if something happened to him. When we got news they'd crashed, she… well, you know what kids are like, right?"

Woodsey looked thoughtful. "Yeah, besides, I've kinda gotten used to having the gangly Pom around myself, but what would *you* do if something happened to Rose?"

"You think I might be overreacting?" asked Henry.

"Yeah, like a big *woman*. Meanwhile, Rose is out there toughing it out and 'being a man'. As you Yanks like to say – who knew!"

Douglas reached the top without further incident, but he was weakening. His arm still bled, despite his rough care of the wound, and he had not eaten in over twenty-four hours. Fortunately, the rounded pate of the mountain was fairly easy to traverse. As he reached the far side he was both pleased and filled with trepidation by what he saw.

A hundred metres or so below him, there began a deep furrow in the mountainside. The wide, brown swathe had clearly been cut through the ferns by a crashing vessel. A further half kilometre down the slope, the gouge disappeared into a small wooded area. He could see something white, almost twinkling, as it caught the sun's rays which pierced the gently swaying canopy. Hoping for the best, he pressed on, mercifully now downhill.

He reached the trough created by the crash in just a few minutes. Climbing down into it, he found its base almost perfectly smooth. "A road!" he said with satisfaction and followed it down to the small copse where he hoped to find the lifeboat.

About thirty metres away he could clearly see that it was indeed one of his escape pods. He dropped to his belly as he also spotted something less welcome. A stab of pain from his arm made him wince but it was a small price to pay.

Sniffing around on the hillside, about a hundred metres to the west, was a dinosaur. It was not a giant, like the Mapusaurus he had become familiar with, but whatever it was, was shaped along depressingly similar lines. Douglas had noted well that the adolescent Mapusaurus were anatomically quite different from the adults. Their heads were much smaller, proportionally and literally; they were more 'leggy' and much shallower in the draught. They seemed a lot more fleet of foot, too, which he supposed was logical given their lighter build and proportionally longer legs. However, their skin colours and tones were very similar to the adults. Perhaps the reds were not quite as vibrant as they were in the mature males, but they were certainly recognisable – *all too* recognisable, to Douglas' mind. The animal before him was similar but definitely not the same. Its snout was longer but its head not as deep as Mapusaurus. He had, as yet, not been up close and personal to any Giganotosaurus, but the colouration on this animal was quite different, anyhow. The monster that had forced him to hide under his own shuttle the night before had been of a completely different shape – a fact discernible even in such low light. The creature before him had no sail across its back and its head was less crocodile and more characteristically dinosaur.

He rubbed his eyes tiredly. He was hurt, he was exhausted and he was alone. Although he could not recognise this animal, Tim's crash course in dinosaur anatomy still served him well. It was a theropod, with a large head, damned big teeth and it was an order of magnitude bigger than him. What else could he possibly need to know?

How about, how to get the hell away from it! The conscious thought surfaced in his mind.

The creature did not seem to have spotted him yet, but if it did, what could he do? It was clearly a predator, measuring easily eight metres snout to tail. He scrutinised it. *If Ah guess correctly*, he thought, *it looks like a youngster, so outrunning it's not even on the table. Damned thing probably weighs more than a prize bull! Ah'll bet its got a similarly sunny disposition, too!*

Not for the first time, on his walking holiday from hell, he was reminded of basic training as he crawled downhill below the tops of the ferns, favouring his bad arm.

Ten metres from the crashed ship he took the pistol from his belt and risked raising his head. The dinosaur was nowhere to be seen. *Could things be looking up?* He dared hope.

He turned to check the pathway behind him and saw the creature sniffing, some twenty metres back, at the patch where he had been forced to dive to the ground. His wounds must have left some blood on the soil. He cursed under his breath as the creature raised its head to look directly at him. "Time to go!" He sprang to his feet and ran for the ship with every ounce of strength remaining to him.

Tim watched the three heavy vehicles fan out alongside the ship from one of the bridge viewports. The huge bulldozer was still a way away, rumbling unassailably across the terrain towards them. "They're here, Captain."

Singh remained bent over the screen where an endless stream of damage reports scrolled.

"Captain?"

"Huh? Oh yes, thanks, Tim. We'd better go and greet them, eh?" replied Singh. *This 'captain' thing's going to take a little getting used to,* he thought, but kept it to himself.

The *New World*'s crash-landing had left a trench fifteen metres deep in the lakeshore. It was now completely filled with water from the lake itself, but the ship's low-lying position brought her mid-level access hatches near to the ground. Tim and Singh arrived at the hatch to find The Sarge already waiting with a small, lightweight aluminium stepladder. Singh, as acting captain, nodded for Jackson to open the interior airlock door. He stepped through and glanced out of the glass portal, built into the door, before opening the outer hatch.

As the machinery hissed, a waft of warm, humid, but very fresh air hit them. Tim helped the temporarily one-armed sergeant extend the ladder the remaining two metres down to the ground below. A small party was gathering, all looking worriedly over their shoulders back in the direction they had come.

"How was the journey?" asked Singh.

Jim Miller virtually threw Rose up into the ship, very quickly following behind. "It won't be making the tourist trail, Lieutenant!" he replied, tersely.

"It's *Captain* Singh, sir," said The Sarge. "Old naval tradition – whoever commands a ship is called captain regardless of rank, sir."

Jim blinked at him, struck temporarily dumb. Finding his voice, he quietly asked, "What's happened to Jill?"

"We're not exactly sure," replied Singh, helping the other climbers off the ladder, one at a time. "Let's get everybody in – we've got a lot to discuss."

"Rose!" Tim called out. "What are you doing here?"

"It's bad on the Pod, Tim. I'll tell you about it – come on," she said, taking his hand and leading him back into the comparative safety of the ship.

Hiro gazed at all the damage within the landing strut chamber with despair. "How are we ever going to fix this mess here, Georgie?" he asked mournfully. "Sekai needs a full factory refit, with parts drawn from all over the world – that is, all over our world, not this one."

"Our first problem will be raising her so we can even work on the problem," added Baccini. "She won't stand on three struts – how do we get her up?"

"I've been thinking about that," replied Hiro.

Georgio looked hopeful. "Oh, good. What have you got?"

"Nothing."

"Hmm."

They sat in silence for a while, listening to the pumps supplied by the relief crew, as they evacuated water from the chamber. At least they could see the damage, or 'the full horror', as Hiro had described it. The huge steel foot at the bottom of the stanchion had taken the brunt of the initial explosion. The hatch which covered the support strut was completely gone, disintegrated by the shell. The hydraulics were ruined but were replaceable. Unfortunately, the strut could not be lowered due to the amount of distortion to the hull.

"We'll need to cut away large sections of the hull to get the landing gear to descend," said Hiro. "If we can lower the strut we may be able to replace the hydraulics. The trouble is, even if we fix this and all the damage to the fuel system and thrusters, I just can't see how we can ever get her space-worthy again."

"No," agreed Baccini, "I don't think we ever shall. We can get her to fly though – I believe that. At least we would be able to move the Pod and hopefully escape the army of lunatics who are going to come after us now."

Hiro sighed miserably, completely in the doldrums. "I wish the captain were here."

"Which one? We seem to have three now," asked Baccini.

"We need a crazy idea."

"Oh, you mean Jill Baines."

"She gave me strength."

"Hey, she's not dead, you know."

"We don't know that."

Baccini was getting very concerned now. Hiro's brother had died before he and Mario had joined the crew, so he had never seen his friend this depressed before. He pulled out his comm.

"What are you doing?" asked Hiro.

"Getting a crazy idea," replied Baccini. A male voice answered his call. "Hello? Is that Tim?" he asked.

Douglas flung himself through the open hatch in the side of the escape pod. The dinosaur was very close behind him now. He activated the closing switch but nothing happened. He tried again and again, finally punching the stud in anger and desperation. A deafening roar blasted through the opening and Douglas had to throw himself to the side as the huge head came for him. He cried out in agony as his arm took more damage.

Reaching for his pistol, he swore roundly and soundly; it was missing. He looked around wildly. "Where the hell is it? *Damnit!*"

The creature was less gigantic than some of the other predators they had encountered, certainly, but compared with a man and in such an intimate space, it was still enormous. It roared again in frustration, causing Douglas to cover his ears. It tore at the edges of the damaged hatch, ripping away some of the plating. Douglas was really scared now. If the damaged superstructure gave way around the opening, there might be space enough for it to reach inside for the prize. "This is it!" he said frantically. He picked up anything he could get his hands on among the crash detritus and flung it at the creature in desperation. "Get gan, ye ugly brute! Ye Godzilla, ye!"

A succession of loud cracks sounded from outside. The dinosaur banged its head, almost comically, as it jumped before making its getaway. More cracks from outside and this time Douglas' frazzled mind recognised them as repeated fire from an assault rifle. The only people on this planet with that sort of weaponry were Schultz's cronies. "Come *back*," Douglas called after the dinosaur, half-heartedly. "Ah'd rather take ma chances with *ye*!"

He sat down in one of the lifeboat's passenger seats, a man completely out of options, but apparently not out of surprises.

An old man wearing very worn looking fatigues and a huge grin stood in the ruined doorway. He held out a sidearm, grip first. "You really shouldn't leave this lying around, James," he said.

"We attack now, *Kapitän!*" Schultz stood toe to toe with Meritus. He knew how lethal she was, but forced himself not to retreat.

"We do not, Doctor," he replied calmly.

"You refuse my order?" she asked, dangerously.

"You have killed enough of my people, Doctor. It ends here. The disaster which has befallen us was all down to poor judgement on your part. You have systematically undermined my orders since we arrived. I told you we should be cautious – treat this like any other military campaign, but no, you continually underestimated our enemy and now look where that's led us."

"We are here because your people were incompetent!" she snapped back. "They allowed a team to set high explosives in the *Last Word*'s rocket exhausts, right under their noses!"

"No, the stampede allowed that to happen. My people didn't stand a chance out there! It had nothing to do with incompetence and everything to do with the resourcefulness of our enemy. Those men and women paid with their lives for *your* arrogance! Did you think that I wouldn't find out about the homing beacon?"

"What homing beacon?" Schultz asked, unconvincingly.

"You activated the beacon upon this shuttle, the *New World*'s shuttle, *James Douglas*' damned shuttle!" Meritus' temper was fraying now. "What did you think would happen once they knew where he was? Were you expecting them to hit us with a leaflet campaign?! And let's not forget that we needed Douglas to gain bloodless, non-destructive entry to the Pod and where the hell is *he* now?"

"You overstep yourself, *Kapitän*!"

"And you overestimate your capabilities, *Doctor*!"

Schultz pulled a pistol from the holster at her hip but Meritus was already pointing his own at her midriff. "Do we shoot, Schultz? Or will you learn your place and start following *my* orders? The *Last Word* was *my* ship and this is *my* mission – fact!"

Very slowly Schultz re-holstered her gun. "This will not be forgotten, *Kapitän*. You will pay for your insubordination."

"*I* am not your subordinate, Schultz. Your grandfather gave me complete autonomy to run this mission as I saw fit to get the job done. Your interference will not go unreported or unnoticed when he arrives. He's a ruthless man ordinarily, but I understand he can be even more vicious when he feels betrayed by family, yes? Vicious and inventive!" He kept his pistol trained on her. "Do you know what, Heidi, I've just decided that you're too dangerous to have around."

The look of shock and fear which crossed her face for an instant was not what Meritus expected. Nevertheless, he knew it would keep him warm on many a cold night to come. He smirked. "Oh, don't worry. I'm not going to deliberately antagonise Grandpa Schultz. I'm simply going to cut you loose. Your part in this is over and we no longer need you. Drop your weapon, holster and all – *now*."

She did as ordered. He motioned with his gun for her to step outside the shuttle. Keeping at least three metres between them, he would not underestimate *her*. He followed the German woman out. "Sergeant, call the men to order!" he barked.

Within seconds, everyone still sound in body stood in ranks before him.

"People," he addressed them. "We have reached a parting of the ways. I'm sure you are all furious about yesterday's debacle – well, it would never have happened had Dr Schultz not activated the homing beacon in this shuttle," he gestured behind him. "She is a liability and I am casting her out. Now, I fully understand how afraid many of you must be of her grandfather, and I will not deny that there is every chance he will find us in the near future. That is why I will give you this chance and this chance *only*, to choose."

"This is outrageous!" Schultz seethed.

Meritus smiled. "Yes it is, isn't it? But so was giving up our position because you wanted to show off the power of the battleship your grandfather paid for. By the way, it's at the bottom of the valley in a million pieces now, if you wish to return it to him, along with a full explanation, when he arrives!

"I, on the other hand, will have possession of the Mars Pod by then. My people will control the fortifications our enemies have, rather imaginatively, created for us. And my attack ship will patrol the skies. If Grandpa Schultz wishes to destroy *our* Life Pod, he will destroy the very point of this whole mission. No, I believe he will come to bargain at our door – and the price, ladies and gentlemen, will be high!

"So, you can go with *her*," he waved his gun indolently in Schultz's direction, "with nothing but basic kit, or you can come with me to win everything we need to conquer the Earth and the future! Anyone wishing to follow Heidi Schultz, or too afraid to go against her grandfather, can fall out now – everyone who is with me, stay where you are."

The ranks eyed one another warily. The crew who still lived were certainly doing it in interesting times these days.

"You have sixty seconds to choose," Meritus added. "Anyone siding with the Schultzes after *that*, will be shot!"

"Anyone who supports Meritus will die!" screamed Schultz. "When my *Großvater* gets here he will make them all die – *slowly!*"

"Thirty seconds," shouted Meritus, unconcerned. "It's team Meritus or team psycho. You can live and work under military law or take your chances in the asylum – *fifteen seconds.*"

Twelve people left the ranks. Meritus noted they were mostly men and probably enslaved by her considerable physical charms. He also noted that only one of them was from the team who arrived with Schultz from the *New World. Well, that's the difference between fear and loyalty*, he thought.

"Are we done?" he called out. "Good. Sergeant, give them basic survival kit and send them on their way, and Sarge, no compasses."

"Yessir." The sergeant turned on his heel and left, calling men to him to carry out his orders.

Schultz glared at Meritus. "You're *dead!*" she spat.

"After you," he said and, turning his back on her, strode back into the shuttle, closing the hatch behind him.

"We need to send a message to the other people," said Cocksedge, once more standing before a gathering in embarkation, pontificating from the staging area at the front of the chamber. "We should offer peace and reconciliation—"

"Are you crazy?" shouted Burnstein, interrupting her. "Reconciliation? We were never conciliated! They've launched one unprovoked attack after another upon us from the start!"

"*Reconciliation, Mister* Burnstein. We're all human beings aren't we? All with the same needs and concerns?"

"Sure, they need to kill a bunch o' folks and don't concern themselves how – they must be *just* like us!" he answered sourly. His statement garnered more support than Cocksedge expected and hoped.

"I'm simply saying," she continued, trying to get the group back on side, "that we should send overtures of peace, not threats. We should invite them here—"

"*What*?!" bawled Burnstein.

"Mr Burnstein, seriously," said Cocksedge. "These constant and aggressive outbursts really are counterproductive. Surely we're all on the same side here? We all seek peace."

"You seek power, lady," stated Burnstein, flatly. "I notice you didn't give the little Indian guy and the priest any opportunity to be at this rally of yours? You may have pulled their shorts down but don't think you can fool me!" Burnstein stood to get a better look at the people around the auditorium. "If we invite these Nazi sons-of-bitches in here, we're through!

"You all know me and how much I've achieved in my time – I didn't get it all from giving stuff away." He opened his arms to encompass the Life Pod in which they all sat. "This asset is what they want and they can't risk damaging it. This is the only power we have. Hell, *I* paid for half of it! If we give it to them, we're dead!"

Burnstein sat down again to a smattering of applause. Cocksedge was furious.

"If by the Indian and the priest, you mean Dr Patel and Mother Sarah, then my answer is this – they're under the thumb of the military and are no longer sound. We are the people and we have a right to vote 'no confidence' and demand another election—"

"To vote for *you*, I suppose?" Burnstein was on his feet again. "I thought the three people voted to govern us were ill equipped for the job and I was right." He pointed angrily at Cocksedge. "Or this limey chick would never have been given the chance to cause so much trouble. I suggested that I run things – I have the experience, after all, both in corporate and governmental politics. If I'd been listened to and followed, this would not be happening and the military would not be hamstrung by this futile – hell, seditious – gathering! Looks like I was right again!

"So if we do have another vote, I say if you wanna live, vote Burnstein!" he boomed.

Mrs Burnstein stood to address the people. This surprised everyone, especially her husband. "I've heard the arguments," she said, "and all I hear from Ms Cocksedge is talk of peace. All I hear from the other side is male aggression! I say let's send the other people a message and see if they will accept talks. It's just a message, what have we got to lose?"

"You treacherous little—" Burnstein spluttered.

Natalie Pearson stood, interrupting him before he could get going. "We're in serious danger," she began, "of making this a futile battle of the sexes. As a woman—"

"We're not the ones attempting to overrule the will of the people!" Cocksedge called from the podium.

"*AS A WOMAN*," Natalie shouted, "I would like to ask everyone to consider Mrs Burnstein's question – what have we got to lose? We have only one thing to lose, the way I see it – *everything*! Even our very lives, if we give those terrorists and murderers free entrance to our home!"

"I only said we should send a *message* offering peace, to see if they will meet," retorted Mrs Burnstein, and with that comment, the universal pendulum became stuck, hard to one side.

"How are you feeling, Jill?" asked Marston. "Our long chat seemed to take it out of you earlier. I'm sorry if we tired you, but you brought us the first news we've had in fifty years."

"I'm fine, Kelly, really. Though, the world did seem to spin upside down for a while there. Now I've slept on it for a couple of hours, I think I'm actually getting a handle on things. How did you even come to be on this mission – if you don't mind me asking?"

"As Mor said, I found the artefact, the ring-pull locked in amber. More or less here, as it happens. That was a little over ten years before I joined the *Newfoundland*. We were all ordered to secrecy and threatened with harsh penalties if we ever talked, but when the *New World* disappeared and time travel became suspected, it all chimed with NASA and they called us back in. It was almost like they were expecting it – waiting for it to happen, you know? I was offered a place on the mission and, as a palaeobotanist, how could I refuse? The chance of walking among the plants and animals of a long lost era of Earth's history was too much to pass up."

"I'm sorry, Kelly," offered Baines.

"Don't be," the older woman smiled. "We've had a good life here in many ways. It's a wondrous world out there. You need to be careful, of course, but Morecombe and I have adapted. If I hadn't accepted this position I would never have met him, after all."

The door hissed open to admit Hetfield.

"You must miss your family, though?" asked Baines.

"Yes, I think of them every day," Marston replied. "But I'll tell you what gets me through. You see, I'm an old woman – descendants notwithstanding, practically all of the family that I knew would probably have died around me by now. Isn't it wonderful to know that they haven't even been born yet and still have their full lives ahead of them? *And*, in the long, long lost future, I will see them all again and around we go – joined forever."

Baines smiled. "I like that, I hadn't considered it."

"There's more to know," added Hetfield. "If you're strong enough, that is?"

"Of course. What is it, Mor?"

"Well, it seems your past may be catching up with you. I'm sorry, Jill. I'm not as quick as I used to be – he got past me."

Baines' heart sank as the door slid open again behind the old man. She screamed and jumped out of the bed, hopping across the room on her one good leg straight into the one good arm of a grinning Captain Douglas.

"James!" She threw her arms around him and kissed him deeply on the mouth.

"Erm…" said Douglas when she finally let him go. "Perhaps Ah should get myself kidnapped more often?"

Baines laughed until tears streamed down her face. "Oh, James," she said, hugging him close.

Douglas looked uncomfortable, muttering something about regulations.

"We're lost a hundred million years in the past with no way home," she pointed out, laughing as she spoke, "and you're worrying about procedure. When you left us…" Choked with emotion, she was unable to finish the sentence.

"There really was nae choice. Ah couldnae stand by and let them take ma ship, or shoot you down because o' me…" he added, awkwardly.

"I thought I'd lost you."

"Aye, but here Ah am."

"What's happened to your poor arm?" she asked, deliberately changing the subject. "Come and sit down. You must tell me everything and then, finally, I can give you this job back. Turns out, being captain's not all it's cracked up to be!"

"No, Jill," Douglas replied seriously. "You've earned it. Ah cannae believe you took that battleship down. It's the sort of fearless leadership our people are going to need if they're going to make it through this. Maybe Ah'm too tied to the rules for this world. We need a more *flexible* approach – Ah can see that now," he admitted, candidly.

Baines seemed to wilt.

Douglas chuckled gently. "You saved me, Jill. Ah would never have got out of there alive otherwise."

"I thought I'd killed you in the attack," she confessed quietly. "I'm sorry, we couldn't get to you."

"You put the lives of your people before your own needs. Ah'd have expected nothing less from you, Captain Baines," said Douglas, his eyes sparkling with pride. "Besides, Ah'm here am Ah no'?"

"To rescue *me*, after I failed rescue *you*," she answered with chagrin.

"They may have named that black monstrosity the *Last Word*, but Ah reckon we had the last word in the end, eh? Ah take it you used the *New World* to drag it over the edge? That was a stroke of genius, Jill."

Baines looked uncomfortable.

"Jill?"

"Hmm," Baines answered, noncommittally. "I didn't know that thing was called the *Last Word.*"

Unwilling to be deflected, Douglas tried again. "*Jill*? Where's ma ship?"

"Erm…"

"I've been thinking about that," said Tim, joining Georgio and Hiro in the *New World's* mess. "You remember all the ballast you were collecting from the riverbed, Chief? Why don't we lorry some of it over here, along with some cement?"

"You're thinking of constructing a prop underneath the ship, to support her while we work on repairs?" asked Baccini. "Trouble is, even if we get the water from there and build some sort of dyke, we would have to do so much digging in an unprotected environment—"

"Not exactly," Tim interrupted the Italian. "*I* was thinking about digging a shallow hole under the ship – as she's supported fully on the ground right now. Once we have our hole, we could build a 'hoop' from concrete and reinforced steel. This would provide a consolidated ring-shaped pad, a bearer, if you like, to prevent the enormous weight of the ship from collapsing the edge as we dig a deep pit under the damaged area. We'll need to shutter the sides as we go down, using steelwork, of course. I mean, I know it would need to be strongly welded or otherwise fixed together, but surely Jim Miller's people can sort that out, right?

"When the pit's complete, we can pump any water out, bring a few lights to bear and work under the ship, away from any possible access from the outside – away from the wildlife, that is. Once the superstructure's removed, we'll have room to lower the strut and repair it. Aside from our enemy, who are bound to come after us, we'd be safe as houses!"

"Support Sekai on a concrete ring and dig a hole under her," Hiro repeated thoughtfully. Suddenly, he snapped back to life. "A ring-beam. Of course! Tim, you're a genius!"

He grabbed the young man and danced him around the landing strut chamber. "I was thinking about it all the wrong way about! I was trying to think of a way to *lift* Sekai – I doubt even Captain Sandip could get us off the ground safely at the moment!" he rambled on. "I never thought about undermining her to create a working chamber!"

"How in the world did you come up with that?" asked Baccini, astounded.

"YouTube," Tim admitted, shamelessly.

"*Che cosa?*"

"I was pondering how Neolithic man managed to raise a five ton stone up onto three plinth stones. It occurred to me that, although I had no idea how *they* did it, I knew how *I* would do it – simply by digging the much smaller plinth stones in, underneath, and then lowering the level of the topsoil. I hadn't given it a second thought until now. Then you asked me how to support a colossal weight on top of a strut and… well, that's it, really," he finished, lamely.

Hiro still had a tight hold on Tim's arms, having obviously switched everyone else off. His focus was clearly shifted elsewhere and, as with all engineers, his grip was powerful – painful, even.

"*Ahem*," said Tim. As he politely attempted to extricate himself, he had to ask, "What's Sekai?"

Dr Satnam Patel also had a head full of calculations. This was the first time he had been able to do anything like this since leaving Canaveral and it was glorious. He wore a contented smile as he pored over the designs for the augmented wormhole drive, somehow provided by Captain Douglas. Despite the war and all their woes, this was essential work. More than that, it was what he knew he was *meant* to do and he was loving it.

"I think we may actually be able to build this thing," he muttered to himself. "The mathematics border on insanity, but theoretically…" A loaded term for any astrophysicist, but at least the proof lay in a canyon about fifty kilometres away, smashed perhaps, but proof nonetheless.

He had only given the schematics and accompanying calculations a high level scan, but the gist appeared to be about something called *wormhole flexure*. This was a new concept to him, but fortunately the designer had thought to append some extremely detailed and useful working notes.

They all assumed their journey through time had been triggered by energy directed at the forming wormhole; more specifically, too much energy. Although that appeared to be broadly true, it was just the beginning. If he understood the notes correctly, a pulse of energy directed at the event horizon of a wormhole caused singularities to form – a possibly infinite number of them. The immense gravity created by any given singularity, could then be used to open a pathway across the universe – across space, in effect. When choosing a *specific* singularity, either at random or by design, direction becomes plottable.

"The trick, then, is choosing the correct one," he mulled aloud.

Powered by singularities, these 'micro wormholes' did not function in the same way as the wormholes they used to travel to Mars and back, and had become familiar with over the last forty years. Though microscopic, they were much more powerful and in essence more aggressive, too. They could tear a hole through reality, creating a shear in space-time capable of transporting a body anywhere in the universe.

Far from 'merely' bending space-time, this was a whole level above the wormhole physics he had grown up with, and to Patel's conservative sensibilities, this new science seemed insanely dangerous.

He began to understand that once the body had moved, potentially any distance through space, this was where wormhole flexure took over. Flexure was apparently like an elastic effect, so gravitically powerful that it could snap any body back to its source, but, as the journey happened *instantly*, it gave the impression of bending space.

Hence the name, he thought.

If one could look back down the wormhole, one would see the staging point as it *was*, millions, or potentially even billions, of years ago.

To arrive where they did, in the late Albian Stage of the Cretaceous Period, they must have followed that wormhole 99.2 million light years out into the universe – crucially, *instantly* – probably somewhere within the farthest reaches of the Virgo supercluster of galaxy groups, if the map appended to the notes was correct. So, 99.2 million light years out, wormhole flexure drew them back to the Earth as it was, exactly that many years ago. Time, in effect, forced space to adjust. Patel rubbed his eyes. Even his prodigious mind would need time to process, and this was the easy bit. Going forward in time appeared to be still more complicated.

"This is dangerous, very dangerous," he muttered. "It's like plugging the national grid into a torch so you can find your house! We should not be experimenting with this kind of science, not even to save ourselves. The effects could damage the very fabric of our universe."

Despite grave reservations, he read on: To go forward in time, a wormhole must, in effect, ride an entropic cascade.

"What the devil is that all about?" He kneaded his brow. "Are we in danger of stamping all over Heisenberg's uncertainty principle, here?"

He continued to paw through the notes and eventually a dim picture of how the process worked began to form in his mind.

Reading a little further, he stopped, shaking his head. Thinking that he must have misunderstood, he reread the passage aloud. "If one looks out far enough into what we shall call 'the centre of the known universe', eventually one will see the moment immediately after the 'big bang' roughly 13.8 billion years ago. From that point, all other points may *indeed* be plotted."

He looked up. "*Indeed*? But we know that's impossible – at no given point can we know both a body's location and its velocity."

To contradict him, an apparently entirely new branch of physics was appended to the section, belligerently stuffed with all sorts of mathematical proofs boasting a workaround for this very problem. They made his head hurt. However, skipping ahead, it appeared that the key was in knowing exactly how far back the *New World* had been sent through time. They had moved not an inch in space; he knew that, from their exhaustive scans and calculations at the time. Furthermore, Sandip Singh calculated the date of their arrival just after they had landed, based on stellar drift. According to this latest information, Singh's workings seemed more or less correct.

"So from that figure," said Patel, thinking aloud once more to help him understand, "we can extrapolate exactly how far we need to go forward, obviously. But this new mathematics seems to suggest that in order to go forward to our own time, we must go forward *twice* that far – factoring for entropic cascade. In order to view the Earth as it was 99.2 million years in the past from *there* – 198.4 million years in the future, give or take an hour or two – and that, from where I sit *now* is, oh, it's out in the Hydra supercluster somewhere apparently! This is crazy!"

He trawled through some ancillary notes. "Never attempt to plot a course straight to the 22nd century because of the constant variances which occur, every nanosecond, in every point of the universe."

He sighed, rubbing his eyes again. "So the safest path is to hop *over* the required future to view it from a much further future and then return back. Otherwise you may obliterate the required future by destroying the accepted timeline...?

"Who wrote this? And what about us altering a future time and messing up someone else's 'accepted timeline'?! I suppose these people didn't care too much about the future, only resetting the past."

He drank a very large cup of coffee down in one. "OK, so we're 198.4 million light years out in the universe, in the future, and we look back down our travel line 99.2 million light years to see our time and our Earth. Then what? Wormhole flexure neatly deposits us back home?"

Patel stood and walked to his apartment's porthole, still holding the empty cup absentmindedly. He looked out over the Cretaceous plains of Gondwana. "Well, if that's all there is to it, I'm surprised I didn't get there on my own!"

Gleeson's squad and their two vehicles had fought their way through the forests overnight. Eventually, they came upon the road which had been smashed into being by the giant bulldozer earlier that morning. It was fairly obviously not a natural highway. After several minutes of 'lively debate' about their best course, he gave the order to follow the road on a general heading of west-north-west, towards the precise coordinates provided by the *New World* as it limped away from the battle on the previous evening. In essence, their bickering ended with the decision to turn left.

After a mile or so, the road curved slightly to the right, suddenly revealing an opening onto a lake-front beach.

"This must be it," said O'Brien.

"Really? A lesser man would yell 'I told you so', about now," called Gleeson from the rear of the vehicle.

O'Brien privately pulled a face. She was about to gun the engine when a huge predator stepped into the mouth of the opening. The giant theropod flicked her tail about angrily, lowered her head and roared.

"Erm, Commander? A word?" she asked.

Gleeson moved forward to sit with her. "What is i— oh."

"Precisely, sir," she agreed. "Now what?"

"I suppose we could shoot it. These 50-cals look pretty useful..." he trailed off under O'Brien's glare.

"We shouldn't just kill every creature that happens across the road, Commander. You know?" she pointed out, reasonably.

"We can't?"

"*No*, sir," she pointed out with a bit more *point*.

Gleeson blew out a long breath of frustration. "OK, I used me last two 'dingo wingers' on that ugly mongrel that attacked us by the enemy ship, last night." He pondered for a moment longer. "Hang on, I've got an idea."

"Oh, yack! Tim, you're filthy. Don't sit there!" said Rose as Tim entered the staff mess to take the weight off his feet. "Let me put this old cleaning cloth down first."

Tim waited impatiently before crashing into the seat. "Thanks, *Mum!*" he sniped.

"How goes the digging?" she asked, setting a cup of tea before him.

"Muddy," he admitted, grumpily. "Are you planning on – no pun intended – mucking in?"

"Of course," Rose answered brightly. "I'm supplying refreshments to the troops."

Tim looked at her balefully. He tasted the tea, gave a shudder and added a note of resentment to his glare.

Rose laughed. "Yes, I'll take a turn. I've never used a shovel – I'm quite looking forward to having a go!"

"It'll pass," Tim grumbled.

"Lucky for you," she continued, "that we thought about bringing a few changes of clothing for you, eh?"

Tim could not argue the point. "We should be able to construct the concentric bearer pad tomorrow. As long as we're left alone," he explained. "Then it's simply going to be a matter of taking it in turns digging, until we're deep enough to carry out the repairs. Lieutenant Nassaki is working on spare parts and an assemblage to allow us to get them into position and install them. It's going to be a lot of work. Especially as it's a cramped space and we can't get many hands on."

He rubbed his face and ran his hands through his hair tiredly. "Glad my shift's over. I'm done for. Lucky the crew quarters are on the *New World* and not the Pod, or we'd have nowhere to sleep. It's kind of the officers to let us use their quarters on a rotation."

Rose nodded, but clearly her thoughts were elsewhere.

"What is it?" asked Tim.

"I was just wondering whether we *will* be left alone," she replied, worriedly. "Those people from the ship you destroyed – I take it a lot of them survived?"

"I would guess so. The ship went over the edge and was damaged to the point where it will surely never be useful again, but it was kind of a slow-motion crash, you know? I'm sure most of their people will have made it. I just hope that when we broke the back of their ship, we similarly broke the back of their war effort." His look of concern mirrored Rose's. "Just pray it bought us enough time, at least."

"It's not just them, though, is it?" asked Rose. "That monster's out there too." She walked to the window and Tim followed her.

"I think it's a Tyrannotitan." He placed one hand on her shoulder in a comradely fashion and one on the sill. He really was shattered. "If I'm right, then I'm wrong, too," he acknowledged.

"Huh?"

"They were supposed to be extinct by now. Twelve or thirteen million years ago, actually, to the best of my knowledge." He chuckled. "For what *that's* worth."

"Your knowledge has got us this far," said Rose, turning to give him a hug. She pulled away but held him, arms straight. "I'm very proud of you, Tim," she added earnestly.

They looked out of the window in silence. Tim felt slightly embarrassed by such praise, but also immensely gratified. In the weirdest and most convoluted manner, he had finally found his place in the world and for the first time knew where he belonged. He was strangely content.

"Do you know if it's a 'he' or a 'she'?" Rose asked.

"The dinosaur? Maybe we will be able to discern that, with research and observation. It's almost impossible to say at the moment. We don't know enough. When examining the fossil record, the only clues to sexing a dinosaur skeleton were more a matter of timing and luck than anything else."

"What do you mean?"

"If an animal happened to be close to laying eggs when she died, trace evidence can sometimes be left in the fossilised bones. Interestingly, this is a characteristic shared with birds from our own time, too, so it's a process well known to science. Basically, when an egg-laying species is about to lay, they suddenly require huge amounts of calcium, and quickly. This 'new bone' forms in the empty voids within the skeleton, and only in females. When they're in season, it's kind of like having a reservoir of calcium on tap. It's called medullary bone. The animals' physiology takes it from there, carrying it through the blood stream to where it's needed, to build eggshell.

"I can only describe it as one of the many wonders of nature. Remarkable, really. Of course, if this is *not* evident in a skeleton, it *might* mean it belonged to a male, but could just as easily be a female who was *not* pregnant. So you see the problem?"

"So, you don't know?"

Tim laughed. "Fair enough, no," he admitted. "Size didn't seem to be a factor within the theropod dinosaurs, nor were there any differentiating features between the sexes, like cranial ridges, things like that. They seemed to be almost indistinguishable, in fact – at least without the rest of the anatomy. From what little we've seen here, I'm damned if I can tell the difference. They must use scent and pheromones to seek a mate at certain times. That would be my guess anyway. As much as I love them, I hope never to be close enough to tell the difference from their odour!"

"Woodsey told me the females were bigger and nastier."

"*Woodsey* told you?" Tim replied, his inflection speaking volumes.

"No, he said that was what you said."

Tim laughed again. "*Now* I'm a real palaeontologist!"

Rose looked at him in bewilderment.

"Sorry, that's an 'in' joke. It seems that all palaeontologists have been misquoted at some point in their career. It's often just down to Chinese whispers, woolly writing or a journalist attempting to make a story more sensational. Woodsey's reasons are probably more prosaic, however, and probably have a lot less to do with gingering up a story and more to do with sexism at your personal expense. He calls it taking the *Michelle*."

Rose did not appear to be joining in with the jocularity. "*Does* he?"

"I suspect this animal might be female, though."

"Why, do you think she might be about to lay eggs?"

"That's hard to say."

Rose looked perplexed. "So, why do you suspect it's female, then?" As they gazed down from their vantage point, high up within the ship, they saw the animal in question, still patrolling around their new roadway onto the beach. Clearly, it had found something of interest.

Tim watched the animal for a few moments and then strode towards the doors. Rose followed him, collecting the dirty towel on her way. "Well? Why do you think it's female?" she called after him again.

Tim stopped halfway through the doorway and called back, "It seems to be in a near permanent strop!"

The dirty towel hit the wall right next to where his head had been.

"Gleeson to the *New World*, come in."

"New World, *here. Crewman Baccini speaking. Good to hear your voice. How can we help you, Commander?*"

"Georgio, we're on the road to you. Do you still have vehicles outside? Around the ship, I mean?"

"*Yes, Commander. In fact the drivers are just returning to them and are about to set off back to the Pod.*"

"Great! Can you get them all to honk!"

"*Eh? I mean, can you repeat that, sir?*"

"Honk! Honk their horns! We need a distraction."

"*Ah, I get you. Please stand by...*"

The comm cleared for a few moments and then a disparate cry of air horns went up, startling the bird life from the trees. The Tyrannotitan also stopped roaring and turned in the direction of the cacophony, sniffing the air.

"Right! O'Brien, do it! Go left! Go, go, *go!*" shouted Gleeson, excitedly.

O'Brien gunned the powerful diesel engine as ordered and the small, tracked vehicle jumped into action, scrambling underneath the angry Carcharodontosaur's tail and onto the beach. The animal snapped back around furiously, giving the four-wheeled personnel carrier behind them the chance to drive past it on the right, smacking the indignant animal's tail on the way through.

"*That* was your idea?" hissed O'Brien, so that no one outside the cab would hear. "*Go for it?!*"

"It worked, didn't it?" Gleeson shot back.

"I'll let you know, sir, *if* we make it to the ship."

"Better put your foot down then, Jen, before that thing tries to use us for a skateboard!"

"Sir," she tried again, delicately. "Next time we need an idea, to save all our lives, maybe we could *bend* the rigorous codes of military conduct and take a vote? *Perhaps?*"

"Perhaps you should concentrate on driving, *Corporal?*" he suggested, bluntly.

The wheeled vehicle left them and the dinosaur behind fairly easily, once they made the beach around the edge of the lake. The tracked vehicle was slower and the continual buffeting from the seven ton predator running alongside them made it more so. The creature was clearly trying to turn them over, instinctual behaviour because most animals tend to be softer underneath.

"Commander!" O'Brien exclaimed as a big nudge sent them into the shallows.

"Keep your speed up, keep your speed up!" shouted Gleeson. "We can't risk getting bogged down."

"I'm trying – it keeps pushing us further in!"

The slow concussive thud of heavy machine guns made them both jump. "What the—" they said in unison.

Corporal Jones had taken to the small turret above and just behind the cab, and was firing into the air. This latest was one loud noise too many for the Tyrannotitan and she broke off, angry and frustrated once more.

A short and bouncy ride later, the armoured vehicle arrived with the others and parked next the crashed *New World*.

"That wasn't so bad now, was it?" asked Gleeson, chipper once more.

O'Brien took her shaking hands from the control levers and turned to stare at her commanding officer, not yet trusting herself to speak.

Chapter 10 | Messages

The young lieutenant ran from the shuttle to where Meritus stood, discussing provisions with a couple of his sergeants.

"Excuse me, sir," he said, skidding to a halt, breathlessly. "We've had a message from the *New World*. Actually, a message from the Pod, sir – signed Alison Cocksedge."

Meritus frowned. "Who?"

The lieutenant nodded understanding. "I looked her up, sir. Apparently she's a British politician, but a minor player. She seems to have been on the rise, with a small but very vocal following, but was pretty unpopular with the silent majority, sir. You know the type, sir. She never did well at the polls."

"What was she doing on the Mars Mission?" asked Meritus.

The lieutenant rubbed his thumb and forefingers together to denote that she had money behind her. "She may have seen a way of fast-tracking her career via Mars, perhaps, sir."

Meritus grunted non-committally. "Alright. What does she want?"

"To open negotiations, sir. According to her, the military action against us was not sanctioned by what she is calling 'the people of the

New World' and she wants to offer a full and frank apology on behalf of the civilian population and begin peace talks, sir."

Meritus' eyebrows shot up. "Does she, by God."

"Apparently so, sir. She's included an encryption so that we can send a return message."

"So, she's working in secret," Meritus commented, mulling over this unexpected turn of events. "Sounds like the actions of a fool or a coward, or a small number of cowards, fearful for their own skins. We might be able to exploit this to our advantage. We seem to have lost Douglas for now, but maybe we can find another way onto the Pod – one which doesn't involve blowing the hell out of it. Right, using the encryption she gave us, send the following message…"

"You crashed ma ship!" Douglas sat with his head in hands, shaking it from side to side in utter disbelief. "Ah cannae believe it, after all she's been through."

Baines hobbled over to him on the crutches Morecombe Hetfield had provided. "I'm sorry, James. The mission went like a charm, we achieved total surprise, but as the enemy vessel went over the edge she managed to bring one of her guns to bear and…" she tailed off.

Douglas looked up at her. Seeing the pain in her expression, he softened. "No, Jill. Ah'm sorry. You did what you had to do and you pulled off a miracle. Forgive me. Ah'd like to hear what happened. All Ah remember is being thrown upside down." His expression darkened again. "There's something *you* need to know, too. We may have friends on that ship."

"Really?" asked Baines, in shocked tones.

"Aye. Please tell me about your last few days and Ah'll fill in any pieces Ah can with what little Ah learned from the enemy camp."

Baines spent the next half an hour explaining all that had happened since Douglas had surrendered himself to Schultz to save her life. Hetfield and Marston sat in on the conversation too, and gradually a three-sided story began to coalesce.

"Hmm," said Douglas, thoughtfully. "Lieutenant Elizabeth Hemmings was a very brave woman. We should all remember her sacrifice, in case Ah never get to write it up in a report. There's just one more piece to the puzzle that Ah havenae told you, Jill. Geoff Lloyd is alive."

Baines was staggered. "What! *How*?"

Douglas snorted. "The man's got more lives than a whole pride of moggies," he said with a wry smile. "You remember how concerned you were that we simply didnae have the facilities to allow him to reform? Well, just maybe he's doing it all on his own."

Baines gave him a sceptical look. "Why do you say that?"

"We were unable to talk freely during our short confinement together, but Ah got the distinct impression that he was nay friend to the Schultzes' regime. He was in a really bad way when Ah left him. He insisted that Ah leave him behind. Not the selfish attitude Ah would have expected from the man."

"He may simply have wanted to stay with them," Baines theorised.

"No," said Douglas, shaking his head. "He was in a really bad way, even before your attack. But reading between the lines, Ah think he favours us. To be perfectly honest, the state he was in, Ah wouldnae have given him long to live, but Ah've made that mistake before. Ah'll no' make it again. If it's in any way possible, Ah'd like to get him back."

"A rescue mission? For *Lloyd*?" Baines was barely able to believe her ears. "Have you forgotten he put us all here?"

"No Ah haven't, believe it or not," replied Douglas with a touch of asperity.

Baines raised her hands placatingly, letting the matter go. "Alright," she agreed. "We'll add that to the wish list, shall we?"

Douglas nodded. He knew the prospect of pulling Lloyd out was, at best, hopeful.

"OK," said Baines. "We'll need to send a secure message to the *New World*. I don't want Sandip doing anything silly, like coming to look for me."

"Heaven forbid anyone should do anything like *that*," Douglas jibed, ironically.

"That was different," Baines answered, aloof. "We needed to get you back, James. The *New World* needs her captain and the triumvirate needs you, too."

"Oh aye, Jill, and Ah'll bet ye a month's back pay that Sandy's thinking exactly the same things about you!"

"I can't let that happen." She directed her next question towards Hetfield, who was taking a deep draught of a wholesome fruit juice he manufactured from local produce. "So, while we're wishing for horses," she continued, "we need certain spares and repairs for the *New World*. What are the chances of this ship flying again, Mor?"

Hetfield spilt his drink all over himself as he fell into a coughing fit.

"She did *WHAT*?!" bellowed Major White, incandescent with rage.

"All I can tell you for certain," replied Burton, "is that the message originated in Cocksedge's quarters. It was encoded and we haven't been able to unlock it yet."

"And you're sure it was sent to the enemy?" asked White, still raising his voice furiously.

"It wasn't sent to the *New World* or any of our operatives in the field. Those are all the facts, Ford, but knowing what a treacherous, lying trout she is..."

White raked his fingers through his hair in agitation. "Right," he said at last, getting his anger under control. "I think it's about time *I* called a meeting! Sam, please make an announcement across the PA, asking everyone to attend embarkation in—" he checked the Pod's chrono, "twenty minutes time. I'll keep my personnel at their posts and I'll get Sarah and Satnam on the horn – let 'em know what we're walking into."

Burton nodded and left the security offices.

Singh and Gleeson shook hands as the Australian and his team boarded the *New World.* "Well done, sir," said Singh.

"To both of us, I reckon, mate," Gleeson greeted warmly in return. "It's good to see you all made it. We weren't quite so lucky, I'm afraid. We lost Pt Jane Ross."

A look of sorrow crossed Singh's face. "I'm very sorry to hear that, Commander."

"Yeah, me too," agreed Gleeson, quietly. "We managed to retrieve her remains on the way back. I'd like to put them in Dave Flannigan's morgue. I assume he stayed with the Pod?"

Singh nodded. "Yes, sir, he did. We'll get her placed there straight away. Unfortunately, we've lost track of Captain Baines too."

Gleeson stopped in his tracks and turned back to Singh questioningly.

Singh nodded again. "We had an extraordinary message from Captain Douglas."

"He's *alive?*" Gleeson interrupted, urgently.

"He was last night," Singh continued. "He sent us a coded message saying he'd broken out."

"Woohoo!" exclaimed Gleeson, punching the air.

Singh smiled. "Yes, sir. More than that, he somehow managed to send us the entire set of blueprints for the time-travelling wormhole drive from the *Last Word.*"

"*Last Word?*"

"Yes," continued Singh. "That's what they called that black monstrosity. Catchy name, isn't it? Captain Baines decided to take *Lifeboat 1* and go rescue him, sir. That was the last we heard from either of them. Once we lost contact, I wanted to take another lifeboat and search for her, but I was *reminded* by the crew that my place was here. Now you're here, that's changed and I intend to leave as soon as I've handed over to you, sir."

"Whoa, whoa, *whoa.* Hang on a minute, sport. You're the only one who can fly this crate now."

"Not so, sir," interrupted Singh. "Hiro and Georgio are both capable pilo—"

"No!" said Gleeson, with finality. "*You* are the senior bridge officer, Singh. Hell's teeth, you should be in charge of this thing! I'm commander in name only when it comes to the running of this ship, we both know that."

Singh was about to interrupt again, but Gleeson cut him off. "No, Sandip. When Captain Baines forced this job upon me, she also impressed upon me that I was responsible for the lives of everyone on the mission. Don't think that I wouldn't risk my life to save her, but we have to consider all those people back on the Pod. If there is any way this ship will fly again, then I think we will need to grab the Pod and go! You know Nassaki's not half the pilot you are. You're too valuable an asset to waste on a wild goose chase, Lieutenant."

Singh's comm beeped. "Singh," he answered.

"*Captain,*" said a female voice.

Gleeson raised his eyebrows. Singh rolled his eyes. "Naval tradition," he whispered. "Go ahead, Rose."

"*We've received an urgent message from Captain Baines. Please return to the bridge.*"

The officers looked at one another in astonishment.

"On our way!" Singh signed off and they ran.

"Was that Jim Miller's kid?" panted Gleeson as they jogged through the ship.

"Yes, sir. She's been helping out around ship. She's doing her best to be useful. When I leave the bridge I get her to monitor comms."

They burst onto the bridge, both shouting, "Report," in unison.

Rose turned to face them, pleasantly surprised by Gleeson's presence. "Commander Gleeson, you're back."

He gave her a friendly smile, asking, "The captain's message?"

Rose blushed. "Oh, sorry, yeah. It was a very short text message. She says: 'Landed badly, but safe now. Do not send rescue – repeat, do *not* send rescue' and that's all, Captain."

"Actually, Rose, now that Commander Gleeson is here, we should all technically call *him* captain now," said Singh.

Rose scratched her head. "Seriously?"

Singh chuckled. "I know, just call me Sandy, it'll be easier all round."

"Has Baines met up with Douglas?" asked Gleeson.

"That's all there was, erm... *Commander*?"

"Commander will do," agreed Gleeson. "*Damnit*! We need to know more."

"She'll be afraid of our comms being intercepted," Singh noted. "I think that's hopeful, though."

"Go on," prompted Gleeson.

"Firstly, she says she's safe, which is great, but also rather hard to understand, knowing that she's crash-landed out there alone."

"So," said Gleeson slowly, catching his drift, "maybe she's *not* alone?" Singh nodded.

"OK, Rose. Do you know how to encrypt a message?" asked Gleeson. Rose shook her head.

Gleeson looked to Singh, who nodded. "I'll show you," he said, approaching her station.

"Send a message to Major White," said Gleeson, making sure they were all on the same page. "Append the message from Jill Baines to it."

As Singh leaned on the console to explain the operation to the teenager, a message popped in *from* Major White. He quickly scanned it and then closed his eyes, letting out an exasperated breath. "Oh, for crying out loud!"

Major White stood upon the stage at the front of embarkation, his expression stern. "Thank you for coming at such short notice," he greeted. "I have a couple of announcements for you all. First, the good news – as you will already have heard, Captain Baines and the *New World* were astonishingly successful in their mission and the enemy warship has been destroyed."

He waited for the exultant whoop of adulation for the away teams' accomplishments to pass. Not for the first or last time, he wished he had The Sarge here, to calm everyone down. Waving for quiet, he continued. "More than that, after the warship died, we received a coded message from Captain Douglas!"

A roar of approval echoed around the large auditorium.

White allowed himself a smile. "More even than *that* – and all you technicians will be ecstatic with this, I'm sure – he managed to send us the plans for the wormhole drive from that ship. The one which allowed it to travel through time at will!"

The most raucous applause yet erupted from the crowd. He had just given them hope of returning home.

White nodded his understanding, once more holding up his hands for quiet. "This is an incredible victory for us, against impossible odds, but unfortunately, my next piece of news is more disappointing – despicable even. Someone aboard this Pod has sent a coded message to the enemy!"

A howl of anger emanated from the crowd. This time White let them sound out for a while before appealing for calm. It would not hurt to allow them to work themselves up against the perpetrator. Anger could send them off kilter, but in doing so might also provide perspective with regards to who was on their side and who was not.

"As Ms Cocksedge seems to have set herself up as a sort of spokesperson for the civilian population, I invite her to join me up here at the podium. Please, Ms Cocksedge," said White, gesturing for her to join him.

A spike of nervous tension shot through Cocksedge at the sound of her name. She controlled it, confident that they would not be able to pin anything on her and even if they did, she would be able to talk it around and make them think she had been acting with everyone's interests in mind. They also did not need to know that she had received a return message – unless it furthered her purposes.

There was much agitation among the gathering and someone shouted, "That *broad* doesn't represent me!"

White singled out Hank Burnstein and his lip twisted to a half smile.

"Thank you, Major White," began Cocksedge, joining him on stage. "Naturally, we're all very relieved to find that Captain Douglas still lives – that's *if* this message is true—"

"Excuse me, Ms Cocksedge," White interrupted. "Can I stop you there? You weren't invited here to speak. You're here to *answer* for the crime of sending out unauthorised coded messages to the enemy."

The crowd exploded.

Daylight was fading, growing darker still under the forest canopy. Dr Heidi Schultz had followed the trail left by the escaping teams from the *New World*, and her stolen armoured personnel carrier, for most of the day. Since her expulsion by the traitor Meritus, her twelve followers had pretty much left her alone, afraid to approach.

She raised her arm, closing her fist. "We make camp here tonight." She led them about a hundred metres into the forest, away from the trail and any dangers likely to approach from it. She spotted a likely tree and began to scramble up. "Get off the ground," she ordered, "and keep your boots on. Use your rations carefully, cold food only – no fires. We move again at dawn."

After millions of years of evolution, they found themselves back up in the trees. Schultz pointedly did not join in the round of arboreal 'goodnights'. She was furious and someone, perhaps everyone, would pay.

Meritus lay down on his temporary bunk aboard the *New World*'s shuttle. In the camp around him, his people had assembled many field tents to provide cover, but he was very concerned about another incursion by a large predator, particularly in the dark. So, taking inspiration from the wagon trains which crossed America's 'Old West' during the 19th century, he had moved his last attack ship to land parallel with the shuttle. Using his three remaining armoured vehicles, he parked two of them nose to tail at one end, creating a box. The third he parked at the opposite end. Utilising salvaged security fence panels, his people fashioned a guarded gateway of sorts to close the remaining gap.

Most of the injured were within the crafts' holds or the vehicles, everyone else was under canvas, but at least they were now afforded some protection. The teams he had sent to strip everything they could use from the *Last Word* advised him against moving people back aboard the ruin at this time. They suspected there might yet be a danger of secondary explosions. Unlike Schultz, Meritus listened to his people before making decisions and their warning seemed sensible.

He sighed. Sleep eluded him. Schultz was out there somewhere, too. *Maybe I should have just ended her,* he thought. He expected her to go to ground, until their relief force arrived with her grandfather, but who could tell with her? She was *beyond* unstable.

Before he had her thrown out of his camp, he knew she had visited the *Last Word*, but he did not know why.

Suddenly, he sat up, banging his head off the upper bunk as he did so. "*Lieutenant!*" he cried, rubbing his head.

The duty officer ran through the shuttle, down to the bunks they had set up in its cargo bay. "Yes, sir?"

Moans came from the injured around him and Meritus suddenly felt like an ass. He quickly donned his boots and led the young lieutenant from the room, apologising to the people he had disturbed.

They made their way, quickly, to the small bridge. "Lieutenant, are we scanning for comm traffic?"

"Yes, sir. We've picked up a few but have been unable to decode them yet. I didn't want to disturb you until we had, but we are working on them, sir. If we had our equipment..." he left the statement unfinished.

Meritus nodded. "I understand. Have you picked up any other signals?"

The younger man looked slightly confused. "We're only scanning for comm signals, sir. Have we missed something?"

"Maybe," replied Meritus. "Take your station, Lieutenant. Check for any signals coming from the *Last Word*."

The officer was obviously surprised but obeyed immediately and without comment. After a few moments going through menus, he set up the desired parameters and leaned back in his seat. "Whoa!" he said.

"What?" snapped Meritus.

"It looks like the balloon's gone up, sir."

254

AD2112 – Patagonia

The old man watched the tropical rain hammer the forest below his window. He looked out from a curved window with an almost 180 degree field of vision, set into the side of his fortress which was in turn built into the side of a rocky promontory. The rainforest, as far as he could see, was his personal domain. Not that it was in any way fit for human habitation. Some of the deadliest creatures in the world lived just outside his window. Heinrich Schultz disapproved of visitors, so this worked well for him.

His thoughts were of his granddaughter, temporarily trapped almost a hundred million years in the past. For all he knew, she might be standing right where he stood now, all that time ago. Of his extensive family, she by far showed the most promise. One day, he hoped for her to succeed him as mistress of his glorious new race, although she was his second choice. He would have preferred a male heir. Operation Dawn was now well underway, so maybe this would change things. Despite being out of contact with his most valuable assets for some time, he instinctively knew they would be performing to the level of excellence he demanded from them. The very sight of his *Last Word* would probably bring the mongrel rabble aboard the *New World* to heel. He would never credit such a motley group with the courage, commitment or strong leadership necessary to defy his plans.

Schultz did not trust anyone, but he knew Meritus to be a strong and resourceful leader. He had chosen him for his abilities. It was unfortunate that the man's commitment to the purity of their cause was so weak. He suspected that Meritus saw the whole venture as merely a way of saving a small portion of the human race. As a native Canadian, it would have been the *only* way to save himself, certainly, and a few of his people, after Canada left the Mars programme under a cloud. The political rift which opened up between Canada and the US had been useful, but the world of the 22nd century was doomed and everyone knew it.

A pragmatist then, thought Schultz, *but he will carry out my orders proficiently until I get there to take command. After that, we shall just have to see.*

The ships making up the rest of his fleet were not yet complete, although they were close. Ultimately, he had access to time machines, so he could invade the past at will. The time and date of his departure was irrelevant. However, there was still the danger that some event in the past might change *his* present. This was the biggest risk of the whole enterprise, so he had been working his people hard. *Harder than usual*, he admitted to himself with a quirk of rare amusement.

The large, beautifully carved doors to his private study buzzed softly. He frowned, turning slowly to face them. "Enter."

They opened to admit his aide.

"Yes?" he snapped peremptorily.

She gave a slight bow. "I apologise for disturbing you, sir, but we have received the temporal signal."

Heinrich Schultz smiled.

"To what crime are you referring, Major?" asked Cocksedge, coolly. "I have committed none." She gave him her maddening politician's smile.

"We know that a coded message was sent to the enemy camp and it originated in your quarters," White spoke clearly so that all could hear.

The assembled passengers and Pod staff were highly agitated and it took a while for the rumblings to die down.

Cocksedge smiled again, turning to the populace. "My friends, did we not decide at our last meeting, that sending a message requesting a peaceful dialogue was our best course of action? I simply carried out my promise to you, the people."

"That's just a bunch o' B.S.," shouted Burnstein. "I never agreed to it – same goes for most of us here!"

White nodded. "Mr Burnstein is correct. You took this upon yourself to further your ambitions. Or was it simply an attempt at collaboration, to save your own skin?"

"Nonsense," Cocksedge called out. "Major White is just trying to use this to sublimate his unprovoked attack upon my person. Furthermore, this is the military, once again, trying to curtail our freedoms. If this continues—"

"Can it, lady!" snapped White, with a flash of temper. "You sent a coded signal to an enemy who are here with the sole intention of casting us out of our home to die! You committed an act of treason against our society and you're *not* gonna double talk your way out of it!"

A loud applause followed and Cocksedge suddenly looked less sure of herself. It was time to roll the dice. "They accepted my offer of a meeting!" she shouted, causing an immediate silence.

Rebecca Mawar, psychic medium and member of the so-called 'paid seats', was taking a little air. A few of the passengers were beginning to take short walks around the compound now, after the teenagers had paved the way for leaving the ship, just before the hurricane struck them about a week ago.

What a couple of days it had been. It was hard to imagine that a battle had taken place just fifty kilometres away and only yesterday. They had *lost* people. Furthermore, a reprisal was expected within the next couple of days. Were that not bad enough, apparently someone had attempted to make a secret deal with the enemy. She shook her head sadly. *We are a curse upon this Earth*, she thought.

Yet, the evening was balmy and beautiful, the sky deep blue under a large, brilliant moon. Mawar breathed deeply in and out, in and out – her heart slowing as she opened her feelings to the world around her.

Peace...

"You are all going to die."

She caught her breath, turning sharply. She was alone. "Who's there?" she asked out.

"You know who I am," said the disembodied voice.

Mario, she thought. *Help me!* She instantly felt the familiar warmth around her shoulders and knew she was no longer alone. The demon laughed and was gone.

Hiro was shattered. Georgio had practically forced him to go for food and rest. He sat heavily at a table in the staff mess. Rose placed a plate of something warm in front of him.

"I'm sorry. I don't have much experience with cooking," she offered.

He nodded gratefully and tried a few mouthfuls. It was not very good but he hardly noticed. *How am I going to get this ship to fly again in the time we have?* he thought, exhaustedly…

Suddenly, he was being shaken. "Hiro?"

The chief opened his eyes and raised his head. Some kind of cold broth trickled into his eye. "Wha'?" he managed to utter.

Singh laughed at him, offering a towel. "I found you asleep in your bowl!"

Hiro looked down at the mess on the table and groaned. It was all over him, too. "*Fantastic*," he said, taking the towel. He cleaned himself up as best he could before turning his efforts towards wiping the table. "I was dreaming about Captain Douglas," he admitted, now more or less awake.

"Oh?" asked Singh.

"Yes, he had just arrived with a load of spare parts and a work crew." Hiro sighed. "Fat chance of anything like that coming my way at the moment."

"Shouldn't we at least wait until morning to try this?" asked Hetfield, barely controlled panic in his voice. "She hasn't been in the air for nearly fifty years – what's another few hours, for God's sake?!"

"We cannae wait," retorted Douglas. "If this doesnae work, we need to know now and Ah'll need to find another way back so that we can get help. According to Jill, there are parts on this ship that we desperately need.

"That's the trouble with you kids," said Hetfield, grouchily. "Always in a rush to be somewhere! And what the hell do you mean *parts*? The *Newfoundland*'s our ship and she's been our home for most of our lives – she's not a junkyard prize!"

Douglas softened slightly. "Ah know, Mor. Ah do understand, but there are lives at stake." He smiled. "Did you just call me a kid?" he asked. "You do realise that a few weeks ago Ah was nearly twice your age?"

"That was a long time ago for some of us, son. And now you come bustin' into my trailer wanting to take it for a ride!"

Douglas laughed and eventually Hetfield did too.

"OK, *Pop*," replied Douglas, kindly. "Ah'm sorry, but we really need to know if this is going to work."

Hetfield sighed and looked across the *Newfoundland*'s bridge to where Marston sat at a science station. She smiled sadly and nodded.

"Alright, Captain. Have it your way," he said. "But go easy on her, she's an old lady now – I know how she feels," he added quietly.

Douglas sat at the pilot's station with Baines in the captain's chair. "This is new," she commented.

Douglas gave her one of his winning smiles. "Where to, Captain?"

"Home, James," she said.

"The signal was only meant to be sent after the *New World* was ours," said Meritus. "This is not good. If Old Man Schultz gets here and finds us in this state – his battleship in pieces and his precious granddaughter in exile – he'll execute us all before he even bothers to land and hear our story!"

"Shall I order a small team to deactivate the signal, sir?" asked the lieutenant.

Meritus shook his head. "No, that will only endanger more of our people. The damage is done now. If that signal has been broadcasting all day, it will have been received. We need to assume that Operation Dawn's second wave are on the way. *Damn!*" he snapped, slamming his fist down on a console.

"Should we move out, sir?"

"Yes, I think we must. *Damnit!* I wanted everybody rested." Meritus thought hard for a moment. "OK, how many people can we move in the ships and land vehicles?"

"We could probably squeeze fifty into this shuttle, sir, if we removed the bunks. The attack ship is only designed to drop a small contingent, but we could *maybe* pack a dozen troops into her. The armoured personnel carriers can carry twelve in relative ease, but comfort aside, we might get twenty into each. It won't be pleasant, but…"

Meritus nodded. "122 places," he acknowledged. "As there are only ninety of us, we may be able to pull this off."

"But, sir," the young officer reminded him, "we have twenty-seven wounded. They will need a lot more space. Do we leave them behind, sir?"

Meritus stared at the lieutenant, whose name was Weber. *An obvious graduate of one of Schultz's 'youth training programmes'*, he thought. "We do not, Lieutenant," he said simply. "At least, not in the way I believe you're suggesting. We will leave them with the land vehicles, a small support staff and a heavily armed guard. I will take a shock team of forty fit individuals, including myself. I will co-pilot the attack ship – you will command this shuttle, Lieutenant."

The young man stood and clicked his heels in salute.

Meritus acknowledged his salute. "I'll let them all rest for two more hours and then we make our preparations to leave."

Chapter 11 | Traitors

She knew it was very late, but she had paced enough. She needed help. Pressing the call button to Mother Sarah's quarters, Mawar stood back and waited for a response.

About a minute later, the doors slid open to reveal Mother Sarah in her dressing gown, her face softened with sleep. "Beck," she yawned. "Excuse me. Please, won't you come in? Can I get you something?"

Mawar stepped into the older woman's quarters, the doors sliding quietly closed behind her. "I'm real sorry, Sarah. I know it's late, but…"

Sarah guided her guest towards a sofa. "I'll get us some tea. Nothing like it for the nerves! It got the Brits through the Blitz, you know," she added with a kindly smile.

After another minute or so she returned with two steaming mugs.

Beck held onto hers like it was a lifebuoy. "Sorry, Sarah," she apologised again. "I just didn't know where else to go."

"My door's always open, Beck. *Always*. Now, why don't you tell me what's wrong?"

"After the incident earlier with that awful Cocksedge woman, I needed some air, to clear my head. As a Native American, I don't expect much sympathy if the bad guys break in here."

Sarah's smile faded. "We won't let that happen, Beck. Ford White is a good man and one of the bravest – regardless of what that odious politician says about him. Don't believe a word of it! Ford will stop them somehow. I haven't written off Captain Baines either. Jill is a lady who always knows how to pull a rabbit out of the hat. If Captain Douglas is still out there too, he will be up to something – you can bet on it!" she winked.

Beck nodded, beginning to feel a little better. The tea was helping, too. Perhaps Sarah was right, maybe it always did.

"When I was outside, Sarah," she began again, "someone came to me. You don't know this, but I went to see Captain Baines before she left on the mission. I know about the death connected with the bridge meeting room aboard the *New World*. She didn't admit to any details, but I sensed it. Whoever it was, is still around and they're evil, Sarah. Truly evil." Her voice shook slightly.

The priest was not really sure what to make of that, simply answering, "It'll be OK, Beck. Anything you need to say to me, you can. You know that, right?"

"Sarah, do you believe in demons?"

They came with the morning light. The explosion shook the entire Pod. Major White had been expecting this tactic but had hoped for another twenty-four hours.

"Game on!" he shouted to his colleagues in their security station. Before leaving his desk he made a Pod-wide address, alerting all security staff to take their stations and for everyone else to gather in embarkation immediately.

As he ran to the main hangar, his comm binged. "White," he answered.

"Ford, it's Sam Burton – I'm in control. We've received a hail from the ship that just blew a massive hole in the ground in the middle of our new compound!"

White slowed to a stop and took a couple of calming breaths. "Direct it through to my comm, please, Sam."

"You're on, Ford. Good luck!" There was a click as Burton signed off.

"This is Major Ford White of *Factory Pod 4*, who am I speaking with?"

"Good morning, Major. This is Captain Tobias Meritus, lately of the Last Word." Meritus' sarcasm was unmistakable when referring to his ruined ship.

"Wish I could say I was sorry about that, Captain, but you know how it is."

"Indeed. I have an offer for you, Major. It was an offer we put forward to one of your colleagues – a Miss Cocksedge, is it?"

White gritted his teeth. "I understand that she made contact with you behind my back, yes."

"I suspected that might be the case, Major. However, I am willing to meet with her, and yourself, within that quaint little fort you have built for yourselves. Shall we say ten minutes?"

"Very well, Captain. Will you be coming alone and unarmed?"

"I'll be coming alone, Major, but not unarmed – you know how it is," he repeated White's words back to him cynically. *"We will land just inside your gates and I will meet you half way. Needless to say, heavy weapons will be trained upon you and your Pod at all times."*

"Understood. White out." He closed the channel and cursed. Opening another comm link, he asked Burton, Patel and Mother Sarah to meet with him in the main hangar. After that, he begrudgingly ordered security to retrieve Cocksedge from her house arrest and bring her down to the hangar too.

"This is it," said White without preamble. "Any final thoughts?"

Patel and Sarah looked afraid but determined.

Burton looked annoyed. "I've just about got this place fixed up again," he muttered.

"I'll try not to do anything that might incite them to launch an all-out attack," said White, sardonically.

"Should we come with you?" asked Sarah.

"No. He asked to see me and *her!*" he answered, pointing at Cocksedge. "That's a brave offer, Sarah, but I'm not willing to risk our entire leadership out there. We know nothing about this guy. And if he works for Grandpa Schultz, he might be a real charmer!"

"You're right," Patel agreed. "But I wish we could be with you, Ford. Good luck, my dear friend." He squeezed White's hand sincerely, in a double clasp.

Mother Sarah pulled White into an embrace. "God go with you. Come back safely to us."

"Yeah, ditto," said Burton, glancing over at Cocksedge. "And if you feel the need to come back alone, that's perfectly OK, too."

White gave him his customary lopsided smile and shook Burton's hand. "Leave a light on…"

Burton nodded. "We're bringing the weapons-mounted lifeboats through from manufacturing now, as you requested. Good luck, mate."

Douglas woke up confused. For a moment he thought he was back in his quarters aboard the *New World*. This room was similar but rather in need of a makeover. A stab of pain from his arm made him gasp. It was still stiff. He sat up and perched on the side of his bed. Gradually, his memory began to catch up with him as he rubbed his face a bit, mussed his hair a bit, yawned a bit and finally stood, stretching.

He walked into the bathroom and splashed a little water on his face, dispelling the last vestiges of the dreadful hours. This was the third such en suite he had used in as many weeks. Looking into the mirror, he experienced a massive bout of *déjà vu* as he continued to greet the day just like the eighty or so other men on planet Earth. However, this time he forewent the shave and the shower, but still needed to take the *et cetera*.

Starting up rocket engines, left dormant for fifty years, had not gone well. In fact, nothing had happened at all. This was not exactly unexpected, but they had simply been too tired to delve into the 'why' so late in the evening, deciding instead to turn in.

Douglas made for the *Newfoundland*'s staff mess. He arrived to find Morecombe Hetfield and Kelly Marston also about to enter for breakfast.

A few minutes later, Jill Baines puffed her way in on crutches. "Sorry, guys. I'm a little slow at the moment!"

"Ah could have brought you something to the bridge, Jill. Save you limping down here," offered Douglas.

"*Now* he tells me," Baines answered, flashing a smile.

Seated around a refectory table, they discussed their plan of action.

"I drained down the fuel system about a year after we arrived here," explained Hetfield. "Once it became apparent we weren't going anywhere, I thought it would protect all of the valves and injectors from getting 'sludged-up' over time."

"That was good thinking, Mor," Douglas acknowledged. "It may just give us the chance we need. Nevertheless, Ah expect we've got a few valves seized closed along the system somewhere. The electrics and electronics seemed to be working – as far as Ah could tell – which is great for us. Ah suspect it's a fuel starvation issue."

"OK. I'm ready when you are, James," Hetfield stated. "Ladies, if you could *man* the bridge?" he added, wiggling his eyebrows. "We'll need you to keep an eye on various readouts and switch things off and on as we need them, please."

"Sure thing," replied Marston. "Come, Jill, let me help you."

A little over an hour passed as the two men checked out the fuel system. They identified a problem within the fuel feed to thruster three. One of the motorised valves was indeed seized. More seriously, some of the fuel trapped within the unit had not only corroded the valve itself but also the chassis upon which it was mounted, destroying the electrics and the electronics too.

Douglas blew out his cheeks. "Don't suppose you have a spare?" he asked.

Hetfield looked at the partially disassembled valve despondently. "We did," he replied slowly. "Trouble is, when Captain Bessel blew the engines he also destroyed most of our spare parts. He wanted to make sure the soldiers with us had no way back to harm our families." He shook his head sadly. "There was no way he could have known, James."

"Aye, Ah know," agreed Douglas. "What about Jill's escape pod? Would there be anything we can salvage there?"

"No, the parts would be too small for this purpose. What we need is another ship to salvage so we can get this one running, to take it to *your* ship for use as salvage!"

Douglas frowned. "What if we used *all* of them?"

"What are you thinking?" asked Hetfield.

"Simply this, the damaged valve feeds into a four-way manifold, yes?" Hetfield nodded.

"So," continued Douglas, "if we forced the damaged valve open and then, taking all four of the smaller valves from the escape pod, placed them *after* the manifold, we could connect each to one of the four injectors *directly*. Ah mean... we'll probably have a fairly horrendous fuel leak, but we don't have to go far. With a bit of clever wiring, and some even cleverer bodging, we might just get a workaround. What do you think?"

"I think that sounds desperate and insane, James, but I'll give it a go!"

Lieutenant Sandip Singh leaned against the food bar in the staff mess aboard the *New World*. "I've called us all together to inform you that an attack has begun against the Pod. We received word just a couple of minutes ago."

A collective groan escaped the small gathering seated around the mess.

Singh continued. "Commander Gleeson is preparing to set off for the Pod in the next few minutes. His strike force will take their armoured vehicle. That'll leave us all but defenceless here. But then, I suppose we're pretty much defenceless anyway, against aerial attack from enemy ships, at least. I..." Singh tailed off, appearing a little uncertain, possibly even slightly embarrassed.

"In principle, I agree with Commander Gleeson's decision to go. Protection of our civilian population is of vital concern, *but*, I can't help wondering whether it's a bad idea leaving the *New World* to fend for herself.

"Even if they focused their efforts on the Pod, our enemies would still have enough manpower to overwhelm us here."

He paused, gauging people's reactions.

"We've taken their capital ship from them. Putting aside revenge for the moment, they must be considering taking the *New World* from us. For logistical reasons alone, she must be a target. So, what do you all think?"

Hiro raised a hand. "Does the commander know we're having this meeting?" he asked.

"Yes," said Singh. "It was his idea. I think he's split, too. Between what he feels is the right thing to do and what he believes is the *wise* thing to do. This places us all in a dilemma. If we can argue for him to stay, I think he will."

"In that case, I think we should protect this ship at all costs. Now hear me out," Hiro forestalled Singh's interruption. "I know you think I love this ship – I don't deny how important she is to me – but this is not about me or my desires. Without the *New World* we simply have no chance of *ever* getting home. Can we put a price on that in potential lives? I don't know, but I think we need to consider it."

After several moments of silence, Singh took his comm from a pocket. "Commander, this is Sandip. Sir, we need to talk."

Meritus stood straight, his feet shoulders' width apart, his hands clasped behind his back. His long coat parted, revealing a holstered pistol as he awaited the Pod ambassadors' approach.

They stopped three paces away.

"Major," greeted Meritus, with a respectful nod.

White offered a similar welcome. "Captain."

Meritus turned to the politician. "And you must be Miss Cocksedge."

"Ms," she corrected him, instinctively.

Meritus raised an eyebrow and bowed slightly. "*Please*, forgive me," he offered insincerely.

"OK," said White. "There's no point in lying, that massive crater in the middle of our compound got my attention. Now, what do you want to say to me?"

Meritus nodded. "Direct. I prefer that. I was sent here to take that Pod from your people, Major. I have always hoped that killing everyone in it would not be necessary. Will you leave peacefully?"

"I can't promise that, Captain. If you take our home, we won't survive anyway. We have little choice but to fight. So, I'm afraid I'm gonna have to refuse your first kind offer. Y'got any others?"

Meritus smiled. *An officer I can respect*, he thought. *Now, let's test the politician.* Before he had chance to invite Cocksedge, she stepped within a pace of him and began speaking anyway.

"Captain Meritus. First, let me say thank you, for agreeing to meet with me. I'm sure that whatever wrongs have been inflicted upon your people by our respective governments may be resolved simply, by us, here. Through honest dialogue, I hope we can realise that we have far more in common than we—"

"Wrongs inflicted by *your* people?" Meritus interrupted.

Cocksedge was thrown off track for a second only. "*Surely*, the American or British governments have done something, taken some privilege or otherwise impinged upon your rights, leaving you no alternative but to take action in this way? I am offering you the *opportunity*—"

Meritus held up his hand for her to stop as he looked to White for explanation.

White rubbed a large hand down his face, ending in a great sigh.

"Major?" asked Meritus. "Care to elaborate on all the things the British and American governments have done to me?"

"I've no idea what she's talking about," replied White, "but if I say I'm real sorry anyway, will you go away?"

Meritus threw back his head and laughed heartily. "*Ms* Cocksedge, I'm here to take the Pod. Can you speak for your people and surrender it to me – yes or no?"

"I can, of course, *speak* for my people and, naturally, we will take your points very seriously—"

"No, she can't," White cut her off, bluntly, "and no, she won't. She's a prisoner under investigation for charges of treason – a traitor. The only reason she's here is because you asked to see her and I was curious what the two of you were gonna talk about. Now, are we done here?"

Meritus laughed again before answering. "There are many ways one can become a traitor, Major – self-serving cowardice being just one of them. However, sometimes, things are simply more complicated than that. Sometimes, one can realise that they have perhaps backed the wrong horse?"

"Captain," White answered, tiredly, "we may have plenty of room in this compound, but do we have to dance around all of it before you get to the point? *I'm* quite *happy* with my 'horse'. It's carried me faithfully all these years. I just can't get behind siding with people who wanna kill half of my friends, just because, in their opinion, they were born in the wrong land. Not to mention all the people who will be wiped from time!"

"Perhaps we should hear more about the captain's offer before we disregard it out of hand, Major," Cocksedge interjected, smiling weakly.

"*Perhaps*," said Meritus, "*I* should make myself clear."

"That might help," White stated simply.

Meritus nodded once more. "We both have the same problem, it seems, Major. I don't disagree with your position. I'm here because I would rather *some* people survived than none at all – but that's perhaps a debate for another day. The problem I speak of affects us all and I can put a name to that problem, Major, and that name is Schultz.

"So, what I'm offering is… an alliance."

"Get down, James. *Get down!*" Hetfield whispered urgently.

He and Douglas hunkered behind a dead tree stump, just under the canopy of the copse where Baines had crashed a couple of days before. About thirty metres or so in front and to the left of them was a dinosaur. Douglas recognised it all too well.

"It's Cuthbert," said Hetfield, quietly.

Douglas shot him a look of surprise. "Eh?"

Hetfield held a finger to his lips. "Careful," he whispered. "He has excellent hearing."

"*Cuthbert?*" Douglas mouthed.

Hetfield grinned. "It's what I call him. We used to have a palaeontologist with us, he did the animals, Kelly did the plants – that was how it worked. Sadly, Vince died years ago from a viral infection, most of us got it but he..." he trailed off sadly.

"Anyway," he continued, changing the subject, "he told me the name of these critters. Tyrannotitan. I remembered the name because it's close to Tyrannosaurus – we all know that one, right? Cuthbert is about ten years old. I've watched him grow from a chick, but he's changing rapidly now. He's making three times the number of kills he used to make and stacking on the weight at a prodigious rate. You can almost *see* him growing, James.

"It was the same with his mother."

"His *mother*?" asked Douglas.

"Ssshh!" hissed Hetfield. "Yeah. She must be about, what, close to thirty now? She hunts a huge territory, so we don't see her that often these days – which is a very good thing, I can tell you. We always know when she's gonna come a-visitin', 'cause Junior over there always makes himself scarce!"

"He's afraid of his own mother?"

Hetfield nodded. "With good reason. She'd kill him in the blink of an eye, *if* she could catch him – which I doubt. At his age they're too fast. Anyhow, he doesn't give her the opportunity and I'd call that a real wise attitude!"

"Fast runner, is he?" whispered Douglas.

"Are you kiddin'? He can run like hell! Way faster than we are – or ever were, speaking for myself," admitted the old man. "If he lives, he'll grow to almost twice his length and ten times his mass in the next ten years. Matilda was the same. It's incredible. Of course, he may not make it, but I hope he does."

Douglas gave him a look of astonishment. "You hope he *does*?"

Hetfield smiled wryly. "James, this is our home and it's a most beautiful home. I make no bones about how dangerous it is – I'll grant you that – but we watched these creatures, within our little valley, grow from *eggs*. They're the closest things we have to children. We've led extraordinary lives here and even if it all ended tomorrow, I wouldn't have changed a thing. Hell, I would never have got with Kelly, if we hadn't been stranded here! What a poor schmo I would have been then, huh?"

The beginnings of understanding came to Douglas as he studied the old man. "And now we've turned up and we're trying to take it all away," he stated, nodding slowly.

Hetfield waved a hand. "No, it's not like that, James. God knows, we're glad to see you. You've no idea how we've missed you all, but the 22nd century? Not so much."

"Ah cannae tell ye how desperately we need the parts from the *Newfoundland*, Mor, but it's your call. Ah'll no' steal them from you."

"I know, James." Hetfield patted him on the shoulder. "And Kelly does. The simple truth is, one or other of us will probably be too slow, or too weak to climb or jump out of the way one of these days and that will leave one alone. I would hate to leave Kelly behind, Captain. You've given me hope that that won't happen now. You don't need to feel bad about it. We're *with* you.

"Now, we'd better see about getting those parts, hadn't we?"

"And what about young Cuthbert over there?" asked Douglas.

"No problem." Hetfield pulled a remote device from one of his many pockets. "I have this area mined, just in case we need to clear a way home. It happens, occasionally."

"I thought you wanted Cuthbert to grow up?!"

The old man chuckled softly. "Watch this."

A loud bang erupted from the ground near the adolescent Tyrannotitan, shocking it to rear in anger and confusion. Hetfield reset his remote and flicked the switch for a second time, causing another small but very load explosion to go off just *behind* the creature. This proved enough, and with a resentful roar the dinosaur ran away from them, climbing the trackway Baines' lifeboat had left in the earth.

Douglas marvelled at the speed with which the animal bounded up such a steep incline. Hetfield was right; they would have had no chance of outrunning it. More astonishing still, it just *kept going*. "That thing must be a hell of a long distance runner," he commented.

"You have no idea," agreed Hetfield. "And you really never want to find out. C'mon, let's get what we need before he recovers and makes his way back."

An hour later, they were safely back within the *Newfoundland* and working on the fuel system once more. Two hours after *that* they were ready for a second attempt. It was a little over an hour before noon and so, assuming they got off the ground without turning over half a kilometre of fuel, ceramic and steel into a second sun, they would have the better part of the day to search the nearby area for the *New World*.

Douglas felt like he had a gut full of hummingbirds. He was nervous of all the things that could wrong, of course, but what really turned his innards over was the thought of seeing his ship again. It had not occurred to him until that moment, just how much he had missed her.

"Hey, Kel," said Hetfield, turning around to face his lifelong partner. "If we're travelling east, I wonder if we'll see Daisy and Gertrude?"

"Gee, I'd love to see them one last time before we leave," replied Marston. "I know it sounds nuts but I can't help it – I'm really gonna miss those girls."

"Girls?" asked Baines.

"If we're going east we should see them," explained Marston. "They usually pass the springtime in that part of the valley." She smiled sadly. "They're beautiful!"

Baines returned her smile. "There's lots more beautiful things to see, Kelly," she said, gently. "I promise."

She turned to face the main view ports and took a deep breath. "OK, James," she said. "We've activated everything we can think of! It's up to you now. *Gently*, please."

"Aye, aye, Captain," said Douglas, beginning the engine start sequence.

Cocksedge's eyes widened with astonishment. "*You* wish to join *us*?" she managed at last. She moved quickly to step behind Major White, grasping his arm. "It's a trick," she said.

White shook her off irritably. "*Now* you don't think we should trust him? I'd ask, whose side are you on, lady? But what the hell would be the point?!"

He turned to Meritus, scrutinising him closely. "Are you on the level with this?"

"We should talk privately, Major."

White nodded slowly. "What if we were to take you inside and hold you hostage?" he asked, devil's advocate.

"Then that would be a mistake," Meritus replied coldly. "You really are better off dealing with me than..." He gestured to his people behind him in the attack ship. "I have some good men and women under my command, Major. However, some of them grew up in a regime not unlike the Hitler Youth Movement. I can control their *excesses*, but left to their own devices, I suspect they might make all the wrong choices. Do I make myself clear?"

"Clearer by the second," agreed White. "I think there are some folks you should meet."

Schultz waded through the shallows of the river crossing. They had followed the vehicle tracks to this point and could clearly see the chewed up earth on the other side, where the personnel carriers had climbed out of the water, up the opposite bank. As she approached midway a sail broke the water off to her right, to the east. *Run or remain still?* she thought.

A huge head surfaced and snorted, clearing its nostrils for air. It began to sniff and then gradually turned towards them.

"Run!" she cried.

Her small party moved as quickly as they could through the shallows, but the resistance of the water, coupled with the slippery, uneven pebble bed, made their going treacherous. They were almost at the far bank when the huge, blood red Oxalaia reached the shallows and stepped up out of the river. Water cascaded from its flanks, its huge, spiny fin blocking the morning sun and casting a shadow across the terrified humans. The water and irregular bed may have offered difficulty for Schultz's team, but to the giant creature it represented no obstacle at all. Before they reached the other side, it was upon them.

Its roar was terrifying. The first weapon in its arsenal, and it worked. Three of Schultz's number fell into the river, their panic to get away causing them to lose their footing. The Oxalaia snapped at all three men, killing them instantly.

The bodies were allowed to drop back into the river, turning it red where they fell. The animal was in a killing mood and obviously decided it could come back for them later, once it had secured its full catch. One of the men was bitten in half, so it allowed itself the torso as a snack to drive its appetite and bloodlust.

Schultz's eyes widened in shock, the rest of her party screamed and the mad scramble for the bank began. The dinosaur snapped like a crocodile but its size and reach was unanswerable. Another two men and a woman were caught in its jaws, just for the briefest second, but the snap carried the force of tons and the huge crocodilian teeth penetrated them all the way through. The beast dropped them like broken blood bags and moving forward, stepped on another man, crushing him into the stones of the riverbed without even seeing him.

Schultz and her remaining five troops made the bank just seconds after they first spotted the creature, the whole devastating encounter happening so quickly that they barely had time to register their peril.

With a firm footing at last, they turned to face the attack. Freeing the small hand weapons Meritus had allowed them, they brought them to bear, and the sporadic crack of small arms fire soon echoed across the valley.

Oxalaia roared in fury as the pin pricks stung its face and chest and forelimbs. With a final snap of defiance, it collected another man from the bank, crushing him in its jaws, but the monstrous animal knew better than to risk serious injury and moved quickly away from the threat. It snapped its enormous head back as it retreated, swallowing the man whole.

Schultz crashed roughly on her behind, breathing deeply. *That was close*, she thought. *For most of my team, too close.* In an instant, she had lost eight of her personnel, seven men and one woman. She glanced at her remaining followers. The only remaining woman, other than herself, seemed to have a damaged ankle from the scramble. Schultz assessed her coldly. *If she cannot move quickly, we may have to leave her behind.*

"Can you walk?" she asked.

The woman got to her feet shakily. Clearly in pain, she nodded bravely.

"Come," Schultz ordered brusquely. "We must go, and quickly!"

"Are you crazy?" asked Gleeson to the small assembly in the mess. "You want to send *me* as a representative?"

The *New World* had received a coded message from the Pod just a few minutes previously and Gleeson, as the senior officer, had been recalled to discuss their new reality.

"Sir," Singh tried. "You're in command, but as you said yourself, I can't leave the ship. Would you rather send *Hiro*?"

Chief Nassaki straightened, momentarily offended, but then shrugged, bowing to the logic of Singh's thinly veiled insult.

"Besides, Hiro's needed here more than *I* am," Singh tried again.

"Ahem," Patricia Norris interrupted them as politely as possible. "Might I make a suggestion?"

"Of course, Doctor," Gleeson invited.

"Maybe Dr Miller and I should go," began Norris. "As we both sit on the advisory council. We could take the wheeled personnel carrier, with an experienced driver, and see what the situation *actually* is."

"That could be dangerous, Patricia," Singh pointed out. "Regardless of what you find back at the Pod, that's not a journey to make lightly."

"I agree, but we can add little to your efforts here. These are, after all, 'engineering' problems. Jim has to go back anyway, to oversee manufacturing of the parts you'll need. Most importantly, it will leave our only armament, that little tank outside, here. In my opinion, where it should be, guarding this ship. Your abilities as a soldier cannot be questioned, Commander. I'd feel easier in my mind if I knew you were protecting the *New World*."

She smiled at the Australian. "Also, I agree with you."

"You do?" asked Gleeson.

"Yes," she stated simply. "I have *so* much respect for your courage, ability and ingenuity, Commander, but regarding this embassy, I think I'd keep you on the reserve team."

Gleeson laughed heartily. "When you're right, you're right," he admitted ruefully.

Norris smiled warmly at him. "If all the talk goes nowhere and we need someone to make them leave, we'll call you," she added with a wink.

"So we're *all* staying here then," Singh stated, eyeing the senior officers.

"Back where we started, mate. Ain't that always the way?" said Gleeson.

"Captain Meritus," Mother Sarah greeted, coldly. "You'll forgive me if I don't shake hands with you."

Meritus retracted his proffered hand, giving her and Patel a smart salute instead.

Patel nodded coolly. "Won't you please sit, Captain?" he said, gesturing to a seat around the large table which dominated one of the lecture rooms within the Pod's science department.

Also present were Major White and Dr Sam Burton, in his capacity as the Pod's chief of operations.

"You will forgive us, I'm sure, Captain," added Patel. "Our *full* leadership is rather *dispersed* at the moment."

Meritus managed a wry smile. "Trust me, I know. I've witnessed their work abroad. Now, shall we continue trading carefully polite, carefully masked barbs or shall we see if we can bring this *unpleasantness* to a profitable conclusion for us all?"

Patel nodded. "We are listening, Captain. We have been attacked constantly and without mercy since we boarded this Pod. Make no mistake we want it to end – but I warn you, not at *any* cost."

Meritus nodded. *Schultz was wrong about these people,* he thought, *as she was about so many things. I see no weakness in them. It's probably just as well, too.*

"Dr Patel," he began, "lady and gentlemen, we've all been weakened by the events which have brought us to this point in time. I don't blame you for meeting our combative stance with aggression of your own. In fact, I admire you for it. I was assured by Dr Heidi Schultz that you were leaderless and soft!" He chuckled ruefully. "The destruction of my ship, and without a true weapon to your name, would suggest otherwise. Yours was a deeply impressive strategy, but *costly*.

"Now, it must be obvious to all of us here, that the Schultzes are quite mad."

"Hear, hear," said White.

"What you don't know, is that there was a beacon aboard the *Last Word*. It was only meant to be activated *after* we'd taken possession of *Factory Pod 4*. However, Heidi sneaked aboard – after your Captain Baines so gracefully delivered my ship to the bottom of that ravine – and activated it. It's been broadcasting for almost twenty-four hours, now."

"Broadcasting what exactly?" asked Burton.

"A signal through time," replied Meritus.

"How?" asked Patel, leaning forward.

"Forgive me, Doctors, but that is a little outside my area of expertise—"

"Your expertise being killing people," stated Sarah, flatly.

Meritus stared at her for a long moment. "To my certain knowledge, you people have killed more than sixty of mine and seriously injured almost thirty more. I can tell you the names of each and every one of them – would you like to hear the roll call of my dead, Mother Sarah?"

She did not answer.

"I have ordered no attack on your people, have killed no one," he continued. "Yet I am here offering peace, when I could so easily have wreaked revenge upon you all."

A stony silence fell as the Pod crew looked from one to another uncomfortably.

Eventually, Patel offered, "We did not begin this violence, Captain. Although you yourself may not have killed any of our number yet, you are part of an expeditionary force to do just that."

"Not necessarily. Since *I* have been here, *you* have been the aggressors, but I did not come here to debate that, or score any points over past mistakes – whoever is responsible for them.

"The important thing is this. Heinrich Schultz, Heidi's grandfather, has a small fleet of warships waiting in the 22nd century to jump here upon completion of our mission. He may well be on his way to join us already. His fleet could arrive at any time."

"Maybe *you* will forgive *me*, Captain," said Sarah, "but if you're about to be heavily reinforced, why would you care about making a deal with us now?"

Meritus smiled. "You have struck to the heart of the matter, Mother Sarah. Firstly, I remind you of my previous statement – the Schultzes are insane. Secondly, we did *not* arrest possession of the Pod away from you before the message was sent. It seems that to do so now, we would have to take it from you by force. I could do this, of course, but it would be a costly action, both in terms of lives and matériel.

"When Heinrich Schultz arrives he will be furious. He will perceive this as an unequivocal failure to carry out his orders. If I do not take this Pod from you now, he will be correct. Heidi may think her familial relationship to that old tyrant will save her, but I have doubts. She was the one to activate your shuttle's homing beacon, which I suspect caused Captain Baines' *overreaction*, shall we call it?"

"You might," said White. "I call it evening the odds."

Meritus smiled again. "Anyhow, I believe Heidi's arrogance and continual disregard for my orders cost us our battleship. She may be able to cast the blame onto me, perhaps, but either way, I expect summary execution when the old man arrives. Like yourselves, I don't believe in sitting around and waiting for the enemy to come and kill me.

"You may well think that, unable to fight my way in here without damaging the prize, I'm simply trying to talk my way in instead. Subsequently, I don't doubt you have reservations about trusting me—"

"You think?" interrupted Burton.

"Quite," acceded Meritus. "But let me explain *my* position—"

"*You* need *us* to save *your* ass!" snapped White.

"Major, whether you decide to accept my offer or not, you will see that I still have significant resources and many loyal personnel at my disposal. Do you really think I will go down so easily?"

White gave him an appraising look. "No," he admitted, grudgingly.

Meritus continued, "What I meant was, let me explain my *philosophical* position."

This comment raised eyebrows around the table, each member of the Pod staff irresistibly thinking about Del Bond, down in the cells.

"I'm no Nazi. I'm simply a soldier," he added.

"Just following orders, huh?" interjected Sarah.

"No!" Meritus slapped his hand, palm down on the table, showing his first sign of irritation. "This has nothing to do with ethics or blindly following orders. I *know* Heinrich Schultz is a monster, but he is a monster with a plan and that plan is to save at least *some* people, when the human world ends.

"I know you guys are all about hope and scientific endeavour, but we all know that Mars is a pipe dream – too little, too late. The human race is doomed. There's no way Mars will be viable to transplant enough of the population quickly enough to save us. You're a man of science, Dr Patel, *you* tell *me*. What do we have, fifty years before the end? Thirty? Twenty, even?"

Patel looked uncomfortable. "That's hard to say with any surety, Captain."

Meritus gave him a look of sufferance. "Come, Doctor. Let's not be coy. Schultz is the only one with a plan to save the human race, but it's a flawed plan. It took an evil genius to come up with such a scheme, so naturally it comes with a certain… *bias*."

He reached for a glass and the pitcher of water in the centre of the table, helping himself.

"Schultz's plan to 'reboot' the human race may be our only chance to continue the story of our kind. However, his selective approach is limited and naïve – let's leave good and evil out of this for a minute. You have the people and the personnel aboard this Pod to recreate all the glories of humanity – *I* know this, but Schultz will have no part of it.

"Together, your brains and resources, coupled with my muscle, could survive this world – possibly forever, if we learn from our mistakes and I suggest, lady and gentleman, that this is lesson one."

A deep rumbling began to shake the water in the pitcher and made the glasses tinkle together on the tray. Gradually the noise became louder. The five seated around the table stood and walked to the window. Approaching from the east were three black objects in the sky. They very quickly grew larger, their nature becoming clear. Three large vessels, all black, roared overhead shaking the very deck plates the watchers stood upon. As the swell died away, Meritus spoke into the sudden silence.

"I would love to let you discuss the pros and cons of this lesson, people, but if I'm not mistaken, that was the final bell."

Chapter 12 | Hope and Damnation

"Thruster three is firing but it's on the fritz, Captain," Hetfield called across the bridge. "I'm increasing the pressure from its pump to 110 percent to compensate. This may blow our temporary pipes and manifold!"

"Hold it together," Douglas called back. "Once we've lifted you'll be able to dial it back, but Ah need everything you've got, Mor. The jungle is holding onto us!"

Outside the *Newfoundland*, fires were erupting around each of the four main lift thrusters. As the behemoth began to move, a terrible groaning and cracking sound came from plant life which had long since accepted the giant ship into its embrace. As earth spilled from the sides of the half-buried craft in giant furrows, an entire mini ecosystem was ripped apart or put to the flame.

550 metres long from bow to stern, over time, the *Newfoundland* had become just another hill in a valley filled with small hills, but it was leaving now. The roar of the rocket motors became frenetic and ear shredding as the Earth's final clutches lost their grip, releasing her to the skies.

"*YEEEAH!*" shouted the bridge crew as the old ship gained altitude, dropping and scattering entire trees like bombs upon the ground below.

Douglas gently turned her to the east and began to move forwards. As they rose, the view of the entire valley blossomed before their very eyes. Douglas found it movingly beautiful, despite his terror of the ancient vessel falling apart or blowing herself up.

"We've left ruin behind us," Hetfield noted with regret. "We always make such a mess of things."

"Aye," agreed Douglas. "We created a crucible of fossil-fuelled irony down there, right enough. But it'll recover, Mor. Nature always survives us – she always will."

They cleared a small ridge of low hills and were about to cross into a larger valley when Marston called out, "Look, Mor! There they are! It's Daisy and Gertrude!"

"Hello, my beautiful girls," cried Hetfield, a tear escaping from his eye. "These are the animals I mentioned earlier, Jill. They must be as old as me!"

Baines stared at the sauropod dinosaurs below them in wonder. They were absolutely enormous, possibly even bigger than the incredible Argentinosaurus they already knew. They were clearly similar, what Tim referred to as Titanosaurs, but none of that mattered to Baines. She began to laugh. Despite all the perils they faced, the sheer spectacle offered by the world they had fallen into was joyous to behold. "They're amazing, Mor. They're *huge*! At a time like this, it may be unwise to tempt fate, but the phrase 'see Cretaceous Patagonia and die' does spring irresistibly to mind!"

Douglas took the craft ever upward to avoid scaring the creatures below them. Both animals craned their necks, turning their heads towards them. Although the bridge crew could not hear them, they clearly saw the animals open their mouths to call.

"Goodbye, Daisy. Goodbye, Gertrude," said Kelly, before covering her mouth and nose with her hands as she tried to hold back tears. Continuing huskily, between her fingers, she added, "Most of our lives we've watched them grow…"

They continued to acquire altitude in order to clear the much higher, more jagged mountains which formed the outer bowl of Hetfield and Marston's little world. For the old couple, fifty years of life was reduced to memory in a blur of emotion, as they cleared the crags and were gone.

"It's not all bad news," said Meritus, eventually. The protracted silence had started to become painful.

White rounded on him forcefully. "What the hell is that supposed to mean?!" His tone was merely a symptom of the anxiety they were all feeling.

"Calm yourselves," said Meritus, gently. "I need to get back to my crew, but before I go, I need your answer. *Do* we have an agreement?"

After looking from one to another, Patel finally spoke. "What form do you see this agreement taking, Captain? We will not allow your soldiers in here until we know a lot more about you and your actual purposes and agenda – no offence," he added sardonically.

"None taken," replied Meritus. "Look, we're out of time here. That much is clear to me, and all of you, I'm sure. So what I suggest is this – I bring all of my people within your ramparts for now, so that we can share in the protection you have industriously constructed for yourselves here. We'll camp right outside your doors, so that Schultz doesn't get any ideas about bombing us. It's my absolute belief that he needs this Pod intact.

"We have many wounded among our number, maybe we could talk about setting up a temporary hospital within your hold, perhaps? But we can sort out the details later.

"Can we make this happen now, before the old man gets his bearings and finds out just what the hell has been going on here?"

They all nodded agreement.

"Very well," said White. "We can agree to that. Before you leave, perhaps you could tell us what you meant by 'not all bad news'?"

"Certainly, Major. Firstly, we are stronger now than we were half an hour ago, even if we haven't yet ironed out the details and secondly, Schultz is a creature of habit with a fondness for dairy produce. He starts every day with hens' eggs on toast followed by a glass of milk." Meritus grinned. "If you haven't already run out of those, I'm guessing you soon will, yes? One of those ships will have chickens and cows aboard."

"Well, thank God for that!" sniped Burton, acerbically. "Just give us a few minutes to round up the men and we'll organise a rustle across the border!"

"I might hold you to that, Dr Burton. It would really break Schultz's stride!" Meritus laughed and then gave a slight bow. "Lady and gentlemen."

A pair of White's soldiers showed Meritus out and back to his people.

"What do you think of him, Ford?" asked Patel, once the doors had closed behind him.

"I think he's fearless, but not reckless," replied White. "But if you're asking, do I trust him?" He considered a moment longer. "I don't know yet."

Singh placed his elbows on the pilot's console and held his head in his hands. The Pod's message had arrived several minutes previously. He called Commander Gleeson to the bridge, but otherwise could not bring himself to move.

The bridge doors opened and Gleeson strode in. Noting the obvious distress emanating from his second in command, he stepped carefully over to the lieutenant.

"What is it, Sandy?" he asked, gently, placing a comradely hand on the pilot's shoulder.

Singh raised his head to look Gleeson in the face, blowing out a heavy sigh. "Commander," he answered wearily. "I assume you heard that bass rumble a few minutes ago? We thought it might be some kind of natural event – a tremor perhaps, knowing the long instability of this area's geology. We've just received a message from the Pod."

"And?" asked the Australian, himself developing a sinking feeling in his gut.

"Three war ships just flew over them, heading east. Clearly, they were en route to the destroyed enemy vessel – will be there by now, in fact."

Gleeson sat, deflating. After the merest of moments, he straightened. "Hang on a minute, Sandy. Listen…"

Singh did as ordered. "I can't hear anything, sir."

"Exactly, there's no fat lady hollering just yet – so chin up, my friend!" He stood and grinned. "It's time to get crazy!"

Singh stood and held out his hand. "I'm glad you're here, Commander."

"I'm bladdy not! But in truth, I've got nowhere better to be. You ready to fight?"

Singh nodded determinedly.

"That's ma boy," said Gleeson, and pulled him into a back slapping embrace.

Heidi Schultz scrambled back down the tree. The view afforded from near the top of the forest canopy confirmed what she already suspected. Her diminished team heard the rumbling of their approach for miles before the ships actually passed them.

Her grandfather's fleet flew approximately half a mile due south of them, as it travelled east towards the last resting place of their ruined battleship. Unfortunately, Meritus had refused them compasses or communications equipment, so all she could do was watch – but as she did so, a wide grin split her face.

The injured woman in their party was beginning to struggle. Trailing ever further behind, she caught up with the rest of their party as Schultz landed lightly on the forest floor.

"My *Großvater* is here," she told them triumphantly. "Now we will see some improvement in our situation."

"Do we return to the *Last Word*, Dr Schultz?" asked one of the men.

Heidi weighed this for a moment.

"No," she decided at last. "We are close to the enemy. We must gather what intelligence we can, before meeting with my *Großvater*. If we return empty-handed after such a debacle, it may well go badly for us. We need a prize. Whether that be information or something more tangible, we shall see. We march!"

The wounded and their guards, from Meritus' detachment, lingered behind long after his aerial advance force had left. As ordered, they remained at the site of the *Last Word*, making every effort to ensure that the injured personnel could be transported as comfortably as possible before setting out.

Their three vehicles were now eating up the miles ravenously as they also followed the now well travelled path created by the stampede and Gleeson's escape.

The flyover of Heinrich Schultz's fleet only incentivised them to further increase their rate of progress. Having chosen Meritus over Heidi Schultz, they knew there would be no safety in lingering to be caught by their former comrades.

In truth, many of them did not really know where they stood on these rapidly shifting sands of allegiance. After Meritus had expelled Schultz from their camp, the majority had simply chosen to stay and live within a framework of military justice and discipline. It was something they understood. Whereas the undisputed architects of their mission promised a rather more capricious form of leadership.

They were all here to save the human race and although most of Meritus' people bore the stoicism of soldiers, many understood that *humanity* required more than just a few living bodies, saved from a ruined world.

They drove towards the one man they believed could offer them life.

The old man stared from the bridge viewports in a state of pure incandescence. Utterly speechless, his fury had risen so instantly that he had not yet had the time to lose his temper. Wrath, such as even he had never known, burned through his every sinew. He shook with it.

Below him was the wreckage of trillions of dollars and years of work.

The hush on the bridge was as silent as space. The crew studied their instruments as if they bore a grudge against them, terrified of the rage which must surely follow.

"Take us down," he managed through gritted teeth. "I want a boarding party to inspect that ship and another team to search the entire site around it. I want to know what happened here immediately upon their return. See to it!" he snapped and strode from the *Eisernes Kreuz*'s bridge towards his opulent quarters within its heart.

Schultz could almost feel the heat of Heinrich Schultz's fury burning her from afar. She knew exactly how murderous her grandfather would be when he found the ruined *Last Word*. She would have to bring him something *very* special to assuage his tyranny – granddaughter or no.

Her squad had travelled most of the day and she now suspected they were fairly close to where the *New World* had crashed.

The road smashed through the forest by Gleeson's small convoy was still easy to follow and, despite injuries, they were making excellent time.

By late afternoon, they came upon the new road created to link the *New World* with the Pod. A mere cursory glance told Schultz that vehicular traffic had travelled along it very recently, in both directions.

"This is a supply route," she stated. "We know that we shot their ship down. Clearly they have sent a rescue or perhaps even a repair team."

"If that ship is still operational, this could place an entirely different complexion on things," she said, smiling wolfishly.

"It will be well guarded, ma'am," one of her soldiers pointed out.

"Perhaps," she accepted. "But we will not let that dissuade us from taking a lesser prize, for now."

She turned to them, animatedly, ordering two of the soldiers to take up positions on the opposite side of the road. Schultz waited with the others. The woman with the injured ankle used low growing brush to camouflage her shape. Everyone else climbed to safer positions within the lower branches, covering the T-junction with a crossfire, and as the afternoon sun began to dip, they waited…

The repair crews aboard the *New World* had redoubled their efforts throughout the day. It was only a matter of *when* the attack came, and everyone knew it.

After doing all they could to help, Jim Miller, Rose, Tim and his mother, Patricia, met up with Singh, Gleeson and The Sarge in the mess.

"We should get back," said Miller. "Can we borrow Bluey to drive us, please? Neither of us is used to driving heavy vehicles and it's a rough road."

Singh nodded but before he could agree, The Sarge spoke.

"I should go with them, sirs," he said, looking between Gleeson and Singh. "We have enemies all around us now. These people must be protected."

"What about your arm, Sarge?" asked Gleeson.

"It's much better today, sir."

"*Is* it?" replied the commander, his slight smile betraying the fact that he thought The Sarge both heroically brave and a damned liar. "If that's the case, Sarge, then I need you here all the more. Those crazies won't pass up a chance to take this ship.

"Don't get me wrong, I know that these folks are gonna be making a very dangerous journey, but I think it could be even worse here, an hour or two from now."

He turned to Miller. "Jim, take Bluey, take the kids and get out of here as soon as you can. Oh, and make sure you call ahead. Major White and Sam Burton should be told that if you don't make the journey in *one hour*, they must send out a rescue party immediately. I don't want to take any chances."

He looked to Tim and Patricia. "I wish you two weren't here at all, to be perfectly blunt. I can't believe Jill took you with her, but here we are. I wish you good luck and hope to see you all soon."

At that moment the rumbling began.

Gleeson rolled his eyes. "Oh, bladdy hell!"

"The bridge!" cried Singh and they all ran.

As they entered the bridge, Singh practically dived for the sensor station. The others followed him in, panting after their sprint across the ship.

The noise was still gaining in intensity but also in clarity as they ran. It was now definitely the roar of a ship's engines.

Singh tilted his head to one side. "That doesn't sound right," he said.

"Bladdy hell, Sandy," snapped Gleeson. "Can you tell me what *is* right about all this? It's a big ship! We don't have any, and unless Santa's decided to come early in a rocket powered sleigh, we're well and truly in the sh—"

"Ssshh!" hissed Singh. "Sorry, sir, but I don't understand. Those are not the main engines of *any* kind of capital ship, they're thrusters. And they're not running properly, either."

"So what's coming?" asked Gleeson, puzzled.

"Running scans," replied Singh. After a moment he sat back slowly, in complete bafflement. "*What the hell?!*"

"We're being hailed," said The Sarge. He stepped across to the pilot's usual station and accepted the call, nodding to Singh to signify that he was now on an open channel.

"Approaching vessel, this is Lieutenant Singh of the USS *New World*. Please state your intentions."

"*Sandy, what the hell have ye done to ma ship?!*" ranted Captain James Douglas.

Schultz heard the low moan of a diesel engine. No, diesel *engines*, she decided. It was difficult to be sure, but she believed they were coming from behind them, along the track they had followed to arrive here.

"Stay out of sight!" she ordered.

Although the afternoon was wearing on, they were fortunate that there was still good daylight. Without the use of infrared, the drivers should find it very difficult to spot them, unless specifically using the machines' basic scanning equipment to find them by other means. Schultz did not think this likely. Within their armour they must feel safe from the wildlife and would expect no other problems in this area.

After a few minutes of waiting in silence, the first vehicle became visible a couple of hundred metres back down the track, behind them. The three tracked vehicles were in convoy, the armed transport leading, as she would have expected. Schultz knew their other armed personnel carrier had been stolen by the bombing team from the *New World*, so these three vehicles together could only be Meritus' people.

Schultz squinted in anger and massaged her temple as she fought to regain control. Her pathetic little squad were only armed with pistols. The magnanimous Meritus had made a grand speech about not wishing to cast out any of *his* people, however misguided, without the means to protect themselves in this violent world.

Her eye twitched again as she seethed in silence. Her companions all looked to where she hid, awaiting her instructions. She had no choice but to shake her head. There was absolutely nothing they could do against the vehicles' armour.

The personnel carriers very quickly drew alongside their position at the T-junction and all turned right without hesitation, clearly heading for the Pod and its compound.

Schultz watched them disappear along the forest road on a more or less easterly heading.

Meritus met with Lieutenant Weber and his two remaining active sergeants. He had waited out most of the day to see if there were any further developments before explaining his plans. Just to cover his bases. However, Heinrich Schultz had made no immediate move on their position, so he must now commit.

"I have made a deal with the crew of the *New World*," he stated. "We will move our ships as close as we can to the Pod so that they make less tempting targets from the air. Our ground vehicles should already be well on their way here."

"A deal, sir?" asked Weber.

"Yes, Lieutenant. As you will all have realised by now, I'm sure, the Schultz plan was the only game in town with regards to saving at least *some* of the human race. I still believe that we're doing good work here, in striving for that. However, I'm sure that it will also not have escaped your notice, that our highest leadership is quite mad."

Weber looked uncomfortable. Meritus did not believe him to be a blind follower of the Schultz philosophy, but he had nevertheless grown up within the regime they created.

"Lieutenant," said Meritus, then began again using the young man's Christian name, "*Richard*, we have all the resources we came for, right here. There are close to a hundred people inside *Factory Pod 4*, many of them scientists of the highest order, all of them fit, most of the women still of child-bearing age."

"But they're the enemy, sir," said Weber.

"Are they, Richard? Just because elements of the Schultz movement have attacked them, quite viciously I understand, does not necessarily make them *our* enemy. We can choose to fight them or we can join them."

Weber was outraged. "*Join* them! They killed sixty of our people, Captain!"

Meritus nodded. "Yes, they did. And I know it's hard to get past that, but we are all soldiers. If we were in their position and about to face the *Last Word* without so much as a proper rifle, I can only hope that we would have acted with so much courage and ingenuity, eh?

"Now don't misunderstand me, I mourn our people, but we came here to do battle and take from our enemy their only chance of surviving this brutal world. We cannot be surprised when they fight back.

"I think joining with them, to save as many people as possible, gives us another option. A better option."

Weber looked suspicious now. "What, exactly, are you suggesting we do, sir?"

Meritus scrutinised the young man for a few seconds before answering. "I think you mean, what are my *orders*, don't you, Lieutenant?"

Weber straightened and clicked his heels in salute. "Of course, that is exactly what I meant, sir."

I wonder, thought Meritus.

"My orders are simple, people. We defend this Pod against any who come to take it, for now. From there, we'll see how things develop. It must be clear to you, that we did not take our objectives prior to the Dawn Fleet's arrival. Heidi Schultz activated the signal beacon in direct contravention of our orders, and in doing so, took away many of the options we may otherwise have had.

"She may well be one of the most lethal individuals I've ever met, but she's no soldier. She has no concept of strategy or procedure, she's just dangerous! And most importantly, I believe her arrogance and dereliction led to the deaths of our comrades as surely as the rather more honourable military actions of the *New World*'s crew – our *former* enemy.

"Grandad Schultz will not rest until he has annihilated us for failing him, and for what he will certainly perceive as treachery.

"The people aboard that Pod are already on his 'to kill' list, so they have nothing to lose by opposing him. Even the ones who are not marked for death seem determined to stand up and be counted with the ones who are. And who can blame them? They also have a weapon in their arsenal that we do not."

"I thought they had no weapons to speak of, Captain?" asked Weber, warily.

Meritus noticed that both of his sergeants, a man named Hans Baier and a woman named Mila Daniels, had so far said nothing.

"There are many types of weapons, Lieutenant. In this instance they have the asset that the Schultzes are desperate to attain – crucially, attain in an undamaged state.

"This gives the crew of the *New World* an edge on a playing field which is otherwise heavily weighted against them. They can strike, but Schultz must be oh so careful when he strikes back.

"They also have their ingenuity, it seems, and their courage. This surely cannot be doubted. We may have lost the *Last Word*, but with cunning and a little courage of our own, I think we can hold this world. I intend to deny Heinrich Schultz this asset he so craves.

"I very much doubt we'll be able to deal with the fanatic – so we will just have to find a way to *deal* with the fanatic!"

The bone-numbing grinding from below, accompanied by some fairly alarming *crack*s and *pop*s, were grating Douglas' nerves. He grimaced like a champion gurner, forcing himself not to close his eyes as the *Newfoundland* landed alongside the *New World*.

Using the largest open area available, the ship had filled the beach, also flattening the edge of the forest. Despite this, his rear portside landing strut was still thirty metres out into the lake.

He was not clear whether the last time the sister ships stood side by side was a hundred million years ago, fifty years ago or a few weeks ago. Somehow it was all three and they both looked rather the worse for wear.

With a final groaning scrape to the accompaniment of a hundred lesser *snap*s, the manoeuvre was finally concluded. They had landed.

The crew of four made their way down to the Rescue Pod carried under the giant ship's belly. From here they could take its lift down to terra firma.

As they lowered themselves, they saw a hatch open on the *New World*, followed immediately by the appearance of a step ladder.

Douglas helped Baines walk between the two ships, supporting her left side while she held her crutches under her right arm.

Marston and Hetfield followed sheepishly behind, naturally overwhelmed by the thought of meeting so many people after so long – at least, it was a long time for them.

Singh leapt the two metres from the *New World*, straight down onto the sand. Sprinting forwards, he threw his arms around his captains.

By the time the others had caught up with Singh, Douglas finally found his voice. "Ah never thought Ah'd see any of ye again," he croaked hoarsely.

He was way beyond salutes or handshakes and made sure he embraced every single one of them, individually, as if making sure they were real.

Singh was shaking his head, laughing through a few unexpected tears. "That was *some* entrance, Captain. Where *the hell* did you find another ship?!"

"It's a long, long story, son," he answered, squeezing his pilot's shoulder affectionately.

Singh nodded, wiping his eyes. "We'd better get inside to hear it, sir. We've got a really big dinosaur in the area and he or she is very unhappy that we're here."

With that he ushered everyone aboard the *New World* for what would undoubtedly be an extraordinary exchange.

"I hate to say it, but we could really use their help right about now," said White, stating what everyone else must surely have been thinking.

The mood of the gathering could only be described as maudlin.

"I've prayed for guidance to help us with our decision," admitted Sarah, in little more than a mumble. "For myself, I just don't know what to think. Since we left our world behind, so much has happened and in such rapid succession, now things seem to be accelerating still further."

"Have your prayers provided you with counsel, Sarah?" asked Patel, kindly.

"I'm not sure," she confessed honestly. "At face value, I see this as an opportunity to strengthen our position, but much more than that, if we can turn an enemy into a friend, then surely that's a good thing, right? Especially as they were on a path towards – and I choose my words carefully – what I can only describe as evil.

"Can we trust this reversal? I don't know. My instinct is to try, but I don't know if that *is* the answer to my prayers or just me wishing for the best." She smiled at her own confusion.

"I think that pretty much sums up how I feel about it too," Burton agreed. "It worries me just how much I want to believe his offer is genuine. Smacks of desperation, doesn't it? And once we go down that road, there won't be any turning back. The enemy will, once more, be *within*."

White nodded. "What do you think, Satnam?" he asked levelly.

Patel stroked his chin and took a while before answering. "It goes without saying that this might simply be a ruse to take the Pod from us, without the more direct military action that could result in extensive damage to the Pod.

"However, I have been thinking for some hours now about what would happen if we turned Captain Meritus' offer down.

"Forgive me, Major, I have the greatest respect for your abilities as a military leader, *but*, the way I see it, they have more resources in terms of trained soldiers and weapons than we could ever hope to match. If we say 'no' we can, at best, die by inches.

"We could drag it out, perhaps, but I can see no way to win against so many and with the hardware they can bring to bear. We pulled off a masterstroke against their battleship. Our teams on the ground and aboard the *New World* executed nothing short of a miracle, in my opinion. It was an extraordinary achievement, but one we will never be able to repeat.

"If that battleship was an end to the affair and Captain Meritus' reduced force were all we had to face, I would give us fair odds. But these new arrivals change everything, and not just logistically.

"We are now impossibly overmatched in terms of matériel and far worse than this, we now face a very different kind of foe.

"Now that we have seen 'the face of our enemy', so to speak, in the guise of Captain Meritus, it seems to me that he is, first and foremost, a soldier. Wouldn't you agree, Major?"

White nodded, but allowed Patel to continue.

"He is an *enemy* soldier, but unless I miss my guess, a man of duty and of honour.

"Again, if the enemy battleship had been all that was sent against us, I think we could hold our own, or possibly even come to an accord with Meritus.

"However, we now know that the true mastermind behind all that has happened is now here, and I doubt very much whether any kind of arrangement could be made with him. We have only his granddaughter to judge him by, true, but as one of his senior captains would rather join us than face his own boss, this would suggest that Schultz the elder is something even worse – far worse, potentially."

He looked at Sarah and squeezed her hand affectionately. "I too, now choose my words carefully. As an Indian man, I believe that myself, and many of the other nationalities aboard this Pod, are in absolute peril for our lives. However, there are many of you who may be able to save yourselves and live within this new regime. It would probably be abhorrent to you all, but you *could* do it, to live. What I am saying is, all of our people are like family to me and I would rather save some of us, than kill us all to save myself and others like me."

The force of his offer hit Sarah like a hammer blow and she broke down. After a moment she rose, through her tears, to stand behind Patel, placing her hands on his shoulders. "Satnam, I would give my life a thousand times, standing shoulder to shoulder with you, before I would live one *day* under that creature's regime!" she spat forcefully.

"Hear, hear," agreed White, standing too. "I swore I would do everything in my power to defend the people aboard this Pod, even if the cost was my life. I won't go back on that now. You're a remarkable man, Dr Patel. I salute you, and we are with you, *all* the way."

"Too right," said Burton, also standing.

Patel got to his feet and reached across the table for their hands. "Thank you, my dear friends. In that case, I suggest we accept Captain Meritus' offer. And in doing so, we either gain a solid ally and secure our position or lose much more quickly, but either way, we go out fighting!"

Chapter 13 | The Chase

"I'll go back to our people on the Pod, James," said Baines. "The *New World* has her captain back. You don't need me here now, especially with my gammy leg! I'll hitch a ride with Bluey. I can make myself useful on the journey by stopping Tim from terrifying his mother, Jim and Rose with his 'dinosaur facts'."

Douglas appeared unsure for a moment. "That could be a dangerous journey with just one vehicle. Ah agree that we should keep the air clear and avoid using the lifeboats – they're too easy for our enemies to track."

"Or shoot down," Baines added, tetchily.

"Exactly," continued Douglas. "So, my instinct is to keep you all here until we can assemble a convoy."

"I see your point, James, but that might be a while, and there is so much going on over there. I think one of us should be a part of it, don't you? I can't do anything here, anyway, with my injury. Besides, when they come for the ship, they're likely to be a lot less gentle than they will be with the Pod. We may well be safer over there."

Douglas mulled over her points. "What you say makes sense, Jill. Ah just cannae shake the feeling that we should wait." He gave her a half smile. "But it's your call – *Captain*."

"Having experienced the big chair, I'm quite happy with 'commander', thank you," she replied.

"Hear, hear," Gleeson chipped in. "And I can go back to just being the bloke who blows stuff up!"

"No," said Douglas with finality. "If you're going over there, it's to take command, Jill. There's no backward step for you. You've done a hell of a job so far and those people will need your determination to get things done. Ah've total confidence in your leadership.

"And you, *Commander* Gleeson, Ah'll need here. Ah expect it's going to get rough. Can Ah rely on ye?"

Gleeson straightened and gave Douglas a smart salute. "Of course, sir."

"Good man," Douglas stated, gratefully. Turning back to Baines, he said, "If you're committed to this course, then you'd better get going, Jill. Please take care and send us a message as soon as you arrive safely at the other end."

It was hard for them to leave, but after making their farewells, they embarked upon their expedition back to the Pod.

A six mile drive would normally have been so routine as to border on banal, but their circumstances were extreme. They would be a lone vehicle on a very rough road through some challenging terrain – terrain potentially filled with terrifying predators. However, by far the greatest shadow cast over their journey came from the new and deadly enemy in the region.

Baines knew that Schultz's forces could attack at will and without warning. Going with the assumption that they would probably need to catch up with events and take stock before making a move, her one hope lay in getting back to the Pod before the enemy could organise themselves. Baines gambled that this would be more difficult now, as Meritus' people were no longer at their rendezvous point to answer any questions. She hoped this would buy them a little extra time.

Meritus' sudden defection also gave her great cause for concern. Even if genuine, their first meeting would surely be rather strained, after what she and her crew had just done to the man. She had great trouble in picturing anyone associated with the Schultzes as the 'forgiving type'.

Bluey broke into her thoughts as he opened a secure comm channel to the Pod. After a moment's delay he got through to chief of operations, Sam Burton.

"Sam, it's Bluey."

"*Reading you loud and clear, Bluey. Go ahead.*"

"We're departing the *New World* now, that's 1725 hours. We expect to be with you within *one* hour. Repeat: we should be with you by 1825 hours."

"*ETA 1825 hours – check.*"

"If we're not there within the hour, mate, you won't waste any time before sending a rescue, will ya?"

Burton chuckled. "*Don't worry – we won't let you guys down. And Bluey, take care. Burton out.*"

Bluey turned to Baines, strapped into one of the cab's two passenger seats. "Well, that's it, Captain, we're on our own."

Their route from the *New World* back to the road was blocked by the vast bulk of the *Newfoundland*. Fortunately, Douglas was able to raise the old ship high enough on her hydraulic struts to allow them to pass underneath.

"Don't come crashing down now, old girl," muttered Bluey, looking up at the *Newfoundland*'s underbelly with concern.

"My dad would be so proud," said Baines.

"How so?" asked Bluey.

"This ship, still basically working after all these years and all she's been through. Those struts are good old US of A quality!"

"*Yeah*," commented Bluey, drily. "That's why I'm not hanging around under here."

Baines smiled. "It's funny, you know. America, Britain and Australia – comrades through some of the worst crises in human history, willing to take the world on together yet still taking the mickey out of each other after all these years. Maybe that's why we're still friends."

Bluey grinned. "That's because no matter how much we like to bicker, we've always known who we can rely on when push comes to shove. Or certainly should do, at least. Nothing changes."

Leaving the shadow of the *Newfoundland* behind, they drove across the beach and joined the road.

The beds were laid out in three rows of ten within one of the smaller holds adjoining the Pod's main hangar.

Major White and Captain Meritus approached Dr Flannigan as he organised the final arrangements.

"Dave?" greeted White.

Flannigan turned, noticing them for the first time. "Major," he greeted in return.

"This is Captain Meritus, our new *ally*." White stressed the word, clearly suggesting that this situation would be under constant review. "Captain, this is our chief medical officer, Lieutenant David Flannigan MD."

Flannigan gave a military salute. "Captain," he said coldly.

Meritus returned the salute. "Lieutenant," he replied. "I hope that we can be of some assistance to your efforts, once a little trust has been built."

Flannigan remained silent. In order to head off any awkwardness before it began, White explained that their allies had two medical doctors on their strength, along with several supporting staff.

Flannigan did not acknowledge this, saying instead, "The temporary field hospital is ready as ordered, Major. You may bring the injured across as soon as you're ready. In small groups, please. We'll need to set everyone up carefully."

White blew out his cheeks in mild exasperation. He knew he was no diplomat; clearly he was not the only one.

"Very well," he said. "Captain Meritus, could you make your first vehicle available for my inspection, please?"

"Certainly, Major. Please follow me."

The agreement to assist Meritus' people with their urgent medical needs had been contingent upon all three vehicles being inspected before they entered the Pod. Once White and his inspection team gave them the all clear, they would be permitted to enter, one at a time.

The hangar was heavily guarded as the first tracked vehicle drove in and reversed up to the doors of the temporary hospital.

The injured were helped or carried from the vehicle by their own people, who laid them out to Flannigan's design. He assigned beds according to the severity of their injuries, having set out curtained-off areas for the most serious cases.

One of the more serious cases made Flannigan cry out in surprise. "For the love of *God*! Not *you* again?!"

"Hello, Dave," the injured man managed weakly.

Flannigan let out his breath in a protracted *wheesh*, but remembering the heroic action which had saved the life of Georgio Baccini from a deadly dinosaur attack, he eventually managed a greeting. "Welcome home, Geoff," he said, gesturing around his new ward, ironically.

White watched the reunion from a distance, wearing his casual lopsided grin. He had forbidden the armed personnel carrier from entering the hangar at all, so the first vehicle, which had delivered Lloyd and the other casualties, returned to collect the third group as the other *un*armed carrier brought in the second.

"I commend you, Major," said Meritus, returning him to the moment. "A very smooth operation. And on behalf of my people, I also thank you."

White nodded. "If we're going to work together, I hope this goes a long way to show *our* good faith."

"Indeed it does," replied Meritus, himself gesturing towards Lloyd. "And in that spirit, I return your man to you."

"Gee, thanks," replied White, sourly.

Meritus chuckled. "But while we're on the subject of good faith, I assume you would *actually* like to know all that *we* know about Schultz's fleet?"

White offered him a wintry smile. "I thought you'd never ask."

The sun slid down the western sky like undercooked pasta on a kitchen wall and beneath it, to similarly flog the simile, the plateau was being hastily tidied and swept, to clear up the mess.

A small armoured bulldozer unceremoniously pushed all of the bodies, human and animal alike, over the edge, while teams of people fenced in a new perimeter around the three forty-metre-long, black warships.

There were still hundreds of Mayor Dougli Salvators milling all over the clearing. The noise of the great ships had initially driven them off into the forest, but they gradually returned throughout the day – much to the annoyance of the clearing and camp building teams.

Their first fence, which faced the forest, had to be reconstructed three times in the first hour. The Mayors kept knocking it over to sniff at the equipment and supplies being distributed around the new compound. Fortunately for the curious little animals, the workers did not wish to have another hundred corpses to clear, so in the end they opted for firing into the air to run the herd back into the forest.

Even this proved only partially successful. Pretty soon, the more inquisitive, or perhaps the more forgetful among the herd, returned again, to see what else they could steal.

After rebuilding their fences for a fourth time, the people on the ground finally resorted to the only barrier which could be trusted between humans and animals – the final 'them and us' – fire.

However, collecting fuel soon proved to be another drain on resources. They quickly worked out, to their further irritation, that they needed a fire every twenty paces or so, to keep the wildlife at bay. Subsequently, progress was slow.

Heinrich Schultz paced his luxurious private quarters furiously, stopping at each window to check if the search team, sent to board the *Last Word*, had yet crested the top of the steep incline from where it lay.

He wanted to know *exactly* what had transpired here. Only then could he punish those responsible, and only *then* could he continue with the mission. Whatever had befallen his battleship, it seemed most unlikely that the *New World*, or more importantly *Factory Pod 4*, were yet in his hands.

His people had clearly left overland and two of their orbital attack ships were also gone. The ruin of the third was now berthed within his new compound, waiting to be stripped for spare parts.

As they flew inland from the sea earlier that day, they had scanned another of his attack craft within what could only be the enemy encampment.

Was the missing one destroyed? He had no way of getting an answer to this or a hundred other questions. Until he made contact with his people, he dare not move forward for risk of compromising their mission. Until he made contact, he was blind.

"Where *are* they?" he seethed. "Heads will roll for this! And *where* is my granddaughter?" For a moment he wondered whether she might have been killed during the apparent upheaval which had taken place here. *That would be a waste,* he considered coolly.

"How long are we to wait here, ma'am?" the man called across the track.

"Until we see someone travelling between the Pod and the *New World*," answered Schultz, irritably. She despised questions, particularly when they regarded her orders. Her people were becoming bored and that was dangerous in its own right. It would make them sloppy.

She decided to throw them a bone. "It may take a day or two, so we should get as comfortable as we can, but make sure you—"

She was cut off by a whistle from another man, adjacent to her but on the opposite side of the T-junction. He had the best line of sight facing west and was pointing along the road in the direction of what she believed to be the *New World.* She craned further around her branch to get a look at what he had seen.

An unpleasant smile turned her lip. "Right, this is it! Everybody back on the ground and stretch your muscles. We have a lorry incoming. I want to take *it* and prisoners. Get ready and wait for my signal!"

Within moments they could all see one of the *New World*'s augmented personnel carriers bouncing towards them over the rough surface of the road. As it drew nearer they also heard the creak and crack of broken timber as it crushed the foliage under its heavy wheels. Its electric motors made virtually no sound among the general noises of the forest.

Schultz let it approach to within twenty metres before stepping out into the road. She fired a single shot at the vehicle's windscreen.

The bullet hit directly in front of Bluey's face, creating a small pit and several radial cracks. The Australian ducked instinctively as he brought the vehicle to a full stop. The screen had stopped the bullet but a few more shots would clearly break through.

Schultz signalled for her people to leave the trees at the side of the road and they walked the last few metres towards their target. She stopped directly in front of the driver, beckoning with her index finger for him to get out.

Bluey looked at Baines, who nodded and grabbed her crutches. "Everyone, stay in the back," she hissed. "They've only seen the two of us. If you get chance to make a break, get out of here and don't wait for us – that's an order. We're going out."

Tim pocketed four of Gleeson's 'dingo wingers' from a pouch attached to the bulkhead behind the cab, just in case he had the chance, or need, for a diversion.

Bluey stepped out of the truck to stand before it. He looked at Schultz and her four troops ranged before him and spat on the ground.

Schultz smiled at his insolence.

Baines eventually managed to lower herself from the cab and made her way around the front of the vehicle on crutches, to join Bluey. "What will it take to kill you?" she asked Schultz, witheringly.

"I could ask you the same, Commander. We did blow you from the sky, did we not?"

"That's *Captain* to you, Flight Officer Schultz. And that's not how I remember it. I remember a feeble parting shot at a completely unarmoured ship. A ship which still managed to land safely. I was very impressed though, considering how we had completely *devastated* your vessel. It must have been one in a million that you didn't miss us. Wouldn't you agree, Bluey?"

"Defo! Surprised they could hit a barn door at three paces, the way they ran that ship. I may not have been there, but I heard the sounds of epic failure from over thirty miles away, mate."

"Yes, yes, this is very amusing," retorted Schultz, "but you will see that I have all of the weapons – and your truck, now. You have only the cutting remarks, it seems—"

She stopped mid-sentence, noticing a flash of movement from within the vehicle. "So, *Captain* Baines, I see that you are not alone," she added triumphantly. "Get them out of there," she snapped, gesturing to her men.

Miller jumped down first, followed by Patricia and finally, Tim and Rose.

Schultz's face lit up like the fires of hell with an expression of almost demented joy.

"Timothy Norris," she breathed. "It looks like I have my prize after all."

Patricia stepped in front of her son, virtually knocking him backwards in her attempt to shield him. "You leave him alone, you *monster!*" she growled.

A terrifying roar split the air from the direction the lorry had travelled.

"We have another visitor to our little party, *Kapitänin*. It seems we will need to expedite." She addressed Baines, ignoring the fierce remonstrance from Patricia Norris. "You know, you have been a nuisance to me for far too long. I was going to kill you now, but seeing the state you are in, I think it will be more *amusing* to leave you here to provide that creature with its dinner."

She nodded for one of her men to get behind the wheel of the truck.

"Get over there, all of you," she gestured with her pistol to the side of the road. As the prisoners began to move, she said, "Not you, *Herr* Norris. Take him!"

"*No!*" screamed Patricia, managing to land a roundhouse punch on one of the soldiers.

In the scuffle Tim surreptitiously dropped something on the ground before he too tried to hit his assailant around the head.

The soldier batted Patricia aside contemptuously, knocking her to the ground, but she instantly jumped back to her feet, launching herself at the men as they attempted to drag her son away.

"You let him g—"

BANG!

"*MUM!*" Tim screamed, his adolescent voice breaking in torment as his mother fell to the earth, clutching a bullet wound in her stomach.

Schultz stood completely calm and unemotional amongst the mêlée, a small wisp of smoke and gun oil spiralling from the muzzle of her gun.

"YOU *BITCH!*" bellowed Baines, but as she began to limp forwards, Schultz's gun raised again, stopping her.

Baines was shaking all over, completely overwhelmed by a fury she could not bring to bear.

Tim was professionally cuffed into oblivion, to control him and for his own sake. The enemy soldiers were already manhandling him into the vehicle, leaving Schultz alone to face down the crew from the *New World*.

Miller was desperate to help Patricia but was unable to move without leaving his daughter unshielded.

"That blood should bring the creature here very soon *Kapitänin*. I am almost sorry that I will not be here to see how it plays out." Schultz turned to leave and then changed her mind. "Oh, and by the way, *Kapitänin*. Break a leg!"

Flashing an evil smile, she leapt lightly up into the truck, which lurched forward forcing them back off the road.

Bluey dived forward to help Jim Miller drag the screaming Patricia Norris out of the way. Before they were even clear, she had already fallen unconscious from shock and pain.

The stolen vehicle turned off the main track, back towards the *Last Word* and the Schultzes' base.

"Taking the parts from the *Newfoundland* will dramatically speed up our efforts, Captain," said Hiro. "We thought we'd have to manufacture a lot of these items. Your arrival was beyond hope."

"I don't suppose you have any weapons on board?" asked Gleeson.

"Sure," replied Morecombe Hetfield, "but most of 'em don't work. I was down to one rifle, which I managed to keep running by cannibalising the others. We have a couple of working pistols but we're down to one clip of ammunition between them. I dare say all of it could be reconditioned with spare parts, but…"

"Maybe we should have given Jill one of those guns," said Douglas, berated by hindsight.

"I doubt it would have done much good, James," said Hetfield. "I was gonna give the rifle to Commander Gleeson – better in the hands of a real soldier, eh? Besides, if they saw any animals that could threaten that truck, the pistol would have done little more than go 'bang'."

"Actually," said Gleeson, "they had some of my 'dingo wingers' in the truck. I had Corporal Thomas show Tim where they were, just in case. I can't imagine they'll run into anything more than animals at the moment, though, Captain. Not yet."

Douglas nodded. "Aye, hopefully not. Right, we need to get those parts from the *Newfoundland* immediately, even if it takes us all night. We can work shifts if necessary, two hours on, two off. Also, Commander, Ah want you to pick two of the six soldiers we have, to see if they can recommission any of Mor's weapons. OK?"

"Yes, sir."

"Right," Douglas concluded, "The Sarge will stay on watch with me – as neither of us will be much use for carrying right now. We'll take a firearm each to make sure no one sneaks up on us unannounced."

He turned to The Sarge. "We'll be like a couple o' one armed bandits, eh?

"The rest of our troops are on fetching and carrying duty. Ah'd like you to organise that, please, Commander.

"Any questions? No? Right, let's all be about it."

Hiro, Hetfield and a small team made for the *Newfoundland* to retrieve as much essential material as they could get their hands on. Meanwhile, Georgio continued to remove the battle damaged components from the *New World*.

The engineers' estimate for a rough and ready fix to her strut and damaged thruster assemblies was forty-eight hours. They had no illusions about the repairs being pretty, but hoped she would at least fly in atmosphere again.

Georgio opened a short range comm channel to the other ship. "Hiro?"

"*Go ahead,*" crackled the chief's voice.

"There's more damage to the fuel system than I originally thought. Strip everything you possibly can from over there. I don't even *know* what else we're going to need."

Hiro's sigh carried across the airwaves. "*Understood. Hiro out.*"

"*Understood,* he says," Georgio chuntered to himself. "All I understand is, I'm not seeing my bed tonight – again!"

"That roar was definitely closer," said Rose nervously, looking back up the road in the direction from which they came.

"I'm going as fast as I can," complained Bluey. "I've only got a bladdy penknife!"

Jim and Bluey were working as quickly as possible to manufacture the most basic of stretchers to carry Patricia Norris, who was mercifully still unconscious.

After a small *crack* from the trees, Bluey emerged triumphant, bearing a stout looking stick approximately 1.3 metres long with a crook at the top.

"Right," said Jim, removing his coat. "Can I pinch your jacket, Bluey? We'll be warm enough carrying Patricia, I'm sure."

He removed his own coat and zipped it up like a canvas tube, stuffing Baines' crutches inside it to fill out the shoulders. Taking Bluey's jacket, he did the same to form the other end. It was basic but, even with the crutches at full extension, it would be strong enough to support Patricia's slight frame.

"We need to *go*!" snapped Rose. Shock made her teeth chatter as angry tears streamed down her face.

Bluey passed Baines his rapidly crafted crutch before bending to help Jim lift Tim's mother.

"Thank you," said Baines, trying it out.

"Will it do?" asked Bluey.

"Definitely, thank you. Don't worry about me."

Another roar made them all turn around anxiously. This time it was *much* closer. Worse still, they could now hear the heavy footfalls of a very large two-legged animal, moving quickly.

"Move it! Into the trees!" said Jim, a croak in his voice betraying his nerves. "Rose, help Jill. Come *on*! Let's get the hell out of here!"

"Wait!" said Baines. She had just noticed three small, cylindrical objects on the ground near their recent altercation. "Look, Tim must have dropped those for us to find. Can you pick them up for me, Rose?"

Rose quickly did as asked. "What are they?"

"Dingo wingers – at least, that's what Commander Gleeson calls them. They make a bang to scare animals away. Thank you. You keep one. Now come on, let's go."

They limped and staggered into the forest hurriedly, but despite the crashing and cracking noises they created while travelling through the brush, they could still hear the unmistakable sounds of heavy pursuit.

The trees were not as densely packed in this part of the forest as Jim would have liked. He felt sure that a determined effort from even a very large creature would probably break or squeeze through the foliage. If it was the creature he feared it might be, the effort was likely to be *most* determined as they had foxed it on several occasions already. Maybe this time their luck would run out.

Don't think like that! Jim chided himself. *I've got to get my daughter out of this, and my friends. Damnit! Why didn't I leave her with her mother! We're here fighting for our lives and I'll bet the most pressing concern in Lara's mind, at this moment, is whether the fine weather we've been having means it's time to break out the summer palette from her makeup bag!* He broke off that line of thought; it led only to resentment. More crucially, the colossal roar from where they turned off the road had stolen his entire consideration.

Baines was falling steadily behind, even with Rose's help. She was also beginning to feel a little woozy. She was unsure whether this was due to the strain of her injury or perhaps the more general stresses of their situation. "Rose," she said, panting heavily, "you must catch up with the others."

Rose wore a queer expression, somewhere between terrified and mutinous. "I'm not leaving you, come *on!*"

"No, Rose, listen," Baines tried again, a little breathlessly. "If you don't apply pressure to Patricia's wound she will bleed out and die. Only you can save her. The men have literally got their hands full and I need my arms just to get around. Please run and save her. *Go!* I'll be fine."

Rose now added confusion to her repertoire. "You're not lying to save me?" she asked.

"I promise," Baines assured her. "Go, *please.*"

Rose nodded, extricated herself from Baines' underarm and sprinted forward to catch up with her father and Bluey, six or seven paces further on.

Jim spotted a rocky outcrop about fifty metres ahead. The ground began to slope upwards, and it seemed to grow much steeper very quickly around the promontory.

"That way," he hissed to Bluey, who trudged behind him.

Rose suddenly caught up with them and dutifully applied pressure to Patricia's gut wound. The injured woman began to moan.

"She's coming round," said Bluey. "We need to get her out of the way fast, mate."

Jim nodded but saved his breath for the final run at the slope.

Back on the road, a huge dinosaur sniffed the earth. It had tracked Patricia's injury like a bloodhound and now began investigating the brush to the side of the road. With the scent secured, it lowered its head, the better to see under the branches. Its gaze burned through the forest towards the escaping quarry. Taking its first steps among the trees, it quickly became entangled in the lower canopy, but the whiff of blood on the air drove it through this awkwardness to begin smashing a way forward.

The fleeing humans could hear the sounds of destruction closing from behind, but were already tiring and unable to increase their rate of climb any further. As they approached the rockface, they saw evidence of a scramble-way, climbing about ten metres.

They stopped at its base, the men eyeing one another with concern. Bluey shook his head. "No way we're gonna get her up there," he stated quietly.

Jim was forced to agree and, with the crashing sounds coming from the forest below them escalating his stress levels, found it increasingly hard to think.

Rose could see they were at a loss and shot off to their left, around the base of the small cliffs.

"*Rose!*" hissed Jim. "Come back!"

Baines' vision was starting to blur slightly and she suspected she was developing a temperature. Now well in the rear, she could see the animal pursuing them. It was moving slowly, its lack of visibility making it cautious. Were it not for her fractured shin bone and the giddiness she was experiencing, she could have outpaced it fairly easily under these forest conditions, at least for a while. She looked ahead. The others were at the foot of the promontory, about twenty metres south of her position. She suspected the animal would run her down before she reached them.

They seemed to have stopped. She could not tell whether they waited for her or were simply unable to proceed further. Either way, if she made for their position she would only bring them unwanted company. Ahead and to her right, a small group of trees grew in a tight cluster.

"Time to test this thing's problem solving abilities," she muttered to herself to keep her spirits up.

She made it to the trees, in which she hoped to trap or at least confuse the animal, and waited. The dinosaur was very close now and within a few seconds she could see its head parting the foliage. She could see it and it could see her.

"Hey! Over here, you ugly brute!" she shouted to make sure.

Bluey turned as he heard Baines shouting. "What the hell is she doing?" he asked in astonishment.

"Something incredibly brave," Jim replied sorrowfully.

A crashing through the brush nearby got their attention.

"Rose!" cried Jim with relief.

"Sshhh! *Dad*!"

"Sorry, sorry," Jim conciliated.

"This way," she beckoned. "I've found a small gap in the cliff. It won't take all of us but we could hide Patricia, while we lead that thing away."

They scrambled after her, struggling sideways across the slope with their ungainly burden. Presently, they came upon Rose's cleft in the rocks.

"You're a genius," said Bluey. "Quick, let's tuck her in there."

Baines' ruse had worked and the creature came on. She waited as long as she dared before darting, as well as a one-legged woman could, between the trees. She could feel her strength failing, despite the adrenalin surging through her system, and tripped over a root, falling headlong. She landed about two metres past the line of trunks and turned quickly but was forced to stay down.

The foul breath of the dinosaur was nothing if not intimate, as its head lunged within a foot of her face. However, Baines' horrified mind laboured more along the lines of rancid and bowel-*squeezingly* close.

She used her one good leg to weakly push herself across the forest floor and out of the animal's reach, while scrabbling around for her crutch. Once she had it in her hand, she rained a flurry of blows down upon the two-metre-long head with the unsustainable strength provided by terror.

It repeatedly lunged at her but the effort only jammed it tighter between two of the trunks.

Baines managed to regain her feet with the help of the crutch, but could only stare in shock at the fury of the creature as it raged to get to her.

The trees began to creak and groan alarmingly, but she was afraid that if she moved, her attacker might get the idea that it too could simply walk around the obstacle pinning it in place. That could well be a game over scenario for her.

As the thought formed in her mind, the dinosaur seemed to relax its efforts, sneezing nameless fluids and mucus all over her trousers; probably as a result of the battering she had administered to its snout with her stick. However, before she could bellow her disgust and condemnation of this latest attack, she realised that the animal had just worked out what she had feared most.

It wriggled and shuffled back, extricating itself from between the trunks with depressing ease. Almost calmly, it sidestepped, craned its head around the trees and, in what was undeniably a crow of victory, it **ROARED!**

"Oh, crap," muttered Baines and summoning the last of her courage, she hollered, "NO ONE LIKES A BAD WINNER!"

Beck felt like the walls were closing in. No matter what she did or how she meditated, no manner of psychic protection proved equal to the task of shaking the presence which seemed to be stalking, rather than haunting her. She desperately needed help to fortify her resistance, but Mother Sarah was incredibly busy with meetings regarding their 'new alliance'.

She had come to rely heavily on Mario and the other spirits who had contacted her since their untimely, and often gruesome, demises throughout this mission. She would have completely broken down without their support. She had never been alone before, not since she was very young and was so grateful when they came to her. However, this was something different. Loneliness had begun to wear her down, gnawing away at her soul, but now she was *afraid* for her soul. This thing that pursued her was too powerful. She was terrified and had no one to turn to. They were all so busy and would probably think her insane anyway. What could she do?

She felt the comforting presence of Mario. He always came to her when she was low; they had become linked, somehow. It was always reassuring, but this thing that seemed to have invaded their plane was more powerful than all of them together.

Mother Sarah had prayers that could be used to fight this evil, she knew, but Beck was no longer sure whether they would work. Although Sarah was convinced that God's power spoke through those prayers, Beck believed that the psychic power actually came from millions of living believers and even, to some extent, from the ancestors who had gone before. Without this awesome power, she suspected that the prayers might merely be words. She hoped, literally prayed, that Sarah was right and she was wrong. She needed God's love now, but did not really believe it was there to save her.

Beck could feel a weight, almost physically bearing down upon her. She staggered to her apartment's doorway and managed to press the open stud before she collapsed across the threshold into the corridor outside.

"So, what are you going to say to her, dude?" asked Woodsey.

"I don't know," admitted Henry. "She said Ma was lying. I don't know if I can let that go."

"No she didn't," replied Woodsey. "Rose said she was *mistaken*, seeing what she wanted or expected to see, rather than what actually was. You can't tell me you think that Cocksedge Sheila's on the level?"

"OK, so why would she make up being punched in the face by Major White?"

"Because she's twisting things to her own ends, dude. She's a politician – one of the slimy ones who suck people in. The major's never struck me as the sort of bloke to go around bashing Sheilas! Besides, if he had really landed one on her, I reckon he'd have left marks to show for it – not just a bit of a convenient nose fountain."

"So *you* think Ma's making it up as well, do you?" asked Henry, crossly.

Woodsey raised his hands in a calming fashion. "Look, mate, this isn't my place to say, but I reckon you and your family have been through a lot with your old man. Am I right?"

Henry blew out his cheeks. "I guess," he admitted, relaxing slightly.

"So, that being said, dude, I reckon your mum is susceptible to being influenced by someone like Cocksedge. Someone who's allegedly suffered at the hands of a man and is now trying to stick it back to him, y' see? She's bound to defend someone like that."

Woodsey placed a companionable hand on Henry's shoulder. "Don't get me wrong," he continued, "if I believed any of this, I'd be right behind her. Everyone hates a bully, right? Whatever form they take. But I'm sorry, I just don't buy it, mate."

Henry looked thoughtful. "So what do *you* think Ma saw, then?" he asked at last.

"Look, your parents arrived just *after* whatever happened, happened, right? So I reckon, the Sheila heard them coming – let's face it, your old man's not subtle, is he? She thought quickly, saw an opportunity and took it. Anyone can palm themselves in the nose to create a tiny injury that looks like a bloodbath, mate – kids have been using that one to skive double maths since forever!"

Henry was becoming more troubled. "I can't let Ma down, dude. Dad doesn't believe her and I know she was making secret plans to move out and apartment share with Alison Cocksedge – before she was arrested."

"That's another thing," added Woodsey. "They arrested her for *treason*. They don't throw stuff like that around lightly. Many countries back home don't even have any treason laws anymore. It's heavy duty, mate."

"That could just be a smokescreen to get the major out of trouble," retorted Henry.

Woodsey held his head in his hands, wondering if he was banging it against a brick wall. "Mate, she was contacting the enemy behind our backs," he tried again, patiently.

"Only to offer peace talks," snapped Henry.

"Alright, let's say that bit's true, it doesn't mean the rest of it's what it seems. I'm no expert, but I reckon I'm pretty good at reading people and I think that Cocksedge would happily sell us all out as long as she came out right."

Henry began to protest but Woodsey held up his hand to forestall him. "Let me finish, mate. All I know is this – I wouldn't let a girl like Rose go, based on *anything* that woman says. Rose hasn't said anything bad about your mum, she just thinks she's wrong. She's got a right to that opinion, mate. Is it worth losing her over?"

Rose slipped and screamed. Flailing, she managed to grab a vine creeping up the rock face. Bluey made sure of his handhold and twisted to offer her his other hand. Jim, bringing up the rear, managed to get the tips of his fingers to his daughter's back to apply just enough force to swing her back to where Bluey could reach her. After a desperate flap, they managed to lock wrists and Bluey pulled the girl up by her arm to a safe foothold.

"Thanks," said Rose.

Bluey nodded acknowledgement and turned to resume his climb.

They could hear a colossal amount of noise coming from the dinosaur below. It sounded furious.

I hope that means Jill's still alive, thought Jim. He scrambled up the last few metres of the gully they had found to climb, gratefully accepting the Australian construction worker's strong hands to help him up the last haul.

They now stood on the top of the small promontory. In front of them, a small plateau ran smoothly back into the hill. If the dinosaur found its way around the sides, their position would offer no protection at all – just an almost sheer drop.

Behind them, things sounded bad below.

"We can't just leave Jill down there," said Jim.

"I know," agreed Bluey. He quickly made a decision. "I'm going back for her."

"I'll come with you," said Jim.

"No," said Bluey, meaningfully. "It won't be long before the Pod sends someone to look for us. *You* stay with your daughter."

Rose was holding on tightly to her father and he could feel her shaking. Exasperated, Jim reached out his left hand to the Australian. "Good luck, mate."

Bluey took the hand and squeezed it. Noticing Rose's tears, he gently wiped them away. "Don't worry, little lady, they'll soon find us and take us home."

"And what about Tim?" she asked haltingly, through shuddering breaths.

Bluey's expression hardened. "We'll get the lad back too. Depend on it!" He nodded to Jim and began his scramble back down the culvert in the rocks.

Rose looked up into her father's eyes. "Dad, I've got an idea…"

Baines' wits were completely scattered. She hobbled backwards slowly as the creature advanced. Now it had her, the pressure was off and it seemed interested to find out what she was before it ate her. Bobbing its head in a very birdlike manner, it sniffed and swayed from side to side to get a better view of her.

Without realising where she was going, Baines backed into a tree. "End of the road," she muttered.

At the sound of her words, the dinosaur hesitated, momentarily confused by such an alien sound.

Despite struggling with nausea, Baines managed to clearly and loudly ask, "What are you?"

A deep belly growl came from the creature in response.

"I guess that's the small talk over then, eh?" She cringed and closed her eyes, waiting for the death blow when a loud bang came from the small cliffs to the south. Judging by the volume and echo, one of Gleeson's dingo wingers had been dropped down the rockface.

The huge beast roared and stepped back, turning around to face the new sound.

"Hey! You ugly galah-brained rooter! Over here!" shouted Bluey. He jumped up and down, waving his arms around. "I remember you from the last time, and I know what you are!" he bellowed. "*You* put the *tit* into Tyrannotitan, you stinking mongrel!"

His taunt seemed to work and the scar faced, veteran theropod matriarch launched herself after him.

Sam Burton was in a meeting with one of Meritus' staff sergeants when the door to his office chimed.

"Come in," he called.

"Sorry to disturb you, Dr Burton," said the operations tech. "You asked me to let you know when the deadline for the transport from the *New World* expired."

"They're still not here?"

"I'm afraid not. Do we give them a bit longer or send a search vehicle?"

Burton shook his head. "We can't wait. Thanks, I'll deal with it."

The man left.

"Please excuse me for a minute," Burton apologised as he opened a comm channel to Major White.

"*White here.*"

"Ford, it's Sam. We've heard nothing from the transport and they've missed their ETA."

"*OK, Sam. What do you suggest?*"

"Bluey specifically said that they would be here within one hour and if they weren't, we should send someone to look for them and not hang around."

"*Right. Understood. Leave it with me, I'll put together a search and rescue team immediately.*"

"Nice one. Burton out."

Major White was also in a meeting, with Captain Meritus. "Captain," he said, "do you remember earlier, when we were talking about good faith?"

Baines almost collapsed after her reprieve, but relief was short lived as she realised that the young, burly Australian may well have just signed his own death warrant to save her.

Coming to her senses with effort, she shouted, "Bluey, *no!*" but it was too late. The creature had taken the bait and all her rescuer could do now was run like hell, while hoping to heaven for a stay of execution.

When the loud bang initially distracted the dinosaur, it also jogged her woolly memory about the other two devices. *Thank God I gave one of these to Rose*, she thought, fumbling in her pocket for the dingo wingers. *At least* someone*'s thinking clearly!*

Bluey made a beeline for the first scramble way they found up the rockface, earlier. He was fairly certain Patricia Norris was safely tucked away, but even so, he did not wish to take the monster anywhere near her, just in case.

The animal smashed its way through the trees behind him, seemingly too incensed to notice the damage she was inflicting upon herself.

Bluey was no more than four metres from the ground when the Tyrannotitan caught up with him. In her haste to catch the Australian, her first lunge missed him by mere centimetres. The *snap* of the massive jaws closing right behind him, the teeth knitting like monstrous shears, gave him all the encouragement he needed to leap up to the next foothold. Unfortunately, the dinosaur was old for her kind and no stranger to prey trying to leap away from her. She judged his next move and leapt too, a relatively small motion for such a giant creature. Although one foot still firmly transmitted her weight to the ground, the movement was enough to snag Bluey's clothing and he screamed as he was pulled bodily from the rockface and flung to the ground.

"*Nooo!*" screamed Baines as she limped towards them with all the speed she could muster.

The Tyrannotitan threw Bluey past the rocks to the softer ground below and he hit the steep incline in a pell-mell roll down the bank. By the time he stopped rolling he had struck his head several times and lay still.

Baines threw a dingo winger, giving it everything she had left. It landed on the ground near the dinosaur's massive, splayed feet. As the creature stepped back and bent to investigate this strange gift, it went off, causing her to roar and rear away from the blast. Her senses temporarily overloaded, she crashed her head into the rockface with shocking force, causing a small avalanche of stones to dislodge themselves. The animal continued to roar, now in obvious distress and pain.

Baines noted that Bluey had vanished from sight, buried by the dense underbrush further down the bank.

After a final shake of her head, the Tyrannotitan spotted Baines once more and lowered her head, making grasping motions with her claws and parting her jaws wide; an unmistakable posture of murderous intent.

A colossal roar was clearly building within the beast's chest, but it came out as a weak and almost comedic whimper of indignation as she was struck on the head by a large rock thrown from the top of the outcrop.

"Get lost!" screamed Rose.

"Go on! *Get out of it!*" her father joined in, also hurling anything he could lift at the creature.

The dinosaur's incandescent rage had, within moments, been replaced by confusion and distress – due in no small part to the anaesthetizing effects of her skull's collision with the rockface. Staggering slightly, she moved away from the thrown stones. When the roar of jet engines batted the treetops from above, she gave up and slunk away through the forest back towards the road. Even in the Cretaceous Period, there had to be easier ways to get a meal. Within moments she had gone, the final cat-like flicks of her tail offering redundant advice that it would not be a good idea to follow her.

Baines' head suddenly swam, blurring her vision completely and she fell to the ground unconscious.

Chapter 14 | The Truth

An armed guard stepped out from the compound gates, holding up a hand for the personnel carrier to stop. Schultz jumped down from the front passenger seat to be recognised, dragging a few branches off the vehicle and throwing them to the side. It had been a rough ride through the forest and she fully expected things to get rougher still when she met with her grandfather.

The soldier in charge of the watch detail clicked his heels and nodded in salute, letting them pass. A few moments later, her driver pulled up outside the *Eisernes Kreuz*.

"Get this vehicle to a recharge station, it works well," she ordered as she stepped through to the rear crew compartment. She nodded to her small remaining force. "He's still under?" she asked, gesturing towards Tim.

"He came round about fifteen minutes ago," replied one of the men, "but struggled so violently I had to cuff him again, ma'am – to prevent him from worse injury."

"Very well," Schultz acknowledged unemotionally. "Take the prisoner in and get him checked over by a medic. From here onwards, he is to receive the best possible care."

She jumped from the rear hatch of the vehicle, made her way past another couple of guards and up into the ship. She had never been aboard the *Eisernes Kreuz* before, but already knew her layout by heart. Presently, she stood before the entrance to the executive suites.

Heidi felt the need to take several steadying breaths before announcing her arrival, but she really should have known better. Her grandfather was surely the most paranoid individual alive – certainly in this age. He would have been watching her from the moment she entered the ship, quite possibly even before that.

The doors slid open before she could even activate the call button.

"*Enkelin*," greeted a cold voice she knew well.

"*Großvater*," she returned the greeting, formally. There would be no hugs or 'how are yous', Heidi was certain of that. Heinrich would only be interested in information, and if he did not like the information she provided…

There was no advantage in pursuing that line of thought. She had never failed him before. So, if blame for the debacle they had suffered could be shifted squarely onto the traitor Meritus' shoulders, maybe her perfect record, and more importantly her life, would be spared.

Heinrich Schultz sat at a small conference table within his quarters, next to a window which looked west, over the edge of the plateau at the lower valleys and plains beyond.

Heidi was grateful that the ruined *Last Word* was beneath their field of vision, where its ghost was unable to accuse her. Heidi's grandfather was almost impossible to fool. She would have to very carefully tell the truth, but not the whole truth, so help her God.

"You may sit with me, *Enkelin*," he said, coolly.

"*Danke, sehr nett*," she replied, courteously.

Heinrich responded by slamming his fist down on the table. "Tell me what happened!" he spat furiously.

So much for being nice, thought Heidi. Over the next thirty minutes she delivered a monologue, explaining all that had transpired since the *New World* left Canaveral. She was quite sure to include the incompetences and ineptitudes of all who had brought them to this point, including the woeful performance of Lieutenant Geoff Lloyd, the man who set them off on the wrong course to begin with, stranding them in this most inhospitable of times.

Over steepled fingers, Heinrich's gaze burned through her. He said not a word, nor did he give away anything to indicate his thoughts. He was the best, yet least compassionate listener she had ever met.

The silence into which her story vanished stretched, testing even the limits of Heidi's great nerve.

"Meritus has betrayed our cause and offered his services and some of *my* personnel and equipment to the enemy," he stated at last.

Heidi nodded. "*Ja, Großvater*," she admitted quietly.

"My battleship has been almost completely destroyed," he added.

She nodded again, mutely this time.

"And you *completely* failed to see these events coming!" he snapped, showing the first signs of wrath.

"Almost all of our people," he continued, furiously, "defected with him, *against* you!"

Heidi lowered her eyes.

"You have most diligently informed me of just how blatantly everyone in the chain has let me down. Now I wish to hear how you so fundamentally lost control of the situation. Please also fill in the details as to how *exactly* you lost the fear and respect of those under your command," Heinrich asked, almost conversationally.

"*Großvater*," she began. It was time to play a dangerous game. "Their numbers allowed them to overcome their fear. Captain Douglas—"

"Who you also lost!" he interjected.

Heidi swallowed. "Captain Douglas commands a fierce loyalty from his crew, they are almost besotted with the man and yet none of them *fear* him. Perhaps our strategy..." she tailed off, sensing imminent and explosive danger.

"*You* criticise *my* strategy," began Heinrich.

"*Nein, Großvater*," she acquiesced immediately.

"You know the price of failure. Tell me, why should you not pay the highest price for your actions here?"

Heidi looked up once more, staring the old man in the eye. It was time to play her last card. "I have the boy."

Heinrich sat back, temporarily thrown off course. "The Norris boy?"

"*Ja, Großvater.*"

He took a moment to consider. "Bring him to me," he demanded.

She stood, bowed and left quickly.

When she returned a few minutes later, two of her guards manhandled a bruised, frightened and very distraught teenager into the suite behind her.

"Remove his restraints and leave us," she told her men.

With his hands free, Tim batted away tears of despair and impotent rage. He straightened, getting control of himself. "I won't help you," he stated. "Whatever you want, the answer is no!"

Heidi watched her grandfather's response, sidelong. He smiled slightly, amused by the boy's hopeless bravado, perhaps even moderately impressed by it.

"Your bearing does you credit, young man. I would have expected nothing less," said Heinrich.

"*You're* murderers and thieves," snapped Tim. "I don't care what you do to me. I will fight you!"

Heinrich chuckled, for the first time looking at Heidi. "Who would have guessed the boy would possess such courage, after his weak upbringing. Blood will out."

Tim scrutinised the old man, a puzzled expression crossing his face. "What the hell is that supposed to mean?"

"It means I knew you would be a survivor," replied Heinrich.

"You don't know anything about me," Tim retorted.

"I know *everything* about you, *Herr* Norris, and your parents."

"My dad was a good man and my mum would never have anything to do with the likes of you!"

"I mean your *real* parents."

Tim caught his breath. The thought of this evil old man knowing more about him than he did himself made him feel naked and even more afraid. "How can you know about my family? They were killed by religious fanatics in a raid on the factory where they worked."

"We know. We orchestrated it."

"*No!*"

"Oh yes, *Herr* Norris," said Heidi, feeling sufficiently confident to join in now. "You see, when people work for my *Großvater*, they don't leave unless he allows it—"

"Which is, of course, almost never," the old man interjected.

"Your parents disobeyed his instructions," continued Heidi. "They tried to flee. It took three years but we caught up with them. I dare imagine they thought themselves safe after all that time." Schultz's lip curled cruelly.

"What had they done?" asked Tim, shocked.

"It's what they did not do. They refused to eliminate people *Großvater* deemed worthless."

"But they died in a random terrorist attack…"

"Like the one which led the *New World* here?" she was grinning at him, mocking now. "We orchestrated the attack on their place of work as final payment for your parents."

Tim looked at the beautiful young German woman with disgust. "*Hundreds* died in that attack," he managed at last.

"It's called misdirection, I'm sure you know the saying about omelettes and eggs, yes? Did you believe that ridiculous story about reconstituted tampons being subversive and against the will of God? The idiots we employed to undertake the attack were ordered to come up with a convincingly misleading cover story. Unfortunately, when working with fringe types, they are rarely equal to anything more than the most menial of tasks. Although," she looked thoughtful for a moment, "perhaps they knew their business after all. The world has had to deal with all manner of lunatic factions over the last century, their insanity played smoothly in the media, barely raising any eyebrows in a world already gone mad. You see, that is why we are going to so much trouble to reboot the human race, *Herr* Norris, we are *salvation*."

"You're *evil*."

Schultz laughed lightly. "Your adoptive father, Dr Edward Norris, said exactly the same thing, when we contacted him. How simplistic your world must seem."

"*What?*" asked Tim, horrified.

"Oh, yes. We contacted him. When he refused to help us, we were forced to arrange his little works accident, I'm afraid."

"You killed everyone I ever had," Tim mumbled quietly, his heart completely broken. He had been fiddling in his pocket while she spoke. Now, with absolutely nothing else to lose, he produced the last of the four dingo wingers he removed from the truck, suddenly launching it across the room into the face of the woman who shot his mother.

The loud crack and flash sent the old man flying backwards into an armchair, while Heidi collapsed to her knees, holding her face.

Tim knew he had mere seconds. He dove across the room and lifted her sidearm from its hip holster and stepped back waiting for them to regain their feet.

"You allowed him to appear before me *armed*!" bellowed Heinrich.

Heidi's face was blackened and her eyes were puffy as she repeatedly blinked to regain her sight.

"Give me one good reason why I shouldn't kill you both now," snarled Tim. "You murdered my real parents, you murdered my dad and today you murdered my mum, you evil witch!" He turned on the old man. "And you! What manner of twisted creature are *you*, Schultz?" The pain and rage on his young face rendered him almost unrecognisable.

"Wait!" shouted Heidi, regaining most of her senses. "Let me ask you a serious question, *Herr* Norris, just one question!"

Tim nodded shakily for her to continue.

"How do you think you ended up being part of this mission, hmm?"

"You know how, my mum's a brilliant scientist. Or she was until you—"

"Yes, *yes*," Schultz cut him off disdainfully, "in a world of fifty billion, there is an endless supply of such people. Were you not curious how you came to be among so many – what do you call them – high flyers? Somehow, among all these tycoons and politicians and celebrities and well-connected scientists, your little mongrel family sneaked aboard. This did not strike you as odd?"

Tim said nothing. He simply stared with hatred.

"*You* are here because of your parents."

"Yes, you killed them – I get it – and now you want to kill me, I understand," he spat angrily.

"Your mother was a necessary casualty. We tried to separate you from her, with your father's help but he refused, despite our most generous offer. We even arranged for you to be split from her on the flight to Mars. Do you remember that?" Schultz laughed again. "She was a weak influence on you, but *you* nevertheless have courage. Do you also have intelligence? I have been told you are a genius, a prodigy. Can you not fill in the gaps yourself?"

A sickening feeling began to take hold within the young man. He raised his left arm to support the pistol in his right which had begun to shake violently.

"If we wanted you dead," Schultz continued, "you would *be* dead. If your real parents had merely been employees, that would have been an end to it. But they were much more than that, much more, and so are you."

Tim's stomach dropped away. "What do you mean?" he asked slowly. His whole body shook now, putting a tremor into his voice.

"I mean it's time for you to come home now, Timothy Schultz."

Tim pulled the trigger.

Author's note:

As with the previous book, I thank everyone working in the field of dinosaur research (and Steve Brusatte for being kind enough to answer my emails and for giving me *Buitreraptor* as a suggestion). These animals have always been a passion for me, and the experts continue to inspire me to write about them. Also as previously, a few liberties have been taken...

Firstly feathers: There is a huge amount of effort going into researching this subject at the moment. It seems likely that many species had at least some form of feathers. Perhaps all dinosaurs did; the final answer seems to be up for grabs at the moment. Even the reasons for having feathers may have differed wildly between the species – maybe even between *a* species, at differing points throughout the animals' lives. Although I have introduced a few species with feathers, notably *Buitreraptor,* I have largely hedged around the subject for two reasons. Firstly, information on the subject is being gathered and is changing at a prodigious rate – and I did not want something so obvious as the look of the dinosaurs to become immediately out of date (this is a major problem faced by anyone writing about dinosaurs at the moment. Most books have to be updated three or four times just in the time it takes to write them!). Secondly, many people have a cherished view of what a dinosaur, particularly the larger and more popular clades, should look like. In terms of the story, this does not really matter or affect events, and as this work is purely for entertainment, I leave the subject open and hope that each reader will enjoy 'clothing' these incredible animals in the way *they* prefer. Feathers or scales – please imagine them as you will.

The arctometatarsalian condition has, as far as I know, never actually been found amongst the carcharodontosaurids; although it is a feature which has evolved more than once, apparently. I think I mentioned this in my notes at the end of book one (at least in the audio book). Tim speculates about the possibility of new animals that may have this trait, but also uses the potential speed and/or long distance running capability this condition was believed to imbue, to scare Woodsey into being quiet for a few moments.

As previously stated in my notes at the back of book one, *Buitreraptor* lived a little later than the setting for these stories, perhaps in the Cenomanian or even Turonian stages of the Cretaceous Period. There are few dromaeosaurids yet known in Patagonia during this period, so I chose this little animal rather than make one up. *Tyrannotitan* lived a little earlier than the setting for REVENGE, possibly in the Aptian stage of the Cretaceous Period. I included this great animal for three reasons: Firstly, to give the great *Mapusaurus* and *Giganotosaurus* a rest after their exhausting efforts following the stampede in book one; animals that size would probably have hunted vast territories, perhaps even hundreds of square miles, so this would seem logical. Secondly, there is no conclusive evidence, as far as I am aware, to categorically prove or disprove the group behaviour of the large theropod carnivores. It may be that they grouped together at certain times of year, or to bring down great prey, but were otherwise solitary; or they may have grouped together for mutual benefit when young, only to become more solitary when grown. Research continues and it is truly fascinating. With regards to my story, as the mapusaurs and giganotosaurs worked in packs (possibly due to a springtime breeding cycle), I thought it would be nice to describe another, similar animal with a lifestyle at the opposite end of the spectrum – a 'lone wolf', if you will. Thirdly, I am a writer of stories and with a name like **Tyrannotitan**, how could I possibly resist?

Thank you so very much for reading,

Stephen.

Coming soon:

ALLEGIANCE

THE NEW WORLD SERIES | BOOK THREE

Stephen Llewelyn